CARAGH M. O'BRIEN

birthmarked

SQUARE
FISH

ROARING BROOK PRESS
NEW YORK

The author is donating a portion of the proceeds of this novel to the Global Greengrants Fund, a non-profit, international grass-roots organization that provides small, pivotal grants to people dealing with environmental destruction. Interested readers may find more information at www.greengrants.org.

SQUARE
FISH

An Imprint of Macmillan

Library of Congress Cataloging-in-Publication Data
O'Brien, Caragh M.
Birthmarked / Caragh M. O'Brien.
p. cm.
Summary: In a future world baked dry by the sun and divided into those who live inside the wall and those who live outside it, sixteen-year-old midwife Gaia Stone is forced into a difficult choice when her parents are arrested and taken into the city.
ISBN 978-0-312-67472-4
[1. Midwives—Juvenile fiction.   2. Dystopias—Juvenile fiction.
3. Midwives—Fiction.   4. Genetic engineering—Fiction.   5. Parents—Fiction.   6. Survival—Fiction.]   I. Title.

PZ7.O12673 Bi 2010
[Fic]—dc22
2010281716

Originally published in the United States by Roaring Brook Press
First Square Fish Edition: October 2011
Square Fish logo designed by Filomena Tuosto
macteenbooks.com

10 9 8 7 6 5 4 3 2 1

AR: 5.4 / LEXILE: HL800L

In memory of my father,
Thomond R. O'Brien, Sr.

Contents

Chapter 1 / *The Baby Quota* / 1

Chapter 2 / *A Small, Brown Parcel* / 9

Chapter 3 / *Rapunzel* / 25

Chapter 4 / *The Folded Triangle* / 34

Chapter 5 / *Shepherd's Purse* / 50

Chapter 6 / *The Obelisk* / 58

Chapter 7 / *Noon* / 70

Chapter 8 / *Life First* / 80

Chapter 9 / *The Doctors of Q Cell* / 93

Chapter 10 / *Blueberries in the Unlake* / 100

Chapter 11 / *The Gilded Mirror* / 114

Chapter 12 / *A Pigeon Visits* / 127

Chapter 13 / *Birthmarked* / 135

Chapter 14 / *A Crime Against the State* / 160

Chapter 15 / *The Yellow Pincushion* / 169

Chapter 16 / *Cooperation* / 178

Chapter 17 / *The Baby Code* / 191

Chapter 18 / *One Chance* / 207

Chapter 19 / *Jacksons' Bakery* / 218

Chapter 20 / *Forty-Six Chrome Spoons* / 232

Chapter 21 / *Happiness* / 249

Chapter 22 / *The Women of the Southeast Tower* / 268

Chapter 23 / *Maya* / 280

Chapter 24 / *A Perfectly Circular Pool* / 295

Chapter 25 / *The Tunnels* / 307

Chapter 26 / *White Boots* / 325

Chapter 27 / *Trust* / 343

Chapter 28 / *Returned Property* / 349

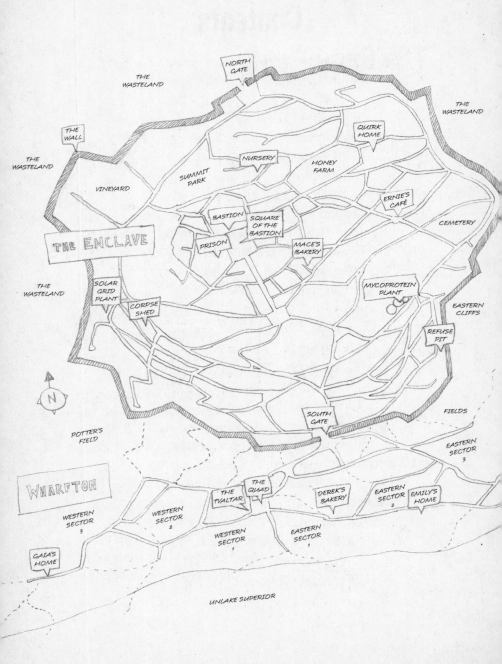

THE
WASTELAND

THE
WASTELAND

NORTH
GATE

QUIRK
HOME

THE
WALL

THE
WASTELAND

VINEYARD

SUMMIT
PARK

NURSERY

HONEY
FARM

ERNIE'S
CAFÉ

CEMETERY

THE ENCLAVE

BASTION

SQUARE
OF THE
BASTION

PRISON

MACE'S
BAKERY

THE
WASTELAND

SOLAR
GRID
PLANT

CORPSE
SHED

MYCOPROTEIN
PLANT

EASTERN
CLIFFS

REFUSE
PIT

N

SOUTH
GATE

FIELDS

POTTER'S
FIELD

EASTERN
SECTOR
3

WHARFTON

THE
TVALTAR

THE
QUAD

DEREK'S
BAKERY

EASTERN
SECTOR
2

EMILY'S
HOME

WESTERN
SECTOR
3

WESTERN
SECTOR
2

WESTERN
SECTOR
1

EASTERN
SECTOR
1

GAIA'S
HOME

UNLAKE SUPERIOR

Chapter 1
The Baby Quota

IN THE DIM HOVEL, the mother clenched her body into one final, straining push, and the baby slithered out into Gaia's ready hands.

"Good job," Gaia said. "Wonderful. It's a girl."

The baby cried indignantly, and Gaia breathed a sigh of relief as she checked for toes and fingers and a perfect back. It was a good baby, healthy and well formed, if small. Gaia wrapped the child in a blanket, then held the bundle toward the flickering firelight for the exhausted mother to see.

Gaia wished her own mother were there to help, especially with managing the afterbirth and the baby. She knew, normally, she wasn't supposed to give the baby to the mother to hold, not even for an instant, but now the mother was reaching and Gaia didn't have enough hands.

"Please," the young woman whispered. Her fingers beckoned tenderly.

The baby's cries subsided, and Gaia passed her over. She tried not to listen to the mother's gentle, cooing noises as she cleaned up between her legs, moving gently and efficiently as her mother had taught her. She was excited and a little proud. This

1

was her first delivery, and it was an unassisted delivery, too. She had helped her mother many times, and she'd known for years that she would be a midwife, but now it was finally real.

Almost finished. Turning to her satchel, she drew out the small teakettle and two cups that her mother had given her for her sixteenth birthday, only a month ago. By the light of the coals, she poured water from a bottle into the kettle. She stoked up the fire, seeing the burst of yellow light gleam over the mother with her small, quiet bundle.

"You did well," Gaia said. "How many is this for you again? Did you say four?"

"She's my first," the woman said, her voice warm with awed pleasure.

"What?"

The woman's eyes gleamed briefly as she looked toward Gaia, and she smiled. In a shy, self-conscious gesture, she smoothed a sweat-damped curl back around her ear. "I didn't tell you before. I was afraid you wouldn't stay."

Gaia sat down slowly beside the fire, set the kettle on the metal rod, and swiveled it over the fire to warm.

First labors were hardest, the most risky, and although this one had progressed smoothly, Gaia knew they'd been lucky. Only an experienced midwife should have tended this woman, not only for the sake of the mother and child's health, but for what would come next.

"I would have stayed," Gaia said softly, "but only because there's nobody else to come. My mother was already gone to another birth."

The mother hardly seemed to hear. "Isn't she beautiful?" she murmured. "And she's mine. I get to keep her."

Oh, no, Gaia thought. Her pleasure and pride evaporated, and she wished now, more than ever, that her mother were there. Or even Old Meg. Or anybody, for that matter.

2

Gaia opened her satchel and took out a new needle and a little bottle of brown ink. She shook the tin of tea over the kettle to drop in some flakes. The faint aroma slowly infused the room with a redolent fragrance, and the mother smiled again in a weary, relaxed way.

"I know we've never talked," the mother said. "But I've seen you and your mother coming and going at the quadrangle, and up to the wall. Everyone says you'll be as great a midwife as your mother, and now I can say it's true."

"Do you have a husband? A mother?" Gaia asked.

"No. Not living."

"Who was the boy you sent for me? A brother?"

"No. A kid who was passing in the street."

"So you have no one?"

"Not anymore. Now I have my baby, my Priscilla."

It's a bad name, Gaia thought. And what was worse, it wouldn't matter because it wouldn't last. Gaia dropped a pinch of motherwort into the mother's teacup, and then silently poured tea into the two cups, trying to think how best to do this. She let her hair fall forward, shielding the left side of her face, while she moved the empty teakettle, still warm, into her satchel.

"Here," she said, handing the cup laced with motherwort toward the young woman on the bed and smoothly removing the baby from beside her.

"What are you doing?" the mother asked.

"Just drink. It will help with the pain." Gaia took a sip from her own cup as an example.

"I don't feel much anymore. Just a little sleepy."

"That's good," Gaia said, setting her cup back by the hearth.

Quietly, she packed her gear and watched as the mother's eyelids grew heavier. She unwrapped the baby's legs to gently pull one foot out, and then she set the baby on a blanket on the floor, near the fireplace. The baby's eyes opened and flickered toward the flames: dark, murky eyes. It was impossible to tell what color they might eventually be. Gaia sopped a bit of clean rag into her cup of tea, absorbing the last hot liquid, and then wiped it over the ankle, cleaning it. She dipped the needle in the brown ink, held it briefly to the light, and then, swiftly, as she had done before under her mother's guidance, she pressed the pin into the baby's ankle in four rapid pricks. The child screamed.

"What are you doing?" the mother demanded, now fully awake.

Gaia wrapped the birthmarked baby again and cradled her firmly in one arm. She slid the teacup, needle, and ink into her satchel. Then she stepped forward and took the second teacup from beside the mother. She lifted her satchel.

"No!" the mother cried. "You can't! It's April twenty-first! Nobody ever advances a baby this late in the month."

"It's not how late the date is," Gaia said quietly. "It's the first three babies each month."

"But you must have delivered half a dozen by now," the woman shrieked, rising. She struggled to shift her legs to the side of the bed.

Gaia took a step backward, steeling herself to be strong. "My *mother* delivered those. This is my first," she said. "It's the first three babies for each midwife."

The mother stared at her, shock and horror shifting across her face. "You can't," she whispered. "You can't take my baby. She's mine."

"I have to," Gaia said, backing away. "I'm sorry."

"But you can't," the woman gasped.

"You'll have others. You'll get to keep some. I promise."

"Please," the mother begged. "Not this one. Not my only. What have I done?"

4

"I'm sorry," Gaia repeated. She'd reached the door now. She saw she'd left her tin of tea next to the fireplace, but it was too late to go back for it now. "Your baby will be well cared for," she said, using the phrases she'd learned. "You've provided a great service to the Enclave, and you will be compensated."

"No! Tell them to keep their filthy compensation! I want my baby."

The mother lunged across the room, but Gaia had expected this, and in an instant she was out of the house and moving swiftly down the dark alleyway. At the second corner, she had to stop because she was shaking so hard she was afraid she'd drop everything. The newborn made a lonely, anxious noise, and Gaia hitched her satchel more securely over her right shoulder so that she could pat the little bundle with her trembling fingers.

"Hush," she murmured.

From far behind her she heard a door open, and then a distant, wild keening noise. "Please! Gaia!" the voice called, and Gaia's heart lurched.

She sniffed back hard and turned to face the hill. This was far worse than she'd imagined it could be. Though her ears remained primed, listening for another cry in the night, she started forward again and trod rapidly up the hill toward the Enclave. The moon cast a blue light on the dark, wood and stone buildings around her, and once her foot caught against a rock. In contrast to the urgency that drove her forward, a hollow, sleepy silence filled the air. She'd made this trip many times before on her mother's behalf, but until tonight, it had never seemed like such a long journey. She knew the baby would be fine, even better than fine. She knew the mother would have others. More than anything, she knew it was the law that she turn this baby over and that if she didn't, her own life and that of the mother were forfeit.

She knew all of this, but for a moment, she wished it weren't so. In violation of everything she'd been taught, she wished she could take this baby back to her mother and tell her, "Here, take little Priscilla. Head into the wasteland and never come back."

She turned the last corner, and there was the light over the arching doors of the south gate, a single, gleaming bulb in a lantern of mirrored glass that reflected the illumination onto the doors and hard-packed ground. Two guards in black uniforms stood before the two massive wooden doors. She let her hair slide forward, covering her left cheek, and instinctively turned to keep that side of her face in shadow.

"If it isn't a little delivery," the taller guard said. He took off his wide-brimmed hat with a flourish and wedged it under an elbow. "Bringing us one of your mom's babies?"

Gaia walked forward slowly, her heart thudding against her ribs. She had to pause to catch her breath. She could almost hear the plaintive wail of the mother behind her, and Gaia feared that she was following behind on her pale, shaky legs. A bird flew overhead with a quick burst of wings. Gaia took another step forward, into the reassuring light of the lantern.

"It's my own," Gaia said. "My first."

"Is that right?" the second guard said, sounding impressed.

"Unassisted," she said, unable to resist a glimmer of pride.

She put a finger on the blanket under the infant's chin, taking a satisfied look at the even features, the little, perfect, convex dip in the skin above her upper lip. The great gate was opening, and she glanced up to see a white-clad woman approaching. She was short, with the healthy girth of someone who ate well. Her face was mature, capable, and if Gaia was correct, eager. Gaia didn't recognize her, but she'd seen others from the Nursery like her before.

"Is the baby perfect?" the woman asked, coming forward.

Gaia nodded. "I didn't have time to clean her," she apologized. "I had no assistant."

6

"This was your first delivery, then? There wasn't any problem with the mother, was there?"

Gaia hesitated. "No," she said. "She was glad to serve the Enclave."

"And when was the birth?"

Gaia pulled at the chain around her neck and pulled her locket watch out from the neckline of her dress. "Forty-three minutes ago."

"Excellent," the woman said. "You must remember to verify the mother's name and address in the quadrangle tomorrow morning to be sure she gets her compensation."

"I will," Gaia said, slipping the watch back into her dress.

The woman started to reach for the baby, but then her gaze flicked up to Gaia and she paused. "Let me see your face, child," the woman said gently.

Gaia lifted her chin slightly and reluctantly smoothed her hair behind her left ear. She turned fully into the light of the lamp that shone over the great gate. As if their sightlines were made of fine, invisible arrows, the gaze of six eyes zeroed in on her scar and lingered there in speechless curiosity. She forced herself to stay still and bear their scrutiny.

The taller guard cleared his throat and brought his fist to his lips in a little cough.

"You've done well, Gaia Stone," the woman said finally, giving her a wise smile. "Your mother will be proud."

"Thank you, Masister," Gaia said.

"I'm Masister Khol. Say hello to her for me."

"I will, Masister."

Gaia let the hair fall free from behind her left ear again. It didn't surprise her that the Enclave woman knew her name. Too often before, Gaia had met someone for the first time only to discover they'd already heard of her, Bonnie and Jasper Stone's daughter, the one with the burned face. The recognition

7

no longer surprised her, but she didn't much like it. Masister Khol was holding out her hands in an expectant manner, and Gaia gently leaned the infant away from the warmth of her left side to pass her carefully over. For a moment, her palms felt light, empty, and cold.

"She's called Priscilla," Gaia said.

Masister Khol looked at her curiously. "Thank you. That's good to know," she said.

"You're going to have a busy time ahead," the tall soldier said. "And what, you're only seventeen, isn't that right?"

"Sixteen," Gaia said.

She felt suddenly, inexplicably ill, like she might throw up. She gave a quick smile, switched her satchel to her other shoulder, and turned.

"Good-bye," Masister Khol said. "I'll send your compensation to your mother's place in Western Sector Three, shall I?"

"Yes," Gaia called. She was already walking down the hill again, her legs not quite steady. She closed her eyes briefly, then opened them and touched her fingers against the dim building beside her for balance.

The moon's light seemed less powerful now than it had before she stepped into the glow of the lantern, and blink as she might, she could not instantly make her eyes adjust to the darkness. She had to stand, waiting, just around the corner from the gate with its gleaming lantern. In the stillness, she could hear crying from somewhere near, a soft, lonely crying. Her heart stopped. For a moment she was certain that Priscilla's mother was close by in the shadows, ready to plead with her again, or accuse her. But no one appeared, and in another moment, when the crying subsided, Gaia was able to continue down the hill, away from the wall, toward home.

Chapter 2
A Small, Brown Parcel

Gaia turned the corner of Sally Row and was relieved to see the glow of candlelight in the window of her home. Gaia was striding forward when she heard her name whispered urgently from the deeper darkness between two buildings.

Gaia paused. "Who is it?"

A stooped form came forward from the alley just enough to beckon to Gaia, and then withdrew again into the darkness. With the one glimpse, she recognized the distinctive profile of Old Meg, her mother's faithful friend and assistant. Gaia moved into the shadow, taking a last look up the row of worn houses toward the light in her window.

"Your parents have been taken by the Enclave," Old Meg said. "Both of them. The soldiers came an hour ago, and there's one that stayed behind for you, too."

"To arrest me?"

"I don't know. But he's there now."

Gaia felt her hands grow cold, and she slowly lowered her satchel to the ground. "Are you sure? Why would they take my parents?"

"Since when do they need a reason?" Old Meg retorted.

"Meg!" Gaia gasped. Even in the dark, secluded as they were, Gaia was afraid someone might hear the old woman.

Old Meg grabbed her arm, pinching just above Gaia's elbow.

"Listen. We got back from the other birthing and your mom was just leaving to find you when the soldiers came for her and your dad," Old Meg said. "I was heading out the back, and they didn't see me. I hid on the porch. It's time you wised up, Gaia. Your mother's an important resource. She's too knowledgeable about the babies, and Enclave higher-ups are starting to want more information."

Gaia shook her head, wrapping her arms around herself. What Old Meg was saying made little sense.

"What are you talking about? My mom doesn't know anything that everybody else doesn't already know."

Old Meg brought her face closer to Gaia and drew her farther back into the darkness. "The Enclave thinks your mother can track the advanced babies to their birth parents."

Gaia laughed, incredulous.

"Stupid girl," Old Meg said, gripping her arm with her clawlike fingers. "I heard what they were saying, what the guards were asking them, and they're not just going to let your parents go. This is important!"

"Ouch! Let go," Gaia said.

Old Meg stepped back farther, looking around furtively. "I'm leaving Wharfton," she said. "They'll be after me next. I just waited to see if you want to come with me."

"I can't leave," Gaia objected. "This is my home. My parents will be back." She waited for Old Meg to agree, but when the silence stretched into doubt, Gaia's fear resurfaced. "How could they keep my mother? Who else will take care of the babies?"

An ugly laugh came from the darkness. "They have you now, don't they?" Old Meg muttered.

10

"But I can't take my mother's place," she whispered urgently. "I don't know enough. I got lucky tonight. Would you believe the woman lied to me? She said it was her fourth, but it was actually—"

Old Meg slapped her sharply, and Gaia fell back, clasping a hand to her sore cheek.

"Think," Old Meg whispered harshly. "What would your parents want you to do? If you stay here, you'll be the new midwife for Western Sector Three. You'll check on the women your mother was tending and deliver the babies she would have delivered. You'll advance her monthly quota. In short, you'll do just what you're told, like your mother did. And just like your mother, it might not be enough to keep you safe. If you leave with me, we'll take our chances in the Dead Forest. I know people there who will help us, if I can find them."

"I can't leave," Gaia said. The possibility terrified her. She couldn't leave her home and everything she knew. What if her parents were released and she was gone? Besides, she wasn't going to run away with a paranoid shrew who slapped her and bossed her around like a naughty child. Gaia's distrust and resentment flared. This was supposed to be a night of celebrating her first birthing.

A cloud cleared across the face of the moon, and Gaia thought she saw a glimmer in the black, fierce eyes of the old woman. Then Old Meg slipped her a small, brown parcel, smooth and light as a dead mouse. Gaia almost dropped it, repulsed.

"Idiot," Old Meg said, grasping Gaia's hand firmly over the parcel. "It was your mother's. Keep it safe. On your life."

"But what is it?"

"Put it along your leg, under your skirt. It has ties."

There was a clatter in the street and they both jumped. Gaia and Old Meg fell back against the wall, huddled and silent, until the slam of a door came from the distance and all grew quiet again.

Old Meg moved her head near so that Gaia could feel the old woman's tepid breath against her cheek. "Ask for Danni Orion if you ever make it to the Dead Forest," she said. "She'll help you if she can. Remember it. Like the constellation."

"My grandmother?" Gaia asked, confused. Her grandmother had died years earlier, when Gaia was a baby.

Old Meg gave her a quick jab. "Will you remember, or won't you?" she demanded.

"I wouldn't forget my grandmother's name," Gaia said.

"Your parents were fools," Old Meg said. "Trusting, cow-ardly pacifists. And now they'll pay."

Gaia was horrified. "Don't say that," she said. "They've been loyal to the Enclave forever. They advanced two sons. They've served for years."

"And don't you think they've regretted their sacrifices?" Old Meg said. "You think they don't feel the costs, every time they look at you?"

Gaia was confused. "What do you mean?"

"Your scar," Old Meg insisted.

Gaia had the impression she was supposed to understand something, but there was no mystery about her scar. It was impolite, even cruel of Old Meg to refer to it now.

Old Meg gave a humph of disgust. "I'm wasting precious time," she said. "Are you coming with me?"

"I can't," Gaia repeated. "And you should stay. If they catch you running away, you'll go to prison."

Old Meg gave a brief laugh and turned away.

"Wait," Gaia said. "Why didn't she give this thing to me herself?"

"She didn't want to give it to you at all. She hoped she

wouldn't have to. But a few weeks ago she started to worry, and then she gave it to me."

"Worry, why?"

"I'd say, in light of what happened tonight, she had her reasons," Old Meg said dryly.

"But why don't you keep it?"

"It's for you," Old Meg said. "She said, if anything happened to her, to give it to you. And now I've kept my promise."

Gaia saw now that the old woman had a small, droopy pack leaning beside the wall, and when she put it on, it sagged around her torso as if she'd just added another decade to her age. She took up her walking stick, and for the last time she brought her withered face near to Gaia's.

"Once I'm gone, be careful who you trust. Use your wits, Gaia," the woman said. "Remember we're all vulnerable. Especially if we love someone."

"You've got that wrong," Gaia said, thinking of her parents. "It's love that makes us strong."

Gaia felt the old woman's gaze upon her, and she looked back defiantly, suddenly feeling stronger. This old woman was a bitter shell of a person who had pushed people away from her all her life, and now she couldn't even say good-bye with any charity. She promised herself she would never become like Old Meg, withered, unloved, cowardly. Maybe Old Meg, with her unsteady hands, was jealous that the midwife job should come to Gaia, and not her.

She felt a brief thrill of promise again. Her parents would come back, like all of the others who had been briefly detained. They would resume their life as before, only now there would be two midwives in the family, with twice the compensations coming in. Gaia might be scarred and ugly, but unlike Old Meg, she had promise and people who cared for her.

Old Meg shook her head and turned away. Gaia watched as she wound her way down the narrow alley toward the far end and disappeared. Then she glanced down at the little package in her hand. By the faint moonlight, she saw there was a cloth tie connected to it. She hitched up the hem of her skirt, feeling the cool night air against her legs, and quickly tied the parcel around her right thigh, arranging it to lie flat along her leg. Then she dropped her skirt and took a few experimental steps. The parcel was slightly cool against her skin, but she could tell that soon it would be unnoticeable, even when she moved.

When she stepped back out on Sally Row, the candlelight still gleamed from the downstairs window of her home, and she kept her eye on the growing trapezoid of yellow as she walked quietly forward. Around her, the neighboring houses were quiet, their curtains drawn over their windows. She considered going to the Rupps' home instead, but if a guard truly was waiting for her, he would find her eventually anyway. It was best to face him now and find out what she could about her parents.

The front porch step squeaked as she stepped upon it, and Gaia could practically feel the expectant house responding to her. In three more steps, she reached the door and opened it softly inward.

"Mom?" she said. "Dad?"

She looked automatically toward the table, where a candle was burning upright in a shallow clay dish, but the chair beside it was empty.

The last wisp of hope that her mother would be there to greet her evaporated. Instead, a man straightened from beside the fireplace, and she instantly took in the black of his uniform and the rifle along his back. Candlelight illuminated the undersides of his jaw and the wide, flat brim of his hat, leaving his eyes in shadow.

14

"Gaia Stone?" he asked. "I'm Sergeant Grey and I'd like to ask you a few questions."

The candlelight flickered in the draft. Gaia swallowed nervously and closed the door, her mind working frantically. Was he going to arrest her? "Where are my parents?" she asked.

"They've been taken to the Enclave for questioning," he said. "It's just a formality." His voice was cultured, low, patient, and Gaia looked at him more closely. He looked vaguely familiar, but she couldn't remember seeing him before at the gate or the wall. Many of the guards were strong, simple people from Wharfton who had been selected for military training and who were proud to earn their living serving the Enclave, but she knew others were from inside the wall, educated men with ambition or a natural bent for strategy who chose to serve. Gaia guessed this man was from the latter category.

"Why?" she asked.

"We just have some questions," he said. "Where have you been?"

She forced herself to stay calm. She knew to answer truthfully; she hadn't done anything wrong. Her instincts warned her to cooperate with him just enough that she wouldn't bring more trouble on her parents or on herself. At the same time, she feared him. His gun didn't have to be pointed at her head to be a threat. As she set her satchel on the table, she realized her fingers were trembling, and she hid them behind her back.

"At a birthing. My first," she said. "It was the last house down Barista Alley, a young woman named Agnes Lewis. She had a baby girl, and I advanced her."

He nodded. "Congratulations. The Enclave is fortunate to have your service."

"I'm glad to serve," she replied, using the polite phrase.

"And why did you go to the birthing instead of your mother?" he asked.

15

"She was already helping another mother. I left a note for her to join me when she was finished, but—" Her note was still on the table beside the candle. She looked around the little room, feeling the traces of fear that erased the usual homey warmth. The bolts of cloth, the baskets of sewing supplies, the chess set, the cooking pots, her mother's half dozen books, and even her father's banjo on its shelf were all askew, as if they'd been systematically searched. Sgt. Grey knew perfectly well why her mother had not joined her.

"So you went alone?" he asked.

"A boy came for me and said it was urgent," she said. She moved closer to the fire, picked up a poker, and stirred the coals. Until he made a move to arrest her, she might as well act like they were just having an innocent conversation. A late-night, innocent conversation to top off the arrest of her parents. She was reaching for a log when he put out a hand.

"Allow me," he said.

She withdrew slightly while he threw two logs on the fire and a shower of sparks lit the room with the anticipation of more warmth. Gaia slid off her shawl and set it next to her satchel. To Gaia's surprise, the soldier took the rifle strap off his shoulder, ducking his head beneath it, and propped the rifle against the fireplace. It was almost as if he were making himself at home, as if some innate courtesy were overriding his formal training. Or he was deliberately manipulating her to try to put her more at ease.

"You said you went alone?" he repeated. "You didn't take your mother's assistant?"

She glanced up at him, noting he had a very straight nose and brown hair cut in the neat military style, short in back and a bit longer over the forehead. Though she could not see his shadowed eyes clearly, she sensed an emptiness there that matched the controlled composure of his other features. It chilled her.

"You mean Old Meg?" she said. "No. I didn't take her. Wasn't she with my mother?"

The guard didn't answer. Gaia frowned, coming closer to him, wishing to see his eyes, to verify the coldness she sensed there, despite his gentle tone and considerate manners. "Why are you here?" she asked.

He turned without speaking toward the mantel and slid off what looked like a little pamphlet or book. He tossed it onto the table with a bit of spin so it landed facing her. She could barely make out the title in the candlelight.

Summer Solstice 2403
Extant Members of
The Advanced Cohort of 2390
Are Hereby Invited to Request
Unadvancement

"Do you recognize this?" he asked.

She had no idea what it was. "No." She picked it up and flipped to the first page, seeing a list of names.

Katie Abel	Alyssa Becca
Mara Ageist	Zach Bittman
Dorian Alec	Pedro Blood
Dawn Alvina	Jesse Boughton
Ziqi Amarata	Zephryn Brand
Bethany Appling	Gina Cagliano
Kirby Arcado	Chloë Cantara
Sali Arnold	Brooke Connor
Francesco Azarus	Tomy Czera
Jack Bartlett	Yustyn Dadd
Bintou Bascanti	Isabelle Deggan

It went on alphabetically for several pages, and on a quick glance, none of the names were familiar. The pages were pocked with tiny pinholes in no pattern that she could see. She shook her head.

"You never saw your mother with it? Your father?" he asked.

"No. I've never seen it. Where'd you get it? It looks like an Enclave thing."

"It was at the bottom of your father's sewing box."

She shrugged, tossing it back on the table. "That makes sense. He picks up all kinds of odd papers to stick his pins in."

"Like what other papers?" Sgt. Grey asked. "Anything else you can think of?"

She frowned at him. "Didn't you ask him this yourself?"

He picked up the pamphlet and slid it slowly into the pocket of his jacket.

"I need to know if your mother gave you anything recently—a list or a record book or a calendar of some sort."

Confused, Gaia glanced automatically at the calendar that hung in the kitchen by the back window. They kept track of when her dad's clothing orders were promised, and when they planned to meet friends at the Tvaltar, and when one of the pullets laid its first egg. It listed her family's birthdays, including her brothers'. Only then did she remember what Old Meg had given her. Gaia's heart fluttered as she thought of what was tied against her leg at that very moment. She didn't know what it was, but if he searched her and found it, would he believe her? She tried to guess, watching the visible lines of his smooth, angular cheeks, and his precise, colorless lips.

"There's the calendar there," she said, pointing to the one on the wall.

"No. Something else. A list perhaps."

"All she gave me is in my satchel," she said. "There's no list."

"May I?" he asked, reaching toward the table.

18

She made a gesture of permission, as if she had a choice.

Sgt. Grey opened her bag and carefully examined each item as he took it out: the squat, metal, dark-blue teakettle and its two matching cups; the herb kit, a pouched towel with vials and bottles of pills, herbs, and serums that her father had sewn for her and her mother had filled from her own stores of medicines; forceps; a metal bowl; scissors; a kit of scalpels; a knife; needles and thread; a syringe; a suction bulb; the bottle of dye that she had not had time to return to the herb kit; and a ball of red twine.

He then turned the satchel inside out and examined the cloth, every seam and ripple of the brown, gray, and white fabric. Gaia's father had lovingly sewn each stitch, making a thing of beauty as well as a strong, practical bag that fit comfortably over Gaia's shoulder. She felt like the satchel was part of her, and watching Sgt. Grey's examination of the cloth and its contents felt like a keen violation of her privacy, all the more because his fingers were meticulous and careful in their movements.

His hands stilled on the cloth, and he looked over at her finally, his expression neutral. She couldn't tell if he was relieved or disappointed.

"You're young," he said.

His comment surprised her, and she saw no reason to answer. Besides, she could say the same thing to him. He straightened, then exhaled with a sigh and started putting her things back in the satchel.

"It's okay," she said, stepping forward to the table. "I'll do it. I need to clean my things anyway."

She extended her hand as he picked up the bottle of dye, and when he didn't instantly give it to her, she looked up into his face. A gleam of candlelight finally illuminated his eyes. The bleakness she'd sensed in him was as real as a flat, gray stone, but it was also tinged by a hint of curiosity. For a moment his measuring gaze held hers, and then he released the heavy little bottle into her palm and stepped back, away from the candle flame.

"I want to know about my parents," she said, forcing herself to remain calm. "When will they be home?"

"I don't know," he said.

"Not soon? Can I see them?" she asked. Why had he relinquished the charade that everything was all right?

"No."

Each of his answers increased her panic, but also her anger, as if a dose of sand was rising up her windpipe. "Why not?"

He adjusted his hat brim over his eyes. "You'd best remember your place," he said softly.

It took her a moment to realize he was reprimanding her for her impertinence. He might have been polite and considerate as long as that was efficacious, but he was a soldier of the Enclave and as such he had power over her that she could only barely imagine.

She lowered her face, her cheeks burning, and summoned up the deferential words. "Forgive me, Mabrother," she said.

He reached for his gun, and she heard the shuffling noise of his black coat as he readjusted the strap over his head to the opposite shoulder so it ran diagonally across his torso.

"Should you find a list, record, or calendar anywhere among your mother's things, you will bring it directly and with no delay to the gate, and request an audience with Mabrother Iris, none other. Is that clear?"

"Yes, Mabrother," she said.

"You will take up your mother's duties as a midwife and serve the Enclave in the birthing of babies in Western Sector Three of Wharfton. You will advance the first three babies of each month to the Enclave, each being delivered to the south gate within ninety minutes of the child's birth."

Gaia took a step back. The prospect of going on with her mother's work without her mother to guide her was horrible.

"You agree?" he insisted, his voice sharper.

Startled, she glanced up at him. "Yes, Mabrother," she said.

"You will be compensated. You will receive a double quota of weekly mycoprotein, water, cloth, candles, and fuel. You will be granted weekly fourteen hours at the Tvaltar, which you may accumulate or give to others as you wish."

She bowed her head, knowing this last compensation would allow her to trade for anything else she might need. It was an incredible pay, essentially double what her mother had been earning, and far more than Gaia had ever expected.

"I am grateful to the Enclave," she said quietly.

"The Enclave knows that you advanced your first baby, unassisted," he said, his voice dropping slightly. "This is a baby that might have been easily concealed, or sold, or given to the mother. The Enclave knows you have demonstrated the highest loyalty, and loyalty does not go unrewarded."

Gaia knotted her fingers together. It was almost like the Enclave knew what indecision had gripped her before she advanced the baby. Though she had done the right thing and was being rewarded for it, she was frightened, too. Did they know also that she had stopped to talk to Old Meg? Did they know that even now she had her mother's parcel tied to her leg? What the Enclave knew or did not know had never mattered before, when she had no secrets.

Now it did. She wished Old Meg had never given her the parcel.

She had a startling realization, and suddenly looked up at Sgt. Grey. She could turn it in right now. Her heart leaped into overdrive. She could ask him to wait, and turn to lift her skirt, and take off the parcel right now and hand it over. That would be the safest thing. She could say she'd never even looked at it carefully and had no idea what it was. The guards could catch Old Meg before she got very far.

She bit inward on her lips.

"Yes?" Sgt. Grey asked. "You've thought of something?"

She turned her left cheek toward him, the scarred side, which she showed instinctively when she wished to hide her thoughts. For an instant, she remembered the keening wail of Agnes Lewis as she begged Gaia for her baby Priscilla. Agnes Lewis! Gaia had hardly thought of the mother as a real person until now. Such mother greed was unnatural and disloyal to the Enclave, and yet there had been something so powerful, so desperate in it. Gaia could not fully close herself to Agnes's pain, and it was inextricably tangled up with the parcel Old Meg had given her, as if her mother had sent her the mysterious gift as an antidote.

"Gaia?"

She shook her head, startled that he was using her first name. It was a complete breach of etiquette. She looked at him curiously. The rigid line of his jaw had relaxed, or maybe it was that his shoulders weren't as stiff.

"Excuse me, Masister," he said. "I thought you recalled something."

A log in the fire adjusted in the heat with a crackling, falling noise, and a flare of light emanated from the fireplace, touching along his stern profile. She needed to confabulate something that would reassure him she had nothing to hide.

She gave a smile that she hoped looked like embarrassed vanity. "I was just thinking I might be able to get some of those boots like they show on the Tvaltar. The cowboy-style ones for girls."

The soldier gave a dry, brief laugh. "You'll certainly be able to afford them. It's your privilege."

She stepped nearer to the table again with a more determined air and began carefully rearranging things into her satchel, setting aside what need to be cleaned. She breathed deeply, forcing her hands to be steady.

The soldier moved toward the door, and Gaia thought he would open it to say good-bye. When he paused there, she looked up again.

"What happened to your face?" he asked.

She felt a familiar kick in her gut, and then a stab of disappointment. Twice in one night. She had assumed he would be too polite to ask, or that he, with any background knowledge of her family, would already know the story.

"When I was little, my grandmother was making candles and she had a big vat of hot beeswax in the backyard," she said. "I walked into the vat." Usually that ended the conversation. "I don't remember it," she added.

"How old were you?" he asked.

She tilted her face slightly, watching him. "Ten months."

"You were walking at ten months?" he asked.

"Not very well, apparently," she said dryly.

He was silent a moment, and she waited again for him to put his hand on the doorknob. She knew what he was thinking. Because she was scarred, she had had no chance of being advanced to the Enclave. In some ways, her case was the supreme example of why it was better to give the babies over within hours. Years ago, they used to leave babies with their mothers for the first year of life, but the mothers were growing increasingly careless, and the children were getting injured or sick before their twelve-month ceremonies. With the current baby quota system, the Enclave received healthy, whole babies the day they were born, and the mothers could get on with becoming pregnant again, if that's what they wanted to do.

No deformed babies were ever advanced, for any reason. For Gaia, one accident had guaranteed a life of poverty outside the wall, with no education, no chance for good food or leisure or easy friendships, while the girls her age who'd been advanced were now in the Enclave, with boundless electricity, food, and education. They were wearing beautiful clothes, dreaming of wealthy husbands, laughing, and dancing. Gaia had seen them once, when she was a child. The Protectorat's sister had had her wedding and for one day, the people of Wharfton had been permitted into a barricaded street of the Enclave to witness the wedding parade. It seemed like a dream to Gaia now, the colors and music, the beauty and wealth. The specials at the Tvaltar paled by comparison. That one glimpse, she later realized, was proof of a life that might have been hers had she not been so clumsy, or if they had instituted the safer policy before she'd been born.

She would make sure that the babies in her care had the opportunities she'd never had, those lucky three every month. If the rest, the other half dozen or more babies were unadvanced, then that was their destiny. They would take their chances with life in Wharfton as she had.

She had no idea if her visage betrayed the shades of her thoughts, but Sgt. Grey was regarding her still with an attentive, expectant expression.

"I'm glad to serve the Enclave," she said finally.

"As am I," he replied.

He turned then, and she watched his fingers close on the knob. A moment later the door closed softly, and she was left alone in her home, with a drafty flare from the fireplace highlighting the silent strings of her father's banjo and the fact that both her parents were gone.

Chapter 3
Rapunzel

WHEN GAIA HAD FINISHED cleaning out her teapot and cups and replenished the herbs she had used for Agnes's labor, she carefully repacked her satchel, keeping it ready as her mother had taught her. Next she straightened up everything that had been disturbed in the guards' search, trying to make the little house feel like home again. Even the two yellow candles on the mantel that they lit every evening in honor of her brothers had been shifted a few millimeters from their familiar spots. Despite the return of order, her sense of unease remained, and when she slumped down in her father's chair before the dying embers on the hearth, she could not relax enough to sleep, even when weariness seeped into her muscles with the gentle heat.

A soft tapping came on the back door. She rose. "Who's there?"

"It's me. Theo. Amy sent me over to see if you're all right."

She pulled open the door and Theo Rupp entered, opening his arms wide. "Scared you, didn't they?" he said.

Gaia gratefully flew into his hug, closing her eyes as the man's strong arms enfolded her. The potter smelled of clay and dust as he always did, and he patted her back with a heavy hand. She sneezed. "There, now," he said, releasing her. "Why don't you come on over and spend the night with me and Amy? You don't want to be alone over here."

Gaia stepped back to the fireplace and threw another log on. "No," she said, taking a seat and motioning him toward her father's more comfortable chair. "I want to stay here. They might be back anytime."

"I didn't actually see you come home or I would have been over sooner," Theo said apologetically. "Amy saw a guard leave ten minutes back and said you had to be here. Was there just the one, then?"

She nodded. "One was enough."

Theo sat slowly, and she searched his face to see if he knew anything more. Theo and his wife Amy lived across the road, and like the other neighbors, they must have seen her parents being taken away.

"Tell me what you know," she said. "Do you have any idea why my parents were arrested?"

"None. Total mystery," he said. "You know, it just happens sometimes. The Enclave takes somebody in, asks a few questions, then lets them go none the wiser. Your parents might have been standing next to someone and might have seen something and now the Enclave wants a little information."

"But if it's that simple, why did they arrest them? Why didn't they just ask the questions here? My parents would have cooperated."

"Don't know," Theo said. "That's their way."

Gaia looked down at her hands and splayed her fingers in the light from the fire. She trusted Theo. She'd known him her whole life, and his daughter Emily was Gaia's dearest friend.

"Do you know anything about my mother keeping a list of some sort?" she asked. "A calendar?"

He pursed his lips together. "Your mother kept lots of lists. There's nothing to that."

"That's what Sergeant Grey wanted to know."

Theo crossed his arms over his chest, his expression puzzled. "Well, for that, they could pretty much arrest every person in town."

Gaia glanced behind him to her father's sewing corner, with the boxes and baskets of material and needles and patterns. Her father's yellow pincushion had rolled under one of the treads of the sewing machine.

"You don't think I need to be worried?" she said, fetching the pincushion.

"I wouldn't put it that way, darling. I'd say worrying won't do you any good."

Gaia glanced up to see him smiling at her, his eyes tender.

"Come over with me now," he coaxed. "Amy will never let me hear the end of it if I leave you here, and Emily will about scratch my head off."

She took a deep breath and shook her head. "I want to be here."

"You'll come to dinner, though, won't you? Later tomorrow? We might hear something by then."

Gaia rolled the pincushion slowly in her fingers, nodding. She was deeply weary now, and with his common sense to reassure her, she expected she would be able to sleep. "Thanks for coming," she said. "I feel much better now. It will work out all right, won't it?"

Theo stood and gave her another pat on the arm. "They'll be back before you know it," he said. "Just get busy doing what you'd normally do. Keep feeding the chickens."

She laughed. "I delivered my first baby tonight."

"Did you! Well! That's what we'll celebrate when you come to dinner. Imagine our little Gaia a full-fledged midwife! Amy

27

will be beside herself. I'll go around and get Emily and Kyle to come, too."

Gaia could see he was happy to have any excuse to get his family together. She smiled, holding the door for him. When he'd gone, she was finally able to slip into her parents' bed, pull up the blankets, breathe in the scent of them, and sleep.

Under a bright noon sun, she carried the third May baby toward the gate of the Enclave, and this time Gaia felt no pride, no residual thrill from the birthing she had just mid-wived. She felt only exhaustion, and the perpetual dread that gnawed at the back of her mind. Her shoes scuffed over the dry brown dust of the road, each step taking her steadily upward toward the wall. She unrolled the long sleeves of her brown dress, grateful the light-weight material wasn't too hot. She twitched her hat forward to keep the sun from her face and noticed that pinpricks of light fell through the weave of the brim onto the baby in her arms.

In the three weeks since her parents had been gone, Gaia had had no news about any of them—Agnes, Old Meg, or her parents—and she was beginning to fear she never would. Her initial terror had grown so enormous and her loneliness so acute that she'd been afraid she would go mad with the simple, desperate need to have her parents back. She'd tried to remember what Theo Rupp continued to tell her, that everything would work out. Only her work had kept her going, and by day she'd learned to school her helpless panic into a needling, exhausting numbness. Her nights were riddled with nightmares.

In the quadrangle, before the Tvaltar, several families had set up market stalls, and the people of Wharfton were en-gaged in lively trade. A few desultory shoppers from the Enclave had wandered down to inspect the wares, and for them, Gaia knew, the prices would go up. Gaia waved to Amy

28

Rupp, who had a blanket spread with bowls Gaia had watched her throw on her potter's wheel earlier that month. Old man Perry sat under a makeshift umbrella of shade with a barrel of water on wheels and a string of cups. A whiff of the vinegar he used to rinse the cups between customers was enough to make her wish for a drink, but she had to keep moving. Another man sold woven mats and hats. Still others sold eggs, ground cinnamon, herbs, and loaves of flat, dark bread.

Gaia heard the chink of coins and saw the smithy exchange a bright blade for several Tvaltar passes. Above, a brace of pigeons flew by on their heavy, loud wings and vanished in a messy nest at the apex of the Tvaltar roof. Several dirty, barefoot children ran through the quadrangle, laughing as they kicked a soccer ball. One ancient mesquite tree cast a pool of shade where several old people had gathered to rest on the rickety stools that always waited there.

"Coming to the Tvaltar later, Gaia?" Perry called, waving himself with a paddle fan.

"Not tonight."

"Suit yourself, then."

Gaia glanced back at the façade of the Tvaltar, and the doors that were closed to keep the interior cool. In the weeks since her parents had been arrested, Gaia had avoided the Tvaltar and its palliative escapism, but now as she saw a pair of young girls head inside, she remembered how the Tvaltar had been a magical place to her when she was little.

Until recently, she'd liked the colorful costumes, the music, and the dancing that splashed across the gigantic screen. She'd liked the short specials about life inside the Enclave, with its fashion and parties and glamour. There were specials about the Protectorat's family, with his advanced son and his own son and his two twin daughters, just a little younger than she. She'd enjoyed the archive reels from the cool age, with all its strange technology, and the nature ones about horses and elephants and other extinct species.

But most of all, when she was very young, she'd loved the fairy-tale stories that took her into a different life. These would stay with her for weeks afterward. She had only to close her eyes on her own back porch, and she would be carried away again to a world under the sea where mermaids sang, or to a land where dwarves lived in a wooded glade, or to a castle tower where a princess under a magic spell slept for years while the dust gathered around her and generations beyond the enchanted forest grew up and had children of their own.

She remembered in particular how on the night of her friend Emily Rupp's fifth birthday, Emily's parents promised to take Emily, Gaia, and their friend Sasha to the Tvaltar to see *Rapunzel.* To add to the excitement, Sasha had never been to the Tvaltar before because her family couldn't afford passes, so Gaia and Emily had the pleasure of anticipating their friend's delight.

"It's huge," Emily explained. "As tall as the Enclave wall, with moving pictures."

They were holding hands, with Emily in the middle, skipping ahead of Emily's parents toward the quadrangle.

"It gets dark before the show," Gaia said. "There are twinkling lights in the ceiling like stars, and on the side walls, other lights go down on a horizon, like sunset. That's how you know it's about to start."

"And people go every night?" Sasha asked.

"No. Well, maybe some grown-ups do. But only if they have Tvaltar passes," Emily said. When Emily leaned close to them, Gaia could smell the cake still on her breath. "My mom got them special. For my birthday."

Gaia just hoped *Rapunzel* was as good as the other shows she'd seen. Her mother had told her that the story had a tower in it, like the tower of the Bastion, and a princess with a very long braid. She, Emily, and Sasha had braided their hair on purpose for the show, and Gaia's brown braids were the longest. Sasha's blond braids were the shortest. Emily's red hair was so thin, they put it into one braid.

Soon they passed through the tall doors. Gaia looked back at Sasha, who was gazing up at the stars in the ceiling with suitable awe.

"What did we tell you!" Gaia said.

Sasha simply closed her lips, speechless.

Emily poked her. "I knew you'd like it. The show hasn't even started yet."

"Come on," Gaia said, pulling at Emily again, trying to lead her down the long aisle that sloped toward the huge screen. People were filling up the benches all around them, talking and laughing in merry voices. Many of the women waved paddle fans idly before their faces, and some of the younger men who'd let their arms become uncovered while working in the fields had bright red burns.

Gaia glanced back for Emily's parents, wishing they would hurry, and then, to her amazement, she saw them start to turn into a row of benches only halfway toward the front.

"Girls!" Emily's mother called.

Emily and Sasha turned obediently, but Gaia tugged at Emily's hand.

"No," Gaia said. "Let's go down to the front. That's where the good benches are. Look! There's plenty."

Emily shook her head. A couple of adults budged past them, jostling them.

"We can't go down there," Emily said.

"Why not?"

"That's where the freaks sit," Emily said.

Gaia didn't understand. She didn't know what a freak was.

31

She and her parents always sat at the front of the Tvaltar. That's where their friends were. That's where it was easy to see. She slipped her hand out of Emily's and turned to take a few more steps down the sloping aisle, toward the front.

"Gaia!" Emily's father called firmly.

But Gaia kept going, like she couldn't help it, like the slope was pulling her down. There were the benches where she and her family had sat the other times that they'd come. There was the boy with the cleft lip, and the boy with crutches. Their parents were mixed among them, still standing, talking to each other. She could see the quiet, moody boy who lived with the artist, and a very small girl whose arm didn't grow right. The girl lifted her hand and waved to Gaia.

Freaks, Gaia thought. *They let the freak families sit in the front.*

"Gaia!" Emily's father said.

She jumped as his hand came to rest on her shoulder. "We're sitting back here today," he said gently.

An usher came toward them. "Hey, Theo. She can sit up here," the man said casually. "She can bring her friends, too, if you want."

Emily's father took her hand. "Thanks. That's all right."

Mutely, she felt him tug her gently. "Come on, Gaia," he said softly. "The show's starting soon."

She realized suddenly that most of the people had sat down now and the chatter was dying down. Turning, she saw the rows of faces and watched as one by one, as if on cue, they all began to turn toward her and Emily's father. Gaia was wearing a new dress, a pretty brown one her father had made for her just the week before, with a soft, curved collar and a bow in the back. Matching ribbons were carefully tied at the ends of her braids. But she knew the people were not noticing her clothes. They were staring at her scar. And as she and Emily's

32

father walked back up the aisle, to the place where Emily and Sasha were already sitting with Emily's mother, Gaia heard whispers. Muttering. She didn't have to hear individual words to know it was pity. The only thing that stung worse was the deeper message: freak.

Not even *Rapunzel*, the most amazing Tvaltar show she'd ever seen, could make Gaia forget what she really was. Just before the end, she begged Emily's mother to let her leave early, before the lights came up, to avoid the staring crowd. To clinch any last doubt Gaia might have had, Emily's merciful mother agreed with her, and took the freak out.

Chapter 4
The Folded Triangle

GAIA BLINKED AND THE MEMORY VANISHED, leaving only a trace of the old shame. Even the worst feeling, with time and familiarity, became tolerable. A pigeon was audibly pecking at the dirt before her feet. Perry had turned back to his friends, and the baby made a small shifting motion in her arms. As Gaia left the quadrangle and continued upward toward the gate, she passed a couple of Enclave men dressed in white and evaded their gazes with the brim of her hat.

Gaia's job was to advance a baby, and that's what she would focus on. Today's mother, Sonya, had not objected or complained. She had known when Gaia arrived that this was a third child of the month, and Sonya had accepted that the infant would be advanced. This, and knowing Sonya had two kept children already, should have made advancing the baby easier for Gaia, but she found the woman's passivity disturbing. She kept expecting someone to react like Agnes had, with tormented, heart-wrenching cries. But no one did, and Agnes had vanished along with the agony of that night. Gaia didn't know whether she'd been arrested or fled, like Old Meg, to the wasteland.

34

Gaia glanced down at the sleeping child and wearily touched his little ruddy cheek. "You'll have a good life," she whispered.

Uneasy, she wiped a strand of her dark hair back over her right ear and glanced up at the banging, sloshy noise of a filthy boy who was washing dust from a rain-collecting panel.

"Are you wasting water?" called a voice from the doorway behind him.

"No, Ma," he said, his sponge dripping over the bucket.

"If you take your hat off, so help me, I'll knock your head off, too. I don't want you burning."

"I got it on."

He nudged his hat back to grin up at Gaia, his teeth white and his feet wet in a dark track of mud. From above, an unseen man laughed pleasantly, and Gaia heard the clink of dishes.

Despite the crude simplicity of the Wharfton homes and the endless work, life outside the wall had a raw decency for a moment. At least no one ever actually starved. Her parents' arrest and continued absence were making her question things she'd taken for granted and see the impoverished community outside the wall with new eyes. Perhaps the three advanced babies from their sector were simply payment for the water, mycoprotein, and electricity the Enclave gave them all. Perhaps the exchange, stripped of its veneer of privilege and promise, was that simple. And was it worth it? She passed another row of sunny, scrappy hovels and wondered if the people behind the rattan shades were watching her progress, secretly celebrating that this was the last quota baby for May.

Eastern Sector Two had reached its quota, too. Gaia had heard the news the day before from Emily's mother, who only pretended to be sorry that her grandchild would not be advanced. Emily was bright-eyed with excitement to be a mother, and her husband Kyle strutted around the wharf with his black hair thrown back, full of muscle-bound pride. Their child was likely to have a completely un-extraordinary life outside the wall, like Emily and Kyle, and grow up to serve the Enclave also. Gaia couldn't quite be happy for them, knowing how they would struggle, but neither was she sad, and that added to her confusion.

As the road ascended, Gaia had a view of the unlake on her right. It was almost possible, from this higher vantage point, to imagine how Unlake Superior had once been full of fresh water, a vast supply that had stretched all the way toward the shimmering southern horizon. Now Wharfton marked the edge of a great, empty basin that sank into a valley of granite, with alluvial fans of boulders and ledges of aspen and wildflowers. Where once there was water, now the only hint of blue came from the washed-out gray of pure distance.

To her left, looming larger with every step that drew her closer, was the massive wall of the Enclave.

The doors in the wall were open this time of day, and as Gaia came around a last bend, she could see through them to the clean, cool-looking buildings behind the wall. Cobblestones opened in wave patterns along the street, and a row of tidy shops with white awnings dropped a layer of inviting shade beneath them. A pair of colorfully dressed girls stood under an awning, peering in a shop window. A young woman in red called to them, and they followed obediently up the street out of sight, their matching yellow hats bright in the sunlight.

"So this is the last one this month, is it?" the guard said as Gaia approached. "The third?"

Gaia knew him well by now. Sgt. Georg Lanchester, the taller of the two guards who had been on duty the night she'd advanced her first baby, had an avuncular, talkative personality, and she had learned that he'd grown up outside the wall before he'd joined the guard. She couldn't help watching his Adam's apple as he talked. A second guard in a matching black uniform and black, wide-brimmed hat glanced at her briefly, obviously bored. Gaia gave him a respectful nod.

"Hello, Mabrother," she said to Sgt. Lanchester. "Any news of my parents?"

Sgt. Lanchester pushed a button on a panel inside the door.

"None that I've heard, Masister. I've heard a rumor as concerns you, though."

She looked up edgily and began to rock, instinctively shifting her weight between her feet to begin an easy rhythm for the child in her arms. Painfully, she pushed the thought of her parents out to the edge of her mind again. "What would that be?"

"They're saying they'll raise the quota to five in June," Sgt. Lanchester said.

"Five!" she exclaimed. "It's never been higher than three, and usually it's one or two. What's going on?"

"I couldn't say," Sgt. Lanchester said. "There's a real desire for babies, apparently. In fact," he leaned closer, "if you happen to hear of any mums as would like to do a little business on the side, completely legitimate you understand, I could connect you up with some very worthy parents on the inside."

Gaia kept her expression completely neutral, but she was inwardly horrified. Had her mother had to deal with this? What would she have done? She certainly didn't want to offend Sgt. Lanchester, but she was not about to start negotiating the trade of babies. That's what he was implying, wasn't he? She glanced at the second guard, but he had moved several paces away and was facing the other direction, out of earshot.

"There'd be some nice Tvaltar passes in it for you," he added, confirming her suspicion.

"Thanks," Gaia said. "It's a thought. I'll get back to you on it."

Sgt. Lanchester nodded, looking pleased. "There's my girl. I

37

knew you were a right one. Completely on the up and up, you understand," he said. "But I'd just as soon you not mention it to anyone but me. Some very worthy families I know, but they'd like to keep it all discreet." He wiggled his eyebrows briefly toward the other guard.

Then he straightened and beckoned to the man. "You should see this baby," Sgt. Lanchester called. "He's a right swell little man."

The guard walked nearer, took a brief look, and said nothing. He was an older man, with slightly graying hair, and square, narrow shoulders. When he stared openly at Gaia's scar, her cheeks grew warm with embarrassment, and she angled her hat brim to block out his face.

The guard grunted and turned away.

Gaia looked past him, curious for another view of the Enclave, and farther up the curved street she could see Masister Khol coming down the hill, her white cloak flapping out behind her in the sunlight. She paused when a man greeted her, and twitched her hood forward as she leaned near to speak with him for a moment.

A middle-aged woman in a blue dress edged past, heading down toward the quadrangle with a basket over her arm. "Good afternoon, Masister," Sgt. Lanchester said, tipping his hat. "Fine day, isn't it?"

As the woman gave a cheery reply, Gaia felt a familiar pang of longing. People from the Enclave could come out if they wished, but very few from Wharfton ever went inside the wall, and then only when expressly invited to perform some service or deliver some good. Not even the farm laborers entered except when they brought in the harvests to store in the warehouses near the mycoprotein plant. Was there no way to earn a place inside the wall? Her desire confused her, mixed now with fear for her parents.

Masister Khol came through the gate. "Ah, Gaia!" she said. "Do you bring us a little boy or a little girl?"

"A healthy boy, Masister," she said politely.

The woman made a little ticking noise. "Girls are very much in style just now. That's okay, though. There are plenty of traditional fathers who still want a little junior. Come to Masister," she said sweetly, reaching for the child.

Gaia leaned the baby gently toward Masister Khol and was startled to feel something sharp against her fingers under cover of the child's wrap. She glanced at Masister Khol, but the woman's face showed no unusual expression. Still, Gaia could feel her shoving something toward her, and Gaia quickly grasped it and tucked it into her pocket without letting the guards see.

"Such a sweet little mouth he has," Masister Khol said. "And he's how many minutes?"

Gaia's pulse quickened. She lifted the locket watch that hung from around her neck, trying to act naturally. "Seventy-two."

"She arrived here a good fifteen minutes ago," Sgt. Lanchester said. He stepped aside to let two of the men from the Enclave pass back inside.

Masister Khol nodded her head reassuringly. "It's no matter. Anything under the ninety minutes is fine. Lovely, lovely," she crooned. She gave Gaia a warm smile. "That's the quota for this month, then, so I probably won't see you again until June. Keep up the good work, Gaia. You're being well compensated, I hope."

"Yes. I have all I need," Gaia said. "I'm glad to serve the Enclave."

"As am I," Masister Khol said.

"And I," Sgt. Lanchester echoed.

"And I," said the second guard.

Masister Khol was turning back into the gate.

39

"Is it true the quota may go up to five next month?" Gaia asked.

Masister half turned back, looking closely at Gaia. "Where did you hear that?" Masister Khol asked.

Gaia glanced at Sgt. Lanchester and saw him shake a quick negative of his head.

"It's just something I overheard around the quadrangle," Gaia improvised. "It isn't true, is it?"

Gaia saw the two guards exchange glances, and Masister Khol frowned.

"You speak as if an increase in the quota would be unwelcome to you," Masister Khol said quietly.

"Oh, no!" Gaia said quickly. "I just want to be prepared."

Masister Khol's reproving expression lightened somewhat. "The Protectorat makes those decisions," she said. "I could not confirm or deny it. But I will say, our babies are going to only the very finest families in the Enclave."

"Don't they always?" Gaia asked.

Masister Khol's smile was guarded. "Of course. The future of all of us depends on it."

Gaia nodded. She knew this to be true. And she sensed that this was not a good time to ask questions. She reached into her pocket, fingering the sharp object Masister Khol had passed to her. When she realized it felt like paper folded very tightly into a tiny triangle, a spark of excitement almost made her jump.

Before Gaia knew it, Masister Khol had slipped back inside the Enclave with the baby, and Sgt. Lanchester opened his hand toward the road behind Gaia.

"There you go, Masister," he said kindly to Gaia. "We don't want to block the way, now. And get some rest while you can," Sgt. Lanchester added. Under the wide brim of his black hat, his eyes were warm with concern.

"Thank you, Mabrother," Gaia said.

She was weary and thirsty, she realized, especially there in the hot sunlight, but more than anything, she was curious about the triangle in her pocket.

"I serve the Enclave," she said.

"And I," the two guards answered in unison.

Keeping her fingers wrapped around the triangle in her pocket, she started back down the main road and veered into one of the narrow lanes of Eastern Sector One. She waited until she had turned several corners, passed a row of merchants, and then, ducking into a quiet doorway, she pulled out the object. It was a small, tightly folded piece of brown parchment, and when she smoothed it open, she was startled to see her mother's handwriting:

Destroy it. Destroy this. Go to WZMMR L.

Gaia frowned at the last letters, surprised at the gibberish. She flipped the paper over, looking for clues, but the back was blank.

"Got yourself a love note?" a man's voice asked.

Gaia turned, quickly thrusting the note back in her pocket.

A short, bearded man was standing in the doorway beside her, shaking out a towel to create a cloud of flour. Her family always bought their bread from Harry's on the west side, so she'd never visited this baker's shop. Now, as he pointed to her pocket, she felt a blush rise in her cheeks.

He chuckled and gave a teasing jerk of his head. "Let me guess. You've got yourself a sweetheart inside the wall, pretty girl like you. Isn't that right?"

Gaia blushed more deeply and turned to face him fully. She watched his friendly expression turn to surprise, then wincing pity.

41

"You're Bonnie's daughter, then," he said. All the teasing was gone, and his voice was quiet and warm, like a loaf of good black bread. His brown eyes, gentle and concerned, lingered on her scar as if he would heal it if he could.

Gaia's surprise rose in her lungs like a swift bright bubble. "You know my mother?" she asked.

He took a quick look up the street, then made a beckoning nod and backed into his doorway again. He had a way of ducking his chin so that his dark mustache and beard concealed his lips.

"You don't remember me, do you?" the man said. "I'm Derek Vlatir. My wife and I lived in Western Sector Three when our kids were little. I've known your parents my whole life. Please come. Come in."

Curious, Gaia followed him into his bakery. In the blue-walled kitchen, Gaia looked around at the two great ovens, the sacks of flour, and a long wooden table with slabs of brown dough upon it. Sunlight gleamed on a row of measuring cups. Through another doorway, strung with a curtain of brown beads, she could see a single counter that served as the front of his shop. Though there was nothing unusual about the bakery, Derek's quick movement to close the door behind them and his furtive glance into the other room put her on alert.

"We only have a minute," he said.

"You've heard something," she said.

He nodded, and she saw now his concern for her went far beyond mere pity for her scar.

"I don't know how else to say this. Your parents are in the Enclave prison," he said. "They've been accused of being traitors, and this morning they were sentenced to death."

Gaia backed against the doorframe. "That's impossible," she said. "They've done nothing wrong!"

42

"That may be," Derek said. He looked back over his shoulder and took a step nearer to her, speaking softly. "But they're set to be executed next week."

"How do you know this?" Gaia demanded, suspicious. Her heart was pounding with fear. He might be tricking her. He might be a guard in disguise testing to see if she herself was loyal or not.

"Listen," he said. "I know this is hard to hear. It's hard for me, too. I've known your parents since we were kids, so when they were arrested, I asked my baker friends inside the wall to try to see what they could find out. I kept hoping I would have better news, and then this morning I heard this. You have to trust me." He held up his hands, as if they could plead for him.

"Why didn't you come tell me?"

"I've tried twice already," he said. "Both times you were out, and I couldn't exactly leave a message. I was planning to come again today and wait for you if I had to. I'm sorry, but your parents aren't coming back."

Her throat tightened, and she clutched her hands into hard fists. She didn't want to believe him, but he had no motivation to lie. The note in her pocket. Had her mother sent it because she knew she was going to die?

"They would tell me," she protested desperately. "The Enclave would at least tell me." Who else knew this? Did Theo Rupp?

He angled his face a little nearer, and it was the sad curve of a faint smile that finally convinced her he must be telling the truth. "It doesn't work that way," he said.

She fought against the oncoming wave of horror. "There must be something I can do," she said.

"I'm sorry," he said quietly. "Your parents were two of the finest people I ever knew."

43

"Don't talk about them like that!" she said. "Like they're already dead. Please, if you have contacts inside the wall, you must have a way to do something. Can't we get in?"

He wiped his hands slowly on his white apron, hesitating. "It's too dangerous," he said. "No one goes in."

"There has to be a way," Gaia pressed. Her nightmares were nothing compared to this. She was suddenly furious with herself for her weeks of docile inactivity. She should have been doing something. She should have been protesting somehow. Instead she'd been serving the Enclave like a stupid little slave! She grabbed her hat off her head and ran a hand back through her hair, thinking rapidly. If the Enclave could execute inno- cent people like her own parents, then she no longer owed it her loyalty.

If there was a chance, any chance at all that she could do something to save them, she would do it. She could go to the gate and demand to see Mabrother Iris as Sgt. Grey had in- structed, and give him the parcel Old Meg had given her. Mabrother Iris was second only to the Protectorat, so the par- cel must be worth something. Even now Gaia had it tied around her leg under her skirt. She'd examined it and knew it con- tained a brown ribbon, closely embroidered with silk threads, but the pattern made no sense to her, just as the note in her pocket at that moment was a cypher. Then it dawned on her. That ribbon was almost certainly the list Sgt. Grey had been seeking.

It was also what her mother wanted her to destroy.

She leaned back against one of the counters, her mind spinning.

"There must be a way through that wall," she said.

Derek stroked a hand slowly down his mustache and into his beard. "Only the gate entrance is legal. Any other attempt to go inside is punishable by death."

44

She approached nearer to him and seized upon her decision as surely as if she'd picked up one of his measuring cups. She had to see her parents. She had to get to them somehow. "I don't care about any punishment. I want you to help me get into the Enclave prison. Can you do that?"

Derek's eyebrows lowered in visible alarm. "Do you realize what you're saying?"

She no longer cared that she was talking like a traitor. "Please," she said. "I need to see my mother. There's something I need to give her that could save her life."

"What is it?"

She shook her head. "You joked that I might have a sweetheart inside the wall. What if I told you it's true, and I need to see him? Forget my parents. Just help me get inside the wall. I'll do the rest myself."

"I can't afford the risk."

"I'll pay you," she said.

He tilted his face slightly, then reached for a brown pile of dough and began to knead it, then roll it neatly into a long loaf. He set it on a floured cloth, then pinched the cloth to make a pucker for the next loaf. If he hadn't been frowning so intently, she would have thought he was ignoring her, but she was certain he was concentrating and the kneading helped him think.

"Derek," Gaia said softly. "You said you had children of your own. I'm all my parents have. They're probably worried sick about me out here all alone. Wouldn't they want you to help me?"

He shot her a glance and dropped the next loaf onto the cloth. "They'd want me to keep you safe," he said dryly.

"But I want to be with them, too. They're all I have. You have to help me get in there."

Gaia stood next to the table and glanced once more out the front door, toward the empty shop. The laughter of passing

45

children came from the street, and a black fly buzzed in the sunlight.

"It's not as simple as you might think, to rebel," Derek said. His hands worked the dough fluidly as he talked, and he never looked up at her. "Speaking hypothetically, of course. People have a way of disappearing when they talk too openly against the Enclave, for one thing. And then, many of our families have sons and brothers in the guard. We can't fight our own families. Many of us have children who were advanced inside, children who would be harmed if we attacked. How could any of us unite to fight against the Enclave, and for what?"

He only convinced her she'd come to the right place. He'd obviously been thinking about rebelling a lot longer than she had.

"Please, Derek," she said. "I've saved forty Tvaltar passes. I'll give you thirty if you help me get inside the wall."

Derek laughed in open amusement. "Thirty passes!" he said. "It wouldn't be worth it for twice that much."

Gaia pressed her fingers onto the wooden table, feeling the layer of flour. "I'll give you forty," she said. "All I have. And water for a week. You must help me."

Derek eyed her curiously. "What do you think you'll accomplish getting inside the wall? In a matter of minutes, you'll be arrested. You can get arrested for free anytime you want. Just walk up to the gate and tell them you've been illegally concealing your mother's list."

Gaia felt the warmth drain out of her face, and knew she was as pale as the flour covering the table. She swallowed thickly.

Derek laughed again, pointing at her. "I was right, then. You've got a transparent face, child, despite that scar."

"Who else knows?" she whispered, her cheeks burning.

"No need to fret. There's a handful of us as have guessed

she left some sort of list with you or Old Meg, though I wasn't sure until now. Other midwives have been approached with the same question," Derek said. "We've been wondering if you'd do something."

"Who are these people?" Gaia said. Why had none of these people talked to her since her parents were arrested? Were they all so afraid?

Derek's lips closed in a firm line, and her suspicions leaped into overdrive. He might just know a few gossipy friends, but it was possible, too, that some people might be finding each other, quietly questioning the right of the Enclave to dictate the rules that governed the people outside the wall. Maybe her parents had been part of such a conversation, and that was all it had taken to get them arrested. She wished she knew.

"The quota's going up to five next month," Gaia said.

"Is that so?" Derek said thoughtfully. He kneaded another loaf, his fingers moving adroitly over and around the dough. He pulled up another tray, and it landed on the table with a light, metallic bang.

"Anybody there?" called a woman's voice from the front room.

"Comin'," Derek said. He gave Gaia a quick look, and she slid silently toward a corner, out of sight behind a black shelf of cans and boxes. He wiped his hands on his apron and turned, his massive shoulders briefly outlined as he slipped through the strands of the bead curtain.

Gaia could hear a customer's voice and Derek's mellow reply. She wasn't certain why she trusted Derek, but she did. He seemed to have more information than Theo Rupp's family, for starters, even if it was bad news. She was beginning to believe there were things her mother hadn't told her, either because her mother didn't trust Gaia, or she wanted to protect her with ignorance. Gaia had had enough of ignorance.

She heard a final good-bye and a shuffle of feet, and then Derek came through the bead curtain once more. Gaia pushed slowly out of her corner hiding spot.

"You're a little thing, aren't you?" Derek said.

She stepped toward the table, deciding quickly. "Tonight," she said. "There's no time to lose."

Derek frowned at her steadily for a long moment, and she straightened under his intense gaze. She would try with or without his help, but she would rather have him on her side. Finally he nodded. He returned his attention to his bread dough, and with a knife, he scored a short mark across the surface of each completed loaf.

"At midnight," he said. "Dress in red."

Gaia gasped. Red was costly, conspicuous, and taboo for those who lived outside the wall. "Do you want me to stand out like a firecracker?" she demanded.

He chuckled, barely looking up. "You don't know much, do you? Red. And bring the passes. You can leave the water behind your parents' house. I'll pick it up later."

She nodded. "I'll leave it on the back porch."

There was a noise from the front room again, a shuffling, expectant noise of another customer entering. Derek wiped his thick hands on his apron again and reached to an upper shelf. She saw him grab a small brown loaf of bread and when he tossed it, she caught it in both hands. "You've got yourself a sweetheart inside the wall, little Gaia," he said, grinning. "Now go."

She let herself out the back door, stepping into the warm sunlight. She knew it was just his teasing way of saying the deal was on, but the word *sweetheart* grated on her. It didn't help that she'd never had one. She hadn't yet met a boy she'd been particularly attracted to, and of course no one could find her appealing. She had a flashing memory of Sgt. Grey's handsome

48

jaw and mouth, and that irritated her even more. She had seen him only that one brief night, and in dim lighting. Yet his symmetrical, shadowed face was etched clearly in her memory. *No doubt he's had his share of sweethearts already*, she thought. Some girls would be attracted to his handsome face, even though he was dead cold within. Well, it wasn't any of her business.

With the loaf of bread tucked against her side where Sonya's baby had been earlier that morning, she strode down the back streets of Wharfton, heading home, but already her mind was hours ahead of her, imagining her return up these streets and wondering how on earth she was going to find something red to wear. For the first time in weeks she had a purpose, and she could channel all the anxiety that had consumed her into a plan to infiltrate the Enclave.

Chapter 5
Shepherd's Purse

T HE ANSWER TO THE RED turned out to be simple. She used dye from her father's tailoring supplies, boiling it in a pot of water over the fire. She dropped in her brown skirt and a hooded white tunic she had worn a year earlier for the mid-summer festival, and watched them in the steaming water. The brown skirt turned a deep, sorrel red, while the white fabric threatened to stay pink. Gaia pushed the clothes around with a wooden spoon, feeling the steam on her face. Then she sat back and again pulled her mother's note out of her pocket.

Destroy it. Destroy this. Go to WZMMR L.

The letters were in some code her mother expected her to recognize, obviously. She raised her head to listen for noise be-yond the stillness of her little house, but there was only the sound of the blacksmith in the distance, hammering on metal with a ringing rhythm, and the soft chirp of a bird in the back-yard as it hopped among the grasses and herbs of her mother's garden. Very softly, the creak of the water urn on its chain, hanging from the eve of the back porch, reminded her that her father was no longer there to lift the heavy urn when it was full. Nothing was right with her parents gone, no matter how much she'd tried to go on without them.

It had taken losing them for her to realize just how exceptional her parents were. They'd built their little home with no more wealth than the other families on Sally Row, and yet their place had always been different, the drinking water a little cooler, the food a bit zestier, the clothes beautifully sewn. Her father had a keen eye for beauty and function, not only in the tailoring of the clothes he made, but in the smallest layout of things in and around the house.

When her mother had first started transplanting herbs to their backyard, they had withered in the fierce summer sun, but her father had designed trellises to filter the light, and he'd devised drainage and beaded condensation cisterns around the garden. He'd spread the soil with cut grasses to reduce evaporation and cut down on weeds. They'd caught rain from the house roof in a rain barrel, the rain from the chicken coop in another, and when these ran dry, he used the rinse water from their bathing and laundry to water the garden. It wasn't a perfect system. One summer they'd lost nearly every herb. Yet often their garden flourished, and they had herbs to share with their neighbors. He'd even transplanted a willow to the back of the yard as a playhouse for Gaia and a source of bark for her mother's medicinal teas.

She remembered the first time she'd gathered shepherd's purse with her mother, long ago, the summer she was nine. Grasshoppers hidden in the dry grass had flown up against Gaia's skirt, and she'd held the fabric close against her legs to keep them from jumping up under it. She'd turned to look behind her and was surprised by how Wharfton and the Enclave looked from that angle. They looked so small, like a town with a hill and a castle she might have built with stones on the beach. Beyond the wall, she could see the towers of the Bastion and the top half of a great obelisk, no larger than her outstretched thumb.

"Gaia, keep up with me," her mother called.

Gaia looked ahead to see that her mother was nearly out of sight down the path that wound down into the unlake. Another grasshopper leaped, landing on her hand, and she whisked it off as she ran to follow. Where the route circumvented large boulders, the packed path was cool under her bare feet, but most of the way lay in bright sunlight, and she felt like everything prickled—the bit of grit between her toes, the grasshopper's flecking at her hem, the itch of heat behind her ears.

The unlake dipped lower into a dry bay of great, rounded stones, and she came upon her mother. This was the natural amphitheater where Gaia and Emily often played Rapunzel, taking turns as the witch and the princess. But lately Sasha had been inviting Emily to play, and not including Gaia. Loss hid in the shadow of each familiar stone.

"There you are at last, dreamer," her mother said. "Look here. I want you to see this, where it's likely to grow. See these broad, soft leaves, almost furry?"

Gaia couldn't see how one plant was much different from the others around her. She put her hands in the pockets of her dress and twisted the material there, making it bunch around her legs. She expected that Emily would be gone again to Sasha's today.

"Gaia. Pay attention. This matters," her mother said.

Gaia didn't know what she was doing wrong. She didn't know why her mother was being sharp with her. All she knew was that Emily should be there with her. Gaia let her head hang and hot mist filled her eyes.

"Hey," her mother said softly. She held out a hand. Gaia couldn't move.

"It's those girls, isn't it?" her mother said.

"I miss Emily," Gaia whispered.

"Sit here," her mother said gently. "Right next to me."

Gaia checked carefully that no grasshoppers were jumping in the area, and then she sat on her haunches, keeping the skirt of her dress wrapped tightly around her legs. She wiped at her eyes.

"Here's the thing about friends," her mother said. "Sasha I'm not so sure about, but Emily, she'll come back around to you."

"How can you tell?"

"I just can. It's something about depth in a person. Now, look closely." Her mother began again, more patiently. And now, as if she were seeing an entirely new plant, Gaia inspected the pale green leaves and stems. Her mother dug the plant out carefully, and Gaia saw the spidery fineness of the roots.

"What's it for?" Gaia had asked. Her throat didn't feel as tight anymore. She sniffed.

"There's my girl," her mother said. "It helps stop bleeding. It helps a mother's belly contract again after she has a baby."

Gaia fingered the soft, furry leaves.

"Want to help me find more?" her mother asked.

And Gaia had nodded. Just that simply, just by needing Gaia's help, Gaia's mother had known how to make Gaia feel better. Not so lonely.

Now, years later, Gaia leaned forward, hugging one knee to her chin. There couldn't be a more perfect mother than her mother. Never had anyone been so intuitive, so generous, so real. And her father was her mother's ideal, balancing match.

Gaia picked up the loaf of bread that Derek had given her and inspected it. Faintly she could see a mark scored in the top crust, the baked version of the single line she'd seen him cut in the loaves in his shop. He'd made no explanation at the time, but now she wondered at it. She glanced up at the two yellow candles on the mantel. She'd kept the tradition of lighting them each evening at dinnertime in honor of her brothers. She thought of the single strand of bluegrass the weaver put into everything he made, and the fresh posies the blacksmith always hung over his anvil. It seemed everyone who had advanced a child remembered the baby in some way, with a mark or a daily ritual.

Ghost brothers had played beside Gaia her entire life, invisible to all but her parents. Perhaps loss was what had made Gaia's mother so tender. Perhaps she hadn't minded being arrested because she hoped she'd see her sons within the wall.

No. Her parents deserved to be free.

Impatience drove Gaia to her feet. All the doors were open to catch any faint breeze. She peered out the open front door, then gently closed it. She lifted her skirt and untied her mother's satchel. Inside was the brown ribbon, carefully embroidered with silk threads. It looked like a pretty decoration a young girl might wear in her hair. It was long enough to wrap around her head several times and knot so the ends would fall down the back, but she didn't put it on. She tried to make out a pattern in the colored threads, but while many of the figures looked like numbers and letters, they were unlike any alphabet she knew. Gaia scanned her mother's note again, side by side with the ribbon, but there was no similarity.

From down the road, she heard the laughter of a child, and she glanced up. There was the "tock" of a ball against a bat. One of them called something in a merry, high-pitched voice, and the lingering, melodic tone triggered a memory.

"Ah!" Gaia gasped.

Letters. The alphabet. The alphabet song. Her father loved to play his banjo and sing, and when Gaia was a girl, one of his special delights had been teaching her to sing the alphabet song backward, starting with Z, Y, X. He had used the code in little notes to her as well. She jotted out the reversal code:

A B C D E F G H I J K L M N O P Q R S T U V W X Y Z
Z Y X W V U T S R Q P O N M L K J I H G F E D C B A

She looked again at her mother's message and began deciphering, switching each letter with its reverse letter in the alphabet so that W became D and so on.

Destroy it. Destroy this. Go to DANNI O.

She slumped back as the mystery only became more puzzling. The message was in her mother's handwriting, but in her father's code. Did they write it together, or did her mother just remember the trick?

The message itself was the same thing Old Meg had told her: go to her grandmother, Danni Orion. But Gaia's grandmother had been dead for over ten years. Gaia barely remembered her, and her parents had rarely spoken of her. It had seemed as though there was something shameful or tragic about her death, and now that she thought of it, Gaia didn't even know how her grandmother had died. She didn't remember a funeral.

Was it possible her grandmother was still alive? Gaia tried to guess how old she would be, and put her in her mid-sixties. Granted, she would be old, but it wasn't inconceivable to live that long. Then again, it might just be her mother's way of telling her to go to the Dead Forest. Frowning, Gaia fingered the piece of brown parchment, turning it over and over in her hand until the paper was warm, and then she reached forward and dropped it into the fire where it flared for a second and shriveled into ash.

If she obeyed her mother's command, she would destroy the ribbon as well. She looked closely at the silk threads, hoping they would resolve themselves into a clear message, but the design was inscrutable.

It made no sense to her. She searched its entire length of approximately three feet, finding a seam where a segment had been sewn on to make it longer, and the threads on the newer segment were brighter. *It's uncharacteristically careful work for Mom*, Gaia thought. Whatever it meant, Gaia couldn't bear to destroy it. She hoped her mother would forgive her.

She wrapped it smoothly around her thumb, coiling it into a neat, soft loop that fit easily in one hand. Sighing, she slid it back into the little pouch and retied it around her leg. She stood up and poked the wooden spoon back in the pot of red dye. Even the wood of the spoon was dyed red now, and the brown skirt was a deep, dark red. The white shirt remained obstinately pink.

"Enough," Gaia muttered. She fished out the skirt and dropped it in a basin by the door. When it was cooler, she wrung it out and spread it on the line behind her house, low to the fence where it would not be visible from the road. She added the last of her father's red dye to the pot and watched in satisfaction as it swirled a dark, bloody color that thoroughly infused the shirt. *If Derek wants me in red, I'll come in red*, she thought grimly. That was one direction at least that she could follow..

Chapter 6

The Obelisk

ALTHOUGH SHE'D LEFT THEM on the line to dry late into the evening before donning them, Gaia's shirt and skirt were still slightly damp when she left her parents' home for what might be the last time. She shivered as the night air came through the cold seams. The red was concealed beneath her black cloak, and she carried her satchel over her right shoulder. If anyone chanced to see her out and about, they would presume that she was going to a pregnant woman.

A cricket chirped. As Gaia approached Derek's bakery, the moon slid behind a cloud, and she felt her heart beat faster as much from anticipation as from her steady climb up the hill. His bakery was dark, and she had to touch along the door to locate the handle by feel. She had just found it when the door swung inward.

"Gently there," came Derek's voice in the dark. She felt him steadying her arm, and she slid silently within. Coals glowed deep in one of the ovens and cast a reddish hue into the room, leaving deep shadows in the corners. She shivered once more in the warmth. Derek's family must be sleeping for no one else was there. In the quiet, the coals made a warm, flickering sizzle.

"Are you ready?" she asked.

"You're certain of this?" he replied. "You could go back home. I could forget we ever talked."

She shook her head. "I have to see my parents."

She could hear his deep inhalation of breath. "All right, then. Are you in red?"

"Yes, under my cloak," she said.

He picked up a bucket with a cloth over the top. "Where are the Tvaltar passes?" he asked.

"Here."

She watched as he held them briefly toward the oven, then deposited them in a drawer.

"Come on, then," he said. And he opened the door.

The inky, violet darkness of the street surrounded them as Gaia followed him out of the bakery, and she inhaled the dry scent of night blooms and grass. Somewhere near there must be a eucalyptus tree she had not noticed in the daylight, because now she could smell the medicinal fragrance of its bark.

In silence, she followed him up the street, then down another. They climbed steadily for nearly an hour, until she was warmed from within and her clothes were completely dry. The moon reemerged, full and perigee, to travel over her shoulder and illuminate the roads as they became narrower and more uneven. The houses grew smaller and more decrepit until the shanty homes seemed hardly more than rootless boxes to echo back the shuffles of their footsteps. She had never been to this area of Wharfton. She thought they were moving away from the wall, but then another turn brought them up against it in a remote place where a limestone cliff merged with the actual stones of the constructed barricade.

"Wait," Derek said softly.

She paused, looking back over her shoulder. Farther away, and downward, she was surprised to see the glow of the gate where so often she had delivered babies. She could even see the small, alert figures of the guards, shrunken by the distance. Along the eastern horizon, the short summer night was already yielding to a hint of purple. She turned back to the hulking mass of the wall, seeing a guard tower above and to her left. She couldn't tell if it was occupied.

Derek was doing something at the base, something that made a quiet chinking noise. She huddled nearer and put out a hand to brace herself on the cool, gritty stone. Close up, infused with ghostly light, the blocks of pale granite looked roughly hewn and patched with lichen, but together they created an unyielding surface that rose six or seven meters high. By the moonlight, she saw Derek remove a large, flat stone. Surprised, Gaia realized it must have been already loose.

"Is it a passage?" she asked.

"Hush," he said. Then he drew her nearer, and she peered down to knee level, where an opening showed a glow of pale light on the other side. The opening was a space barely larger than the underside of a kitchen stool, but by crouching and crawling, she could make it through. *This is it*, she thought. *I'm going inside the wall.* She dipped her head into the opening, breathing in the fusty, earthy scent.

"Take this," he said.

"What is it?" She looked back to see a bulging towel in his hand.

"Dough. When you get through, I'll move the stones back in place. Take the dough and spread it like mortar between the stones."

"But what if they see me?" she asked.

"You'll be behind a hedge, near a refuse pit. It's unlikely anyone will be looking. But you have to fill in the mortar or the loose stones will be seen during the day. You understand?"

Gaia nodded, taking the towel.

"Then hide your cape and keep the hood of your tunic up," he said. "You'll be able to walk a bit like that, unnoticed. The Bastion servants often walk about the streets at night, and the guards don't bother them."

She nodded again, but she was becoming increasingly afraid. She had no idea where to go once she was inside, and no one else to help her. She had only the vaguest idea of where the prison was.

"Thank you, Derek," she said.

"Whatever you do, don't try to get out again this way by daylight," he said. "They'd catch you in a second, and when they realize that mortar isn't mortar, they'll start looking for me."

"I promise," she said.

She felt his heavy hand on her shoulder, and then his mouth was close to her ear. "Do you know where you're going?" he asked.

"The prison," she whispered. "Near the Bastion."

"Go up," he said. "All the trouble lies uphill, near the obelisk. You can use it for your landmark. If you need help, look for a baker with a black oven. Mace Jackson. He's friendly. I'll put out the word for you."

Gaia wished he could tell her more.

"Up with the hood. You don't want to distract them with all that beauty," he added. He tugged her hair briefly in a friendly way. "Now go find your sweetheart," he said.

She ducked her head, set her hands inside the rough surface of the wall, and crawled forward toward the light. She had barely passed through when she heard Derek closing up the gap behind her, and she looked back. Even now, the gap was vanishing as Derek's two flat stones filled the hole. With shaking hands, she rolled the dough out of the towel and wedged it into the seams around the stones. Despite the streetlight farther along the road, it was dark in the cavity where she was working, and she fumbled with the dough, scraping her fingers as she tried to smooth it in. At last she had wedged in all she could.

She turned again toward the inner street and saw the refuse pit on her right. Rubbing her hands on the towel, she tossed it in with the refuse and then swiftly took off her black cape and tucked it under a pile of broken earthenware crockery. Then she straightened her red tunic and skirt, and slid forward toward the street and the streetlamp that glowed there. A bug pinged against the glass globe and flew back into the warm darkness.

Her fear mixed with a thrill of promise and hope. She would find her parents. Maybe she would even see her brothers, too. In theory, any boys she met who were nineteen or twenty years old might be her brothers. She wondered if she could recognize them purely on a family resemblance. How amazing that would be.

She was instantly aware of how clean everything was inside the wall. Every building was whitewashed, so that even by night, a little bit of light went a long way. On the narrow streets, the doorways were set on high sills over clean-swept gutters, and she saw frequent drain grates, so she knew that what she'd heard was true: the rain was saved from the streets, saved for recycling into drinking water. *It would take work, but we could do the same thing outside*, she thought. By the occasional streetlights, she could see urns hanging in some of the windows, large, decorated ceramic water holders that would keep the contents cool even in the scorching heat of midsummer. That, at least, was the same.

Gaia walked firmly and quickly along the dark streets, startled when her motion triggered streetlamps to come on while she passed. Thin, white light from the little bulb in each lamp was magnified and reflected around her. Whenever there was an option of which direction to take, she chose the way that sloped uphill. Eventually she came to a main street, wider than the others, bordered with finer row houses. She had a glimpse of shadowy vegetation coming over the white walls, and in one place she recognized the leaves of an apple tree, so she knew gardens were tended on the other side. It was all just as she'd seen in the Tvaltar specials, only better because now it was real.

Twice she passed other women traveling in pairs, all dressed in red. They barely glanced at her as she drew the hood of her tunic near her face and kept on. Once a solitary old man passed her, and then several young men, but they all ignored her, and with growing confidence, she realized Derek had been right: she was taken for a servant. At last, as the sky began to lighten in the east, she came to a graveled open area with several closed shops, and then farther above, a wider, stone-paved square with an enormous building at one end that stretched the entire width of the space. This, she realized, must be the Square of the Bastion. Arched arcades lined two sides of the square, and a prodigious obelisk monument dominated the center, black against the distant purple of the sky.

Gaia stepped under an arcade and rested beside one of the wooden columns. Near the obelisk, a pair of men were hammering at a platform, a single lightbulb illuminating their work, and their rhythmic bangs echoed around the square.

At right angles to the largest building, the Bastion, along the fourth side of the square, were several functional looking buildings behind tall iron fences. A tall, brick archway separated two of them, and beyond, Gaia glimpsed a smaller courtyard. She was starting in that direction when she heard a cry that made her pause.

It was the cry of a baby, and the noise keyed directly into

Gaia's nervous system, setting her on high alert. She scanned the buildings for the noise, and above the arched arcade she saw a window with a light glowing behind a curtain. The cry subsided, then came once more. An arm reached out of the window and pulled a shutter closed. Gaia listened intently, but then the only noise she could hear was the distant voice of one of the workers while the hammering paused. Unnerved, she pulled her cloak closer around her. That might be a baby she herself had advanced.

She examined the building, looking for signs that it might be the Nursery, but she judged it was more likely to be a private apartment, like others above the shops of the arcade.

"It's okay," Gaia whispered, calming herself. She was all right so far, but she was impatient to know more about her surroundings. It was daunting to realize how little practical information she had gathered from the Tvaltar specials she'd seen. They had focused on celebrations and holidays, when what she could use now was a guidebook with a decent map.

Gaia drew back farther as the clatter of marching feet approached, and suddenly four guards appeared in the tall, brick archway. They stomped loudly past Gaia, and she saw that in the midst of them was a fifth figure, a man whose hands were tied behind him and who stumbled along on bare feet. They marched toward the massive building at the end of the square and up the shallow stairs to the great door. It opened to admit them, and all five men disappeared inside the Bastion.

Gaia shivered. She turned again to the archway the guards had come from, and now she was certain the prison lay beyond it. Glancing up, she saw a small tower above and to the right of the arch, its dark angles silhouetted against the ever-brightening sky. If a guard were surveying the square, she would be visible where she stood. Turning sharply to her left, she skirted the edge of the building and circled around to the back. More barred windows met her gaze, and with them her hopes sank. How would she ever get into the prison to see her parents? And worse, how would she ever get them out?

"Hey! You there!" a voice called.

She jumped nervously and turned.

A tall guard was ambling toward her. "What are you selling?"

"Nothing," she gasped. "I was just—"

"Get along, then. No gawking. You won't see nothing from here. Come back later at noon, and you'll get your view."

Gaia stepped back a pace. "Yes, Mabrother," she said. She turned and hurried away, barely noticing her direction in her eagerness to leave him behind. She heard him laugh, and the noise sounded brittle and cold to her ears.

The sky was becoming gradually lighter, with a tinge of yellow, and more people were coming out into the streets. She kept walking, afraid to stop, afraid to go too far downhill again in case she got lost. Above, people hung out lines of laundry between the buildings, and as she looked down, she marveled to see that everyone wore shoes, even the children. Old or young, everyone looked healthy and well fed.

Outside the wall, it was common to see someone with a scar or a deformed hand or crutches. But here in the Enclave, where there were no deformities or handicaps of any kind, her scar would seem even more freakish. Anyone who saw it would know she was from the outside, and she walked in perpetual fear that someone would peer closely inside her hood. Once a young boy looked up into her face and pulled the hand of the woman beside him. "Look," he said, pointing, but by the time his mother turned, Gaia had concealed her scar again.

By late morning, Gaia had wandered much of the area around the main square. She was thirsty, tired, and afraid. As she saw it, her choices were to seek help from Derek's friend

Mace, if she could find the baker with a black oven; try to find Masister Khol at the Nursery in case she might help her the way she'd helped with passing her mother's note; or keep a low profile until night, when she could escape again through Derek's hole in the wall. She searched in vain for the bakery and the Nursery, passing a graveyard, a bicycle shop, several warehouses and cafés, and the mycoprotein factory before circling back to the square again.

Then, as noon drew near, the square began to fill with people. In her anxiety, she studied their faces under their hat brims and gauzy hoods, watching for Masister Khol or a young man who could be one of her brothers, but as the faces turned into dozens and then hundreds, she despaired of finding one she might recognize. Gradually she noticed a pattern in the vivid colors of their clothing. The guards wore black. Red-clad female servants passed frequently, some with arm baskets or young children by the hand. Sturdy men and women of all ages wore blues and grays and browns, and she guessed these were a middle class by their relaxed airs and the jovial way the men slapped each other on the back. Children darted by in yellow and red and green, their wide-brimmed hats tilting with speed, while a separate class of elegant men and women wore only white that gleamed in the sunlight. Those in white lingered in loosely knit social groups nearest the Bastion, where there was a row of shady pecan trees, and they laughed and talked idly, occasionally giving coins to their children to buy a trinket or a drink from a vendor.

Gaia returned to the corner of the arcade to stand with her left side partially concealed by a pillar. Several other young women in red converged just in front of her, gossiping softly, and as guards started coming out of the tall, brick arch of the prison, she overheard the tallest girl say: "No, I don't think so. He wouldn't dare be absent."

66

"Oh, my gosh. He's in front of the Bastion! Near the Protectorat's family!" another girl said.

Gaia looked toward the mansion. The large double doors were thrown open, and a white-clad man and woman strode forward. Hints of gold gleamed in the fabric of their clothes, and the woman wore a wide-brimmed hat with stunning white feathers. Behind them came another couple even more dazzling than the first, until more than twenty people were scattered along the terrace in front of the mansion. They mingled with the other people dressed in white in an easy flow up and down the terrace steps. The Protectorat's family and friends bore themselves with an unstudied grace that was even more impressive live than it was on the Tvaltar.

"Rita actually danced with him?" giggled one of the girls.

The tall girl spun around in response, and Gaia guessed she must be Rita. Her features had an arresting, sloe-eyed vitality, combined with hair the rich color of honey that spilled out from the edges of her red hood. "Are you suggesting I would lie about something so trivial?" Rita asked in clipped tones.

"You? Lie? Oh, never," said the other girl.

Gaia felt the flick of Rita's eyes and knew she was seen. For a sharp instant, she felt the intensity of Rita's scrutiny, like a cat scratching its paw over a bug, and then dismissal.

"Keep your voice down, Bertha Claire," Rita said to the giggling girl.

"He's just so dreamy," the girl teased, and Rita slugged her in the arm.

"Ouch! Okay," Bertha Claire said, still smiling. "Did you hear he was promoted?"

Even without looking at her directly, Gaia felt Rita shoot one last glance in her direction, and then turn her shoulder away. Gaia couldn't hear Rita's response.

Gaia looked again at the people on the Bastion steps, and

this time she saw him: a tall, serious young man in a black uniform with a rifle slung over his shoulder. His black hat shaded the top half of his face, but she was near enough to recognize the angle of his jaw and the steady line of his mouth. She knew instinctively that Sgt. Grey was the guard the girls were gossiping about. He absently lifted his hat and ran a hand back through his hair. Beside him stood a blond guard, a taller young man, who nudged Sgt. Grey and nodded in the direction of the girls.

Gaia looked quickly toward the jail before there was a chance she could meet his gaze.

"He's looking this way! Rita!" Bertha Claire squealed.

There was a hushed flurry of conversation among the girls, and then Rita's voice: "Would you stop? What are you, twelve?"

Gaia deliberately drew farther back behind the pillar.

By the jail, rows of prisoners were being filed behind the iron fence, and Gaia scanned each face fearfully, looking for her parents. The men and women looked weary, their faces as gray and worn as their prison garb. Some had their hands tied behind their backs, but others held each other in frightened embraces, their eyes scanning the crowd and the platform before the monument. Nowhere did Gaia see her parents.

Gaia heard a thudding noise, and then a ripple of silence expanded outward from the center of the square where the platform stood. Two nooses had been slung from a beam, and the noon sun shone brightly on the gray ropes.

"Oh, no," Gaia whispered, clenching her fingers into fists.

A prisoner, his hands tied, had fallen on the steps to the platform, and Gaia saw him rest there, unmoving, until a guard came and raised him ungently to his feet to push him up the steps to the gallows. His brown hair was mussed, his clothes filthy, but his eyes were alight and defiant. He was followed by a young woman whose hands were also tied, and she needed the guard beside her to help her keep her balance. Her black hair had fallen across her pale features, and her shoulders sagged in her gray prison dress. When she reached the top step and turned to face the crowd, there was an audible murmur from the spectators.

The prisoner's belly thrust outward and up in the unmistakable bulge of pregnancy.

Chapter 7

Noon

"OH, MY GOSH. SHE'S HUGE," said Bertha Claire.

"Would you hush up?" Rita snapped. "It's an abomination."

Gaia's outrage surpassed her shock. By her guess, the woman was due to deliver within days. She could not fathom any crime that would merit such a punishment. Why couldn't the Enclave wait another week, two at most, until after she had delivered? They must all realize that killing the mother would mean killing her innocent baby, too.

Instinctively, she stepped down from the arcade and began to walk toward the platform. A guard threw a burlap bag over the man's face.

"This verdict is wrong!" the prisoner yelled. "It's our right to marry and our right to have a child!"

Gaia could see his wife say something softly to him. With his hands tied behind him and the sack over his face, he leaned toward her, and then Gaia saw something that broke her heart. The condemned man blindly shuffled his foot over toward his wife's until his boot met hers. His wife began to cry. The guard threw a second burlap bag over her face.

"No," Gaia breathed.

The prisoner cried out again, his voice breaking: "Spare my wife! I'm begging you, spare my child!"

Gaia looked around, incredulous that no one was intervening. It was a torture game, wasn't it? They couldn't really go through with this. She took another step forward, stumbling against a bearded man.

"Watch yourself!" he snapped.

Gaia heard a disturbance from the prisoners by the jail, and she looked over to see her mother's face. Her mother had pushed forward to the fence and gripped it with both hands; she was staring hard at Gaia across the crowded square.

"Mother," Gaia whispered. She expected her mother to yell, to say something to the guard who was now fitting a noose around the male prisoner's neck, but her mother looked only at Gaia with a mute, pleading expression. She shook her head slightly, her lips bitten inward, and Gaia knew clearly what the message was: Do nothing.

Shocked, Gaia took another step toward the platform. The guard was putting a second noose over the pregnant woman's head now.

"Stop!" Gaia said.

The people around her turned and withdrew from her. Their expressions were a mix of confusion and contempt. She took another step forward and held out her hand. "No!" she cried.

But a hand on her arm held her back. "Idiot!" came a voice in her ear. "You want to see us all killed?"

Gaia, frozen, turned to her right and found Rita's scathing eyes millimeters from her own. She watched as Rita's glare widened in surprise at her scar, and then Rita released her arm. On the platform, the two prisoners, hooded and noosed, stood side by side, their feet touching. The woman's head bowed beneath her hood as if she were crying, and her belly, enormous under her gray dress, seemed to shake with her grief.

71

Gaia looked to the people at the Bastion, and her shock turned to horror. No one was stopping this execution. It seemed impossible, but someone there must have ordered this murder. Why?

Glancing toward the black-clad form of Sgt. Grey, she was startled to find his eyes upon her and Rita. In that instant, she perceived that he knew, somehow, who she was. *Stop this*, she thought, aiming all the power of her outrage in his direction. His hand clenched on his rifle strap, but otherwise he did nothing.

Her gaze shot back to the platform as the guard spoke in a loud and terrible voice:

"Patrick Carrillo and Loretta Shepard. You are found guilty of a most pernicious crime against the State. In flagrant disregard for the laws of the Enclave and the natural order, you have violated the Genetic Screening Act for Advanced Citizens, you have married your siblings, and you have incestuously conceived a genetic abomination. For this, the sentence is death. Let you be an example to others who would so defy the will of the Enclave."

There was one last cry from the man, a protest that Gaia could not understand for it was cut off by a banging noise as the trapdoor beneath the prisoners was released and they both dropped to their deaths.

An awful, loaded silence weighed in the courtyard, and not a soul spoke. The only sound was a creak from one of the ropes as the bodies swayed slightly below. Around her neck, the chain of Gaia's locket watch grew heavy. She could feel the second hand ticking off the instants before the entombed baby would notice the distress of its mother's body. First it would feel the lack of movement, the thinning oxygen, the sluggish heart. Gaia only dimly grasped why the parents had been condemned, but she fully understood the death sentence happening to the child.

"No," Gaia whispered. She clutched the hard, round weight of her watch through the fabric of her shirt.

"I don't know who you are, or where you come from," Rita said, gripping her arm again and speaking in a low voice. "But you'd better leave. A hundred people heard your outburst, and any one of them could decide to turn you in right now."

Gaia barely registered her warning or noticed that several people were still watching them. She couldn't spare a look for her mother or Sgt. Grey. Her mind was entirely focused on the baby. "I must get to the prisoner," Gaia said.

"It's too late," Rita said, twitching her red muslin hood forward to shade her cheeks from the sun. "They're dead."

A desperate urgency was beginning to boil in Gaia's blood. She turned for the last time to Rita.

"You don't understand," Gaia said. "I have to go."

Gaia hurried through the thinning crowd toward the platform. The guard at the platform loosened the rope from above, and another man below collected the male prisoner's body and laid it unceremoniously facedown on a cart. Gaia arrived just as the woman's body was being lowered. Mercifully, the men left the burlap sacks over the heads while they slipped the nooses free to use again another time. Without looking, Gaia instinctively felt her locket watch circle into the second minute, and she began to panic.

"Where are you taking the bodies?" she asked the man with the cart.

He looked at her, frowning. "Are you from the family, then?" he asked.

"Yes," she lied. "I'm supposed to stay with them until the others come."

73

"I was told they couldn't come until sundown," he said doubtfully. "Too disgraced to come earlier, not that I blame them. I'm to store the cadavers out of the sun. Will you be paying me?"

"Tonight," she said. "My uncle will pay you tonight."

He looked at her curiously. "What's wrong with yer face?"

She turned her cheek away.

"Come, girl. What's wrong with yer face?" he repeated.

She turned to face him again and felt the barely restrained fury in her own expression. "Do you really think that matters at a time like this?" she said coldly.

He tipped his cap at her. "No offense intended, Masister," he said.

"Quickly, now," she said.

The man did not move quickly, but he took up the two long handles of his cart and wheeled it over the bumpy cobblestones toward a quiet back street. Gaia felt hope seeping out of her with every meter they traveled. She knew the longer the baby remained without oxygen, the greater the chances of brain damage and death.

They arrived finally at a narrow street. Off the end of it was a passage so narrow the cart could barely fit through, and then finally there was a small yard with a shed where the man lodged the cart.

"They're likely to smell in a few hours," the man said. "They're safe enough here if it's vandals your worried about. If you like, you can wait at the pub around the corner. You'll see anyone arriving."

"This is fine," she said.

He looked skeptical. She busied herself with righting an empty barrel so she could appear to settle on it in the shade.

"Suit yerself, then," he said, and ambled toward the road.

As soon as the man's back was turned, she stepped inside

74

the shed and closed the wide wooden door. Cracks of sunlight came through slits in the wooden walls, and a spiderweb-covered window let in another block of grimy light, but Gaia was in such a hurry she barely noticed.

She felt for the woman's pulse, but there was none, and a quick look at the woman's neck persuaded her she had died instantly from a broken neck. Gaia ripped at the woman's dress, exposing her pale, mottled belly. Pale streaks of blue crossed beneath the skin, and a heavy, unnatural clamminess clung to her, but Gaia pressed her fingers firmly against her still-warm stomach. There was no movement within, no flicker to indicate the infant might still live, but certainly the baby's heart had continued to beat, circulating oxygen through the placental blood, even after her mother was dead.

Gaia closed her eyes and paused. She had never performed a blade delivery. She had seen her mother do it almost a dozen times, but only when the mother's life was at risk, and in most of those cases, the mother had died afterward. But here, the mother was dead already. There was nothing to lose, and there was a chance—a remote one certainly, but a chance—that she could save the baby inside. It took her less than an instant to realize she had made her decision already, the moment she'd seen the mother drop through the hangman's platform.

She reached into her satchel and swiftly chose the short, sharp scalpel in her toolkit. She cut low and firmly below the woman's belly button and gasped as the sweet-scented blood oozed sluggishly around the blade. There were three layers of muscle to cut through, tough but flexible, and when she reached the layer of the womb she had to be careful not to hurt the baby. She steadied the womb surface with one hand while she again drew the blade firmly. Next came a gush of amniotic fluid with its strong, earthy smell, and she could see the pale blue body curled inside. Gaia reached in and pulled gently, bringing out a baby no larger than a loaf of bread. The limp legs dangled. A cream-colored, waxy substance clung in patches to his skin. Gaia smeared the bloody, mucousy covering off the baby's face and suctioned quickly with a rubber bulb. She secured her own mouth over the infant's lips and nose, ignoring the taste of blood. Gently, with hardly more than a puff, she breathed into the child. She saw his chest rise slightly. She gave the infant's chest three compressions, then tried another couple breaths of gentle air.

Nothing happened. She turned the infant facedown and gave his back a firm slap, then breathed into him again, willing him to respond. She tried another round of chest compressions, then another. His body remained limp and unresponsive, and Gaia fought against tears of frustration. She was too late. It had been too long. He was dead like his father and mother, killed by the Enclave before he ever had a chance to breathe its corrupt air.

She listened to the baby's beatless chest, checked his air passages once more, and breathed into him again, doing instinctively what she hoped was right and wishing more than ever that her mother could be there to help her. After another series of chest compressions she paused, peering at the little lax face. "Please," she whispered. She had given up her chance to see her mother. She had risked her own life to help him. He must somehow live.

"What are you doing?" a voice said quietly.

Gaia had not heard the door open behind her. She turned swiftly, clutching the baby in her arms, the evidence of the dead woman's mutilated cadaver obvious beside her.

The man was no one she knew. His dark hair fell in sloppy bangs over his forehead, and his face was pale. "You're mad," he said in awed tones. He backed slowly from the door, shock written in the expression of his face. She saw his boot heel

76

catch on a stone in the bright green grass and he nearly fell. "Boris!" he yelled.

"Please," she said, following after him. "I was trying to save the baby. You must—"

He shook his head, backing quickly away as if he was afraid to turn his back on her. "You stay away from me," he said. Then he yelled again. "Boris! You'd better get out here!"

Gaia was terrified. Glancing back at her bag, she grabbed the scissors and cut the umbilical cord. Then she threw her tools back in her bag and snatched it up. She couldn't leave the lifeless baby behind. Panicking, she blew a last puff of air into his lungs, scooped him into the front of her tunic, and flew out the door. As footsteps came running in her direction, she scrambled rapidly up onto the top of the stone wall that enclosed the yard. She slid over, scraping her hand, and dropped into a pile of steaming compost. The rich, putrid smell swept over her, but she was back on her feet in a moment, scrambling through a garden to a gate. She pushed through, still carrying the baby and her satchel. A long alleyway opened before her and she ran.

Voices rose in alarm behind her, announcing their pursuit. She fled along the alley, turned down a wider lane, looking desperately for a bakery or any familiar street. She glanced behind her to see soldiers chasing her on foot, their rifles pointed, and she shrieked in fear. Around the next corner, four more guards appeared on bicycles. She bounded sideways, crashing through another gate, into another garden. A group of ladies in white straightened to their feet around a table set with silver and lemonade, calling out. Gaia ran past them, seeing another gate leading out of the garden.

She pushed through it, catching her satchel on the latch. She stumbled, freed herself, and looked desperately for an escape.

"There she is. Catch her," cried a man's voice.

She shrank back against the gate and looked frantically back at the women in the garden. It looked like she had disturbed a post-execution card party, and the genteel ladies were watching her with curiosity and alarm. Their white hat brims hovered at expectant angles.

"Help me," she pleaded.

Soldiers closed around her. One pulled roughly at her satchel, and the other tugged at the baby.

"No!" she yelled, yielding the satchel but holding on to the baby with all her might. With wild eyes she struggled back from them, crouching against the wall, protecting the baby tightly in her arms.

The soldiers boxed her in. She could see their shiny boots, their black-clad legs, the petrifying apertures of their rifles. Her heart was beating erratically against her lungs, and she gasped for breath. Never had she been so terrified. Her hood had slipped back during her desperate run, and she kept her gaze down, knowing her disarrayed hair covered her scarred face.

"We've got her, Cap'n," one of the men said.

"Hold your fire."

Gaia tucked the little head of the baby against her throat, gently cradling his shape close to her warm skin. One of the soldiers stepped nearer, and she winced when he pulled her hair back to reveal her face.

"Would you look at that now," the unfamiliar soldier said quietly.

Gaia blinked, her cheeks burning, and anger rising as she knew she was being examined: a freak and a criminal. She jerked against the guard's grip, but since he did not release her hair, her scalp stung with pain.

A tall, blond soldier moved forward next. "I believe we've found your missing girl from the outside, Captain," he said in a light, cultured tenor.

Gaia looked through the group of men. Capt. Grey stood there in the sunlit street, his black uniform unruffled, a new glint of braid over his left breast pocket. It was he who had called to hold fire. Under the black brim of his hat, his expression was unyielding and firm.

With her face still twisted upward, she patted the baby to indicate the real crime in their midst. "Look who's been murdered," she said scathingly. "*Captain.*"

He betrayed no reaction. "Take her to the prison," Capt. Grey said. "Leave the baby with her for now. I'll notify the Nursery we have a new delivery."

The guard holding her hair finally released it, but only to hustle her roughly to her feet.

"But, Captain," the blond guard said. "It's the abomination."

Gaia saw Capt. Grey's eyes flash swiftly, and then his voice was calm. "It's a baby, Bartlett," he corrected. "And a healthy one by the look of it. The girl's skills are obviously too good to waste. The Protectorat will hear of it."

Gaia gasped at his description of the baby. Before she even looked down, her throat felt the first tentative movements of the baby she held there so possessively, and then she eased the little weight against her shoulder, untangling his body from the sticking, damp fabric of her tunic. The infant boy's head rolled with a familiar bobble, his skin showed a mottled red, and with a lurch of his uncoordinated arms, the baby gave out his first, mewing cry of outrage: outrage at being alive.

Chapter 8
Life First

THE PRISON WAS NOT what Gaia expected.

There were no dark, dank walls of stone or chains or piles of dirty straw. The blond guard, Sgt. Bartlett, and four others led her into a small, well-lit, antiseptic chamber and left her there with the baby. From Gaia's side, the door had no handle or keyhole, but there was a small opening at eye level. Opposite the door, a window with clean panes of glass was open to the faint breeze, but when she went near, she saw bars on the outside, black barricades that sliced the view into rectangles and matched the dread that constricted her heart.

The baby in her arms needed more care, and she wished she had her satchel, or at least something to feed him. Without even a blanket to wrap him in, she continued to swaddle him in the front of her red tunic, which was stained and damp with blood.

"Little pumpkin," she muttered. "Little motherless lump."

She shivered as a vivid memory of what she had just done to his mother flashed through her mind. She couldn't help wondering if the dead woman's family would try to track down the child. She didn't even remember the woman's name.

Loretta something? She began to wish she'd kept a record of the births she'd helped with. She could recall them all so far, but in time, it would be easy to confuse them. Gaia remembered the ribbon in the packet on her leg and she was more convinced than ever that it was her mother's record of births. When the guards found it, they would soon guess that it was valuable, and she would be in even more danger for concealing it.

Swiftly she pulled up the hem of her skirt and removed the pouch. Glancing quickly at the little opening in the door to see that no one was watching, she untied the strings and took out the brown, silk-sewn ribbon. The markings made as little sense to her as ever, but she knew anyone would recognize it as a code. She stood, holding the baby, and turned her back to the door. Gently cradling the child's warm little head against her throat, she walked to the window. Did she dare to throw the ribbon away, to toss it out to the chances of the wind? Below, she saw a narrow street. She was several floors up, and beyond the black bars, she could see the roofs of the buildings with their neat white tiles, their solar panels, their black and white cisterns of water, their pipes that spanned from roof to roof, and their whitewashed chimneys. One of the chimneys was wider than the others, and built of black brick, and she realized she could smell the baking of fresh bread.

"The baker," she whispered.

If only she'd located Derek's friend earlier. If only she could get the ribbon to him. Footsteps approached in the corridor, and she was forced to decide: throw the ribbon out the window, or keep it only to have the guards take it from her.

Quickly sitting cross-legged on the floor, she set the infant on her skirt. Then, with both hands she smoothed her long brown hair back behind her head. Rarely did she expose her scarred face so bluntly, and her fingers were unaccustomed to tying ribbons in her hair, but she fumbled the ribbon twice around her head in a band, then knotted it in the back as she had seen other girls do.

She finished just as eyes appeared in the opening of the door, and then she picked up the baby and scrambled again to her feet.

It was Capt. Grey who entered first, followed by Masister Khol, Sgt. Bartlett, another guard, and an older man carrying a small case with a handle. With an air of authority, the older man touched the glasses on his nose and came forward for the baby.

"A table," the man said, and Sgt. Bartlett instantly stepped out.

"Are you a doctor?" Gaia asked.

He was already taking the baby out of her arms, and she had no way to refuse.

"Be careful," she said.

The guard returned carrying a small table covered with a sheet of white paper.

"What are you going to do?" Gaia asked, as the doctor set the infant on the table. She looked anxiously to Masister Khol, but her face was impassive.

"Take her away," the doctor said. He took out a rubber and metal contraption, fitting it in his own ears as he leaned over the baby.

Gaia saw the guards coming for her and backed into the corner. "Wait!" she said. "You aren't going to hurt him, are you? I think he's okay. He just needs to be nursed and bathed. If you have some purified air for him—"

The doctor turned sharply. "Purified air? You mean oxygen? What do you know about oxygen?"

She drew back farther, but the guards grabbed her from both sides, their fingers biting into her arms.

"You have oxygen outside the wall?" the doctor demanded. He sounded furious.

Gaia shrank between the guards. "No," she faltered. "I just saw it given to distressed babies on the Tvaltar. Is that wrong?"

The doctor eyed her intensely for one more moment. Then he turned to Capt. Grey.

"You're wrong about her, Captain," he said in a dry tone. "She's dangerous. I'd put her down immediately if I were you."

Gaia gasped, her gaze flying to Capt. Grey's. He simply nodded to the guards, and they pulled Gaia toward the door.

"Be careful with him!" Gaia called. "Look after him, Masister."

Masister Khol didn't even turn her head as Gaia was pulled from the room, and Gaia's confusion and fear multiplied.

"Please," she pleaded with Capt. Grey over her shoulder. "They won't hurt the baby, will they?"

"If you'll cooperate with the guards," Capt. Grey said, "we can talk in a minute."

She took an anguished glance at the baby, and then at Capt. Grey's stony face. His eyes were cold and unyielding, but something in the intensity of his gaze made her stop struggling. The guards moved her quickly down the hall, down a flight of stairs, and then another. They seemed to be moving deeper into the prison, and she saw more doors with little peek panels in them, all closed. Lightbulbs, spaced along the ceiling, came on automatically as she and the guards passed into their range, and the conspicuous electricity was further proof she'd entered an alien world. For an hour or so, they left her in a small, windowless chamber, checking on her occasionally through an open slot in the door. Then a buzz sounded and the door opened, and her escort moved her again. They came at last to a short hall with another barred window at the end. Here the guards stopped, and one of them opened the door to an office, guiding her inside.

Gaia saw a desk and several chairs, a lamp and a phone, and

what she guessed was a computer, the first she'd ever seen in real life.

"Do you want me to tie her, Captain?" said one of the guards.

Gaia turned to see Capt. Grey entering through the door.

"Please," said Capt. Grey.

Startled, Gaia felt rough hands behind her quickly cross her wrists and tie them together. It took all her pride not to squirm, and then the man let her go. A strand of hair had come loose from her ribbon, and her locket watch had slipped out to hang loosely over her red tunic. When she tossed her head to flip the hair out of her eyes, it slid forward again along her left cheek. She fixed her gaze on Capt. Grey's face, waiting impatiently for him to look at her directly so she could gauge his intentions.

But his eyes were on the object in his hand: a lemon-shaped pincushion, with all of its pins pushed into the sawdust so that only the pinheads sparkled on the surface. Gaia gasped. *Mine,* she thought, and knew he had gone through her satchel. He slowly took off his hat and set it on the table beside the pincushion, and for the first time she saw his full face. His eyebrows were black, his features more even than they'd seemed once by candlelight. He turned to the guards.

"Leave us," he said.

The men left promptly, closing the door. In the ensuing silence, Gaia's heart beat so heavily in her chest she was afraid he could hear it. When she twisted her wrists to test just how tightly her ropes were tied, she felt a bite in her skin. Capt. Grey stood behind the desk, not speaking, and with the tapered fingers of his left hand, he gently turned his hat once upon the desk. She was unprepared for his calm, dispassionate expression when he finally lifted his gaze.

"You do realize what trouble you're in, don't you?" he asked. His voice was low and unexpectedly resonant in the small space.

She slowly shook her head, and wished all her hair was loose so she could hide her exposed scar. She saw his gaze shifting over her face, studying her with thoughtful, unnerving precision.

When he frowned, his eyebrows lowered in a pensive line. "Gaia," he said. "You've violated the cadaver of a traitor to deliver a baby which, by all rights, ought to be dead."

She wondered if he realized he was using her first name, as if they'd been friends once. "I thought he was," she admitted. "But I had to try."

"Why?" he asked.

She stood straight. "It's what I do," she said simply.

"Deliver babies?" he verified.

She nodded.

"No one told you to do this? You aren't working for someone?"

Puzzled, she frowned at him. "Who would ask me?"

When he didn't answer, she remembered how Sgt. Lanchester had asked her about babies for a price, and she wondered how much of a black market there was. Or perhaps there was someone else who would want this baby, someone who disagreed with the Enclave. She was grossly ignorant, she realized. But that was because she was innocent, if he would just see it.

Capt. Grey picked up a pencil and tapped the eraser lightly on the pincushion. "Gaia, I'm going to ask you once more if you know anything about your mother's records."

She felt the skin on the back of her neck prickle and wondered how he could not have noticed the ribbon that held her hair back. "Captain Grey, I don't," she said.

His blue eyes shot suspiciously to hers, and she knew he'd registered her emphasis on his formal title. "I know you're lying," he said. "I hoped you would realize on your own that turning over the record is the right thing to do."

85

"Why is it important?" she asked.

"Hasn't anyone explained to you how this all works?"

"What is there to explain?" she asked. Through the prism of the Enclave's injustice, she saw her life in Wharfton with new clarity, and she could barely contain her sarcasm. "We advance a quota of babies, and let's face it: not one of them ever grows up and wants to come back to us, so they're obviously happy in here. Until you decide to execute a couple of them. In exchange, we get the glory of serving the Enclave and decent water and rations, just enough so we can keep a fairly expendable population living in poverty outside the wall. We're a sort of reserve for when the Enclave needs extra soldiers or field hands or babies. Am I right? Or is there some other explanation I'm missing?"

Capt. Grey paced a few steps to the window, frowning, and then turned.

"I see you have a voice after all. Why don't you sit down?" he said.

"Why don't you untie me?" she countered.

"I can't," he said.

Now she was surprised. "But you're in charge."

He gave a brief, bitter laugh. "I'm doing what I can for you, though I've no idea why. It's obvious to everyone else that I ought to turn you over to Mabrother Iris without delay. I'm probably being tested. But I've also gotten to where I am by using the gray edge of the rules and doing my own thinking. So, it's within my prerogative to interrogate you before I turn you over."

"Or let me go," she said.

He took a step nearer, his eyes steady and intent. "I don't think I can do that," he said slowly.

"Why not?" she asked. "Keep me until night and then let me go. I promise to disappear and never come back." Even as she said it, she knew it was a lie. She hadn't seen her parents yet, beyond that glimpse of her mother, and she had to find some way to rescue them.

He gave a half smile and leaned back on the desk, partially sitting on it. "Let me tell you something," he said. "The people who founded the Enclave planned carefully for years to build this oasis from scratch. We're the ones who developed the post-oil technology. We harnessed the solar and geothermal energy that we needed to grow the mycoprotein and purify the water. It's because of us that there's enough food for everyone, inside and outside the wall. Without us, most of your ancestors would have died wandering the wasteland, nomads hoping to find some peaceful settlement. But you found us, you leeched off us, and we decided to make it work."

Gaia resented his little lecture. Much of this information, or propaganda, was common knowledge via the Tvaltar, but the postcard version of the Enclave left out little things like executing pregnant women. As far as she was concerned, that made everything else she'd learned from the Tvaltar suspect, too.

"If you're really so superior and civilized," she said, "shouldn't you feel an obligation to be even more generous and compassionate to us? Like maybe start by not calling me a leech to my face?"

He frowned and held still for a moment, as if she'd startled him with a new idea. She wondered how much he, too, had been told what to think.

"I demand to be released," she said. "And I demand you release my parents as well."

Still frowning, Capt. Grey picked up the lemon pincushion and tossed it once as he spoke. "There's one problem, one that might inspire your own compassion. The Enclave made a miscalculation. It started with too small a population inside the wall."

"Why is that a problem?" Gaia asked.

Capt. Grey paused before continuing. "Our children are dying. Not all of them, but far more than used to. And our mothers are increasingly infertile."

He had her attention now. "What do you mean the children are dying?" she asked. "How? Why?"

"Different causes," he said. "There's a rise of hemophilia. That's our biggest concern."

"What's hemophilia?" she asked.

He tilted his face slightly. "They bleed to death. From any little scratch."

Gaia found this hard to believe. She had once seen a woman bleed to death after she delivered a baby, but that was different. Capt. Grey turned his gaze toward the window, where the cool light from outside traced his profile. She could see the pale skin on the back of his neck, below his dark hair, where the edge of his black collar met his skin, and it seemed incongruous to her that such a young man should have his responsibility.

A knock came on the door. Capt. Grey dropped the pin-cushion on the desk, strode to the door and opened it, but Gaia could not see who was on the other side.

"A little more. Ten minutes," Capt. Grey said quietly.

She grew nervous again as he closed the door. She couldn't help feeling he was the only thing stopping the hungry, savage system just outside the door from swallowing her up, and yet she was afraid to trust him. He was part of the system, too.

"Listen," he said. "We're at a pivotal time." He took a step nearer and she involuntarily backed up, her fingertips touching the cool wall behind her. His eyebrows lifted in surprise. "I'm not going to hurt you."

She had no reason to believe him. As far as she knew, he represented everything about the Enclave that she despised most, from the execution to the arrest of her parents. Yet she kept her chin lifted. "I know that," she lied.

His eyes pierced into hers, and then, to her alarm, his gaze dropped to the pocket watch on her chest.

"May I?" he asked.

She refused to answer.

He lifted the watch carefully, and then slid the chain to lift it off over her head. Her neck prickled in the wake of his brief touch, and she didn't exhale until he'd moved away again, back beside the desk. He rested both hands on the desk, and tilted his face downward so that the top of his dark hair showed in an oddly vulnerable way. Could it be he hated this interrogation as much as she did? She didn't understand him at all.

"Let's try it this way," he said finally. "Did your mother give you a signal in the square today? Was saving the baby her idea?"

"Of course not."

"Your watch? Where'd you get it?"

"It was a gift from my parents. It helps me keep track of contractions and how much time I have to advance a baby."

He worked the catch and the locket lid flipped open. She knew what he read inscribed inside the tiny round cover: *Life first.* He clicked it closed in his fist.

"And the pincushion?" he asked.

"My father's," she said. "He's a tailor. Remember? You arrested him."

She watched his eyebrows narrow in a brief frown, as if reminded of something. The watch disappeared into his pocket, along with the pincushion.

"I still don't understand what any of this has to do with my family," she said. The pain in her wrists was adding to her impatience. "We've always served the Enclave loyally. I never would have come inside the wall or done what I did for that baby if you had just left us alone. Why can't you just let us go?"

Capt. Grey shook his head in a stubborn way she found maddening. "We can't. We need answers. The problem comes from the inbreeding, both in the original settler families and the advanced children," he said. "Without the midwife records, we don't know how the advanced babies from outside the wall might be related to each other. They're growing up now, and cousins and even siblings have married here, as you saw today. Advanced people are required to pass a genetic screening before they can become engaged. It's usually just a formality to make sure engaged couples aren't closely related, but in some cases, the marriage is forbidden." He frowned, shaking his head. "I'm not explaining this well. The issue is bigger than just the marriages between advanced people. We need to diversify the genetics of our population or soon we'll all be infertile or hemophiliacs or who knows what kind of genetic freaks."

Gaia was amazed, and then angry. "Why should I care? You inside the Enclave have had every advantage, and yet you've done nothing by comparison for us outside the wall. Why should we try to save you now?"

"You still don't understand," he said. "You're the ones with every advantage. Be grateful we've left you alone. Your entire people are the real survivors of the climate change, and it's made you tough. Even you, Gaia. How many babies survive the sort of burn that covers your face?"

She turned her face away, stung. "This burn was not life-threatening. It just made me ugly and undesirable so the Enclave didn't want me."

He shook his head impatiently. "Not the burn itself. The pain. The infections that might have followed. The bleeding."

Gaia breathed in rapidly, painfully, as if he had physically hurt her. She hated that she was scarred, and none of his logic

90

was going to persuade her there was anything good about the burns she had endured.

"I never wanted this!" she said, her voice cracking. She bit her lips hard against an impulse to cry.

Capt. Grey was very still. Then he came around the desk again, near to her, but she refused to look at him.

"Gaia," he said softly.

His gentleness only confused her more. She focused on the corner of the gray walls, and when she felt his hand touch lightly on her shoulder, she flinched away.

"You don't understand," she said scathingly. "Children on the outside of the wall suffer, too. They bleed, too. They get fevers that rage for days and then kill them. And their mothers grieve when they die. What good is all your power—" she jerked her head to indicate the lamp, the computer "—when you leave the rest of us to suffer? When you can kill a woman who is nine months pregnant? What kind of society is that?"

He backed toward the door. His eyes, which had seemed so alive and warm for a moment, clouded over and grew distant. "Those two today knew they were advanced from outside the wall. They knew they had to pass the genetic screening to become engaged. They lived with our advantages and our laws all their lives, but when the results showed they could be siblings, they still decided, selfishly, to get married and conceive a child." His jaw shut stubbornly. "We would have wasted precious resources on their child, and then he would have died before his tenth birthday, long before he could sire a healthy child of his own. Even his parents knew that."

"You're defending murder because their child could be a waste of resources?" she demanded. "Is that what you're telling me? Guess what. The baby's alive. Now what?"

She could see a new degree of pallor in his cheeks, and he evaded her gaze.

Fury shot through her as she guessed he was probably letting that doctor kill the baby. "You're a coward," she hissed. "That's it. Turn me over to Mabrother Iris, or whatever you call him. Give me your worst. I have nothing more to say to you." She strode over and kicked her heel against the door. "Hey!" she called. "Get me out of here!"

Capt. Grey made no move to restrain her further, and she hated the way he retained his composure. As he reached for the door handle, his eyes met hers briefly. "I'll do what I can for you, Gaia," he said in a low voice.

"Like that will be much," she spat out.

She only made him laugh briefly, and she was too angry to care that there was an acrid edge to his mirth. Then he opened the door and called a guard. "Sergeant Bartlett," he said, "take her to Q cell. Make sure she has something to eat, and a shower, and clean clothes. Bring her personal effects to me, and then I'll need a courier."

"Yes, Captain," Sgt. Bartlett said, and briefly saluted. Three more guards surrounded her when she stepped into the hall, as if she were a highly dangerous person who could overthrow any number of burly men with her hands tied. She raised her chin proudly.

"Be good, Gaia," Capt. Grey told her, his voice grave. She still refused to look at him, but she could feel the heated flush of anger again in her cheeks. "Cooperate with the guards. For your own sake," he continued.

"Be good yourself, Captain," she said bitterly. "If you know how."

Chapter 9
The Doctors of Q Cell

"MAKE IT QUICK," the female guard said as Gaia stepped into the shower. Gaia hurried out of her red skirt and tunic, slipped her feet out of her shoes, and handed the pile out to the guard. She kept back the ribbon and hooked it over a knob out of the guard's sight. Already she missed the familiar weight of her pocket watch around her neck.

Stepping into the shower, Gaia marveled that the water came out warm, whole streams of it, from a pipe in the wall. The waste of energy astounded her. And the soap was a soft, blue bar that foamed readily on her skin and in her hair. Such luxury in a prison was beyond her wildest imaginings.

"Out!" called the guard, and passed her a cloth towel, followed by underclothes and a gray tunic that fell past Gaia's knees. Her skin tingled under the coarse fabric of the garment, and her fingers fumbled as she hurried with the three white buttons down the front. There was no comb, but Gaia did her best to smooth the tangles in her hair, and then tied it back again with her ribbon.

The guard looked at her skeptically when she stepped out, clean and dressed. When Gaia reached for her shoes, the guard pointed her to a pair of worn loafers instead. Gaia slipped her narrow feet inside, discovering as she did so that the shoes were too big.

"You'll have to hand over the ribbon," the guard said. "Like as not they'll cut yer hair off in Q, anyway."

"Until then, I might as well keep it," Gaia said.

The female guard, an elderly woman with muscular arms and a hard jaw, squinted at her. She grunted, turning away, and for an instant Gaia thought she was assenting. Then the guard turned back rapidly and backhanded Gaia hard across her right cheek, hitting with such force that Gaia's head snapped sideways on her neck.

Gasping, Gaia fell to the stone floor, and the guard yanked the ribbon out of her hair.

"You'll learn not to be smart," the guard said.

Gaia bit back tears, pressing her fingers to her throbbing cheek. She watched despairingly as the guard added her ribbon to the pile of her shoes and clothes.

"Enter!" the female guard yelled, and Gaia's familiar escort of guards reappeared as if they'd been waiting just outside the door.

With her cheek throbbing, she straightened to follow them. The men walked her down several corridors, and more flights of stairs until the place began to smell musty, as if fresh air rarely penetrated this far within the walls. When they reached the end of the last hallway, one of the guards opened a large wooden door and stepped aside.

Gaia peered inside, and saw only a dim, empty hallway, shadowed in gray.

"I'm supposed to be fed," she reminded Sgt. Bartlett.

"Fancy that," he said coolly, and gave her a little shove forward.

"Is this Q cell?" she demanded, turning.

But the guard closed the door.

"When will I see Capt. Grey again!" she called.

She heard a laugh, and the peek hole in the door opened sharply. "I doubt you'll be seeing him again, though I'll tell him you asked. He'll be touched, I'm sure." Sgt. Bartlett's voice deepened, and his brown eyes were sharp in the metal rectangle. "Let's just hope you haven't screwed up Grey's career for him."

Gaia felt an urge to poke her fist through the peek hole to smash the man's eyes, but he closed it then, leaving her to blink against the darkness.

She turned, listening, waiting for her eyes to adjust, and pressed her cool fingers against her sore cheek. She was in a short hallway, and farther ahead, it turned a corner. She heard soft voices of women. She walked quietly, curious, and heard her belly rumble with hunger. Because of Capt. Grey's directions to the guards, she had been expecting some food, and now she wondered if they had disobeyed him, or if he had just said it in her hearing so she might think he was on her side.

With her fingertips touching lightly on the wall, she progressed forward to the corner, and there, as the room opened up to a large, high-ceilinged cell, Gaia paused. Three small windows were open high above on her left, casting a soft gray light into the room and illuminating half a dozen women who stood in pairs or sat on the wooden benches. They were all dressed in gray, as she was, and they all had cropped hair that fell in bangs over their eyes and reached, in back, just to the napes of their necks.

Gaia searched each face eagerly, hoping to find her mother, but though most of the women were her mother's age or a little older, none were familiar. Disappointment slid through her like a stone into a deep lake. The women were silent, their expressions watchful.

Finally one of the sitting women stood and came forward, holding out her hands. "I would say welcome," the woman said. "But this is hardly a place you'll rejoice to be. I'm Sephie Frank. And who are you, child?"

"I'm Gaia Stone," she said.

There was an instant hum of surprised voices.

"Bonnie's daughter?" Sephie asked, peering closely at her face. "Do you know where she is now?"

"No," Gaia said. "I thought she was here, in prison."

"She was with us for a few days," Sephie confirmed. "When she was first arrested. But then they moved her out of Q cell. That was when, three weeks ago? We saw her from a distance during the execution this morning, too, but not to talk to her."

"How about my father? Have you seen him?"

Sephie looked quickly at the other women, and their voices stilled. Someone coughed into her hand. Dread, like a double dose of gravity, pulled at her bones. It was possible the situation was even worse than Derek had told her.

"What do you know?" she asked quietly. Her voice dropped on the stone floor and rippled outward into an ominous silence.

Sephie stepped nearer and put a gentle hand on Gaia's arm. "Your father's dead," she said. "He was killed trying to escape. Weeks ago."

"No," Gaia said. "It can't be true." Her knees sagged, and Sephie guided her to a bench. "I heard his execution was scheduled for next week."

The women looked at each other. "I'm sorry," Sephie said.

Gaia shook her head. "All this time, I've been serving, delivering babies. Certainly someone would have told me." Her voice faltered. Could it honestly be true? Her sweet father, who sewed so beautifully, who brought a gentle laugh and a wise word to everyone on the street, who played the banjo like a devil was riding him, who radiated joy in the presence of her mother—how could he be gone and she not know it? Gaia felt a shudder of pain knock through her.

"I'm sorry," Sephie repeated.

Gaia was dazed with disbelief. Her father could have suffered. She couldn't bear to think it. With no idea of where he'd been killed, she imagined him running wildly through the green wheat field toward the wasteland, his brown shirt flapping out behind him, his hat flying wide, his strong body bucking as shots drove him facedown into the waves of grain.

"Please, no," she moaned. She'd risked her life to come into the Enclave. To save him and her mother. And she was too late.

"But your mother's living," Sephie said.

"For how long? Isn't she scheduled to be executed?"

Gaia looked from one face to another, and their confusion gave her hope.

"We haven't heard that," Sephie said. "It's possible, of course, but no one here has heard that." She lifted her hand against her chest. "When you went after the baby, she must have been proud."

"How can you know that?" Gaia said, her voice tight.

"It's what she would have done herself."

The other women murmured their assent, but Gaia remembered her mother's silent message: do nothing. Now that Gaia knew her father was dead, it made more sense. Her mother had wanted Gaia to be safe, to protect herself.

"Gaia, everyone knows what you did today, saving that baby," Sephie said. "Even here we heard about it. You've forced people to think."

Gaia was in shock, but her eyes were adjusting more completely to the gloom of the cell, and now she made herself scan the features of the women around her. Brown-haired Sephie had a gentle, sad face that reminded Gaia of a full moon, with widely spaced gray eyes and a small mouth. This woman had known her mother, here, in this cell, and now, when Gaia needed kindness most, Sephie was offering it.

"Why are you all here?" Gaia asked.

Sephie's eyebrows lifted in surprise. "We're physicians."

"But why are you in jail?" Gaia insisted.

"Unbelievable," one of the other women said from the farthest bench. She was a white-haired woman with startlingly black eyebrows and a narrow nose, and she looked back unflinchingly at Gaia. Strangely, her lack of sympathy helped Gaia pull herself together, back from the edge of despair.

"Be quiet, Myrna," Sephie said. She sat next to Gaia on the bench and smoothed her skirt in a tidy way over her knees. "We're all accused of crimes against the state, like falsifying the results of genetic tests, or helping women who want abortions, or not killing faulty babies."

"You've done that?" Gaia asked, astounded.

"I say we're *accused*," Sephie corrected. "As accused doctors, we can be kept here at the will of the Enclave and brought out only when we're needed. It's absurd, really."

It sounded atrocious to Gaia. "Why do you cooperate?"

Sephie smiled, and several of the women shifted on the benches. "What choice do we have?" Sephie said. "If we refuse, we'll be executed like that couple today. It's not like we're in our childbearing years anymore. If it weren't for our expertise, we'd be expendable already."

"I don't understand," Gaia said. "Your families and friends must object to this. Can't they get you out?"

Sephie shook her head. "You're so naïve, Gaia. I'm afraid you'll find not everything is rosy in the Enclave. Our friends are afraid, and rightly so. Besides, every now and then one of us is cleared and released. We live for that possibility."

Gaia gazed upward, toward the middle of the three windows where there was a distant square of gray sky. The more she learned about the Enclave, the more she felt betrayed. It was like they'd deliberately deceived the people outside the wall, making them believe life inside the wall was this ideal existence, this golden life, and all the while it was this beautiful place of cruelty and injustice. This place had killed her father, one of the best, dearest people imaginable. The Square of the Bastion had been filled today with a multitude of seemingly normal but utterly heartless citizens. Would she have become like all the others if she had been raised here, too?

"I don't understand this place," Gaia said.

The black-browed woman on the farthest bench gave a mirthless laugh. "Join the club," said Myrna dryly.

Gaia leaned forward, hiding her face in her hands. Her right cheek was swelling with a new bruise, and the scarred skin of her left cheek was familiarly rippled against her palm. Her new loss hurt far more, yet it had no outward scar. Her hair slipped forward around her like a curtain, and she gave a moan of despair. Her father. She felt a weight in her heart that made it hard to take a breath. It was possible that the one glimpse she'd had of her mother that morning might be the last she would ever have.

"There, there," a dark-skinned women crooned, rubbing a soothing hand on Gaia's shoulder.

The kindness triggered the tears Gaia had tried to hold back, and sobs wracked through her. Sephie tried to pull her against her for comfort, but Gaia curled away from them all and hunched in a ball along the wooden bench, her face to the wall. For a long while, Gaia was lost to blind, wordless misery. No light or tender words could penetrate her sorrow, while over and over she silently cried out for her lost father. Someone tucked a blanket around her and something soft under her head, and then sleep mercifully overtook her.

Chapter 10
Blueberries in the Unlake

As a girl, Gaia taught herself to lie so carefully in her sleep that she never became entangled in her mosquito netting, but when morning turned the sky a rosy, dry pink and it no longer mattered to be still, she sometimes rolled, half asleep, until the skin of her cheek touched unexpectedly against the cool, gauzy material. Then the blind expectation of suffocation woke her fully. She would gasp before she remembered, *oh, it's just the bed net.* Then she would settle back on her pillow and stretch a languid hand upward toward the apex of the gossamer tent.

The summer she turned eleven, her parents moved her bed from the loft to the back porch where she could catch any breeze. One morning the wind chime was silent, and the great heavy water urn was motionless on its chain. Water had condensed on the outside surface, and the drops slicked together near the bottom for her to watch as they swelled and fell.

She slipped her bare feet to the worn boards of the porch and pushed the mosquito net aside to see the soft summer light infusing the air of the backyard. She could see the rain barrel at the corner of the porch, and beyond, near the slope, the laundry lines and the chicken coop.

A pullet had laid her first egg two days before, and Gaia was curious to see if she'd laid another. Lifting her blue nightgown to keep the hem from skimming the grass, she felt the coolness of dew brush her ankles. She had almost reached the coop before she saw that the door was unlatched and ajar.

With a sinking feeling, Gaia looked inside the coop. The pullet and another layer were both missing, though the six others were contentedly on their roosts. Seeing Gaia, the chickens let up a noise and started out past her toes, ready to feed on the bugs in the uncut grass.

Gaia flew back across the yard and jumped loudly onto the porch. "Mom!" she yelled. "Dad! I think someone stole two of our chickens." She hurried through the kitchen, crossed the living area and peeked behind the curtain to her parents' bed. Two lumps were sprawled among the blankets, and her dad's hand was curved upon her mother's shoulder. "Mom," she said again.

Bonnie lay closest to the window, hunched away from her father, and it struck Gaia that it was odd for her parents to be in bed later than she was. Uncertain, she clutched the curtain and drew one foot on top of the other.

"I think someone stole two of our chickens," Gaia said again, more quietly.

Then her mother did a peculiar thing. She lifted an arm over her eyes so her face was lost behind her elbow and she murmured one soft word: "Jasper."

In answer, Gaia's father put a kiss on her mother's shoulder and rolled to put his feet on the floor.

"Hey, sunshine," Jasper said to Gaia. "Let's let your mother get a little sleep, shall we? She came in late last night." He was already reaching for a shirt, and Gaia stepped back, letting the curtain fall.

She felt odd, as if she'd witnessed some small, silent, previously invisible language between her parents that excluded her, and then he came around the curtain, fully dressed. He smiled at her and rubbed his unshaven jaw.

"Get your shoes," he said softly, and she shoved her bare feet into her loafers.

Her father preceded her, his broad shoulders and easy gait conveying no sense of alarm, and with his calmness she felt her own uneasiness receding. He handled the latch for a quick inspection, then opened wide the door so she could see under his arm to the dim interior and the empty roosts. Dust motes flickered in a beam of sunlight.

"Definitely gone," he said. "And you're sure you locked the coop last night?"

She nodded up at him. "They were all there then. I'm positive."

His eyebrows lifted and he pushed out his lips, then took another look at the latch. "Well, whoever took them did it quietly. You didn't hear anything in the night?"

She said she didn't. While he collected the eggs, she looked back at the porch, to the bed net falling like a pale gray veil from the hook above. She realized then that some stranger must have been this close to her in the night. She took a step nearer her father.

"Don't you worry," he said, his voice warm and reassuring. He cradled five eggs along one arm. His free hand came to her shoulder, and she linked her arm around his waist. "Let's go pick some blueberries for your mom. We'll be back before she even knows we're gone."

"Like this?" she asked, plucking at her nightgown.

He smiled at her attire. "Definitely. Though we should take the hats. And buckets. I'll get them. Meet me around front."

By the time Gaia walked around the house, he was coming out the front door, minus the eggs, and carrying their hats and a couple of one-liter buckets. He held out his hand to clasp hers warmly, and then he began to whistle a low, complicated tune. Gaia felt a little shy in her nightgown as they passed the waking houses, but as they descended a narrow dirt path into the unlake, she liked the light, airy way the blue fabric floated around her knees. The brim of her hat created a familiar shadow above her eyelashes, and she could smell the sweet scents of the big bluestem, honeysuckle, nannyberry, and wildflowers that grew in sweeping patches between the rocks.

Once they passed below the bay of boulders, they were soon among the blueberries, and Jasper handed her a bucket. The first berry dropped with a metallic ping into the bottom.

"Who do you suppose stole our chickens?" Gaia asked. "Can't we do anything about them?"

"Like what?"

"I don't know. Go look for them?" It sounded unlikely as soon as she said it.

Her father adjusted his hat back on his head so she could see his face. His brown eyebrows were drawn in thick, expressive curves, and his jaw line was strong, with a shadow of stubble delineating it from his neck. His complexion, slightly darker than her own, was a rich tan color, and it ran deeper on his forearms where his sleeves were usually rolled back.

"Think about it, Gaia," he said gently. "Whoever took those chickens must have needed them a lot more than we did."

She was surprised. "But does that mean anyone could take anything from us and you wouldn't care?" she asked.

He returned to picking berries. "No. Of course not."

There were many things about her parents that she'd begun to wonder about lately. A few weeks earlier, Gaia had gone to her friend Emily's birthday party. Emily and Kyle and Gaia had been the only three at the party, and Gaia had enjoyed herself hugely. Then, only yesterday, Gaia had discovered that Sasha and two other girls had been invited to Emily's party, too, but they had all refused to go if Gaia would be there. Gaia's mother had been completely unconcerned by the news. "Yes, I heard about those catty girls," she'd said when Gaia told her. "Emily's a real friend."

Now her father, too, was undisturbed by events that troubled Gaia. It should matter that people were mean to Gaia and stealing her family's chickens, so why didn't her parents get upset? Maybe, as her mother had once said, it had something to do with depth.

When she looked up at her father again, he had moved farther away, and beyond him the unlake sloped steadily downward. Clumps of birch and aspen flickered their oval leaves, but mostly the view encompassed brush and grasses and wildflowers.

"Dad," she called. "Did you ever know anybody who knew what it was like when the unlake was full of water?"

He looked up from under the brim of his hat and waved her over. "No. It's been empty for going on three hundred years." He pointed. "They piped most of it south, and then the springs dried up."

"Who's 'they'? What happened to them?" She came nearer and picked a few more berries.

"I don't know, really," he said. He picked steadily as he talked. "There are other people out there, somewhere, because we still get a few wandering in from time to time. Maybe a

104

dozen in the last decade, like Josh, that storyteller over in Eastern Sector One. You remember him. One winter a horse came in, all saddled up, but it died shortly after."

"Really? What happened to its rider?"

"We don't know. I was a teenager then. We searched a long time out in the wasteland, but we didn't find anyone."

Gaia was fascinated by the possibility of other people and other times. "What was it like, I wonder. Way back."

Her father smiled. "In the cool age, people used to have satellites passing electrical signals all over the world, and cars and roads and all those things we see in the films at the Tvaltar, but that's all gone. It all took energy. Like magic."

"What happened to it all?" Gaia asked.

He put a hand on his hip and arched backward briefly. "The cool age ended when the fuel was used up, and it was too late for the masses to adjust, I guess. Crops failed. Some illness. A few wars. They couldn't move around what little food they could grow, I guess. It takes a lot to feed people, Gaia. We forget. We're lucky here. There are smart people running the Enclave, and we don't do so badly ourselves outside the wall."

"Do we have to worry about running out of food?" she asked.

He smiled at her. "Not really. We'll hatch a couple more chickens."

"No. I mean all of us."

Her father wiped his forehead and resettled his hat. "I don't think so. We had the wheat ruined by hail once, but even then, there was plenty of mycoprotein."

"Emily told me mycoprotein is a fungus."

"She's right, really," he said. "They discovered it and refined it back in the cool age. They wanted to have a food they could grow even in the dark, in case some catastrophic event covered the world in clouds. Now they grow it in the Enclave, in those big fermentation towers you can see."

She looked up the hill, over the wall, to the right of the obelisk and Bastion towers until she found a row of orange silos. "So, as long as we get along with the Enclave, those of us outside are safe, too," she said.

Her father leaned over and tugged her braid. "You're quite the worrier today, aren't you? All because we lost a couple chickens."

As she used to do as a little girl, she squinted to measure the white obelisk against the height of her outstretched thumb.

"What are you doing?" her father asked.

She lowered her hand. "I do it for luck," she said. "My thumb's the same size as the obelisk."

He flicked the brim of her hat. "Let's head back. Your mother should be up."

The winding path through the boulders and shrubs of the unlake was steep in places, and rarely wide enough for two. Gaia scampered ahead.

"Is Mom okay?" Gaia asked.

He nodded, following after her. "Your mother's fine," he said. "She just had a tough night."

"Did she advance another baby?"

"She did."

"Has there always been a baby quota?"

"No," he said slowly. She loved how he always answered her questions, no matter how involved they might be. "It was a gradual thing, I guess. Back when your mother and I were children, there were some new families who came to Wharfton. They weren't used to our ways, and they were rough. The parents drank, and I'm sorry to say it, but sometimes they neglected and hit their kids. People in Wharfton asked the

Enclave to do something about it, so the Enclave took the worst abused children to raise inside the wall."

He passed a big berry to her. She held it on her open palm while he talked, watching the pale bloom of blue slowly warm to a deeper, shiny purple in contact with her skin. "That sounds okay," she said.

"It helped. A lot," he agreed. "But then, some people, especially families who were struggling to feed their kids, started wondering why some of their children couldn't go inside the wall. It didn't seem fair to them that the irresponsible parents were, in a way, being rewarded for abusing their kids."

Gaia understood that. It seemed, from the Tvaltar specials, that the girls inside the wall had everything she wanted, like books and pretty clothes and friends. "So then what happened?"

"Well, the Enclave discovered it was better to take children who were very young. They adapted better. So they offered to take in babies who were just a year old, and they compensated the families, too." He rubbed his fingers together, signaling money. "It was all voluntary at first. But then, just a few years before your oldest brother Arthur was born, the Enclave started requiring parents to bring their one-year-olds to special selections four times a year. It was a kind of competition, and the Enclave would take the strongest, liveliest babies."

Gaia wrinkled her nose. She scrambled up on a nearby boulder and swung her legs to dangle over the edge. "Didn't some of the parents mind?"

"Some did, of course. But others saw it as a great opportunity. You know, Gaia, in a way, each baby belongs to the community that supports its mother, whether that's a poor mother with a bad temper, or a loving mother with patience to spare, or an ambitious mother who wants the best opportunities for her child."

"I don't know," she said. "It kind of sounds like people in Wharfton were selling their babies to the Enclave."

He shook his bucket, looking inside. "It never really felt like that," he said slowly. "When Arthur and Odin were chosen to be advanced, it was a duty and an honor to advance a baby. We knew our boys would never lack for anything. And most important, they told us the advanced babies could come home to us when they turned thirteen if they wanted to."

"I didn't know that," Gaia said.

"That's because nobody ever has. They all choose to stay in the Enclave. The advanced children are genuinely happier with their adoptive families there."

Gaia gazed out at the horizon. "Arthur and Odin stayed, too, didn't they?"

Her father nodded slowly. "Later, maybe a couple years after you were born, the Enclave made advancement random, with a quota of the first babies born each month. It was more fair, and it's been like that for the last decade. I have to admit: in many ways, it works better than taking the babies when they were a year old. People are used to it now. And they still get compensated for each baby, too. It helps out the rest of the family."

"So you got paid for advancing Arthur and Odin?"

"We did."

Gaia glanced up at her father. "Do you miss them?"

He gave a lopsided smile. "Every day. But I have you."

"So why didn't Mom have more babies?"

"She's tried to, actually. But it looks like you're it for us."

Gaia pulled up a stalk of grass and broke off the bits of seed at the end. "Is that why she had a tough time last night? Does she not like delivering babies when she can't have any more herself?"

He took off his hat and ran a hand through his hair before

108

putting it on again. "I don't know how to answer that, Gaia. Your mother's a very strong woman. I know that much. Last night, your mother and Old Meg went to help Amanda Mercado. She had twins."

"Twins!" Gaia said.

"Yes. Twins. Two boys."

Gaia's smile fell. "But, did she advance both of them?"

Her father inhaled deeply, and then sighed. "That's the thing. Amanda needed to keep one and advance the other. The quota this month is two, and your mom had already advanced one baby."

"So what happened?"

Her father's lips compressed in a thoughtful line. "This must be confidential," he said. "Do you understand that?"

"I'll never tell," she promised.

"I don't want you even to talk to your mother about it, not unless she brings it up first. Don't nag her with questions."

"I won't. I promise." With a mix of pride and curiosity, she clutched her bucket tightly in both hands.

"Your mother let Amanda choose which baby to keep," he said. "Both babies were small, but the first one born weighed a little more and looked a little stronger. The second was a tiny little frail fellow. Guess which one Amanda decided to advance."

Gaia closed her eyes against the sunlight and pictured two small newborn baby boys wrapped in identical gray blankets. Their eyes were closed, and they were waiting peacefully for a decision. The only difference was that one was slightly bigger and rounder. She opened her eyes.

"Amanda kept the littler one," Gaia said.

Her father's lips curved in a sad smile. "You're right. Why?"

"She thought—" Gaia struggled for the right words. "She figured the bigger boy would do all right in the Enclave, but the little one, even if he doesn't make it, she can care for herself, with all her love."

Gaia's father lowered his face and drew his hand over his forehead so that she couldn't see him well. For a moment he stayed there, unmoving, until Gaia worried that she'd said something wrong.

"Dad?" she said.

He lowered his hand and his smile was even more lonely than before. With his thumb, he gently brushed the tender, scarred skin of her left cheek. He had a way of making her feel like she was even more precious to him because she was ugly, and it always twisted her up inside.

"You're a wise little girl, Gaia Stone," he said gently. "I wonder what will become of you when you grow up."

She relaxed her hands on the bucket. "Do you think Amanda's boy in the Enclave will ever know he has a twin brother outside?"

Gaia's father leaned back on one hand. "I doubt it. They'll tell him he was adopted from the outside, that's no secret, but they won't know anything about his family out here."

"Did Mom give him the freckles?"

"She always does, to every baby she delivers."

Gaia glanced down at her own left ankle and saw the four faint brown marks.

"In honor of Arthur and Odin, right?" she asked.

"That's right. You've kept that secret, haven't you?"

She murmured her agreement. She hadn't even told Emily when she saw the same freckles on Emily's ankle, and she never would.

"Did you ever think I might get advanced?" she asked.

"It was a possibility."

"Until my accident?"

"Yes."

Gaia looked at the freckles again. "I wonder if those babies will ever grow up and compare freckles and wonder why they all have the same ones."

"It isn't very likely," her father said.

"Why does Mom really do the freckles then?" Gaia asked.

Her father turned his face in profile, up the hill toward Wharfton. "It makes her feel better, I suppose. The same reason we light the candles at dinnertime."

"Do I have a twin inside the wall?"

He laughed. "No. Sorry. Just Arthur and Odin."

Gaia liked making her father laugh. "Do they know about me?"

"I don't see how they could. I'm sure they'd like you if they knew you, even though you ask a lot of questions."

"I still don't get what the problem was for Mom last night," she said. "The bigger baby was the first one out, right? So she followed the law by advancing the second baby born this month, just like she was supposed to."

Her father held out a hand to help her jump down from the boulder. "True. But your mother gave Amanda the choice. That's the difference. For your mother, it was an opening in the law, and your mother normally follows the law to the letter. If she bends it even once, even a little, it makes her question the whole thing. Come on. Let's go."

Gaia led the way up the path again, thinking deeply. She liked that he thought she was wise, that she was trustworthy with secrets. She was pulling the threads of their conversation together into one, weighty question. When they reached the lip of the unlake, she turned to her father. "Did last night make Mom question whether it was right to advance Arthur and Odin?" she asked. "As if she had a choice?"

For the first time in her life, her father turned his back to her. He took a step toward the horizon and stayed there, silent.

111

His fingers twisted in the seam of his pants and twitched there, as if he might absently fray a hole into the cloth. Gaia faltered, wishing she could take back her question.

"I'm sorry, Dad," she said quietly.

As he turned slowly to face her again, his eyes retained a lost, ashy glow. "You always have a choice, Gaia. You can always say no." His voice was strangely hollow. "They might kill you for it, but you can always say no."

She didn't understand his intensity, and he was frightening her. "What do you mean?" she whispered.

He took a long, slow breath and seemed to remember where he was. "It's all right, Gaia," he said. "There are some things, once they are done, that we can never question, because if we did, we wouldn't be able to go on. And we have to go on, every single day." He smiled, more like his old self. He lifted his bucket to click it against hers. "Your brothers are better off in the Enclave. We can still miss them sometimes, even though it was the right thing to let them go."

She watched him warily. Then he flicked the brim of her hat and fell into step beside her. "Come on," he said, his voice warm and coaxing again. "Those big green eyes of yours are making me hungry."

"Dad," she drawled. His nonsense made her smile. "They're not green. They're brown."

"Right," he said. "Brown. I get them mixed up. I beg your pardon."

By the time they arrived home, Gaia's mother was frying peppered mycoprotein patties. Gaia ran up the ladder to her loft to change while her father rinsed the blueberries and made coffee. With biscuits, honey, and blueberries crowding the patties on their plates, they went to eat on the back porch. Gaia looped the strap around her mosquito netting to clear it away, and they hitched three chairs forward toward the railing.

The wind chime let out a faint, tinkling noise, and Gaia's gaze fell on one of the chickens under the laundry lines. It seemed like ages ago that she'd discovered the theft, and compared to other losses, it hardly mattered at all.

"Who do you think stole our chickens, Mom?" she asked idly. She smeared a bite of her patty in honey, and savored the peppery sweetness on her tongue.

"Somebody hungry," her mother said.

It was practically the same thing her father had said.

Gaia's mother looked untroubled and rested, and Gaia realized that her father must have taken Gaia away from the house on purpose to give her mother a bit of time to herself. Normally, such an idea would have hurt her feelings, but now it didn't. Wonder brought a new stillness to her, as if the whole round earth had paused for a moment. *How wise my parents are*, she thought. *How kind they are to each other.*

Her mother glanced over and smiled. "Not hungry?"

"No, I am," she said.

Her mother's eyes grew more perceptive. "Your father told you about the Mercado twins, didn't he?"

Surprised, Gaia shot her gaze to his. He nodded.

"You did the right thing," Gaia said.

Her mother took a sip of her coffee and held the cup comfortably before her lips with both hands. "You know," her mother said. "You don't have to be a midwife when you grow up. That's all right with me."

But Gaia looked past her to where the solid weight of the water urn was suspended from the rafter. The last drops of condensed dew had evaporated away, leaving the creamy surface smooth and cool. A quiet certainty settled inside Gaia, beautiful and blue and grateful, like her own invisible lake.

"No," she said. "That's what I want to be. Like you."

So her training began.

Chapter 11
The Gilded Mirror

Days passed in a nightmarish haze for Gaia. The bleak reality of Q cell was so complete, so utterly opposite to her memories of life outside the wall, that it seemed to obliterate her previous existence entirely. Her hair was cut. She was given a bed, a plate, a cup, and a spoon, and told to keep her things clean. A tasteless mycoprotein stew was provided for her three times a day, but Gaia had no appetite, and she absently shared her food with the other women, who were glad to eat her portion. Tired, grieving, and with no hope, Gaia hardly noticed the cell life around her, even when Sephie urged her to walk with them in the yard outside as they were permitted to do once each morning and once again after the evening meal. She kept expecting to hear word of her mother's execution, but there was no news.

The doctors were often called away during the day, and sometimes they came back animated and invigorated by the practical exercise of their skills, but more often they returned quiet and morose. Myrna, especially, was often called out, and she invariably returned in a grim, taciturn mood.

"Come, Gaia," Sephie said one morning. "I need you to assist."

Gaia was sitting on the bench, staring in a glazed way at a bit of sewing that had been left in a pile, but she glanced up at Sephie's kind face. She tried to stir herself, knowing that Sephie had treated her with gentleness since she'd first arrived in prison.

"Yes," Sephie said, smiling and beckoning. "I've been told to bring an assistant, and it's time to expand your training."

Gaia stood slowly. "I'm allowed to leave?"

Sephie laughed lightly. "Apparently. Under heavy guard. We've been talking it over, and there must be something about you that the Enclave can't figure out. They're cautious that way. Clearly they would have had you killed by now, based on your crimes, but there must be some reason they want you alive. What could it be? Maybe they're saving you to use for leverage with your mother, or they're saving your mother to use for leverage with you. What makes you both so valuable, I wonder. You don't have friends higher up, do you?"

A flicker passed through Gaia's mind as she wondered if Capt. Grey had somehow negotiated for her life. She shrugged now. Life seemed pretty pointless to her at the moment, with her father dead and her mother on death row. What happened to her didn't much matter to her anymore.

"None of that," Sephie said firmly. "Up. We're going to deliver a baby. That should please you."

Gaia looked around automatically for her satchel, but then recalled they had taken it from her. Her watch, too. She stood slowly, feeling like her movements were underwater. Sephie linked her arm through Gaia's and guided her toward the door. "Heads up, now," Sephie said. "I knew you should have been eating more. You're weak as a new cat."

Gaia took a deep breath. "I'm not hungry."

"Well, then. Stand up straight and look like you can be useful. And try to straighten your hair a little."

Gaia felt a ghost of a smile. "You sound like my mother," she said.

"Is that right?"

Gaia ran a tired hand through her hair, still unused to the short ends at the nape of her neck. "My mother wanted me to tie my hair back more often. She told me I called attention to my . . . to myself by letting my hair fall in my face all the time."

The wooden door was being opened with a heavy, grating noise.

"She was right," Sephie said.

Gaia looked quickly out at the guards, half expecting to see Capt. Grey, but the men were unfamiliar. She hung back.

"No," Sephie whispered urgently, and gave her arm a sharp pinch. "Hello, gentlemen," Sephie said courteously to the guard. "My bag, please. I do hope you didn't forget the fetoscope this time."

Sephie passed the bag—a heavy black item with large handles—to Gaia, clearly expecting her to carry it for her, and then she started rapidly down the hall, leaving Gaia and the guards to catch up. The gray halls and staircases passed in a blur, and Gaia forced her heavy limbs to hurry after Sephie. At the last door, they were given two straw hats with distinctive gray and black hatbands and ordered to keep them on. When they finally stepped out from under the arch into a bolt of sunshine, Gaia gasped at the brightness of it. An effulgent wash of fresh air invaded her lungs, and she blinked back in surprise. She felt like she had emerged from a tomb, with all the shock and wonder of someone returning from the dead.

It was market day in the square, and noises and colors were vibrant on every side. It was easily ten times, no twenty times bigger than the simple exchange that happened in the quadrangle by the Tvaltar outside the wall. Tables and awnings filled the area around the obelisk, and the aisles bustled with people of every class, all reaching and laughing and exchanging money. A delivery boy with an overflowing basket of bread on the back of his bike rang his bicycle bell as he tried to weave through the crowd, and someone stopped him to buy a loaf. The hubbub of noise was merry and full of life. Gaia absorbed a quick impression of squawking chickens, bright yellow and green fabrics, and the shine of copper pans before she and Sephie were hurried down the street, surrounded by an escort of four armed guards. She noticed more than one curious glance in their direction, but Sephie walked as if she were oblivious both to the guards and the attention. She seemed to know precisely where to go, and when, after a few minutes of steady walking, they arrived at a blue-painted door, it was Sephie, not one of the guards, who rapped smartly on the door.

"Persephone Frank?" said a young man, opening the door.

"Who else?" Sephie said dryly, with a quick jerk of her head toward her guards.

"Thank goodness," the man said, shaking her hand. "Tom Maulhardt. I was afraid we couldn't get you. My wife Dora's having her first baby, and everyone says you're the best—" He was cut off by a muted cry from above. He went pale. "This way," he said.

Gaia followed Sephie in and heard one of the guards close the door behind them. As Sephie was striding rapidly up the stairs, Gaia lingered in the foyer, reveling in the sensation of being out of her prison and away from the scrutiny of the guards. This was what she'd missed: freedom.

Slowly she slid off her hat. Glancing left, she was curious to see the brightness of a living room. This was more like what she'd expected from the Tvaltar specials. Sunlight streamed through enormous panes of glass, touching on a pair of yellow couches that bracketed a low coffee table. A glass chess set was poised on the table, ready for the next move, and with a pang she thought of her father, who had loved to play. The polished wooden floor was partly covered by a white carpet, and a TV was mounted on a wall between bookshelves. Gaia had never seen so many books in one place, nor such graceful, pretty sculptures. A bronze nude child, waist-high, tipped a watering can over her crouching sister, and a trickle of real water dribbled out of the can.

"Hurry, girl," Sephie called impatiently.

Gaia lifted the doctor's bag and hurried after Sephie. She followed the noise of the laboring woman, turning a corner and entering a bedroom that was as light and airy as the rest of the house. On an enormous, four-posted bed, a young woman lay panting, her mousy hair askew, her eyes wide with fright. Gaia was surprised to see no one else there: no supporting mother or aunt, no sisters making extra food in the kitchen or standing ready to help. This woman was more isolated than most of the mothers she knew outside the wall.

Sephie was already talking soothingly to the woman and taking a pair of gloves out of her bag. "Here, now, Masister Dora. You're fine," Sephie said. "Tie my dress back, Gaia," she said, handing her an apron. Sephie worked competently, helping to ease the woman into a more comfortable position and preparing to examine her.

"Are you staying?" Sephie said to Tom.

He took an anguished look at his wife, and nodded.

"Good, then be of use. Support her back. Move those pillows," said Sephie. When the young man still looked uncertain, Sephie spoke to Gaia sharply. "Gaia."

But Gaia was already moving, seeing precisely what needed to be done. It was like being with her mother, with all the familiarity of a progressing labor and the woman's fear and pain, and yet it was different, too. In her last weeks outside the wall, Gaia had been in charge, responsible for every decision, and it was a relief to slide back into an apprentice role. As Tom held Dora's hand, she grew calmer, and Gaia could see that the labor had not progressed as far as the cries she had heard as they entered the house had seemed to indicate.

"It's a breech," Sephie said abruptly. "Is she full term? Not early?"

Tom looked confused. "She was due next week."

Sephie nodded, frowning, and steadied the woman's knees as she had another contraction. Gaia knew that a breech birth, with the baby arriving bottom first instead of head first, could be more complicated and take longer. At least, with the baby full term, its hips were as wide around as its head, and it was less likely to get stuck. She'd helped her mother deliver half a dozen breeches, but she hadn't done it herself yet, and she was glad again that Sephie was there to know just when and how to turn the baby as it came through.

"It's a frank breech," Sephie said. "She's not too far along with the timing of these contractions. I think—" she paused, still concentrating. Gaia watched her feel the woman's stomach, gently smoothing her hands around, with a confident little prod here and there. "Yes," Sephie said. "Let's turn it."

Gaia's eyes widened in surprise. "Can we?"

Sephie was already climbing onto the bed beside Dora. "Do you have any vodka?" she asked Tom. "And a hot water bottle? We need to slow this down."

Gaia was more shocked then ever. If Sephie was wrong, if she delayed this birth in some way, it could only be more dangerous for the baby. Yet, already Sephie was talking calmly to the patient, explaining that she intended to try to manipulate the baby upward in her uterus, turn it sideways, and then, gradually, turn it again so its head was downward. Gaia put her hands where Sephie told her to, gently and firmly identifying the little elbows and knees within the woman's distended

119

belly. She had never done this before, never dreamed of doing it. She imagined the protest of the baby within, and feared the umbilical cord might wrap around the infant's chin or knees. But Sephie worked steadily, keeping Dora calm, letting her rest between contractions, and when, later, the baby girl was born smoothly, head first, Gaia was awed at Sephie's skill.

"She's beautiful!" Tom said, clutching Dora's hands. "She's a miracle!"

Sephie wrapped the child in a soft white blanket, passing her to Dora to hold, and Gaia had a flashing memory of the first baby she'd delivered alone. She, too, had passed a baby to its mother, but she had known she would take it away again within minutes. This child was home to stay, with loving parents and the promise of wealth and privilege. Why did it make Gaia ache with sadness, when she should feel triumphant?

Sephie was quietly cleaning up her belongings. Gaia looked through the black bag for a teapot, for an inkbottle and needle, without success.

"Don't you do any freckles?" Gaia asked.

Sephie looked up. "What do you mean?" She turned her head toward the baby. "I didn't see any. They may show up later."

It felt so strange not to honor Arthur and Odin like she always had with her mother, but of course, Sephie wouldn't be familiar with her mother's pattern. "What about the tea?" Gaia asked.

Sephie's eyebrows lifted in curiosity. "What tea?" she asked, and waited for Gaia to explain.

As the silence stretched, Gaia finally realized that Sephie had no idea what she was talking about, and then guilt kicked in. She had promised her father never to tell anyone about the freckles, but now it had slipped out. Gaia spun toward the window, her mind reeling with a new possibility: the tattooed freckles were not only a secret way to honor her advanced brothers. Her mother signed those babies. With four carefully arranged pinpricks, she tattooed her own all-but-invisible mark on every baby she delivered. The tea itself was merely a distraction, a comforting, soothing ritual to honor the mother and midwife together. The soporific trace of motherwort in the mother's tea would leave no lasting mark. But that tattoo would last forever.

"What are you talking about?" Sephie said, crossing to the window.

"I meant the motherwort." Gaia tried to smile naturally at her, but she knew she was terrible at lying. "We give motherwort in some tea to the mother, and wash a little bit on the baby to prevent freckles. Don't you do that in here?"

Sephie eyed her closely one last time, and then turned back to her bag. "I don't know what you were told about motherwort, but it has no effect whatsoever on freckles." She reached for Gaia's arm, and Gaia was surprised by the cool strength in the woman's hand on her skin. "They're superstitious barbarians outside the wall, no offense intended."

Gaia straightened, but Sephie was already releasing her.

"We're leaving now," Sephie said to Tom and Dora.

The couple were profuse in their thanks, but Sephie, looking tired, waved dismissively and reached for her hat. "May you have many more children to serve the Enclave," she said.

"Let me give you something," Tom insisted, following them downstairs.

"No. They'd only confiscate it anyway," Sephie said. She put on her hat and signaled Gaia to do the same.

"Please, Persephone. There must be something I can do. Dora and I, we're so grateful. I'm sure I'm no one to question the Enclave, but—"

Gaia turned at the door and saw Sephie put her hand on

Tom's arm. "No," she said seriously. "It's my privilege, coming here. I'm honored to be part of your lives at this moment. Enjoy your child and your beautiful wife. You owe us nothing."

Gaia felt Tom's eyes flick to hers, and by his sudden, sharp gaze, she had the feeling this was the first time he'd looked at her closely, despite all they'd gone through together. When his gaze settled on her scar, she could feel both his curiosity and his pity.

He cleared his throat, looking uncomfortable, and then his lips curved in a deliberate smile. "At least let me give something to your assistant," Tom said. "I'm sorry. What's your name?"

His effort at graciousness didn't fool her. When she didn't answer him, Sephie gave her a sharp look.

"She's Gaia Stone," Sephie said. "The girl from outside."

He nodded, as if several pieces had just clicked together in his mind. "The one from a couple weeks ago? With the convict's baby?"

"Yes," Sephie said.

Tom ducked slightly to put his hand inside a drawer in a small desk beside him. "It's nothing much," he said. "But please, take it." He extended his hand toward Gaia and she looked down to see the gleam of a small gilded mirror, the hinged type that ladies used when adjusting their makeup. She felt herself go pale, staring at it. What could she possibly want with a mirror? Was he mocking her?

Sephie took the mirror for her and thrust it firmly into Gaia's stiff fingers.

"Thank you," Sephie said. "You're very generous."

Gaia could not trust herself to raise her eyes, not without revealing the fury and shame she felt at being treated like a freak. Again. She fumbled for the door handle, muttering a good-bye. She pulled the door open. The four guards who lounged nearby in the shade looked over. She would have dropped the mirror and crushed it underfoot right there except Sephie grasped her arm sharply. "Behave yourself," she whispered savagely. She thrust her black bag into Gaia's hands and took the little mirror.

The men came forward as Sephie said good-bye to Tom. Gaia's mind was spinning with all she had seen and discovered this morning: Sephie could turn a breech baby; the ankle freckles were a signature; Gaia was famous for saving the convict's baby; her service was of no more value than a glass trinket. She pulled the hat low on her forehead, feeling the faint scratchiness of the straw and wishing she still had long hair to hide her face.

Sephie fell into step beside her, and her pace was unhurried. The guards retreated slightly behind them, and Sephie linked her arm lightly around Gaia's waist.

"You're not bad as an assistant," Sephie said.

Gaia shrugged.

"But you've got something to learn about manners," Sephie said. "You embarrassed me back there."

"I embarrassed you!" Gaia said. She glanced back at the guards and brought her voice down. "He insulted me. What could I possibly want with a mirror? A chance to see my hideous face up close?"

Sephie looked at her strangely. "It was a token. He couldn't give you anything more significant. You're a prisoner. It probably belonged to his wife, Gaia. It was a gesture of respect and gratitude."

Gaia could not immediately accept what she was saying. She took her arm out of Sephie's so she could walk without the pretense of being her friend.

Sephie sighed. "Fine. But you might give people a chance. Not everyone is treating you like some hideous monster."

They reached the wide street that led up to the Square of the

123

Bastion, and Gaia could hear the noise of the market as they approached. Now that they were getting closer to the prison, she didn't want to go inside, and she didn't want to waste the chance to look around her by being in a bad mood. She looked around at the passing people, the shop windows, and the pigeons that pecked in the gutters. Despite herself, she watched for the familiar form of Capt. Grey, and then she was annoyed with her disappointment at not finding him. She smelled baking bread, and turned to look for the source. *Stupid*, she chastised herself. She should have been looking for Derek's friend's bakery all this time.

She scanned the street actively, looking for brown loaves of bread, or a hanging sign with the familiar etching of sheaves of wheat, but there were none, and the scent vanished. They reached the Square of the Bastion again and the bustling activity of the market.

Barrels stood filled with cabbages and potatoes, and a stall was hung with dainty blue and white dresses for toddlers. Gaia could see delicate smocking on the front of one. *My father would love this*, she thought with a pang. He'd relish the whole market, and especially the sartorial handiwork. She owed it as a tribute to him to live as fully as she could, even as a prisoner.

She saw apples, and even, on one carefully displayed plate, six oranges. A seventh had been sliced in wedges. She had never eaten one, but she'd seen them in a picture book. Now the bright color called to her like a magnet, drawing her in.

They passed so close that Gaia could smell the sliced wedges, and her hunger became so keen that saliva flowed around her teeth.

"Are they really oranges?" Gaia murmured to Sephie.

Sephie turned briefly in the direction Gaia was looking.

"They're outrageously expensive," Sephie said. "Usually the owners of the orange trees eat them all themselves, or give them as gifts to the Protectorat's family. But once in a while there are a few for sale. You getting your appetite back?"

"Yes."

"Good. I was beginning to worry."

The guards, now that they were so close to the prison, surrounded Gaia and Sephie again, but not before Gaia saw a red-clad girl step up to the orange seller.

The girl took out a purse of coins, and as the guards nudged Gaia along, Gaia kept gazing back over her shoulder, watching the exchange. When the girl reached for one of the oranges, her hood fell back slightly and sunlight gleamed off her blond hair: Rita. She was the girl who had tried to advise Gaia during the execution, the one who had warned her to keep quiet.

Gaia stumbled against a cobblestone, and Rita looked up. For one instant, her dark eyes met Gaia's gaze, and her mouth rounded in a silent O.

"Careful there," Sephie said.

One of the guards steadied Gaia from behind and hustled her toward the arch. Gaia lost sight of Rita, but as she replayed the moment in her head, she thought she recognized a glimmer of pity in the other girl's eyes. Or had it been sympathy? Perhaps Sephie was right. Perhaps Gaia, in her quickness to assume people were mocking her, failed to interpret how people really looked at her.

Gaia lowered her head as the shadow of the arch fell upon her. She handed back her hat and was escorted deeper into the prison. Soon she and Sephie were back in Q cell, but even when the heavy wooden door was shoved loudly closed behind them, Gaia knew she was no longer lost to the despair that had gripped her at the news of her father's murder.

She had rediscovered what it was like to be alive and hungry.

She had realized that the freckles were more than just a tribute to her brothers.

She was going to survive this internment and find a way out.

Chapter 12
A Pigeon Visits

THAT NIGHT, GAIA ate her first full meal in weeks. The image of the oranges haunted her, and the memory of the sweet scent was like a mist of pure color before her nose. She craved one of those oranges so badly it was like an illness. And this made her laugh.

"What's so funny?" Sephie asked.

"I could about kill for an orange," Gaia said.

The doctors laughed, and the sound was an unaccustomed counterpoint to the noise of their spoons grazing their plates. As Gaia ate her beef-flavored stew, she fingered the little mirror that Sephie had returned to her, flipping it over, thinking of how much her life had changed in such a short time. Less than three weeks before, she'd seen such luxuries as those in Tom and Dora's home only at the Tvaltar, with a sheen of glamour and impossibility. She'd never guessed that oranges could be available for a price in an open market five kilometers from her home. She'd never known a breech baby could be completely turned in the womb. She had still believed both her parents were alive. This was a different world inside the wall, cruel and enticing both.

"It's a pretty bauble," one of the women said. Her name was Cotty, and her soft black hair curled thickly around her lined face. She picked up the mirror now, eyeing herself in the glass, and she made a little primping motion with her bangs that made Gaia smile.

"Keep it," Gaia said.

"Oh, no. I couldn't."

"I have no use for it," Gaia said.

Cotty handed it back, patting Gaia's hand in the process. Cotty's fingers were a rich, even brown, several shades darker than Gaia's tan hand. "Don't say that," Cotty said. "Everything has value in here. You'll see. You can trade it for something you want."

"Maybe with a guard," Sephie said. "For food. Or knitting yarn."

"Or a novel," Myrna added.

Gaia held it doubtfully. "How was your day?" she asked Myrna politely.

Myrna's striking black eyebrows lifted while she slowly took another bite of her bread. "I performed a surgery on a burst appendix, thank you very much for asking."

Gaia thought at first she must be joking, but Sephie asked her a question or two about the procedure, and Myrna answered curtly.

"Gaia was a steady assistant today," Sephie said. "You should take her with you next time. Teach her a thing or two."

Myrna's level black eyes studied Gaia for a moment. "They should have left her outside the wall where at least she could do no harm to anyone that matters," Myrna said.

Gaia's resentment flared, but she did not respond.

"Really, Myrna," Sephie said mildly. "Give her some credit."

"Who's been tending the mothers in my sector since I was arrested?" Gaia asked.

Cotty, Myrna, and Sephie exchanged glances but didn't speak.

"Haven't any of you been going out?" Gaia asked more urgently.

Sephie set a hand on Gaia's knee. "Be calm, Gaia. None of us has ever gone outside the wall. That's nothing new."

"But then, who's taking care of my deliveries?" Gaia asked. "Did the Enclave send out some other midwife?"

"There must be half a dozen midwives out there," Myrna said carelessly.

But Gaia shook her head. She and her mother had been the only midwives in Western Sector Three, and they were often shorthanded.

"Perhaps—" she began, thinking aloud. Could the mothers be going to Western Sector Two to find a midwife? Did they go into labor alone, with no help? She shook her head, frustrated, and with her last bite of bread she stood to pace the room. Stuck here in prison, she was no good to anyone.

Above there was a fluttering at the window, and Gaia looked up, startled to see a pigeon sitting on the ledge of the center window. The other women made no comment, as if it would take more than a pigeon to rouse them from the protective apathy that cocooned their hearts. Gaia secretly hoped the bird would fly in and stir up the gloomy cell with its flapping wings and chaos, but it merely hopped on the sill, made a squawking noise, and flew away again.

Gaia turned slowly to see the women: Cotty, Sephie, and Myrna sat on two benches, the last crumbs of their dinners before them. Four other women rested on the other two benches, none of them speaking.

"When's the last time any of you looked out those windows?" Gaia asked.

They looked at her, and then their faces turned upward.

Myrna muttered something that no one answered. Gaia walked to the nearest bench, and bent to look beneath it. Sephie cleared her feet out of the way.

"What are you thinking?" Sephie said.

Gaia gave the bench a little pull, and then a little shove. It had been nailed to the floor, but the nails were rusted and old. If she could get out that window, she could search for her mother again. "Get up," she said, and Sephie and Myrna stood.

"I don't believe this," Myrna said.

Gaia gave the bench a good kick, and it rattled free from its nails. "Help me," Gaia said, and Sephie took an end of the bench so they could carry it over beneath the third window.

By now the other women were up, examining the other three benches. Two were securely bolted down, but the last was soon wrenched from its old nails. The excitement in the cell was palpable as they carried the second loose bench under the window, too.

Gaia looked up at the windows, judging their distance above the floor of the cell to be five meters or higher. Each bench was a couple of meters long, but stacked on each other, they would only come as high as Gaia's chest.

Myrna was the first to go back and sit down. "Tell me when any of you grows another two meters," she said.

But Gaia wasn't ready to give up. She hauled one bench to the corner and tipped it up. Then she angled the lower edge out · slightly to create a makeshift ladder. Bracing herself against the wall, she climbed the tipped underbelly of the bench, standing unsteadily on the top edge.

"Don't fall," Sephie said.

"Go ahead and fall," Myrna said. "Cotty here will sew you up. Just don't break the bench or we'll have nothing to sit on."

Gaia climbed back down and looked closely at both benches, seeing if the answer lay in breaking one or both of them, and constructing a ladder from the pieces. But she had no nails, and no tools, and the benches were sturdily made. She looked up again longingly at the windows.

Then Cotty made a little coughing noise from the doorway to the bedrooms.

"Would these help?" she asked. She held two blankets, and Gaia knew there was one for each of the prisoners, a total of eight in all.

"Wait, Gaia. Do you know what's on the other side of that wall?" Cotty asked.

"Is it any different than what's in here?" Myrna asked.

Gaia ignored Myrna's pessimism and answered Cotty. "Does it matter? If we can look out, we can climb out. We'll find a way."

What seemed impossible gradually began to change. They had to stop when it was time for the evening walk, but afterward they continued. Working together, Sephie, Cotty, and Gaia experimented with tying the two benches together, overlapping the wood and wrapping the blankets tightly around them. The squares of sunlight that shone through the windows lifted along the wall toward the ceiling and then vanished as the sun went down. Evening gloom filled the room before at last they leaned a solid structure into the corner of the cell. It reached more than three meters high, but fell short nearly two meters from the window. The distance was daunting.

"It's all right," Gaia said. "Myrna, go listen at the door. Sephie and Cotty, help me up."

She climbed gingerly up the benches, gripping hard at the wood and digging her knees into the blankets' folds. She could smell the cool, gritty stone of the wall against her face and once, when her balance shifted, she could feel the whole structure begin to fall away.

"Push it in!" she said urgently. "Hold it against the wall."

131

The other women came to help, too, steadying the structure from below. Gaia caught her breath, and turned, keeping her back to the wall. Sweat broke out on her face and neck as she slowly straightened, standing on her heels on the uppermost ledge of the tied benches. Her eyes were still a good ten centimeters below the edge of the window, but now she lifted her left hand, holding the mirror she'd received that morning, and extending her arm upward, she was able to look into the bit of glass, and out to the violet sky and the roofs of the twilit city.

Gaia gasped with pleasure and amazement, instantly forgetting her precarious footing.

"Can you see anything?" Sephie asked from below.

"Yes. The city," Gaia said. "And the sky."

Below, the women murmured their approval and excitement.

"Can you reach the window?" Cotty asked.

Gaia nodded. "If I turned, I could, I'm sure, but I can't turn while I'm up here."

"Is there anything to attach a rope to?" Cotty asked.

Gaia squinted into the mirror, inspecting the edges of the opening. "I don't know."

"Come down. Quickly," Myrna said. "The guard's coming."

Gaia scrambled down in a panic.

"Hurry!" Sephie said.

All eight women tore at the blankets, pulling them apart, and they dragged the benches breathlessly back to their old places. "Quick, you there," Sephie said, pointing. "To your beds!"

Half the women fled so that when the guards came around the corner, there were only a few women left sitting in the dim common room.

Gaia's heart was racing. She kept her arms crossed, her eyes down, and in the dim light she saw a dark spot on her wrist. It was a narrow line of blood, and she hid her scratched wrist quickly beneath the sleeve of her other arm, applying pressure."Persephone Frank?" the guard said.

Gaia felt Sephie stiffen beside her on the bench. Her round face had never looked so much like the moon, solemn and distant.

"Yes?" Sephie asked.

"Yer to come with me," he said.

Gaia looked up in dread, not knowing what this could mean. Myrna stood.

"What are you taking her for?" Myrna said in her dry, hard voice.

The guard said nothing.

"It's late," Myrna pressed him. "Will she be back tonight?"

Sephie turned and gave Gaia a quick hug. "Be careful," Sephie whispered. "Stay strong."

"Sephie!" Gaia whispered, suddenly afraid for her.

Sephie turned to hug Myrna, too, and her pale fingers clutched the fabric on Myrna's shoulder into gray puckers. Then the guard was taking Sephie's arm.

"Release me," Sephie said, wresting her arm free. "I'm coming."

Cotty began to sob, and the other women came from the bedrooms, disturbed by the commotion. "Sephie!" they cried.

But Sephie was preceding the guard out the door, her chin level, her calm expression steeled to endure whatever might come. The heavy door closed with a tight, suffocating bang.

"What will they do to her?" Gaia asked in a hushed voice, turning to Myrna.

Myrna shrugged, turning toward the corner, running a hand slowly along the wall.

"Myrna!" Gaia demanded. "What will they do?"

Myrna sent her a scathing glance. "Why ask me, idiot? I don't know anything."

"But, don't you care?" Gaia asked.

Myrna turned away without answering, closed her eyes, and leaned her forehead against the wall. She lifted one heavy fist and rested it near her face, as if the only thing she could bear was to merge herself into the stone. In that one stoic, lonely gesture, Myrna revealed an intensity of suffering that stunned Gaia.

"Oh, no," Gaia whispered, refusing to believe that harm could come to Sephie. Sephie was so good, so generous.

Gaia sagged down upon one of the benches. Slowly the other women, even Myrna, went to their beds, but Gaia kept her gaze on the third window and the deepening purple square of sky. She didn't know what she was listening for, but she listened late into the night, not daring to think of her mother, hoping only that the guards would bring Sephie back.

Chapter 13
Birthmarked

T HE FIRST NIGHT AFTER SEPHIE was taken away, Gaia tried to rally the others to help with the benches again, but Myrna, sitting stubbornly, spoke in a low, sharp voice. "You're putting all of us at risk with your foolish games."

"But we could escape," Gaia said.

"*You* could," Myrna corrected her. "Or you could drop to your death on the other side. Even if you used the blankets to make a rope ladder, as I'm sure you've been thinking, the rest of us couldn't all climb up to the window. Some of us couldn't even fit through. As soon as the guards discovered your escape, the rest of us would be killed as accomplices."

Gaia looked around the room, seeing the truth reflected in the other women's eyes. She was certain she could escape. Positive. But how could she endanger the others?

"At least you have a shred of a grasp on reality," Myrna muttered as Gaia sat, her eyes on the windows above, her dream slowly fading into dusty ashes.

"It's all right," Cotty said quietly, leaning near to pat Gaia's knee. "We'll find another way out. At least you started us thinking."

Or pointlessly, hoping Gaia thought, not certain whether the women were better off or worse than they'd been before she came.

Over the next few days, they heard nothing of Sephie or of Gaia's mother, not from the guards, and not from anyone they chanced to see when they went out of the prison to tend to patients. Gaia woke often at night, restless with grief for her father and anxious about her mother. In the lonely darkness, she would try to comfort herself with memories of happy times outside the wall, little things, like the fried eggs and honey bread she and her father had made for her mother's birthday breakfast, but the images would evaporate until she was left with only the sound of Cotty breathing from the bunk opposite hers. Then she would return to thoughts of escape, and her mind would circle fruitlessly until exhaustion, near daybreak, would finally tumble her into a last, fitful cycle of sleep.

Weeks passed as Gaia became Myrna's assistant, often inciting her sarcastic tongue. Gaia never complained. The work was a distraction from the grief and fear that haunted her, and always she hoped that she might learn something of her mother when she was out of the prison.

Twice they were lined up behind the fence outside the prison to watch other executions: one man was accused of smuggling a woman in from outside of the wall to hire out as a prostitute; another was accused of buying blood on the black market for his hemophiliac son. There were public floggings, too, for a teenage lover who was caught sneaking into a girl's home, and a woman who carelessly contaminated a vat of mycoprotein at the factory. Gaia winced with each whiplash.

But there were good things, too, Gaia found. Now and then, a guard would deliver small tokens to the doctors in the cell, items that led the doctors to think their work was appreciated and that soon one of them might be freed: a book, a small jar of honey, a skein of wool and new needles, and an anatomy chart.

Then once, miraculously, an orange was delivered.

"How could this be?" Myrna said, lifting the orange out of a small box and letting a green tissue fall away. She turned the fruit in the light of the window so that the porous peel glowed orange before the women. "Who would send this, and how could it make it past the guards without getting filched by one of them?"

Gaia reached for the orange sphere, wondering at its cool weight on her palm. She was reminded of what Capt. Grey had once said, that cooperation in the Enclave was rewarded, and it seemed to be true. "Maybe that man you stitched up yesterday owns an orange tree," she suggested.

Myrna lifted a card from inside the box and angled it toward the light. Farsighted, she tilted her head back slightly to read it. "It's to you. Gaia Stone, Q Cell. But it doesn't say who it's from."

"Me?" Gaia said, puzzled, taking the card and pondering the small, neat handwriting. "Could it be from Sephie? Could she be free after all?"

Cotty reached for the orange, and Gaia passed it over, watching as the older woman lifted it delicately before her nose. "Who cares where it came from," Cotty said. "It's an orange. I haven't eaten an orange in years."

Gaia laughed. "Well, let's have it now." As if the orange were a jewel divided among them, the women held up their sections to the light before eating them. Gaia savored her section, biting it in two, letting the bright, juicy taste of it pucker every cell on her tongue before she swallowed. She glanced up to find Myrna still watching her thoughtfully.

"What?" Gaia asked.

"Nothing."

But Gaia felt a shiver of warning along her arms. She knew what Myrna was thinking. Sephie couldn't have sent in an orange. And this token had nothing to do with how well Myrna had treated some patient. Someone had an interest in Gaia, someone with enough power to deliver an orange through prison walls.

Gaia bit through a piece of tangy peel. *Who was it,* she wondered. *And why her?*

One late afternoon, when Myrna and Gaia had finished delivering a premature little girl, Gaia glanced up at a trio of soldiers relaxing before a café and was startled to recognize one of them as Capt. Grey. She and Myrna were surrounded by four armed men, but Gaia hardly noticed the escort anymore, and when she stopped, an escort soldier trod on her heel.

"Hey!" he said.

"Sorry," Gaia murmured, and she paused to wiggle her heel back into her loose shoe.

Capt. Grey lifted a small white coffee cup, tipping his head back so she had a clear view of his fluid profile as he swallowed. To her eyes he looked thinner, but he wore his customary black uniform and broad-brimmed hat, and carried himself with his usual loose-limbed ease. If she had allowed herself to think of him at all during her weeks in prison, it had been to dismiss him as a cowardly cog of the machine, a man who would let an innocent baby get killed. But it struck her now as outrageously unfair that he was free while she was a prisoner. How dare he be enjoying a cup of coffee! With friends even!

"Guard! Hold there!" Capt. Grey commanded.

The soldiers stopped and came to attention. Myrna stopped too, and though Gaia was compelled to stay beside her, she averted her face.

"What is it, Captain?" Myrna said brusquely.

Gaia could hear his boots approaching over the cobblestones, and still she kept her gaze studiously on a flowering vine that grew on the wall beside her. He brought a faint scent of coffee with him, a scent from freedom. A savage spike of jealousy twisted through her before she could control it.

"Has your apprentice been useful?" Capt. Grey asked, his voice quieter now that he was near. Gaia was struck by his cultured, smooth tone, so different from the harsher voices of the guards she'd grown accustomed to.

"She does tolerably," Myrna said.

Gaia was surprised enough to turn back toward the older woman. Her black eyes regarded her frankly from under her straw hat, and then she lifted her eyebrows faintly. This was the closest thing to praise that Gaia had ever heard from Myrna.

"I'll bring her back to the prison," Capt. Grey said.

Gaia looked up to see him nodding at the surprised sergeant.

"Proceed, Sergeant," Capt. Grey said decisively. "I'll be responsible for Masister Stone."

"Yes, Captain." The guard saluted.

Gaia absolutely did not want to be left with him, but she had no way to protest. She looked at Myrna in time to see her expression return to its customary ironic lines. With a peremptory huff, Myrna took the doctor's bag from Gaia's grip, leaving her hands free of their usual burden. A moment later, the guards were in step around Myrna, and they were turning the corner. Their footsteps faded on the cobblestones, and Gaia heard a clink of china from the café on the corner as the rest of the world went on.

Gaia was left alone with Capt. Grey. It was unexpectedly painful to be standing in front of him, even though this was the closest she'd been to freedom since the dismal day she had been captured and taken to the jail. She looked past him, down-hill, wondering if she dared try to run, but a quick look at his agile physique reminded her he could easily stop her.

"You're doing well?" he asked finally.

At his quiet voice, she peered up into the shaded line under the brim of his hat. His blue eyes regarded her with the steady gravity she remembered from before, from back before she'd known what he was truly like, and a tinge of color rode high along his cheekbones. *Why,* she thought. *Why do you care?*

A breeze swirled her gray dress against her legs, and she instinctively smoothed the material. "As you see," she said coldly.

He pivoted beside her and gestured an invitation with his hand. "Walk with me."

"Do I have a choice?" she asked, and then she wished she could take it back. He didn't deserve to know she was angry with him.

But he simply murmured "Ah." When he began to walk, she was compelled to fall into step beside him.

It was a clear, beautiful afternoon, and they were gradually ascending a sloped street in one of the quieter residential areas, toward a neighborhood she'd never visited. The tinkle of a wind chime stirred from over a window. Purple and white phlox cascaded cheerfully over the top of a nearby stone wall. Sunlight sifted through the weave of her straw hat, casting freckles of light on her nose and cheeks that shifted, out of focus, as she walked.

When she'd first peeked into the Enclave, the physical place had seemed like a paradise to her, all white walls and purity. Then when she'd witnessed the first execution, she had been shocked by the brutality beneath the façade, and she'd believed there was nothing here she could trust. Gradually, on her trips with Sephie and then Myrna, she'd seen a practical side to the Enclave: the routine of the thriving market, the steady work of the doctors in Q cell, and the satisfaction and dignity that came with working well, even when they had little hope of freedom. Many hard-working, decent people kept the foundry, glass factory, and mills going to produce useful goods. There were things to respect here, lives that weren't all brutality.

This new area had a quiet loveliness to it, an inviting atmosphere that matched the heady scent of the honeysuckle. It felt older somehow, more settled, unhurried. The white of the homes was more of a cream color, and there were more shade trees and wider sidewalks. A park opened along the summit of the hill, and children ran after a soccer ball, their voices bright and intense. Though the area looked nothing the same, it kind of reminded her of the unlake. If she weren't a prisoner and he weren't a guard, they might have been two companions taking a leisurely stroll on a warm summer afternoon. But she was unwilling to let down her guard. This man was not a friend.

"I hope the orange was ripe," he asked.

"That was you who sent it?"

He slid his hand in his pocket. "A friend told me she saw you looking at them at the market." His voice dropped to an easy resonance. "Well, 'drooled' I think, was the word she used. I would have sent more, but they're hard to come by."

She remembered the other gifts for the doctors. She glanced up at his profile. "Did you send the yarn? The book and things?"

He met her gaze briefly. "I suggested it to the Protectorat. You've made a lot of people think, Gaia. He's had some pressure about the doctors in the prison lately, and sometimes little things help."

So he *was* responsible. She thought of the day they'd received the orange, and the way the mood in Q cell had lifted slightly since then. It was still prison, it was still horrible, but there was a little hope there now. A pigeon mingled among several wrens at the side of the road, pecking at crumbs, and she stepped passed them and up the curb. *I should thank him*, she thought, but the words stuck in her throat.

"I was put on the decoding detail for your ribbon," he added.

Her nerves buzzed with alarm. They had discovered, then, that the ribbon was a code. How long would it take to decipher it, or had they already? She glanced up and found his expression pensive.

"I should say, I was put on it *at first*," he corrected, his voice dry. "Then I was moved to a less sensitive assignment. Apparently, I'm not trustworthy where your case is concerned."

She peered ahead up the road and gripped her hands together before her. "I should be grateful, I suppose," she said.

"Why is that?"

She shrugged and let sarcasm tinge her answer. "With your keen mind, you probably would have deciphered it in a few days."

"So you knew it was the record?" he asked.

She'd made a mistake, she realized. "No," she lied.

"Do you know what it says?" he asked.

She folded her arms around herself. "Why are you asking me this? I have no interest in cooperating with you. If you want to coerce me, of course you can try. But I won't willingly tell you anything. The Enclave killed my father." Mentioning him brought back the hurt again.

Capt. Grey paused beside a stone wall, leaning both his hands on it and directing his gaze toward the view. "That shouldn't have happened."

She let out a strangled laugh. "No? You don't think so?"

"We make mistakes, too," he said quietly.

She almost laughed again. Did he realize how absurd he was? The Enclave didn't just make a few mistakes. The whole system was inherently unethical, and he was admitting only the tiniest chink. She followed the direction of his eyes and saw the gray, sloping expanse of the unlake, smoky blue toward the horizon, while at the near edge, the shabby houses of Wharfton were almost completely concealed behind the hill-side and the wall. Anyone living here and seeing this view regularly could easily overlook Wharfton and forget its struggling people even existed. The peculiar beauty of it seemed to mock her, as if it, too, thought her losses were insignificant.

She twisted her fingers together. "You didn't even tell me he was dead." Her voice came out with a catch. "You could have told me, anytime, but you didn't."

Capt. Grey turned slowly then to regard her. "I'm sorry," he said.

Until then, she hadn't realized that was what she wanted to hear. She knew it wasn't Capt. Grey's fault, particularly, that her father had been killed, but someone should have told her, and he was the one who had been in contact with her before. For an instant, she was near to tears, and then his apology released a pent up dam of questions within her.

"Where is he buried?" she demanded.

"I can find out."

"Where is my mother?"

His eyes flicked strangely. "I don't know," he said.

She took a small step toward him. "Is she still alive?"

"I don't know that, either. I haven't heard of her death."

"You don't know much, do you?" she asked.

The brim of his hat kept his eyes in a line of shadow, but he stood quite still, watching her intently. It occurred to her that his watchfulness could well be an act, a learned shield for his feelings when he was disturbed or uncertain.

"You know," he said mildly, "I'm making an effort to speak courteously to you."

She folded her arms more tightly around herself. She cared nothing for his courtesy or his chastisement. "Excuse me," she said bitingly. "I forgot. I'm supposed to be grateful to you, aren't I? You sent me an orange. Consider us even."

His eyes narrowed. "I didn't—"

She heard a sudden intake of his breath. His gaze was directed above and behind her, to where a pair of women had paused on a higher street to look down at them. Their white dresses shone in the sunlight, and even from the distance, Gaia could tell they were both very pretty. The older woman wore a wide-brimmed hat, but the younger woman was holding her hat by the strap, and her blond hair, unfettered, blew lightly in the wind, causing her to hold it back briefly with her slender fingers. A slight flutter of those same fingers might have been a wave of greeting, but Gaia couldn't be sure.

"Let's go," he said abruptly, and began walking more rapidly along the street.

"Who are they?" she asked. She had to lengthen her stride to keep up with him.

"My mother and sister," he said.

"But they—" Gaia was confused. They were obviously of the wealthiest class, the sort of people whose families didn't give up their sons to the guard.

"Do they know the Protectorat?" she asked, wondering that they didn't ask for a favor to get Capt. Grey out of his service.

He turned toward her again, and she saw a flash of dark pain and anger in his eyes. Then he looked at her strangely, as if she'd said something odd.

"He's my father," Capt. Grey said.

Gaia came to a standstill, stunned. Capt. Grey. He was Capt. Leon Grey. Formerly Leon Quarry, the oldest son of the Protectorat.

"I know about you," she said wonderingly.

He drew out the sardonic syllables of his reply. "Is that right?"

Capt. Grey took another two steps and turned to stop, too. He looked over his shoulder, but with the angle of the hill, they were no longer in view of his family. Gaia's mind was struggling to reconcile what she knew of this young man, this captain of the guard, with what she knew of the Protectorat's son. The advanced one. Leon was the boy who had vanished from Tvaltar coverage years ago. Now she understood why he'd looked vaguely familiar when she'd first met him: in her own childhood, she'd seen images of him as a boy, images ten meters tall. But he'd changed. Completely.

"I don't understand," she said.

His lips hardened in a straight line as he seemed to make a decision.

"Come," he said, and with that he took her arm and guided her forward again, more urgently this time, and at the next turn, he took her left onto a narrow road that led downward, farther away from the center of town.

"Where are you taking me?" she asked.

But he didn't answer. In a few more paces, he opened a metal gate by reaching inside to a latch, and guided her into a garden. Closing the gate, he led her down a slope, toward a back corner of the garden, under the shade of a lofty white pine tree, to where the coolness smelled of the pine needles, both the green ones above and the brown ones that formed a cushiony layer beneath her shoes.

"What is this place?" she asked.

"It's safe, for now," he said. His cheeks were flushed, and he took off his hat to wipe his brow. "The Quirks who own this place are old friends of the family. They spend most days in the Bastion, and shouldn't come home until late."

She peered past a row of apple trees and up a grassy slope to where a gracious, stone house was painted a clean, mellow cream. The white tile roof and arched windows created a welcoming picture, and though it was far from fancy, the simple elegance made her guess that this home and private garden were even more valuable than Tom and Dora's pristine white home. Purple and yellow flowers proliferated in abundance, proof that water was used here to assure decoration, and white boulders dotted the area in a harmonious, random pattern, providing natural places to sit.

A high, stone wall protected the garden on three sides, and the fourth side was open to a cliff with a spectacular view of the unlake and the distant southern horizon.

"Stay back," he said, when she would have walked nearer to the cliff. "We don't want to be seen."

She glanced down, then stepped back into the shade of the pine. She turned to Capt. Grey, and her amazement hit her again.

"I can't believe you're Leon Quarry," she said.

"I thought you knew."

She shook her head. "How would I? You're completely different from the last time I saw you on the Tvaltar. What happened to you?"

His neat fingers clenched the rim of his hat in his hands. "I joined the guard."

There was so obviously more to the story that she almost laughed.

"What does the Protectorat's son want with me?" she said.

He peered at her. "It wasn't an accident that I saw you by the café. I've been waiting for you. I know you have some answers we need, and I think I can help you," he said.

She lifted her eyebrows, doubtful.

"Listen, Gaia. The Enclave is getting ready to interrogate you for the last time," he said. "It won't be me. They have an

146

expert. They want to know about the ribbon, and they want to know about the ink."

"The ink!" she exclaimed.

"There was no pen in your satchel, but they claim the ink bottle is evidence you wrote notes at a birth, information that was transferred to the permanent code on the ribbon later."

"But I don't have any notes," she exclaimed. "I don't know anything about a code."

"Gaia," he said, coming nearer. "They're deadly serious. If you know anything, anything at all, they'll get it out of you. It's far, far better to cooperate with them right from the start. They reward loyalty. They always have."

She staggered back, bracing herself against the black trunk of the pine, feeling a bead of sap against her thumb.

"I don't know anything," she insisted.

His mouth was closed in a straight line. "Then you'll die."

Gaia instinctively clutched a hand to her chest. He hardly seemed to care what he was saying, and yet he'd brought her here on purpose to warn her. It made no sense. She scrambled for a solution. She would have to leave the Enclave. Immediately. She would have to come back later for her mother since she wouldn't do her any good dead. She glanced to her left, toward the cliff. Would it be any worse to jump now, and take her chances running away from Capt. Grey? "Can't you let me go?" she asked. "Right now?"

He shook his head. "Even if I did, orders are to shoot any unescorted prisoner on sight. You'd be dead in five minutes."

She hesitated, indecisive. "If I tell them something," she said in a small voice. "I don't see how it could help, but if I tell them something, will they let me go?"

Capt. Grey lowered his face into his hand, pressing his fingers with visible pressure against his forehead. His hat dropped softly to the ground. "This can't be," he said in a low voice.

His reaction only made her more afraid. "Wait, Captain. Please. There has to be a way out of the Enclave."

He turned pained, angry eyes to her. "What do you know?" he said. He grabbed both her arms, pushing her backward until her foot hit against a root and she stumbled. Her hat knocked back and fell to the ground. He gripped her harder. "For your own sake. Tell me!" he insisted.

It was her parents' secret. She had promised never to tell. How could she know telling wouldn't make things worse?

He shook her again. "Gaia, tell me!"

"The freckles," she said.

His arms loosened infinitesimally, but his expression remained urgent. "What do you mean? What freckles?"

"We put a pattern of freckles on each baby," she said. "I don't know how it would help. It would only track some of the advanced babies back to me and my mother. I guess to Western Sector Three."

His grip loosened further until he was just holding her. "What are you talking about?"

She instinctively angled her foot outward. "It was in honor of my brothers. I didn't realize it could be important until recently," she said. "Whenever a baby was born, my mother would sit with the mother afterward for a bit, drinking tea. She would have me put pinpricks of ink in the baby's skin. It was part of my apprenticeship."

"A tattoo? Did she write anything down? Did she have the ribbon with her?" Capt. Grey asked.

She shook her head. He released her, but stayed near, his expression puzzled. She reached up to rub her tender shoulders where his strong grip had hurt her.

"Can you show me?" he asked. "Do you have the marks yourself?"

She stepped into the sunlight, and bracing her shoe against

a boulder, she smoothed her skirt up her shin to expose her left ankle. Pointing, she traced the area on the inside of her left ankle, where the smooth, tawny skin was marked by four seemingly natural freckles in a simple pattern.

•

•

•

•

"Four dots," she said. "Three in an almost straight line, and one farther below. Like the three stars of Orion's belt and one for the point of the sword."

"They're the same on every baby?" he asked.

But before she could answer, Capt. Grey was moving.

He pivoted before her to sit on the boulder and propped his left ankle on his right knee. With one rapid movement, he shucked off his left boot. A black sock followed, and then, almost savagely, he pulled up the black leg of his pants to expose his ankle.

There, faint but clearly visible, were three freckles arranged in a line, and a bit lower, to the left, was a fourth. Gaia stared, unbelieving.

"I'm from outside the wall," Capt. Grey said, his voice barely more than a whisper.

Her eyes shot to his and held. "My mother was there when you were born," she said. "She birthmarked you." Her mind scrambled to put it all together. Her mother had advanced Leon into the Enclave. "What's your birth date?" she asked.

He blinked slowly in her direction. "My birth date? It's April fourteenth, twenty-three ninety," he said. "Why?"

She was both disappointed and strangely relieved. "You're not my brother," she said, and warmth tinged her cheeks. "You're the same year as Odin, but a different day."

He closed his eyes briefly. Gaia felt an overwhelming urge, a compulsion to trace her mother's mark, and she gently reached forward to touch his ankle. He winced back, looking up at her curiously.

"I'm sorry," she said, withdrawing. Her finger tingled from the feel of his skin.

"Do you realize what this means for me?" he asked.

She shook her head.

"Do you have any idea who my parents are? My biological parents, I should say."

She shook her head again. "I'm sorry. No."

"The information wouldn't be in that ribbon, would it?" he asked.

"It could be," she said, hesitating. She locked pleading eyes to his. "I don't know the code," she said. "Why does it matter who your biological parents are? You were raised in here. You said yourself your father is the Protectorat. What could be better than that?"

He was putting his sock and boot on again swiftly.

"I'm sure you remember the Protectorat Family Special of *How We Are Family*," he said in a tight voice. "The Protectorat's first wife couldn't have children, so they adopted a son—me." He stood to stomp the boot on. "Then my adoptive mother died, and my father married a second wife, Genevieve, a fertile woman who gave him three children of his own."

Gaia was thinking quickly. "So those women you called

your mother and sister today. They're technically your step-mother and stepsister, through adoption. Right?" she said.

"Technically. But wave your magic wand, little Gaia. We're *family*," he drew out the last word, as if it were written all in capital letters with music in the background.

She drew back slightly, disturbed by his dark sarcasm. "I'm not sure you really know what a family is, Leon," she said quietly.

He let out a laugh. "No kidding. Thank you. And it's 'Leon' finally. There's a breakthrough."

She drew her arms across her chest. "I don't understand you," she said.

He ran a hand back through his dark hair and frowned at her. "It doesn't matter about me," he said. "What you need to understand is that the freckles will only make them more desperate to decode the ribbon. The freckles are like a brand."

Gaia was shocked. "You're going to tell them?" she asked, incredulous.

He turned to face her, his eyes piercing into hers. "No. You are," he said.

She backed away from him. "I am not."

"You are," he insisted. "You have to convince them you're cooperating. You have to try to unravel the code. Don't you see it's your only chance? If you resist, they'll kill you. But if you help them, they'll see how valuable you are. Think of Sephie."

"What about Sephie?" she asked.

He straightened, his expression surprised. "They released her," he said. "Persephone Frank is back home with her family. She's practicing medicine as if nothing ever happened. Didn't you know?"

She let out a laugh of astonishment. "I don't believe you."

"It's true. I could show you, but we don't have much time."

But Gaia was stupefied.

"She told them to look for the tea and the motherwort," Leon continued. "She convinced them you have knowledge you're not consciously aware of yourself."

"She betrayed me?" Gaia asked.

Leon shook his head, trying to explain. "No," he said. "She cooperated. She cooperated, and they let her go."

Gaia struggled to see it from his point of view. "But you said yourself it's like a brand. If I tell the Enclave about the freckles, they'll be able to identify all the babies advanced by my mother." Something puzzled her. "But don't they know that already? Don't they have their own records?"

He shook his head. "They know which people are advanced, obviously. That's no secret. And they have their birth dates. But they don't know their birth parents, or what part of Wharfton those parents are from."

"And the people with the freckles?" she asked doubtfully. "Would it help them?"

He twisted a twig of pine from the tree above him, and fiddled with the needles. "I suppose they'd be even more careful not to fall in love with each other," he said.

"What do you mean?" she asked, affronted.

He shook his head, frustrated. "People here, inside, who were advanced from outside are discouraged from marrying each other. It's a kind of civic duty for an advanced person to marry someone who was born inside the Enclave, and in a similar way, advanced people have become desirable as spouses to the people born inside. Are you with me?"

"It sounds like you think people can control who they fall in love with," she said.

"It's not really like that. It's possible for two advanced people who fall in love with each other to marry, as long as the genetic screening shows they're not related, but it's considered a waste of their genetic diversity." He closed his eyes, shaking

152

his head. "*Our* genetic diversity," he clarified. "I'm one of them. One of the advanced."

It sounded to her like he was still grappling with the basics of his identity.

"Didn't you realize you were from outside the wall?" she asked. "You knew you were adopted." She watched a faint ruddiness rise in his cheeks.

"Until five minutes ago, I thought I was my father's bastard," he said. He twisted the pine needles into a tangle and let them fall.

"And was that worse?" she asked softly. "To be a bastard from inside the wall?"

He'd been looking away, but now she saw him refocus on her, and his lips curled in a kind of self-mockery. "You don't miss much, do you? It was worse. I'd by far rather be a legitimate nobody from the outside than be the Protecorat's bastard."

"And that's saying something," she said.

He let out a brief laugh, and looked at her, his eyes warming with wary gratitude.

"You could still be the Protectorat's bastard, but from outside the wall," she reminded him.

"Not if you know him. He would never touch a woman from outside the wall."

A breeze moved through the pine needles with a soft, rushing noise, and Gaia heard a bird make a clicking noise in the garden.

"I'm sorry," he said quietly. "That's how he thinks. Not how I do."

"It's all right."

She looked down at her hands, wondering why she understood him, why it was becoming easier to talk to him, even about things that were intensely personal. He wasn't who she'd thought he was, not underneath.

"Why Orion?" he asked. "Why not some other constellation?"

She braced her foot against the boulder again and looked at the little marks on her own ankle. "Orion's my mother's maiden name." She spoke slowly, pondering the design. "You could see the Orion tattoo there your whole life and never guess it means anything."

"Until you know," he said. "And then it means everything."

She nodded.

When she lowered her foot to the ground, she felt a strange tingling in her ankle, as if the freckles on her skin there were somehow aware of the matching freckles concealed again now on his ankle. *Does he feel it too?* She wondered.

"We need to go," he said. He lifted both hats from the ground and brushed the pine needles off before he offered hers to her.

"Thank you," she said.

He gave her a long, unsmiling look and spoke gently. "My pleasure."

An unfamiliar awkwardness gripped her, coupled with a tight tug in her lungs, and she reached instinctively for her missing locket watch. She found only the buttons of her dress and touched them self-consciously.

"That reminds me," he said. He pulled her locket watch out of his pocket and held it toward her. "We're finished with this."

She frowned at the familiar object in his hand, hesitating. "You keep it."

"Why?" he asked. "It's yours. It still works. I kept it wound for you."

She shook her head. "It belongs to a free person. I have no use for it now. Besides—" She couldn't say it, but the object was defiled for her, ruined by the unknown eyes that had examined and prodded it.

Leon slowly closed his fingers over the watch and slid it back into his pocket.

"Gaia," he began. "You told me once to be good, if I knew how. I wish—"

She waited, unwilling to meet his eyes, hoping he would go on. When he didn't, the silence stretched between them like invisible cobwebs. In the dimmest part of her, she realized she might have wishes, too, elusive wishes that belonged more to a girl in a garden than they did to a captive.

Leon cleared his throat. "That baby," he said finally. "The one, you know, from the executed convict. I thought you'd want to know. It turns out that baby made its way to the black market."

Gaia's eyes widened. Could he have arranged it? The significance of his news was not lost on her. If he had saved that baby, he had done so because of Gaia. For her. And it couldn't have been easy. "Thank you," she said.

He turned his hat once more in his hand, then dipped his head to put it on and started through the garden.

Gaia followed him out and waited as he carefully closed the gate, causing a light click. It meant a lot to her that he'd given the doomed baby a chance. And the orange. He had done what he could for her, just as he'd said he would, and even though he remained a guard and part of a corrupt system, she was grateful.

They were nearing the center of town when she stopped a moment to catch her breath. She glanced up to find him studying her, but with a new easiness. Gaia smelled freshly baking bread and instinctively turned to the alluring scent. She looked up a small lane, and there, hanging from an iron bar, was a wooden sign with a carved sheaf of wheat.

"Buy me some bread," she said quietly.

He slid his hands in his pockets and leaned back in a friendly way for a moment. "That, Masister Stone, is impossible."

Pleasure shot through her, and she saw he was almost smiling. She stepped closer to him, until the buttons of her dress nearly touched his chest, and when she tilted her face to look up into his, their hat brims all but met. She felt unbelievably bold, and she liked it. She heard him breathe inward. His pupils dilated, and he seemed to freeze for a moment, but he didn't draw back.

"Leon," she said softly. "I may go into that prison and never come out again. I want some bread."

His keen blue eyes narrowed slightly, and then she saw him lick his lower lip. She had trouble breathing. It struck her how handsome he would be if he ever allowed himself to smile, and then, naturally, she felt her own lips begin to curve, encouraging him.

Leon backed up a half step, closed his eyes, and nodded.

A flash of embarrassment hit her. Her cheeks burned with a rush of color. She had actually believed, for an instant, that she was attractive to him. And he had kindly pretended to forget, for an instant, that she had a half-hideous face. She grew dizzy with mortification.

"Forget it," she muttered.

"No," he said, and though he didn't meet her eyes, he grasped her wrist tightly and drew her up the lane, into the bakery. The warm, yeast-laden air carried a rich, healing scent that permeated her face and filled her lungs as she entered, easing some of the shame she felt.

"A loaf of black bread, Mabrother," Leon said, releasing Gaia.

The baker's eyes flashed from him to Gaia in her gray prison uniform, and then back, revealing nothing. Rubbing her wrist, Gaia looked over the tall counter and saw what she was looking for: a vast brick oven, black as night. As the baker wrapped the small crusty loaf in a sheet of brown paper, she studied his face, memorizing his sharp nose and bushy white brows. His arms were muscled, his white apron dirty with dried bits of dough. When he took Leon's coin, he gave a brief nod and dropped it with a clink into a box behind the counter.

"Will there be anything else, then, Mabrother?" the baker said. His voice was rich and round.

"No. Thank you," Leon said.

"I serve the Enclave," the baker said.

"And I," Leon said.

"And I," Gaia whispered.

The baker gave her another sharp look with his small black eyes. Then he took a step back and gently placed his hand on the brickwork of the oven. Nothing more. It was a small, natural gesture, but seeing it, Gaia felt her heart slide against her ribs. It was a message, a sign, and when she met the baker's eyes again, he nodded infinitesimally. She looked hurriedly away, stepping out of the shop before Leon would notice.

She didn't dare to look back into the bakery, but she knew the baker would be watching her still. He was Derek's friend. She'd forgotten his name, but she knew he was to be trusted. She could barely hide her thrill.

Leon passed her the small loaf of bread. "Do you have a pocket?" he asked. "It will hardly do to march in with everyone seeing I've bought you a gift."

She took a gulping bite of the loaf, nearly moaning with the tasty goodness of the clean, warm bread and her new speck of hope. On instinct, she offered it back to him. His eyebrows lifted with surprise. He took a quick glance down the narrow lane, but they were alone. He broke off a piece and bit into it with white teeth.

Gaia tucked the remaining piece into the sleeve of her dress. Wouldn't the others be amazed when she came into Q cell with real, fresh bread to share? There would be a small bite for each.

Leon swallowed and his expression sobered. "Please remember," he said. "Cooperate with them."

"How soon should I expect this interrogation?"

"Soon. Tomorrow or the next day."

She licked her tongue over her teeth for the last taste of bread. It wouldn't do her any good to know a baker if she was lost in an interrogation deep in the prison. She needed to get to him soon. As they returned to the main road, Leon adopted a purposeful pace, and Gaia hurried beside him.

"There's something I don't understand," she said. "Why are you in the guard? If your father's the Protectorat, why are you serving the Enclave like any uneducated man from outside the wall?"

"You forget. I am from outside the wall," he said dryly.

"That isn't what I mean," she said.

They had reached the square now, and Gaia slowed at the sight of the arch leading to the prison. A heavy, late afternoon shadow slanted across half of the square, though light was still bright on the yellow stonework of the Bastion itself. The building had different significance to her now that she knew Leon had grown up inside it, part of the Protectorat's family.

"My father disowned me," Leon said abruptly. "It's no secret. I'm in disgrace, and yet they feel compelled to keep an eye on me. What better place than the guard?"

They were nearly at the prison entrance now, and Gaia was afraid he wouldn't have time to tell her before they were surrounded by other guards. Even now, people in the square were watching, curious to see a guard talking tête-à-tête with a prisoner.

"What did you do?" she asked.

She saw his profile turn toward the Bastion, as if he could see through its walls to the people within, and then he turned his ironic gaze upon her.

"A crime against the state," he said, his voice cool.

The change in him was startling. Gaia didn't understand what he was telling her, or even if he was speaking the truth. She did know that only something that hurt deeply could make a person so bitter.

"I'm sorry," she murmured.

His eyebrows lifted in mild surprise and a hint of disdain. "Don't be," he said. "I got just what I deserved."

They passed beneath the stone arch, and he signaled to the two guards who stood before the wooden doors.

"Take her to Q cell," he commanded. "She's clear."

"Yes, Captain," the guard said.

Gaia slowly took off her hat and felt the chill of the stone walls settle around her as the door closed, leaving the sunlight and Leon outdoors.

Chapter 14

A Crime Against the State

THAT NIGHT, as Gaia shared her fresh black bread in Q cell, the other women were openly astonished that Leon had bought it for her. She was tempted to tell them about the freckles and her fear that she would be interrogated again soon, but she had a new fear now. What if one of them passed on anything she said to the guards? She had trusted Sephie, and even though Leon had argued that Sephie had not betrayed Gaia, it felt like betrayal to her. The women were even more astounded to hear Sephie was free and back to her old life.

"So then, there's hope," Cotty said. "Any of us could be set free."

There was a buzz among the women, and Gaia saw the light in their eyes. Hope was intoxicating. One of the women giggled. Only Myrna, sitting apart and reading a frayed book by tilting it toward the light from the window, continued to look unimpressed. When she glanced up from under her black eyebrows, Gaia knew Myrna guessed there was more to her story.

"Watch out for him," Myrna said.

Gaia looked away in confusion, beginning to blush, and

that seemed to confirm something for Myrna. She nodded, setting a finger in her book as she closed the pages.

"Don't underestimate the Enclave," Myrna said. "They're using him, just like they're using all of us."

"Even you?" Gaia said.

Myrna gave a short laugh, as if Gaia amused her. "I'd say so. They've taken everything from me, and I still work for them."

The other women's voices quieted.

"Pay no attention to her," Cotty said.

"No," Gaia said. "Why, Myrna? Why do you do it? Why don't you give up, or walk away and get shot? What keeps you going?"

"Good gracious," Cotty said.

Myrna stretched her jaw and looked coldly at Gaia. "Truthfully? I can't stand to think of being outlived by the idiots."

Cotty and the others began to laugh, and Gaia thought she understood what Myrna meant.

"I want to hear about Captain Grey. What's he like?" Cotty asked. Her open, curious expression made her seem younger, despite the lines in her dark face. "I mean, I used to see him with the Protectorat. Everyone did. But I've never talked to him like you have. He's an awfully handsome young man."

"Does everybody know he's the Protectorat's son?" Gaia asked.

Cotty and the others exchanged glances. "I'd say so," Cotty said.

Gaia felt like a moron.

"You didn't know!" Cotty said, laughing. "I tell you, these people outside the wall. It's like you're from another world."

Gaia crossed her arms defensively. "It's not like I'd never heard of him," she explained. "I just didn't realize that's who he was."

"Oh, this is great," Cotty said. "I want to hear all about it."

Gaia wasn't sure how to answer, but she could see the others, all except Myrna, were watching her curiously. They welcomed any topic that distracted them from their own bleak prospects, and she was learning what power existed in the smallest news from outside the prison walls, but she wasn't certain what she could say about him. Besides, she still felt like she ought to have known who he was somehow. As if it made a difference. Gaia picked at a last crumb of bread on the gray fabric that covered her lap. "I don't know," she hedged.

Cotty laughed. "You like him!"

"No," Gaia protested.

But the other women were smiling now, too, and Gaia could feel her cheeks getting warm.

"That's ridiculous," Gaia said. "I hardly know him. Besides, I know how hideous I am."

Cotty leaned her head back against the wall, and her shoulders looked relaxed and comfortable for once. "You know, I thought so at first," Cotty said. "But you get used to your face. I always watch the pretty side of you now, and the other side sort of vanishes into a blind spot."

The others murmured. Gaia was frankly disbelieving. She'd lived with her own ugliness for so long, hiding it behind the curtain of her hair whenever possible, that there was no way she'd believe anyone else could find her pretty. Unbidden, she pictured Leon walking beside her, and realized he'd positioned himself on her unscarred side. It was natural to avoid her disfigurement; it didn't mean he could find her pretty.

Even if he did almost kiss her.

She closed her eyes and repressed a groan.

"What's he like?" said Brooke, another one of the prisoners. Brooke was a tall, gangly woman with deep circles under her

162

eyes and a long, narrow nose. She set aside the anatomy chart and smiled encouragingly.

Gaia looked down at her own hands. *What does it matter if I indulge them?* she thought. "It's hard to say. When I first met him, he had just arrested my parents, and I was afraid of him. He seemed serious and cold to me then. Really cold, actually. Now I think it's more that he's reserved," she said. She frowned. "He's quite courteous and well spoken, which makes sense now, I suppose." She remembered the baby she'd delivered from the hanged mother and how he'd saved it. She couldn't tell them about that, either. "I used to think he could be cruel," she added quietly, "but now I'm not so sure." *He could be manipulative*, she thought, glancing briefly at Myrna. The discovery that he was from outside the wall was too personal, too confidential to tell them, and for some reason she didn't want to tell them that the orange was from him, either. "It's hard to reconcile his gentle manners with him being in the guard. It's like he doesn't fit anywhere."

The women nodded. "Well, and the bread was certainly a surprise. He must have a generous streak in him somewhere. He was raised in the Bastion, you know," Brooke said.

"Until they kicked him out," Cotty added. "When was that? Two . . . no, three years ago."

Gaia glanced at the other women to see this was common knowledge among them. "He hasn't been on the Tvaltar for longer than that. Do you know why?" Gaia asked.

Cotty passed Gaia a skein of blue wool. "Roll that for me, would you?" she said. "He was on pretty regularly until he was ten or so. Then he faded out. They started doing more individual profiles of the younger kids. I don't know. I was kind of curious about Leon."

Brooke nodded. "Me, too. But then it became a respect-our-privacy thing as the kids got older."

Gaia found the end of the yarn and absently passed the first few loops of it around three of her fingers. "Why did they disown him?" she asked.

Cotty made a clucking noise. "It was all very hush-hush. He must have been, what, around sixteen then? It was about the time of that unfortunate accident with his sister, too. Fiona. A tragedy, that."

Gaia looked around expectantly, hoping one of the other women would elaborate. Cotty's knitting needles made a steady clicking. Myrna was sitting with her book open again, conspicuously refraining from joining the gossip.

"What happened to her?" Gaia asked. "I mean, I remember she died in an accident, but how?"

"Fiona fell," Brooke said. "From her bedroom window one night. Broke her neck."

Gaia felt an eerie tingle of alarm, remembering the way Leon had warned her away from the cliff in the garden. She wondered if he had been thinking then of his stepsister. "After Fiona's death, there was hardly ever anything about the Protectorat's family on the Tvaltar," Gaia said, remembering more now. "Genevieve. I remember a photo of her crying at the funeral."

Brooke nodded, and Cotty made a sympathetic humming noise. "Very unfortunate," Cotty repeated. "The whole business. Best not to talk about it."

"But what did Leon do to get disowned?" Gaia pressed. "What's a crime against the state?"

The women looked nervously at each other, but no one spoke until Myrna turned her flat black eyes on Gaia. "It's a genetic crime," she said.

"Like what?"

She looked at Cotty and Brooke.

"Like what we're accused of," Cotty said.

Gaia remembered what the doctors had first told her, but

she was confused. "How could Leon have falsified genetic tests or helped with an abortion?"

Cotty and Brooke said nothing. Gaia looked around the circle of women, and then finally to Myrna.

"He slept with his aunt," Myrna said.

"No," Gaia said, aghast.

Myrna shrugged, looking at her book again. "It's what I heard."

Gaia turned beseechingly to Cotty. "Is it true?" she whispered.

"No," Cotty said, scowling at Myrna. "That was just a rumor. There were all kinds of crazy rumors, not half of them true, I'm sure. His Aunt Maura is ten years older than him and a very genteel, married woman. I'm sure she'd never do such a thing. Myrna, you should know better than to torment the girl."

Myrna merely rolled her eyes as if she found them both incredibly boring.

"But then, what did happen?" Gaia asked Cotty.

"Well, I don't know exactly. Nobody knows," Cotty said. "We could gossip until we're blue in the face, but nobody has any facts. Frankly, I thought it was pretty disgusting, all the speculation there was. For a while there, it sounded like he'd slept with every girl in the Bastion, which was obviously not true. Anyway, he took his mother's maiden name, Grey, for his last name and joined the guard, and we didn't hear much more about him."

Gaia slowly rolled more blue yarn around her fingers. "Why didn't this gossip make it outside the wall?" she asked.

"I'm sure it did," Cotty said. "It must have. Maybe you just weren't listening."

Gaia must have been twelve or thirteen at the time, she reasoned. Her parents, never much for gossip, might have talked about it a little, and Old Meg certainly would have talked about it, but it hadn't made an impact on Gaia. She had known that

Fiona had died, but she certainly hadn't registered Leon's new last name. Perhaps his scandal had been overshadowed by the mourning.

Now she pondered the little bit she knew, troubled by the sordid possibilities. She couldn't believe Leon had slept with his aunt. The idea was sick. It would violate everything decent she knew about him. She could not believe it, but certainly something had happened to cause his disgrace. He felt he deserved it.

That was the key. Her hands stilled on the ball of yarn, and she let her gaze drift up to the windows. No matter what the rumors were, Leon believed he'd done something wrong, some evil that warranted exclusion from his family and a life in the guard. That existence, carrying out the Enclave's laws without question, had stymied everything else in his nature, and in essence, he'd chosen that. He'd chosen to surrender his own ethics. He'd chosen to become callous.

She glanced up at Myrna to find the older woman looking at her through tired eyes. She felt a chill around her heart, remembering Myrna's warning: they'll use you. And him.

"Give it enough time, and this place will destroy even you," Myrna said softly.

Gaia stood, handed the ball of yarn back to Cotty, and walked into her bedroom cell.

After dinner, while the others were walking in the courtyard, Cotty sewed a pocket inside the waistband of Gaia's dress for her. "In case you get more bread," Cotty said, patting the fabric smooth before she gave back the dress. "Or anything else. You can smuggle in treats for us."

Gaia smiled, thanking her, but she doubted she would have more opportunities to walk with Leon as Cotty was obviously implying. Gaia pulled the dress over her head.

"Can I ask you something?" Gaia asked softly, working the buttons. "Have you known Myrna long?"

Cotty gave a brief laugh and poked her needle into a spool of gray thread. "You want to know why she's so mean, don't you?" Cotty said.

Gaia wouldn't have put it that bluntly, but now she nodded.

"She has a heart, I know that," Cotty said slowly. "But I think she pushes people away before they can disappoint her. I heard she was married briefly, long ago, and it ended badly. I know for certain she's been thwarted about wanting to start a clinic. She argued that we need a blood bank for the hemo-philiacs and a teaching clinic for doctors, but the Protectorat flatly refuses."

"Why?" Gaia asked.

Cotty shook her head, putting her spools and scissors in a little box. "It was one of the founding principles: no hospitals, no extreme medicine. Just antibiotics and morphine. They thought anything more just catered to the weak. It was a choice about resources, brutal but necessary. Now Myrna thinks things have changed."

Gaia gazed up at the three windows, puzzling over the pos-sibilities. "She's a good doctor. If she were in charge, more people might live longer."

"I agree. But the Protectorat has his point, too. There's no shame in dying. His focus is on the whole population, what's best for everyone, not what's best for an individual. He and Myrna just come from different perspectives."

"And he's in charge," Gaia said dryly.

Cotty made a soft clucking noise, and Gaia glanced over to see her warm, crooked smile. "Don't you worry about Myrna," Cotty said kindly. "She's mean, but she's smart. And she's not like Sephie."

"How do you mean?" Gaia asked, puzzled.

Cotty gave a sideways, apologetic glance. "I don't like to speak ill of someone who's not here. Let me just say, it's easy to like Sephie because she's so warm and friendly. But when she has to, she'll always choose the easiest route."

Gaia grew uncomfortable, not certain what to say.

"I'm sorry," Cotty continued. "I was only trying to say, you can count on Myrna." She rubbed the bridge of her nose thoughtfully. "Maybe that's why she's here."

That night, when the others were asleep, Gaia took out her little mirror and tried to see her face in the darkness. It was pointless, of course. The little oval mocked her by reflecting only the near-black of the night shadows, as if she herself were invisible. She ran her thumb slowly over the smooth surface of the glass, and then slid the mirror into her new pocket. At night, with nothing to distract her, she missed her mother and father so intensely, the loneliness invaded her heart like a cold, soundless mist. Myrna, Leon, and even Cotty—these new people in her life didn't know her. They didn't know who she really was inside, or the intricate workings of her heart. There was nobody now who really loved her, she realized.

Nobody but her mother, wherever she was. Gaia had a flashing memory of her mother standing at the edge of the back porch, her face turned up toward the sunlight, squinting and half smiling as she reached up to untangle the strands of the wind chime.

You really should brush your hair back, Gaia. Let me braid it for you.

Unbidden tears crowded against Gaia's eyelids. Her hair was short now. Her mother was gone. She turned her head against her flat mattress, automatically keeping the tender skin of her scar upward, and told herself she would not cry.

Chapter 15
The Yellow Pincushion

I<small>T WAS BARELY LIGHT</small> when the guards came.

"Gaia Stone!" a man's voice yelled.

She rolled out of bed, her bare feet hitting the cold floor.

Myrna ran in and gripped her arms tightly, pulling her near in a sudden, fierce hug. "They're here for you," she whispered tersely. "Stay strong. Remember, whatever you do, whatever you say, your first job is to survive."

Gaia clutched at her, terrified, as the guard entered the bedroom and jerked Gaia away.

"Shoes!" he yelled. "Where are your shoes?"

Gaia looked to the floor, where the shoes lay, and Myrna picked them up and thrust them to Gaia.

"Quickly!" the guard yelled again, and the instant her shoes were on, he grabbed her again and roughly tied her hands behind her back.

"Where are you taking her?" Cotty asked.

The other women came from their rooms, too, and watched in horror as the guards hurried Gaia toward the door. As one of them began to cry, Gaia was reminded of the day they took Sephie away. She had one last look over her shoulder at Myrna, who was standing alone under the windows while the other women grouped together in a terrified hug. Myrna's stony face was harsh with bitterness, and her fists were clenched rigidly at her sides.

"You hear me? Your first job is to *survive!*" Myrna repeated.

The door banged shut behind her. If Gaia had ever believed the older doctor was indifferent to her, she knew now she was wrong. What Cotty had said was true. The sharp commands, the sarcasm: these were Myrna's version of affection, and now Gaia clung to Myrna's last words of advice.

The next moment, Gaia was being hauled up the stairs and along another hallway. She was barely able to keep on her feet, and she was prevented from falling only by the rough grasp of the guards who held her arms, one on each side. When they reached the main entrance, she looked around desperately, hoping to see Leon, but there were only more unfamiliar guards dressed in black. Half a dozen of them fell into step around her as they left the prison, passing under the stone arch into the cool, dim air of the deserted square. A swirl of fog enshrouded the obelisk in the middle of the square.

With a jolt, she remember the first day she was there, when a man was dragged to the Bastion at dawn, just as she was being dragged. Later the pregnant woman and her husband had been hanged. Terror coursed through her, and her feet refused to propel her forward.

"Come now," the guard on her left said roughly, jerking her so that she half fell out of her loose loafers.

Gaia gasped in pain as her tied hands twisted in the tight rope, and then she lunged forward between the guards. When they led her straight toward the Bastion, Gaia's alarm mushroomed with the cold air in her lungs.

"No," she whispered.

"You'll come, and no more fuss," the guard said in her ear.

Gaia recoiled, but the two guards lifted her by her arms up the stairs, and plopped her back on her feet when they arrived at the door. As they waited for the door to be opened, Gaia had her first chance to catch her breath. One of the guards leaned nearer, and lightly lifted the bangs that had fallen forward over her eyes.

Gaia jerked her head back, glaring at him.

"Ha," the man said, his breath sour in her face. "I thought we had a pretty one here, but she's right disgusting."

The guard in the front turned slightly. "That's how we know we've got the right one," he said briefly. "Her scar."

Gaia burned with resentment, but anything was better than the unthinking panic she'd felt before. She stood straighter now, eyeing the first guard coldly. His eyes protruded and a mottled, bulbous nose overhung his lips as he leered at her. Pride took hold and saved her from reacting to him. She turned her gaze forward, toward the door.

The guard gave her arm a sharp pinch, and she gasped.

"Think you're better than me?" he whispered.

She clenched her teeth, hoping desperately that this man would not be in charge of her for long.

"You're nothing but a cheap slut from outside the wall," he hissed.

Then the door opened, and she was ushered into a lighted hallway that smelled unexpectedly of some faint perfume. The guards fell silent and after a last shove, they allowed her a little distance.

She was standing in a vast, open space that was completely antithetical to the plain, practical façade of the building. Nothing she had ever seen on the Tvaltar had prepared her for this sight. A pair of potted gardenia bushes, responsible for the pure fragrance, stood at the bottom of a grand, white staircase that ascended in a double curve upward, out of sight. White tiles, with smaller inlays of black tile in a whimsical, geometric pattern, graced the floor. Beyond the staircase, the walls seemed to be made entirely of French doors and she saw the green light of a solarium behind the panes. To Gaia's immediate left and right were enormous matching wooden doors, both sets carved with figures and trees.

Gaia stood waiting among her guards, grateful for their silence, and then, unexpectedly, she heard a snatch of childish laughter come from somewhere in the back of the house. A small boy of two or three years came running around the corner in a bright blue nightshirt and a pair of fluffy pink slippers that were clearly too big for him. He carried a small yellow ball. His laughter was a bright, joyful noise, completely incongruous with the desperate situation she found herself in, and she stood still, caught in anticipation, knowing that any moment he would see her and the guards.

He was moving so fast that he'd gotten partly past their group before he saw them, and then he skidded in his slippers, his laughter abruptly gone. She watched his foot catch against his own ankle, and then he was down, sprawled in a blue heap on the white tile, and his ball was jarred loose from his hand. Instinctively, she took a half step toward him, but strong hands held her back.

The small yellow ball skidded forward across the white and black tiles, landed before her, and proved to be her father's lemon-shaped pincushion. Gaia was astounded. By what circuitous route could the pincushion have traveled from Leon's pocket to become this child's plaything?

The next moment, an older girl of nine or ten came running around in the path of the boy. Her blond, wavy hair stood out around her pink-cheeked face in a glorious haze.

"Michael!" she called, her voice breathless with mirth. "If you don't give me back my slippers—" Her voice broke off as she saw them, and she stumbled to a stop. The boy scrambled forward to grab the pincushion just as she ran to him, crouching to scoop him up into his arms.

"Aunt Genevieve!" she screamed. She was backing up the way she'd come, carrying the heavy child.

A third person now came wrathfully around the corner. "What on earth?" she demanded.

Gaia stared. This was the woman she'd seen only the day before, when she was walking with Leon: Genevieve Quarry, the Protectorat's wife. And she looked furious.

"Britta. Take him back to the kitchen. Immediately," Genevieve said to the girl.

As the children backed away another step, and then hurried away, Genevieve stormed forward.

"How dare you," she demanded, her cultured voice scathing even at a hush.

"Excuse me, Masister Quarry," the guard said. "I was told to bring her to Mabrother Iris first thing."

Gaia felt Genevieve's piercing gaze turn to her, and she instinctively backed up.

"Then do your job," Genevieve said contemptuously to the guard. She rapped on the door to Gaia's left, and instantly it was opened from within.

"Get this rabble out of my foyer, Winston," Genevieve said.

"I beg your pardon," Winston said smoothly, stepping aside and gesturing Gaia's group inside. "An oversight that will not be repeated."

Genevieve was already disappearing toward the depths of the house. "Miles will hear of this," she said over her shoulder, and her quiet voice carried clearly.

Winston was a stocky, middle-aged doorkeeper with a small mouth and little expression, even when he was being scolded. He merely nodded again, hurried them inside, and closed the door.

173

Gaia expected Winston to chastise the other guards, but he said nothing, leading them down a hallway. "Watch the step there," he said courteously, pointing, as he preceded them down two stairs, and then guided them down several passages. Gaia passed a row of tall windows, each offering a glimpse of the fog and the denser silhouette of the monument.

When Winston led them next up a staircase, a practical, boxy one with narrow treads, Gaia had the impression the Bastion had two distinct functions: the beautiful, gracious home that Genevieve and the children inhabited, and the no-nonsense part that she was entering as a bound prisoner. *In a way, it's only a more extreme version of the society I already live in,* Gaia thought, *another division, like the one that separates those who live inside and outside the wall.* She had just seen where the worlds collided.

"Here, one moment," Winston said finally, pausing before a tall, wooden door. Other similar doors lined the hallway. There was a carpet runner down the center of the hall and windows at both ends.

Winston knocked, and a voice invited them in. Gaia stepped into a large, airy room, lined with books and carpeted with a sumptuous rug that muffled her footsteps. A yellow canary made a skittering noise in a cage by one of the windows.

"What's this?" An annoyed voice spoke, and Gaia saw a small, gray-haired man with glasses and slumped shoulders peer at them from over a desk. His white clothing had trim, tailored lines without appearing to be strictly a uniform. It was a peculiar desk, with a glass top and a light shining through it from below, so that the man's face was lit under his chin and nose and eyebrows, giving him an unearthly appearance.

"It's the scarred girl from outside," the guard said. "Gaia Stone."

"I can see that," the man said irritably. "What's with the rest of you?"

174

The guards stood stupidly for a moment.

Winston cleared his throat. "Thank you," he said to the head guard. "We can take it from here."

The guard set his jaw stubbornly. "She's dangerous. I'm supposed to take every precaution."

"Indeed," Winston said. "And you have done so. Let me show you out."

Gaia was left standing beside the door as it closed gently, and the last noise of the guards and Winston could be heard receding down the hallway. Her hands were still tied behind her and her gray dress was rumpled from all the jerking she'd been subjected to, but she took a deep breath and told herself to remain calm. She stood quietly, waiting. Based on what the guard had told the Protectorat's wife, she realized the old man must be Mabrother Iris. *He doesn't look like a torturer*, she thought cautiously, *and this seems more like a library than a prison cell*. But still. She wondered briefly what would have happened if, weeks ago, she had reported to the south gate with her ribbon and asked to see Mabrother Iris, as Leon had advised her to do.

He adjusted his glasses, his attention still on his desk. Gaia took a slight step forward and noticed that the top of the desk was like an enormous television set, but with a dozen screens overlapping at once.

"Come," he said impatiently.

As Gaia stepped silently across the thick carpet, he touched the top of the desk with his fingertip, and a scene appeared: a father beside the unlake, and a red-haired woman dandling a baby before her. The sun was just coming up, and both parents were dressed in simple work clothes. The woman let her hat fall back and hang from the strings around her neck. They were smiling and their mouths moved, but Gaia couldn't hear their voices.

"Yes, come here," the man said, beckoning her to come stand beside him. "Precisely here. Not too close," he said, wrinkling his nose as if she smelled.

"Are you Mabrother Iris?" she asked.

"Watch," he commanded, pointing to the screen.

Gaia looked more carefully, and when she realized the woman in the screen was Emily, she impulsively smiled. "Oh!" she said. "I know them! Emily's had her baby, then. Is it a boy?"

"Yes," the man said.

She was puzzled. "When was she in a movie?" she asked.

"Unbelievable," the man muttered to himself. "It's *now*, girl," he said. "There's a camera focused on them now. They're taking a morning walk before they go to work."

As Gaia grasped what he was saying, she realized there must be cameras aimed strategically around Wharfton. She'd always supposed there were a few informants in Wharfton who relayed information to the Enclave, but she hadn't guessed there were actually cameras spying on them in real time. That's how the Enclave seemed to know everything as soon as it happened.

"Do you have cameras everywhere?" she asked.

"Watch now," the man said. "This is a lesson for you."

"If you're Mabrother Iris," she said nervously. "Do you know where my mother is?"

The man gripped Gaia's arm with unexpected strength and pushed his face near to her own. "Of course I know where your mother is. But now, you need to watch this."

He slapped his hand down upon the desk so hard the images vibrated for a moment. Gaia was stunned that he spoke of her mother in the present tense; that he knew where she was.

With a surge of hope, she obediently turned her gaze to the screen on his desk and saw a raven, huge and black, settle on the stones by Emily's feet. Kyle pointed it out with big, goofy

176

gestures, but the baby was far too young to appreciate a bird, and instead continued to gurgle at his mom. Gaia could see Emily say something, laughing.

Mabrother Iris pushed a little button on the edge of the desk. "Take out the bird," he said.

At first nothing changed, except that Emily passed the baby to his dad. Then there was a blur of black at the edge of the screen and the parents simultaneously jumped in alarm. At their feet, the bird was reduced to a motionless mass of feathers with one crooked foot pleading upward. The camera view zoomed out, shrinking the image of the parents, who were running with their baby as fast as possible back toward the houses of Wharfton. Emily's auburn hair flew wildly behind her, and though there was no sound, Gaia saw that she was crying out in panic and fear.

Chapter 16
Cooperation

"W HY WOULD YOU DO THAT?" she asked, uncomprehending. She had known the Enclave could be systematically cruel, as when they executed prisoners in the Square of the Bastion, but the bird had been harmless. The cruelty was so pointless. The horror of it, the scope of his power, made her cold. As Mabrother Iris turned deliberately, watching Gaia intently, she backed away.

"You commanded a soldier on the wall to shoot the bird," she said. "What if his aim had been poor?"

Mabrother Iris lifted his tinted glasses and propped them in the gray hair on top of his head. The pupils of his eyes were preternaturally dilated, reducing his irises to the narrowest rings of pale blue. "I need to be certain I have your entire cooperation," he said.

"Or what?" she asked, breathless. "You'll kill me?"

He tilted his face slightly, contemplating her with fathomless eyes. "No. Emily's baby, maybe. Or Sephie Frank. You liked her, didn't you? Or how about Leon?" His voice was deceptively casual.

"You wouldn't."

"How about your mother?" he added.

She shook her head stiffly, her mind scrambling to keep up with each evermore painful threat. "I don't even believe she's still alive." The hard truth hit her again. "You lied to give yourself more leverage."

The man stepped nearer the desk again. "Maybe not so stupid after all," he muttered, and touched the desk with his fingertip.

A new screen popped up, and in spite of herself, Gaia stepped near again to see better. It was a view of three women sleeping in a semi-circular space enclosed by stone walls. Gaia could see they were on cots, with gray blankets. It might have been a black-and-white photo, it was so devoid of color and motion, except that once a curtain swelled in a silent wind. Gaia tried to make out their faces, to glean any clue from the scene that would show her where they were. She saw a black chain leading to one of the beds. Could the women be shackled?

"You can't tell now," he said. "But the middle one's your mother."

"Where are they?" Gaia asked, peering closely, willing the woman to roll over so she could see her face and be certain.

The man touched the desktop, and it went dark. Gaia blinked and stepped back several paces until her legs hit against a chair.

"Perhaps," he said slowly, lowering his glasses over his eyes again, "if you cooperate, I could arrange for you to see her."

"Could you really?"

"Indeed I could."

Torn, Gaia twisted her fingers into fists behind her back, instinctively straining against the ropes. Mild as he looked, she understood that he had the power of life and death over all the people he could see in his screen desk. Conversely, Leon had told her the Enclave rewarded loyalty. The choices were clear:

cooperate and see your mother. Resist, and she'll be killed. Gaia felt sick to her stomach.

"Sit, please," Mabrother Iris said.

She sat gingerly on the edge of the upholstered chair behind her, touching the cushiony satin behind her back with her fingertips for balance. If only she knew what her parents would want her to do. Since her father had been shot escaping, he must have believed that anything was better than cooperating with the Enclave, even death. But her mother lived still. Had she found a way to resist and still be alive? Gaia couldn't bear to think that anything she might do could put her mother in even greater danger. "What do you want me to do?" Gaia said, her voice small.

For the first time, Mabrother Iris's lips curved in a slight smile. "There," he said. "I knew you'd be reasonable. You've always served the Enclave well, aside from that one ridiculous aberration after the hanging."

Gaia's cheeks flamed. "Yes," she improvised. "I'm sorry. I didn't know the laws then."

He shrugged. "Your training was left to chance, essentially," he said. "You no doubt absorbed some misguided ethical sense that saving a baby's life is more important than obeying the laws of the Enclave. But our laws exist for the greater good, and it's not for you to flout them."

She lowered her face, hoping she looked suitably humble. This man believed, completely, that what he was doing was right. That made him even more terrifying. Mabrother Iris resettled his glasses on his nose and turned to touch the screen again.

"I need you to tell me what you know about your mother's ribbon," he said.

Gaia tensed, remembering Leon's warning. "I don't know much," she began. "I think it's a code. I was told to keep it safe and not to lose it." She neglected to add that her mother had warned her to destroy it.

"Who told you this? Your mother?"

She shook her head. Hopefully Old Meg was long gone by now and safe in the Dead Forest. If not, she had probably perished on the way. Gaia hesitated a second, then remembered how ruthlessly Mabrother Iris had commanded the shooting of the bird. She could not resist him now. "Old Meg," she said. "She was my mother's friend. She gave the ribbon to me the same night my parents were arrested."

He frowned slightly, and Gaia guessed this was something he had not known. It gave her a modicum of hope. Maybe he would decide she could be useful to him.

"Where is Old Meg now?" he asked.

She averted her eyes, looking at the tall windows to her right. She could see the top of the obelisk emerging through the fog. She shifted uncomfortably on her chair, her hands still tied behind her back.

"Answer me!" he said sharply.

Gaia jumped. The canary made a cheap from its cage. "She left," she said. "She said she was leaving town."

"No one leaves town," he said. "Did she say where she was going?"

Gaia swallowed hard. "To the wasteland. To the Dead Forest."

Mabrother Iris's eyebrows lifted in amusement.

"What is it?" she asked.

"The Dead Forest doesn't exist," he said. "It's a place from a fairy tale."

She was confused. "But—"

He was shaking his head now, his eyes warming slightly through the tinted lenses. "I keep forgetting you're a child," he said. "From outside the wall, no less." He paused, and rubbed his chin. "This could take some time, I see," he mused. He leaned over the picture table and pushed a button. "I need a room prepared," he said softly. "No, the third floor. And you might as well arrange a shower and fresh clothes for her. There's a slight stench."

Gaia felt her face redden, but she tried to resist her first reaction of shame. It wasn't her fault the prison didn't give her a chance to clean herself frequently. The man was inspecting her.

"Are you thirsty?" he asked.

She nodded. She hadn't eaten that morning. The man reached over to a teapot she hadn't noticed before on a nearby table and poured a cup of tea. The redolent aroma drifted across the room, and she was wondering how she would drink it with her hands tied when he lifted the cup to his own lips.

"Tell me more about the ribbon," he said.

Her thirst, hardly noticeable before, now intensified, and she eyed his cup enviously as he cradled it between his fingers.

"I don't know anything more," she said.

"You promised to cooperate," he reminded her.

"I know," she said. "I am." She struggled to find the right words. "Ask me something."

"Did your mother bring the ribbon with her when you went to deliver babies?"

"No," she said.

"Did she ever show it to you before the night Old Meg gave it to you?"

"No," she said. "I didn't know it existed."

"Did your mother ever write you notes with unusual alphabets?"

Gaia's heart jumped in her chest. She licked her lips. "No," she said.

"I can tell when you're lying," he said mildly.

182

"No," she repeated. "My father was the one who liked to play games with letters and songs," she said.

His eyebrows lifted again. "So is it possible your father made this ribbon?"

The idea intrigued her, and she shifted her gaze to his. "That makes sense," she said slowly. "He was a tailor. He did all the sewing for our family." She realized now it was possible, even likely, that her mother had told her father about the babies, and her father had recorded the information with the silk thread in the ribbon. He was the true record keeper.

Mabrother Iris leaned back against the picture table and relaxed one leg over the other. "That is a shame," he said dryly. He'd apparently come to the same conclusion she had.

She narrowed her eyes. "Because you killed him," she said.

The man was rubbing his chin again.

"Why?" she asked. "He was the most gentle man who ever lived."

He turned his gaze slowly in her direction. "He killed two guards."

"Trying to escape? I don't believe you."

"Trying to get to your mother."

The ache in Gaia's heart tightened a little more, and for a moment she closed her eyes and imagined her father wrestling with guards, trying to get to her mother. That made sense to her. That was her father. She glared resentfully at the gray-haired little man. The canary made another skittering noise in its seeds and let out a note of birdsong.

Mabrother Iris set down his teacup and walked over to a little cabinet, opened a drawer, and pulled out a small bottle. He strolled by the windows and stopped there to hold it to the light, gazing at it. Gaia inhaled quickly, recognizing her ink bottle.

"Let me tell you a little about this ink," he said. "It's ocher, mixed with clay, alcohol, and an antibiotic." He twisted it idly in the light, inspecting the opaque, brown color. "It's crude enough, but functional," he said. "It's the addition of the antibiotic that's unusual, especially given that antibiotics are illegal outside the wall. Did your mother make this ink?"

She thought fast. He must know at least as much as Leon had known before they talked in the garden, she realized. Did he already know about the freckle pattern because of what she'd told Leon the day before? If Leon had relayed this information to Mabrother Iris, this could be a test for her, one she had to pass. On the other hand, if Leon had kept her information secret, she would be revealing it needlessly to her enemy.

"Gaia?" the man said. He came nearer to her and slowly untwisted the lid. "Don't waste my time, Gaia," he said ominously. He dipped the tip of his pinky finger into the ink and held it up before his eyes.

"It's for the freckles," she said.

He gave a satisfied smile. "Now we're getting somewhere," he said. "Explain."

Briefly she explained the custom her mother had of giving tea to the mother, and the four quick pricks of ink in the baby's ankle. She watched him closely as she spoke, but she could not tell if she was revealing something he'd never known before. She was afraid. The freckle pattern was the last secret she knew. There was nothing left to tell. If they wanted her to reveal anything else, she would not be able to help them, and then what? They might kill her. Would they torture her first, or would they harm the innocent people she cared about?

There was a silence in the room when Gaia finished, and she could hear only a faint buzz from the picture table, and a muted clanging noise from out in the square.

"Can I see my mother now?" Gaia asked, afraid.

184

Mabrother Iris turned away with a brief, humorless laugh. "What's the hurry, my dear? We've just begun."

He put the cap back on the ink bottle and dropped it ungently in the little drawer of the cabinet. He brought out a sheet of paper and a pencil. He set them on the table beside her, and then he glanced at her arms and frowned. He touched another button on the picture table.

"Send a guard up." In the interval while they waited for a guard, Gaia sat stiffly on her chair, growing increasingly uneasy. Mabrother Iris picked up his teacup and went to stand gazing out of the window. Something about his casual unconcern for her chilled her deeply, and when she glanced over at his narrow, white-clad shoulders, his prim little shaded glasses, she felt a degree of loathing that surpassed any she'd felt before. Her dislike of him made her even more afraid, until her cold fingers were trembling.

She remembered what Myrna had told her and tried to hold on to it: *survive*. That was the goal. So far, she was surviving, but only at the cost of giving up her parents' secrets. What would her mother think of that?

A light knocking noise sounded on the door behind her, and Mabrother Iris told the guard to untie Gaia. Her arms and shoulders prickled and ached when at last her wrists were free, and she rubbed her cold, stiff hands together until they tingled.

"The room is ready, Mabrother," the guard said.

Gaia started at the familiar voice, and turned slightly to see Sgt. Bartlett, his fair hair carefully combed and his expression neutral. She instantly looked away, not wanting to reveal by her manner that she recognized him. It was possible, just possible, that Leon had arranged to have his friend there, but she had no evidence that Sgt. Bartlett would be at all inclined to help her.

"Good," Mabrother Iris said. "Remain by the door."

Gaia heard him retreat behind her, and then Mabrother Iris turned his attention back to Gaia. "I want you to draw the freckle pattern," he said, handing her the pencil.

She hid her surprise. It would be simple to show him the pattern on her own ankle, but he apparently he didn't know about it, which could only mean Leon hadn't told him. Gaia took the pencil in her cold, clumsy fingers, and forced them to grasp it. Aware that the guard behind her was also watching, she carefully drew the familiar pattern:

                                        •

                                    •

                            •

                                          •

"That's it?" Mabrother Iris sounded surprised. He spun the paper toward himself. "So simple," he added in a different voice, as if that made sense to him. "What does it mean?" he asked.

Gaia shrugged a shoulder. "I don't now. It's like part of a square."

Mabrother Iris was still looking at the paper, or she was sure he would have known she was lying. She thought the hint of the Orion constellation was a connection to her mother's maiden name, Orion, but if he didn't recognize the pattern, she wasn't going to fill him in.

"So every baby your mother advanced to the Enclave, every

baby from Western Sector Three, has these freckles," Mabrother Iris said. "These same freckles?"

"Yes. She sometimes helped deliver babies in other sectors if she was needed, but they would be comparatively few."

"But those babies, too, would be in your mother's code," Mabrother Iris said.

Gaia couldn't be certain. "I expect so," she said. "I don't know." It made her feel acutely uncomfortable, cooperating with him. Honesty, even partial honesty, had never felt so wrong to her. Her gaze shifted longingly toward the windows. The fog had lifted now, and she could see sunlight on the pale stone of the obelisk.

"What makes you think the ribbon code is about the quota babies?" she asked.

"Come. Look at this," Mabrother Iris said. He was standing beside the screen desk again, and he guided Gaia closer. On the top layer was an image of her mother's ribbon, but now it was increased in size so that a section of it was wider than her hand, the silk markings easy to see.

She gripped the pencil tight in her fingers, willing the little lines to resolve themselves into a pattern she could identify, but the symbols looked more like doodles than any letters she'd ever known. She sensed that Mabrother Iris was watching her face closely, and she tried to concentrate. Her effort only made her more confused and anxious.

Beside her, the man sighed.

"I'm sorry," she said quietly. "I'm trying."

"There's no question that we'll eventually decipher it," he said. "We can see that it's a record of births." He pointed to one group of symbols. "These, clearly, are numbers. They repeat, with variations." He pointed to another group, and then another, but she couldn't see how any of them were related. "The other figures are the names of the parents. Combined with the Nursery's birth date records from when the advanced babies first arrived inside the wall, we can figure out the birth parents of our children from outside the wall. At least from Western Sector Three. So far, your mother is the only midwife we can find who kept records."

"Have you asked the others?"

"Obviously."

Gaia wondered if her mother had heard about these investigations, and if that was why she had given her ribbon to Old Meg a few weeks before she was arrested. Gaia frowned, and Mabrother Iris tilted his face, watching her.

"You have another question?" he asked dryly.

"Why didn't you keep track of the birth parents before?" she asked. It seemed an obvious thing to do.

He lifted an eyebrow, leaning back slightly. "Why, indeed. There was a misguided idea of equality and fairness—all babies from outside the wall were equally worthy, so there was no need to track their heritage, theoretically. They were true members of their Enclave families, with all the rights of blood. No ties to the outside. That was the principle decades ago, when the Enclave first rescued babies from abusive parents on the outside. Furthermore, the anonymity was supposed to elevate everyone's sense of responsibility: there was a community obligation to raise all the children, to create an Enclave that was best for everyone. Absurd, of course. Parenting doesn't work on a massive scale. By its very nature, it's individualistic. Yet even the Protectorat's family believed in the anonymity once."

Gaia thought of Leon, adopted by the Protectorat and his first wife. No one knew who his biological parents were.

"There were practical reasons, as well," Mabrother Iris continued. "Some of the more shortsighted parents outside the wall objected to advancing their children. They wanted to trace the adoptions and reclaim their offspring. In one case, a

188

grandfather actually broke into the wall and tried to take a two-year-old he thought was his grandson. The parents inside the wall wanted to be sure that could never happen, and so we had to promise there were no records. No records connecting specific babies to specific birth parents outside."

Mabrother Iris faced her directly, and his gaze grew somber.

"Your mother's code—or your father's, I should say—is vitally important now."

She couldn't hide her frustrated confusion. "I still don't see why," she said. "What good does it do to know who the parents are? If you just care about the genes, wouldn't it be simpler and more precise to test each person's DNA?"

He looked at her curiously. Then he ran a finger along the edge of the picture desk, frowning in thought. "You're turning out to be quite an interesting mix of ignorance and information," he said, with an odd note in his voice. "Do you know what DNA is, exactly?"

She hedged, trying to recall what her mother and father had taught her, back in the evenings when they had walked together by the unlake. "I know it's a person's genetic code, and each person's code is unique, like a fingerprint."

Mabrother Iris frowned. "True, for a start. We've taken the DNA of many families within the wall. People we're worried about. Now we're linking traits for health problems with the genes. Some of the simpler ones, like recessive hemophilia, we've known about for a long time. Others, like infertility, are far more complicated."

"So can't you just take the DNA of all the people outside the wall, too?" she asked. "That wouldn't be too invasive, would it? Can't you tell, then, how people are related?"

He shook his head. "That would be like adding more hay to the haystack when we're looking for one needle. The DNA alone without the family relationships is far less valuable when

189

we want to identify a specific, significant gene. But that's beside the point. From you, we need to know the birth parents of the advanced babies from Western Sector Three," he said. "That's our top priority. Your code is the key to that information."

"But—" Gaia was still confused.

"Trust me," he said ironically, nudging his glasses. "Do your bit. Decipher the code." He pushed a button, and a long piece of paper began to roll out of a side slot of the picture desk, then another. He pulled them out and handed them to her. "This is the first half of one side, enlarged. If you find you need more, let me know."

Gaia took the enlarged copy of the ribbon; every silk thread was clearly visible and impenetrably obscure. Mabrother Iris made a gesture toward Sgt. Bartlett, who started forward.

"You've undoubtedly asked my mother to do this same thing," she said. "Why do you think I can solve it when my mother can't?"

His smile didn't reach his eyes. "Because you're smarter." He took off his glasses and polished the lenses with his handkerchief, and when he looked up, his strange, dilated eyes seemed to look right through her. "You have twenty-four hours to prove you can help us on this. It's not a game."

Chapter 17
The Baby Code

S GT. BARTLETT ESCORTED Gaia to a small, clean room with pale yellow walls and a large window. A wooden desk and chair lined one wall, and a simple cot, made up with sheets, pale gray blankets, and a pillow, lined the other. A narrow door led to a compact bathroom, and Gaia could see folded white towels on a shelf beside the sink. A clean gray dress hung on a hook over a pair of tidy black shoes.

She stepped to the window, which also overlooked the square, but from even higher up. It was open a hand's width at the bottom and rigged to open no further. She could see the white roofs of the prison and other buildings, and in one yard, a quiet place where the sun didn't touch yet, a woman in red was hanging laundry on a line. What she wouldn't give to trade places with that woman right now.

Sgt. Bartlett cleared his throat from the doorway, and she turned sharply. She hadn't even realized he was still there.

"The clean clothes are for you after your shower. Do you need anything else?" he asked.

She searched his brown eyes, and for the first time, she saw a yielding in them. He was young, too, she realized. Maybe a bit older than Leon. His lips were fuller, with more color, and his features were even and tanned. He was taller than Leon and broader through the shoulders. Where Leon was pale, grave, and intense, Sgt. Bartlett had a confident, natural insouciance, despite his serious work.

"Does Leon know I'm here?" she asked.

His eyes flickered before his expression became politely neutral again. "I'll inform him."

"May I have something to eat?" she asked. "Some water?"

"Of course," he said.

She slumped into the chair. At least they didn't mean to starve her. In her fingers, she clutched the printout Mabrother Iris had given her. She'd never been much of a reader—there had been few books outside the wall—and the task of deciphering the code seemed insurmountable.

"I need something to write with," she said. "And clean paper."

"They're in the drawer," Sgt. Bartlett said, gesturing toward the desk.

"Ah," she said. She glanced up again at the blond guard, and it seemed to her that he was lingering needlessly. His fingers clenched against the side of his leg, causing the fabric to twitch suddenly. The mannerism struck her as familiar, though she couldn't see why it should.

"Is there something else?" she asked finally.

She saw him hesitate, and then he stepped fully into the room and closed the door behind him.

"Is it true the freckles mean a person was born in Western Sector Three?" he asked.

Startled, Gaia tried to remember precisely where she'd been in her conversation with Mabrother Iris when Sgt. Bartlett entered the room. He had untied her just before she drew the freckle pattern, she recalled. She nodded slowly. "Yes."

He closed his eyes briefly, and Gaia knew it was more than simply an idle question.

"If I have the freckles—I'm not saying I do—but if I do, I'd want to know who my parents are," he said now, his voice urgent. "If you could help me, I'd be grateful."

She half expected him to pull up his trouser leg and take off his boot right then to check for the freckles. "I don't know the code," she said helplessly.

He looked confused, disappointed. "But you must know something," he said. "Didn't your father tell you anything?"

She stepped to the desk and smoothed the papers on its surface, inspecting the first line closely:

The symbols didn't look like any alphabet she'd ever seen. She rubbed her forehead, fighting back the despair and fear.

"Think," Sgt. Bartlett said gently. "Think of everything your father ever taught you. It must be there in your mind somehow. Was he an educated man? Did he speak other languages?"

"He was just a tailor," she answered.

Her father had been an autodidactic tailor who had never needed a pattern for cutting out material. He'd been able to visualize in his mind how every scrap of fabric would need to be cut, even for the most complex garment, and he never made a mistake. But also, he'd loved games and tricks and codes and patterns. She remembered again the way he sang the alphabet song backward. He'd played the banjo for hours, inventing his own tunes.

Pulling the chair near, she sat before the desk, frowning. She could do this. She must, somehow. She would think of her father and his sewing things and his capable, wide-knuckled hands. She would use every hint she had and try to read her father's mind. As her gaze unfocused, she heard the rhythmic sound of his foot working the treadle of the sewing machine, half humming, half clicking. But then sorrow, like an underground stream, seeped into her mind, slowing her thoughts. In so many ways, she wished he were there with her.

"If only he were alive," she muttered.

"He is. In you. Somehow," Sgt. Bartlett said. When he smiled encouragingly, a faint glimmer lit his brown eyes. "I need to go." He hurried to the door. "I'll be back later with food. If you need anything else, a dictionary or anything, I'm supposed to get it for you."

She swallowed, nodding, her eyes already scanning over the symbols, looking for anything that might be familiar, that might be a clue. He shut the door softly as he went out, and Gaia sank her chin into the palm of her cool, smooth hand.

Forget the running clock, she told herself. *Forget that Mother's life depends on my cooperation. Think only of Dad.* She closed her eyes and heard the treadle sound again. She summoned a mental image of him sitting near the window at his machine, hunched over to peer at the fabric as it passed under the speeding needle. He always stopped when she came near, sitting back and stretching his arms over his head. His brown eyes were kindly, warm, and his voice overflowed with laughter. Then he would lean close and pull one of her braids with a little, teasing jerk she could still feel. "Hey, squirt."

It hurt to think of him, even the happy memories, but she tried to summon what she knew. Because of his reverse alphabet song, which she'd remembered when her mother sent her the note about Danni O, it was likely he'd done some reverse of letters. On inspiration, she pulled the mirror out of her pocket, and tried looking at the symbols through that:

"This is impossible," she muttered. It looked just as indecipherable this way.

Another hour passed, and the only thing she gained was a neck crick from tension. She flexed her arms in a stretch and leaned back. She'd found several symbols that repeated, but not in any way that made sense to her. She was getting nowhere.

She was hungry, too. Standing, she went to the yellow door and tried the knob. It was locked. She knocked on it, wondering how she was supposed to ask Sgt. Bartlett for something if he wasn't there. There was no reply.

At least she could drink from the sink. As soon as she entered the little bathroom, she decided to clean up. The shower water was hot and delicious on her skin, strangely comforting when her mind was in turmoil. She opened her mouth to the warm spray, drinking. Soon she was dressed in clean clothes, and she found a ball of socks in the pocket of her new dress. She pondered the socks, remembering her father's lemon-shaped pincushion, and wondering again how that boy could have gotten it. The same thing could happen, she realized, with any information she gave Mabrother Iris. Once it was out of her hands, she had no control over where it might end up or how it could be used.

Then again, it wasn't like she had a choice at this point. Until she deciphered the code, she had nothing to bargain with. She needed to at least appear to be cooperating if she was ever going to see her mother. She had to keep trying.

As she stepped back into the little yellow room, softly rubbing her short wet hair with the damp towel, she noticed the top paper with the code had blown to the floor. Her eyes, unfocused for a moment, simplified the code to a pattern of blurry lines, and for an instant, she thought she saw something. She blinked rapidly and leaned nearer. As she reached down for the paper, it was gone, whatever it was, and the dazzling confusion of symbols was as baffling as ever.

"What did I see?" she asked herself.

She dropped the paper to the floor again and walked back into the bathroom, determined to retrace her steps.

"I must be going mad," she muttered.

She stood in the bathroom doorway, looking over at the code on the floor, and squinted. From here, the code looked like lines of color against a background of brown. Due to the angle and the distance, the background emerged conspicuously as narrow bands of brown, regular stripes.

"Read between the lines," she whispered, letting her eyes focus normally again.

This time, when she set the paper on the table, she tried looking at it not for each individual symbol, but for the space between the lines.

There was a knock on her door, and she backed toward the window, trying to smooth her wet hair with the towel.

Leon opened the door, carrying a tray. Her lips opened in unspoken surprise. Her mind scrambled back over memories of their last conversation, and the bread he'd bought her, and Myrna's awful pronouncement of his crimes against the state.

"Take this," he said, thrusting the tray toward her. She tucked the towel under her arm and took the tray while he looked quickly down the hall and then carefully shut the door.

"What are you doing here?" she asked.

"I came to see if I could help," he said. "Are you making any progress?"

Her heart constricted with doubt. "Did Mabrother Iris send you?" she asked, setting the tray on the desk. "Do you know anything about my mother?"

He gave her a peculiar, puzzled look. "I came myself," he said. "As soon as Bartlett told me you were here. I haven't heard anything about your mother." He straightened slowly, his expression grave.

"I'm sorry," she said quickly, holding her damp towel in both hands. "It's just—" She was afraid of being manipulated, and the truth was, Leon did something to her. She might as well admit it to herself. Even now, she felt better just having him there. Strangely charged, too. He was still watching her with his pensive, guarded expression, and she finally threw up a hand. What if he was a tool of the Enclave? It wasn't like she had anything to lose.

"I thought I saw something," she admitted. "A sort of optical illusion. But I wasn't sure."

"What was it?" he asked.

She reached over the bowl of soup and picked up the roll of black bread, casting her gaze over the code again. "I don't know. It was there when my eyes were unfocused, I think." She took

197

a nibble of the bread, and as if that triggered her hunger, she was suddenly ravenously hungry. She bit off a huge bite.

"Careful you don't choke," he said. He took off his hat and set it beside the tray, watching her with a frown. "I'm glad to see this situation hasn't affected your appetite," he added dryly.

She had a perverse desire to laugh. Or cry. Or both. She finished chewing and swallowed.

"Good bread?" he asked.

She nodded. If he said anything nice to her, anything gentle, she was going to burst out sobbing.

He nodded, too. "Let's see this mysterious code."

She swallowed thickly. As he leaned over the desk to inspect the papers, she stepped nearer to him. He braced a hand on the table, flipping the top sheet over and twisting it in different directions. She consumed the last bite of her bread. His shoulders were broad, and she could smell the clean fabric of his black coat, as if sunshine still clung to him.

Somehow that, too, confused and troubled her. She wanted sunshine of her own.

Get a hold of yourself, she thought sternly. She turned to step into the bathroom and hang up her towel, and as she did, she took a furtive look at herself in the mirror. A hint of moisture on the glass softened the harsh clarity of the image, and for once she forced herself to look directly at her face. *This is the face of a girl who may die soon*, she thought. Beauty was irrelevant. Her right cheek was faintly flushed from her shower, and her brown, short hair lay in damp, untidy waves around her brown eyes. The left side of her face was scarred a blotchy red-brown from her earlobe to the tip of her chin and up across her cheek to her eyebrow. The tender skin looked as if someone had taken a wrinkled page of tissue, soaked it in colored glue, and stuck it madly across her face. *A mask*, she thought, not for the first time. It looked like she wore a hideous, permanent mask. Anyone who said anything to her about it not being that bad was clearly lying.

Cold, sobering reality steadied her nerves once more. She needed to solve the code. Nothing else mattered.

"Gaia." Leon's voice came in an undertone from the doorway. "What's the mirror for?"

She jumped self-consciously, then realized he meant the little hand mirror she'd left on the desk.

"Just an idea," she said. "It didn't help. My dad liked reversing things, like we had a funny backward alphabet song."

"Maybe you need a bigger mirror," he said. He held out the code and gestured toward the mirror over the sink.

She considered, then took the paper from his fingers. Holding up the page before the mirror, she was about to wipe the glass dry when again she caught a glimpse of something, just a hint of recognizable letters. Puzzled, she looked more closely, but the shapes shifted, and again it was a jumble of enigmatic symbols. She let out a grumble of frustration.

"What is it?" Leon asked. He was standing just behind her shoulder.

"I keep thinking I see something," she said. "But then it's gone."

He leaned nearer to her, so that his arm nearly brushed her shoulder, and she instinctively shrank from him, keeping her gaze on his eyes in the mirror.

"May I?" he asked politely, and then he used the towel to wipe the last vestiges of steam from the mirror. Gaia felt strangely crowded in the little space, even when he withdrew his hand again, and her lungs grew tight with the strain of breathing beside him.

She focused intently on the mirror, her eyes scanning the

spaces between the lines, and then all of a sudden she saw something. She held her breath. Peering nearer, she was suddenly sure. She had been looking at the symbols, trying to find a pattern in them. But the pattern was *between* the symbols, in the negative space.

"Look!" she said, pointing.

Leon looked as baffled as ever.

"Here," she said, turning with the paper and pointing to a gap between two symbols. "It's going backward now, but there are letters between the symbols. Oh, look!"

"I don't see it," Leon said.

She was flushed with excitement, and she impulsively grabbed his arm. "Here, I'll show you," she said, and pulled him back to the room with the desk. She laid the paper flat on the table, and picked up two of the pencils. Laying them along the horizontal lines between the symbols, she created a border above and below a line of characters.

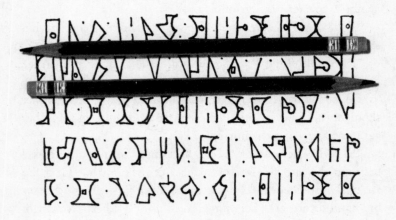

"Look *between* the symbols," she said, pointing. "There are backward block letters in the spaces. Going backward." She started on the right and moved left, bit by bit. *G, L, M, V, Y, L, M, M, R, V, L, I, R.*

Watching his face, she saw the exact moment when understanding came to him. His smile spread warmly, and his blue eyes lit up with excitement.

"What's it say?" he asked. "May I?" He took the paper again and went back into the bathroom to hold it before the mirror. She knew what he would see, and she was already thinking ahead to the next step. She took out more fresh paper from the desk and quickly jotted with her pencil.

A B C D E F G H I J K L M N O P Q R S T U V W X Y Z
Z Y X W V U T S R Q P O N M L K J I H G F E D C B A

"Oh, Daddy," she muttered, torn between sadness and satisfaction. "If this is it, you're too amazing." She was impatient now, and she practically snatched the paper out of Leon's hand when he brought it back.

"What are you doing now?" he asked.

But she didn't answer. She transcribed the letters from the top line of the code onto a clean sheet of paper, and used her reverse-alphabet to change the letters into their opposites. Puzzled, discouraged, she added the next line. She was halfway through the second line before she realized she was spelling names she knew. The names went right to left, like the backward letters, and something was still wrong with the dates, but there they were:

```
- R E P S A J - R S X Y - X W
I R O - E I N N O B - E N O T S
O L - L L I W - R S X Y - W T - N O
Q Z - E L O O P - Y M A - O C R U T
```

Her parents. Jasper Stone and Bonnie Orion. The backs of her ears tingled oddly, as if feathers there were invoking a message from beyond the grave. Gaia covered her face with her hands and dropped her head upon the table.

"Gaia," Leon said softly. "What is it?"

He was crouched beside her at the table, his face on a level with her own, and when she looked at him, her eyes were brimming with tears.

"It's my parents," she said. "They started the record when they advanced their first child to the Enclave. My oldest brother. It lists my father's name first, and then my mother's." She scanned the next set of symbols. "Each word is separated by one of these little circles or squares," she said, pointing. "This part, this repeating R S X Y part, must be a date. Mabrother Iris figured that much out. I don't know how the numbers work yet, but I know this designates my brother's birth."

"Is his name there?"

"No. Babies don't keep their names when they're advanced. Only their birthdays. My father must have been thinking of that. It's not so much about the babies. It's really more . . ." she struggled for the right words.

"What?" he asked.

She ran her hand slowly down the code, knowing now that she could decipher every name, and that she would find the names of many parents she knew back home. "It's a record of loss. A record of parents' loss, baby after baby."

An abyss was sucking her inward and down. She was stunned to find that her own parents' names commenced the list, and yet it all made sense. Gaia had always known that her parents had given away her brothers, but having it spelled out before her in painstaking stitches of silk brought the loss home on a completely different emotional scale. The candles were lit every night. The freckles were tattooed on each baby her mother delivered, as if each one was another son or daughter that Gaia's mother couldn't keep. The list went on and on, she realized, for hundreds of names. Her mother alone had turned in two or more every month, and that was just from Western Sector Three. All those babies. All those losses.

"What have I done?" she muttered, stricken. She had continued it. She, Gaia Stone, in her duty to meet her monthly quota, had personally turned over six children to the Enclave.

"Gaia," Leon said. "Take it easy. You're all right."

"No," she said, clenching her hands into fists and hugging her arms around herself. Only now did she understand. She had sent those innocent babies away from simple, loving parents to become citizens of the Enclave like the ones who had filled the Square of the Bastion when the pregnant woman was executed, people who condoned the imprisonment of their doctors, people who allowed the suffering of children outside the wall, the prolonged imprisonment of her mother, the death of her father. "What have I done?" she repeated, her voice breaking.

"Shhh," Leon said.

She thought her heart would burst in her chest, and then Leon pulled her to her feet and wrapped his arms around her.

"No, Gaia," he said into her ear. "You can't blame yourself. You did what you thought was right."

She was too appalled to cry. "That doesn't mean I'm not responsible. I took those babies from their mothers. I gave them to this—to this *insane* society." Her voice became shrill. "And what about right now? I'm helping them right now with this code!"

She tore free of his arms and grabbed the code, ripping it in half. "I'm as bad as you are!" she said. "As any of you!" She crumpled the papers and threw them away.

Leon stood with his hands open, and his eyebrows lifted in

shock, giving his face a raw, hurt expression. She burned inside with the knowledge she'd somehow betrayed herself. If she could have clawed the truth out of her own chest, she would have. Her crime went deeper than following or breaking any laws. She had advanced those babies to a life that undermined anything in them that might be decent or humane. Advanced! The word itself mocked her.

"We're not all bad," Leon said. His voice resonated with quiet conviction, as if, despite everything that had happened, he'd just discovered this to be true.

"No? Then why are we still talking here?" she asked. "Why haven't you opened that door and helped me escape?"

The time to cooperate was over.

Until he realized that cooperation meant complicity, Leon was as guilty of supporting the Enclave as Mabrother Iris himself.

A clanking noise came through the window from the square below.

Leon turned to look out.

"What is it?" she asked.

Gaia stepped beside him to gaze below. A group of red-clad girls was being led across the square toward the Bastion. Through the gap at the bottom of the window, Gaia could hear the girls crying out in alarm and confusion, even as several guards tried to hush them.

"What's happening?" Gaia repeated.

"I don't know," Leon answered, his voice low. When she looked up, his eyes were intense and troubled. "I'm going to find out." He collected his hat and strode toward the door.

"You're not leaving me here," Gaia said.

Leon had a key he was fitting into the lock. "I must," he said. "I can't get you out now. It's complicated. You have to remember, your mother's well-being is tied to your own. Keep working on the code. See if you can find out who my—" He paused, and his eyes flashed darkly before he looked away from her. He picked up the crumpled pieces of code she had thrown and set them side by side on the top of the desk.

Gaia's heart slowed to a cold, hard rhythm. It all made sense now. He wanted to know his parents. That was why he had come to help her. He was like Sgt. Bartlett. Or Mabrother Iris. She had been used, just as Myrna had warned she would be.

She quietly reached for a pencil and slid it toward her across the desk. "Fine. You want to know your parents?"

"Wait, Gaia," he said. "It's not like that."

Her heart was a bitter stone in her chest. She could use information herself. She didn't know how yet, but she would find a way. There were all kinds of weapons. "What's your birth date again?" she asked coldly.

She watched a hint of color redden his cheeks and lips, and the color made his blue eyes all the more vivid. She couldn't tell if he was anxious or ashamed or both. She didn't care. She steeled herself against his physical appeal and picked up the pencil, waiting. A banging noise came again from the square below.

"It's April fourteenth, twenty-three ninety," he said.

She bowed her head briefly and jotted it down. She didn't know how the system worked for dates yet, but she would figure it out. She smoothed the two ripped pieces of the code and lined them up together at the seam. "I'll see what I can do," she said numbly.

"I'll come back for you," he said. "As soon as I can."

She doubted it. She turned her back to him, already taking her seat again at the desk. Now that he knew how the code depended on reading the negative space, he could tell Mabrother

Iris, and together they could unravel the entire ribbon. They didn't need her anymore, not even for the dates. She was completely and utterly expendable. She heard him open the door, but she didn't turn to see him go.

"Please, Gaia. You're safe here for now. Have a little faith in me," he said, his voice hardly more than a whisper. The next moment, he was gone.

Chapter 18

One Chance

ONCE GAIA REALIZED the first two names were her parents', and that the record must correspond with her oldest brother's birth dates, figuring out the numbers was a tedious but fairly straightforward matter. Her oldest brother had been born on February 12, 2389, and the symbols before her father's name were:

She had mistakenly first translated "I H C B – C D" into "R S X Y – X W" using the letter reversal system, but when she worked backward from the numbers of his date, and threw in the mirror effect, she discovered which letters her father had used for numbers. B C H I had to match 2389. From there, it was a simple substitution system: A = 1, B = 2, C = 3, and so on until J = 0. Similarly, D C became 43. She was stumped until she realized February twelfth was the forty-third day of the year. Instead of using months, her father had assigned a number for each of the 365 days in the year, so that her oldest brother's birth, Arthur's birth, on February 12, 2389, was simply listed as 43-2389.

Gaia should have felt pleased that she'd worked out the code, but instead she felt flat inside, defeated. She couldn't escape the guilt that had seared into her once she'd realized how inherently wrong the baby quota was.

She was deeply puzzled about her parents, and she wished she could go back and listen more carefully to conversations she had had with her father about her brothers. Obviously, he had omitted telling her about the ribbon, but he had talked about the freckles. Her parents must have been far more conflicted about advancing their sons than they had ever revealed to Gaia. Either that, or they had truly believed they were doing the right thing, the best thing for their children, even though they missed them terribly and continued to love them long after they were gone. Could the two opposite things both be true?

She scanned further down the code, to where the year changed to 2390, and then she found the parents who matched Leon's birth date: Derek Vlatir and Mary Walsh. She closed her eyes and leaned back, stretching the kinks out of her neck as she tried to absorb that Leon was Derek's son. The Vlatirs probably had lived in Western Sector Three back when Leon was born. If Leon hadn't been advanced, he would have grown up as a baker's son outside the wall. Leon might have become a completely different person: maybe even trustworthy.

It was dark by the time Gaia worked out the code, her soup long gone, but a single spiral bulb in the ceiling had come on automatically as the sun set. The light went off if she was very still for a length of time, concentrating. If she waved an arm, it came on again. A tiny white box with a red pinpoint of light was positioned in an upper corner of the room, and that, she guessed, was the motion detector.

She stood before the window, gazing down at the quiet city while her tired gaze followed the streetlamps that descended in slow curves away from the Bastion. No one was out. The girls in red had not reappeared. The stillness smelled like the stones of the square down below.

Leon had not returned.

No surprise there, she thought.

She touched her hand to the smooth pane of glass, wondering what Leon would give to know his father was Derek Vlatir. She wondered, also, if she would live to see Derek again and tell him his son had become . . . had grown to be . . .

Gaia closed her eyes and tilted her face against the cool glass. She didn't know what to think about Leon, but whenever she did think of him, an odd, tight feeling constricted in her chest. She wasn't just angry at him. She was disappointed, too. Deeply. It didn't matter that he was just doing his job, like any good soldier. She had thought she could trust him. Worse than that: she'd been stupid.

She slumped back on the bed, looking at her mess of notes on the desk. *I should rip everything up and throw it all down the toilet*, she thought. That would be proof she wasn't cooperating anymore. Yet the gesture wouldn't do her any good with no one there to see it.

She pressed her face into her hands, rubbing her eyes.

When there was a quiet rap on the door, she sat up suddenly and the light went on. She must have fallen asleep. The door was opening, and her heart leaped with anticipation. When she saw it was Sgt. Bartlett with another tray, she was crushed. *Stupid again!* she thought. Leon wasn't coming. As she reached for the tray, the sergeant's gaze went first to the desk, and then flew to Gaia's face.

"Did you figure it out?" he asked.

"Maybe. It's hard to be sure," she prevaricated, taking a bite of the bread. The stale, dry taste was heavy in her mouth, but she was hungry. Food came at strange times here. "How late is it?"

"Around midnight. Can you tell me who my parents are?" he asked.

She stopped chewing as an idea came to her. She swallowed. "Do you know anything about my mother?"

He looked confused. "No. Is she here? In the Bastion?"

"I believe so. I'm trying to find her," she said. "How badly do you want to know about your own parents? Enough to let me out?"

The sergeant leaned his broad shoulders back against the door and crossed his arms. Muscles bulged under the black fabric. "It would be too dangerous," he said.

She let out a dry laugh. "For you or for me?"

He seemed to consider, and then he dug his fingers back through his blond hair in a way that struck her as very young. "Both," he said. "It isn't possible. Believe me. Anybody who helped you would have to be willing to leave the Enclave forever. Don't even ask."

Leon obviously felt the same way, she realized bitterly. "Then don't even ask me who your parents are," she said. "You can wait like everyone else until it pleases Mabrother Iris to share the information."

He gave her a long, scrutinizing look, and then he picked up the empty glass from the tray and stepped into the bathroom.

Jerk, she thought. She took a nibble of the white cheese while she heard the water running, and when Sgt. Bartlett came back, she thought he looked pale beneath his tan. When she reached for the glass of water, he held it back a moment longer than was natural, and she saw he was watching her keenly. With an infinitesimal nod, he indicated the glass.

Suddenly on alert, she reached for it again, and she saw a message written on the palm of his hand:

Her gaze shot to his. His lips were closed in a grim line, and he was watching her closely. "You must be thirsty," he said in a normal voice.

Afraid to turn, afraid to look, Gaia lifted the glass with trembling fingers to her lips. *Oh, no,* she thought. They'd been watching her the whole time. What she'd thought was a motion detector had to be also a camera. They'd seen her with Leon, and they'd seen him leave. Her mind raced. They were watching her with Sgt. Bartlett right now. Could they hear what she was saying, too?

It was all she could do not to scream in frustration. She took another bite of her cheese, chewing slowly, and Sgt. Bartlett went back to lean against the door in his former position. She saw he had his hand fisted tightly in his pocket. In fact, a faint tremor of tension was visible all through him, now that she was watching for it. She hoped it wouldn't show to whomever was watching.

"What happened to those girls?" she asked, trying to make it sound like she was beginning an idle conversation.

"What girls?"

"I saw them earlier in the square," she said. "It looked like they were being rounded up and brought to the Bastion."

He shook his head, puzzled. "I don't know who you saw," he said.

She grew impatient. "Before. When Leon was here. Haven't you talked to him?"

Sgt. Bartlett glanced away from her in a way that instantly put her on alert. He seemed to be choosing what to say, and she realized he, too, was caught in the problem of needing to appear as if he had not told her they were being watched. Why had he warned her about the camera? He seemed to make a decision, and his brown eyes were serious as he gazed at her.

"He was taken to meet with the Protectorat," he said. "Shortly after he left this room earlier today. No one's seen him since."

"Well," she said dryly. "Let's hope he and his father are having a nice chat."

He turned toward the door. "If you'll excuse me," he said. "I'll be back for the tray in ten minutes," he said. "Help yourself to more water if you want it." He nodded toward the bathroom.

Water? She wanted to scream. What she needed was to get out of here. She gripped her fists together and turned away.

The door closed softly behind him, and she let out a whoosh of pent-up air. What was she supposed to do now? A camera was aimed at her every move. She was afraid to look up at the little white device in the corner of the ceiling, but she was certain now that that's where the camera lens was hidden.

A burst of realization hit her: the camera didn't reach the bathroom. And that was where Sgt. Bartlett had gone. Trying to look unconcerned, she walked first to the window, then to her tray to take the last morsel of bread, and then, with her glass, she headed into the bathroom. She stepped around the corner, closed the door, and stared at what she saw on the mirror glass:

1 Chance
October 24, 2390

Sgt. Bartlett had written the message with the wedge of blue soap that lay by the faucet of the sink. Her heart pounding, she dampened a corner of towel and rubbed frantically at the soap on the mirror. *October 24, 2390*, she thought, repeating the date in her head to memorize it.

Her hand went still on the glass.

She already knew that date. That was her brother Odin's birth date. She instinctively drew her fist to her lips.

"I can't believe this," she whispered. "He's my brother."

Could she be sure? What if there were other advanced babies born on the same date? The answer would be right in the code.

Checking the mirror one last time to be sure it was clean of any evidence, Gaia walked back into the yellow room. With a soft clink, she set the glass on the tray, and then stepped before the code. It took her several minutes to look up his birth date, but it was clear that only her parents' names were listed by that date. Sgt. Bartlett was her brother Odin. Unquestionably. Her mind was racing.

Sgt. Bartlett's blond hair and fair complexion made no sense to her because she and her parents were all dark. But it was possible, she supposed. Not all children looked like their parents. He was going to be astounded by the news.

When he returned, she must be ready for anything. She put the little mirror in her pocket. Doubtless Mabrother Iris, or whoever had been watching, already knew what she had discovered—she'd been quite open with Leon while she was unraveling it, but she'd do all she could not to reveal anything more on her own. She ordered all her notes in a pile so they'd be ready for her to grab.

There was a soft rap on the door and Sgt. Bartlett opened it. Expectant, she took one look at his face and knew he had a plan, but more extraordinarily, she saw an echo of her father in his brown eyes. Now that she knew to look for it, the faint resemblance was unmistakable. She was struck with pleasure, and then fear.

"We have seventeen seconds to get out," he said quietly.

Gaia grabbed her papers and flew after him down the hall.

He led her down a narrow staircase, up another, through several doors, and around half a dozen corners. At a closet, he pulled out a red cape with a hood.

"Go through the school courtyard," he said. "Move slowly, straight through the school, and go out the opposite door. You'll be in the street. From there you'll have to find your own way."

"Where are you going?" she asked. She hadn't expected to split up from him so soon.

"That's my business." He was putting on a brown shirt and a dark hat. "Quick," he said. "Who are my parents?"

She gripped his hands tightly. "Bonnie and Jasper Stone from Western Sector Three," she said. "You're my brother."

His cheeks went pale as incredulity and amazement made him frown. He stared intently at her face, as if memorizing and testing every feature.

"How is that possible?" he said.

"It's true." She knew it in her bones, in the deepest fiber of her being. "You're Odin Stone. You have an older brother, too, who was also advanced to the Enclave. I don't know who he is here. Our father's dead. Our mother's imprisoned, but I don't know where."

There was a noise from above and shouting. Terrified, she reached for him, and he crushed her to him for an instant.

"My sister," he said, his voice cracking. "It's worth it, then." He pushed her away. "Go! Now!"

There was another shout and loud footsteps on the staircase above, and then she gripped the knob of the door and pulled. She heard more shouts behind her, but didn't dare to look back. She could only hope Sgt. Bartlett was getting away. She pulled her cloak carefully around her face and walked across an open courtyard, shadowed and hollow-sounding with night. It was painful to keep her stride normal when every instinct urged

214

her to run. Glancing up, she saw a woman closing a window, but the woman paid no attention to Gaia below.

When Gaia reached the door, the knob opened smoothly in her fingers. She had to push with her shoulder to make the heavy wooden door open, and her fear increased again. What if the next door was locked and Sgt. Bartlett had sent her to a dead end? A light flickered on in the hallway and illuminated cream-colored walls. To her right, the hallway opened on a little room with a fireplace that glowed with coals.

An elderly woman in white glanced up from beside the fireplace. "Good evening, Masister," the woman said in a sleepy voice.

Hardly daring to breathe, Gaia said, "I serve the Enclave."

"And I," she murmured, turning back to the fire.

Feeling like an imposter who could be exposed at any moment, Gaia walked purposefully down the hallway, passing closed doors and a tall, old-fashioned grandfather clock that ticked quietly in the stillness. At the end of the hall, the passage opened in two directions, and on impulse Gaia turned left, the darker direction. She had progressed only a dozen paces when she realized she'd made a mistake. She was in a kind of dormitory, with two rows of beds. Her arrival caused a light to go on automatically above her, and the blanketed shape on the closest bed turned in her direction.

"Where've you been?" a girl's voice whispered, sounding annoyed and curious.

Gaia backed up a step. The person sat up further, and Gaia could see she was a teenage girl in a white nightgown, close to Gaia's own age. Brown curls framed an oval, open face with a straight nose and a generous mouth. Her eyes were growing rounder, and she instinctively pulled the blanket up toward her chest.

"Who are you?" the girl said, her voice still quiet.

"My mistake," Gaia said, backing up another step.

If the girl let out an alarm, Gaia would be caught. Gaia pulled the hood of her cloak nearer the left side of her face, but the movement was another mistake. The girl gasped.

"You're that girl with the scar!" the girl squeaked.

"Shh!" Gaia said. "Please!"

Gaia turned and fled as quickly as she could, retracing her steps and continuing in the other direction. Around another corner, she found a large wooden door that matched the first one she'd come in, and she opened it firmly. Soldiers were running down the street, and she backed up, waiting until they passed.

She slipped through the doorway and into the street, heading away from the direction the soldiers were going. Her heart lurched with every step, and she couldn't get her bearings. She wanted to go downhill, but whenever she tried to, she saw more soldiers, so she was forced to head uphill. Finally she came to a street she recognized. A café was brightly lit, and men were laughing loudly in a group by the bar. If she headed uphill, she would come to the garden where she and Leon had talked once. If she circled back, she might be able to reach the bakery with the black oven, but that was close to the Square of the Bastion again, where there would certainly be more soldiers. She didn't know what to do.

At that moment, the men in the café burst into laughter, and two of them came out, calling good-byes. They headed toward the left, and on impulse Gaia turned back, west, toward the square.

She hurried now, losing her nerve. It seemed she could hear footsteps and voices all around her. Walls boxed her in on the right, and lights bolted on above whenever she came to a streetlamp with a motion detector. Cameras, she feared, could be anywhere. She turned a corner, and saw a group of soldiers approaching from the other direction. Her heart sank into her black shoes, but there was nothing to do but keep walking toward them, hood up, shoulders square.

She was about to enter the ring of light from a streetlamp when she heard a sharp, low voice from her right.

"Stone!"

A thick-bodied, short man beckoned to her from a dark doorway, and she almost wept with relief. Ahead, the soldiers were picking up their pace, on line to intersect with her.

"Quickly!" the man said again, but Gaia was already speeding toward him.

He pulled her in with a strong hand and shut the door behind them. Gaia was in a narrow passage with a low ceiling. The air smelled of garbage and urine, but as she hurried behind the man, she could see a warm, yellow light ahead of her. He pulled her through another door and closed it tightly, sliding a bolt across it.

Gaia had never been so happy in her whole life. Before her, warm and massive, stood the hearth of the black-ovened bakery.

Chapter 19
Jacksons' Bakery

THE BRICK OVEN WITH its massive chimney bisected the bakery into the front shop area where Leon had only the day before bought her a small black loaf, and the back work area, where now Gaia stood catching her breath. The warm smell of bread welcomed her like an embrace. A great wooden table stood in the center of the room with a lamp above casting a circle of light upon it. The white string for the lamp had a small measuring spoon tied to the end as a pull tab, and the metal gleamed from use. A teenage boy and a no-nonsense woman stood quietly before the oven, their sleeves rolled up and their hands flecked with flour and bits of dough. Just then, the back door opened again, and a young girl of nine or ten with bright pink cheeks hurried in. The girl threw back the green hood of her cloak, grinning.

"You found her!" the girl said.

The baker ruffled her light brown hair in a loving, proud gesture that reminded Gaia of her own father. "Didn't I tell you she'd come?"

"How did you know?" Gaia said.

The woman wiped her hands in her copious apron. "We've

been watching for you nonstop since we heard you were moved to the Bastion. If ever you had a chance to get free of the guards, it would be now or never. Mace was hoping you'd try to come to us."

"I was looking, too," the girl said excitedly. "I was supposed to call 'Stone!' to you, and if you showed me your scar face, I would take you in."

Gaia slowly pushed her hood back and watched the curiosity on the girl's face as she inspected Gaia's scar.

"Exactly," the girl said, sounding satisfied.

Gaia smiled, but she knew she wouldn't be safe there long. "I was seen coming in with you," she said, turning to the baker. "You can't keep me here or you'll be in trouble."

"I don't think so. That was a sauna parlor, there, where I found you," the baker said. "They'll just think you were working the late shift."

Gaia was baffled. "A sauna parlor?"

She saw the baker and his wife hesitate.

The girl clarified in her open, childish voice. "He means it's a brothel."

The baker clapped a hand to his forehead.

"What?" the girl said. "It's a very discreet, high-class brothel. Tell them, Oliver."

"Real nice, Yvonne. Thanks," the teenager said, blushing. His mother looked murderous. "Hey, Ma. It's not like I go there. I just told her—"

"Enough," her mother said. "Why don't you go up on the roof and keep an eye out? Tell us if any guards start up our street."

The teenager ducked his head and vanished up a narrow flight of stairs.

The baker cleared his throat. "Ah. Well. Here's a nice introduction to our family. My precocious daughter there is Yvonne,"

219

he said, nodding at the girl. "I'm Mace Jackson, and this is my wife Pearl. That was Oliver."

Pearl came over and gave Gaia a big hug.

"What you've been through I can't begin to think," she said in a gruff voice. She gave Gaia a roll of warm, buttery bread, swirled with cinnamon and sugar, and pushed her gently onto a stool. Her kindness should have made Gaia relax, but she could feel anxious jitters in her veins as she sat down, and though her mouth watered, she couldn't take a bite of the cinnamon roll.

"What's our plan?" Gaia said to Mace.

"It depends on what you want to do," he said.

She took a deep breath, holding the roll between dainty fingers. "What are my choices?"

"I could get you out of the city at daybreak," he said. "Oliver and my apprentice, Jet, often go out for wood, and they could take you with them in the bike cart. It would be risky, but I think it could be done."

Gaia remembered the carts drawn by bikes that occasionally came out of the wall. She pictured herself hiding in one, maybe under some sacks. She'd be in danger of discovery every time the cart lurched over a bump or a guard poked the sacks.

"Is there any other choice?" Gaia asked.

"You could stay with us," little Yvonne said. "We have an extra bed in my room."

Gaia glanced from the girl to her mother as Pearl shifted backward slightly. Though Pearl's expression remained concerned and kindly, there was sorrow in her gray eyes that Gaia didn't miss.

"Thank you, Yvonne," Gaia said gently.

The girl took a step nearer and tilted her face in a bashful smile. "It was my sister's bed," she said. "I know she'd want you to use it."

Pearl cleared her throat in the silence.

"But not for long," Gaia said. "It wouldn't be safe for you."

"We're safe enough, as long as you stay inside," Pearl said. She hesitated, and then touched her chin with her knuckles in a thoughtful manner. "My other daughter, my Lila—she died last year from complications of hemophilia. We decided then, all of us, that if we could do something to help the people outside the wall, then we would. We didn't guess that a girl would show up on our doorstep, let alone the one who saved that convict's baby, but here you are."

Gaia lowered her gaze for a moment, doubting she was worthy of their kindness. "Do you think the people outside the wall could have helped save your daughter? Is that why?" she asked quietly.

Pearl shook her head, her eyes dry and lost-looking for a moment. "No. Nothing that simple. We just don't want any other family to go through what we've gone through."

Mace was rolling up his sleeves. "We're thinking a generation ahead, if you get my meaning. For the whole Enclave, the way we're supposed to. My family carries the recessive gene that leads to hemophilia, and so, well—" He stopped himself. "That's neither here nor there."

"No, please. I want to know."

She saw Mace and Pearl exchange a glance. Then Pearl leaned her knuckles on the edge of the table as she sat on a stool.

"There's too many of us now carrying the hemophilia," she said. "There's children like Lila all over the Enclave, and their families are all grieving. I don't know if we need to advance a ton more children or just open the gates permanently, but it's time to start working with the people outside the wall. They're the ones who are going to save us in the end."

As Gaia pondered Pearl's altruistic explanation, it changed

221

how she saw the people of the Enclave. This family's loss was being played out all around the city, everywhere a child died. The problems of inbreeding, she realized, had already affected real families.

Mabrother Iris was trying to solve that problem on a massive scale. And yet, she didn't see how identifying the parents of advanced babies from Western Sector Three would help. There must be more to it, something Mabrother Iris had not told her.

"You understand it's dangerous for us to say this," Mace said. He looked at Yvonne. "This can't go any farther than this room."

"I know, Daddy. I didn't say anything."

"Have you heard some girls were arrested today?" Gaia asked.

"They weren't arrested. They were taken to a special school," Pearl said. "Some boys were taken, too."

"And why were they chosen?"

"They all had a certain freckle pattern on their ankles," Pearl said.

"Oh, no," Gaia groaned. She closed her eyes and bent her face into her hand. "It's started," she whispered. The Enclave had already made a move based on what she'd told them. It was her fault! She looked up again, blinking. "They're going to control more and more," she said. "Who gets taken without notice. Who you marry. Who gets to keep their babies. Can't you see? We have to stop them."

Mace let out a laugh. "You're taking this way out of proportion," he said.

"No," she disagreed, stepping nearer to the table. "We have to stop them before it gets out of control." Her mind leaped ahead. "We have to get rid of the wall."

222

Mace lifted his hand. "Nobody's ripping down any wall," he said calmly.

"I don't understand," Yvonne said. "What do the freckles have to do with getting married?"

Gaia leaned closer to Yvonne so she could speak to her at eye level. She forced her voice to stay calm. "The freckles show that an advanced person was born in my neighborhood outside the wall. That's all. But for some reason, the Protectorat cares especially about those people, enough to take them tonight."

"And you think he'll experiment on them or something?" Yvonne asked, her eyes widening.

Gaia didn't know what to tell her. She glanced up at Pearl.

"No," Pearl said soothingly, putting her hands on the girl's shoulders. "He wouldn't do that. Gaia just got a little excited, but she's just guessing at things, aren't you, Gaia?"

Gaia glanced at the girl with her large, solemn eyes. The truth was, she didn't know what the Protectorat's plan was, but she was certain he had one, and that she was missing an important piece of the puzzle. "I think," said Gaia, making a decision. "That you'd better help me get outside the wall. As soon as possible. I don't want to get you all into trouble."

"No," said Pearl. "I don't believe in this tear-down-the-wall agenda, but you need to stay here, with us. You'll be safe here, and you can think through your plans rationally. There's no immediate hurry. Whatever help you need, we'll give. Isn't that right, Mace?"

His dark eyebrows were set in a line, and he nodded.

Gaia took a deep breath, and finally took a little bite of the bread in her fingers. It was so good, so moist and buttery and rich, that she made an involuntary crooning noise in the back of her throat.

Yvonne laughed. "See, Mom? I'm not the only one who

makes that noise. Don't we make the most incredible cinnamon rolls?"

Gaia swallowed, smiling. Something about Yvonne reminded Gaia of Emily when she was little, and she couldn't help liking her. "Yes. They're spectacular."

"Would you look at the time?" Mace said. "We've got some work to do. Yvonne, go and get Oliver back down here. Then see if you can't catch some sleep before school. Take Gaia up with you. She's not leaving today, in any case."

Pearl was already dumping a huge pile of dough onto a floured board, and she punched it powerfully with her fist before she broke it in quarters and started kneading.

Gaia slid out of the way.

Yvonne pulled her hand and grabbed an extra cinnamon roll on the sly. "Come on," she said, and scampered up the narrow wooden staircase, her feet making a quick, merry clatter. It took Gaia a moment to realize why the noise surprised her so much: it was a sound of happiness, and she hadn't been around laughter or happiness for a long, long time. She took a deep breath, deliberately forced the tension to ease out of her shoulders, and climbed up after the girl.

Gaia awoke to the noise of a door closing downstairs. The room she shared with Yvonne was in the back of the apartment over the bakery, and for the three nights she'd been there, she'd been smelling the bread in the ovens all through her dreams: warm, buttery dreams that soothed her heart and gave her hope that everything might still work out all right. She missed her parents, and for some maddening reason, she missed Leon, too. She had despised him as the worst sort of betrayer when he left her in the Bastion, but based on what Sgt. Bartlett had said, he had been detained by his father. It seemed likely to her that he was enjoying a nice cup of tea with

224

his father and Mabrother Iris right now, happy to finally be back in their good graces. But maybe, just maybe, he was trapped in the Protectorat's web as much as she was.

She wished she could have gotten more information out of Sgt. Bartlett—Odin. She pondered her brother. Did he have any memory at all of his life before he was advanced, she wondered. Did his old name register in any deep part of his mind? She knew so little about him, but he'd done a brave thing, helping her. He had done it without even knowing yet that she was his sister, too. She hoped he was okay.

Late morning light dropped in at the window, barely touching the white curtain that covered the lower half of the glass and swayed gently. Just outside, the leaves of an aspen flickered. A bee flew against the window with a faint thud, failed to find the opening several inches below, and flew away again.

Much as she felt safe with Mace's family, Gaia knew she couldn't stay. It was too dangerous for them, and she had to resume her life somehow, somewhere. There must be a way to find her mother still, now that she was out of prison. Tempting as it was, she couldn't destroy the Enclave single-handedly, so she needed a realistic plan.

She considered all her options, even the bad ones. If she left the Enclave and Wharfton, she had no idea where to find the Dead Forest. If it even existed. Mabrother Iris had been so certain it was a myth. As far as she knew, her grandmother, Danni Orion, had been dead for years, but now she wondered if her parents had used the terms interchangeably: dead and Dead Forest. She shook her head. She had been very young when her grandmother disappeared. All Gaia could remember of her was a gilt-edged monocle she had worn on a beaded chain around her neck, for she had been intrigued by the way it caught the sunlight. And then, gradually, Gaia had understood one thing clearly: her grandmother was gone and was never returning. She had been as good as dead.

Gaia circled back to the cipher of Old Meg. The Dead Forest must exist. Everything else Old Meg had said had turned out to be true. How could Gaia find her mother, rescue her, and take her to a place she couldn't locate?

Another cinnamon bun might help.

Gaia sat up and slipped on the soft tan dress that Pearl had given her. There was a row of small white buttons down the front, and the waistline nipped in before the skirt filled out again with no concern for conserving fabric. She couldn't help flipping back the hem to inspect the workmanship of the seams. They were no finer than what her father might have sewn outside the wall, but the cut of the dress was distinctly different from the outside style. More feminine.

Footsteps beat a hollow rhythm on the stairs. She was reaching for her shoes with her toes when Mace's hand braced on the doorjamb, and he hauled himself up the last step and into the room.

"Hello," he said, smiling his sweet, broad smile. He was panting from exertion. "You're up, then."

She gave him a little smile, and smoothed back her brown hair. It was getting a bit longer by now, long enough to get in her eyes but not long enough to stay behind her ears. He sat opposite her on Yvonne's rumpled bed. The girl was long gone with her brother to school. At least that much of what Gaia had believed about the Enclave was true: the children all went to school during the day. Yvonne had told Gaia that she was learning about adding glucose from the honey farm to the mycoprotein vats, and Oliver was studying solar panel technology.

For a few short days, even though they were in danger every minute that she stayed with them, they had absorbed her

226

into their family. Their loss of Lila shifted like an empty shadow about the rooms, strangely familiar to Gaia. Yet, unlike her family's loss of Arthur and Odin, the Jacksons' loss was raw. They evinced no mitigating belief that Lila was alive and better off someplace else, and in that way, the Jacksons' loss seemed worse.

Gaia fingered the ruffle of a little pillow on Lila's bed. Mace leaned forward and gently slid it out of her hands to hold it himself. "She was younger than you," he said. "Not yet thirteen."

"I'm sorry," she said softly. She noticed a sizable bruise on Mace's arm and wondered if he had a mild version of hemophilia himself. "Wasn't there anything they could do to treat your daughter's illness?"

Mace shook his head. "One doctor was trying to. She tried injecting patients with a blood-clotting protein, but many of them developed antibodies and died anyway. The Protectorat shut down her research and put her in jail. He accused her of starting a hospital."

"Myrna," Gaia said.

He tilted his face, interested. "Myrna Silk, yes," he said. "I accept the Protectorat's decision. It's not about curing one child. It's about solving the problem on a larger scale, maybe with a genetic breakthrough, for all of us." He turned the pillow over, and she watched him trace his strong finger over two initials embroidered in purple thread: L. J. "But still. I miss my girl."

Gaia leaned across the space between the beds to rest her hand on his. She didn't know what to say, so she simply stayed quiet with him. After a long moment, he put the pillow back on Lila's bed.

"Tell me something," he asked gently. "Are you sure your mother's still alive?"

She pushed the hair back from her forehead. "I saw her sleeping in a round cell. On Mabrother Iris's screen desk. He has a camera on her and two other women. That was four mornings ago. She was still alive then."

"A round cell?" He sounded surprised.

"Well, the walls were curved. I saw a curtain move in the wind, so it has a window. I don't know if the window has bars." She stood to pace, wrapping her arms around her waist, but she could only take a couple of steps in the little room before she had to turn again.

Mace was pulling absently at his ear. "I may know where your mother is," he said.

Gaia inhaled sharply. "Where? What do you know?"

He spoke thoughtfully. "I've heard there are three women in the southeast tower of the Bastion. The room you're describing sounds like the place. It's a special cell they keep for important people. A pregnant political prisoner there has a midwife and another attendant with her all the time, so she can't do anything to herself or her baby."

"And you think the midwife is my mother?"

"It's possible," he said. "The prisoner was moved there around the same time your mother was taken out of the prison."

"How do you know all this?" Gaia asked.

"There's a woman at the Nursery who's friends with my wife. They go way back, and they still get together for coffee every couple of weeks. She's the one who told us about the political prisoner."

"Masister Khol?" Gaia asked.

His eyes flashed. "You know her?"

Gaia's heart lifted with another burst of hope. "She gave me a message from my mother once. I think she might help us. Do you really think that's where my mother is?"

Mace crossed his massive arms over his chest. "I'm almost

positive. Your mother would be kind to a pregnant prisoner, wouldn't she? Even if your mother was a prisoner herself?"

Gaia laughed and pushed her bangs out of her face again. "My mother would be kind to the Protectorat himself if he were pregnant. That's what she does." Her mind was leaping ahead, trying to figure out how soon she might be able to get to her, and how she would get her free. A tower sounded bad, but not as hopeless as Q cell. Her excitement slowed.

"The camera," she said. She slid her hands into the pockets of her dress. "There's a camera aimed at the women in the tower."

"Ah," Mace said. "That's another problem, then."

They couldn't just cover up the camera, she realized. She didn't even know how she'd get back into the Bastion, let alone into a tower prison cell. She sat on the bed again. If only she had Leon to help her.

Wrong, she thought. Leon couldn't help her. Even if he weren't off passing tea cakes to the Protectorat, he would probably keep telling her to cooperate. And where had that led her?

"What do you know about the Dead Forest?" she asked. "Mabrother Iris said it didn't exist, that it was only something out of a fairy tale. But a friend of mine said she was going there."

Mace's eyebrows jogged up and down, and he pushed out his lips in contemplation. "I don't really know about it," Mace said. He eyed her warily. "If it exists, it must be way out in the wasteland, or past it. You're not thinking of going there?"

"Where else is there to go?" she asked. "We can't stay here. If they catch us again, I know they'll kill us. It's amazing they haven't already. As long as I was cooperating, there was a chance they would let me go, but I ran."

"You don't know they'd kill you," he said.

"Why not? They hang people all the time for less. Why not kill me, when I really *am* a traitor?"

He leaned back, resting his weight on one hand. "It depends on your perspective," he said. "Think from the Enclave's point of view. It's true you saved that convict's baby. Very high profile maneuver, that. And, you broke out of the Bastion. On the other hand, you have valuable skills as a midwife. You also have a lot of potential, genetically speaking."

Gaia eyed him curiously. "You mean, they would keep me alive because I could become pregnant?"

Mace lifted a hand. "Why not?"

She flushed with indignation. "I'm not some cow they can use for breeding. And there's nothing extraordinary about my genes just because I'm from outside the wall."

He shrugged. "Perhaps not. But you are from Western Sector Three. There are many ways to be a criminal or a hero. Don't forget that."

Gaia leaned against the doorframe and idly rubbed a little dent mark in the blue wood.

"You know that soldier you said you escaped with?" Mace said.

"Sgt. Bartlett," she said. She hadn't told them he was her brother.

"I found out today that he's disappeared. I don't mean arrested. He was seen outside the wall, asking questions about your parents, and now he's gone."

Gaia felt relief for her brother, and then a stirring of hope. There might be other ways out of the wall, and maybe Sgt. Bartlett had gone to the Dead Forest.

She turned again to Mace. "I need to know everything I can about the Dead Forest. How far away it is, who goes there, how to find it. Is that where you get your wood?"

Mace shook his head, his expression puzzled. "There are

some windfalls east of here, left over from a blight a few years back. That's where we get our wood."

She came near and sat beside him on the bed. "I need to know what's out there," she said softly, but with growing conviction. "I'm going to find my mother somehow, and when I do, I'm taking her to the Dead Forest." As she said it, she realized this had been her plan all along, no matter how crazy it sounded.

She studied his heavy profile, with his large nose and ruddy cheeks. Then he clasped his warm hand upon hers. "I can't say I know anything about the Dead Forest, but don't worry," he said. "We'll think it all through carefully. I'll talk it over with Pearl, and we'll find a way."

Her gaze fell again on Lila's small embroidered pillow, a tangible reminder of loss. And courage. Her mother was still out there, alive and needing her, and Gaia wasn't going to give up.

"I'm all she has," Gaia said. "If I can't free her, nobody will."

Chapter 20
Forty-Six Chrome Spoons

I T WAS YVONNE'S IDEA to make the mask. She first suggested that they just cover Gaia's scar with flour and cinnamon, but since the uneven surface of Gaia's left cheek would still be conspicuous, Yvonne suggested a true mask.

"I don't see the point," Oliver said. "All of the Enclave is on the lookout for her now. She's been on the TV broadcast for the last three nights. She'll never even get close to the southeast tower. As soon as anyone stops her and looks closely at her face, they'll see her mask and know it's the girl with the scar."

"Not if it's a good mask," Yvonne argued.

"And not if she's a boy," Pearl added.

It was night, and they'd pulled shades over the windows of the bakery. Licks of firelight were visible in the cracks around the iron door of the brick oven, and within, trays of bread were baking. The redolent, yeasty smell made the kitchen warm, and the lamp above the table made the shadows withdraw to the corners. A pot of leftover soup from dinner was cooling on the hearth. Gaia gazed around at the wooden paddles, the wheeled racks with tray after tray of dark, baked loaves, and pale, white loaves that still needed their time in the oven. She didn't know when Mace and his family ever slept, and now, at nearly mid-night, they were still up and working on a plan to help her get to her mother. Mace had left to try to talk to Masister Khol.

Gaia looked doubtfully at Pearl. "I may be ugly, but I'm no boy."

Pearl sat beside her at the table and took Gaia's slender fingers in her warm hands. "Mace's apprentice isn't much bigger than you," Pearl said. "We have extra clothes for him here, and if we pad you a bit in the right places, we can disguise your figure."

As Gaia realized they were in earnest, she could feel nerves jangling in her belly. She pulled her fingers free from Pearl's. "But will a mask really work?"

Pearl took Gaia's chin in her fingers and tilted her face to the light. Gaia submitted to the inspection and kept her gaze on Pearl's eyes. She knew what Pearl saw.

"How did this happen, child?" Pearl asked gently.

It was such an old story that Gaia should have been inured to telling it again, but somehow, because these were her friends, it bothered her more to tell it. "When I was a baby learning to get around, I walked into a hot vat of beeswax. Not into the liquid wax, you understand, although some had dripped out. I walked up against the vat itself."

Pearl frowned, and traced her thumb gently along Gaia's sensitive jaw line. Her wide, no-nonsense face was hard for Gaia to read. Then she reached for Gaia's hands again and inspected her palms, one by one, turning them upward as a fortune-teller might.

"It doesn't fit," Pearl mused aloud. "Why aren't your hands burned, then?"

Gaia curled her fingers closed, confused.

"When a baby's falling, she tries to catch herself with her hands," Pearl explained. "You would have burned your hands first."

233

Gaia shook her head. "That would depend on the height of the vat and the angle I was falling. I don't actually remember it, but that's what I've been told."

Pearl tilted Gaia's face toward the overhead light once more before she released her. "I know burns, Gaia," Pearl said. She pushed up the sleeves of her dress and showed her own muscular arms, the pale skin flecked with little streaks of brown, a myriad of new and older, fading scars. "When you work with hot trays and ovens all day long, you naturally get your share of nick burns, and worse from time to time. A burn such as yours—well. I wondered if someone did it to you on purpose."

Gaia drew back from the woman. The only people who could have hurt her like that were her parents.

"It was an accident," Gaia said quietly.

"What does it matter now?" Oliver asked. "Can you cover it up?"

Pearl settled her sturdy body back on her stool, and slowly nodded. Gaia dropped her gaze to her hands in her lap, wishing she could erase what Pearl had said.

Yvonne clapped her hands together. "I knew it! Mom once made the most amazing mask for me for school. I was supposed to be this ghost girl, and nobody even recognized me. Tell her, Mom. You do it with a crepe, right? And flour mixed with spices to make just the right color powder. Right?"

As a silence stretched out, Gaia felt Pearl's eyes on her even when she wouldn't look up. Her wrists had healed from when she had been tied several days before, but the skin was still tender when she tentatively pressed on the marks. She couldn't bear to think that her own parents might have burned her, but she couldn't forget it, either.

"I'm sorry," Pearl said gently.

Gaia sniffed once. "I just know you're wrong," she said.

Pearl gave her shoulder a quick squeeze. "Then I'm wrong," Pearl said. "Come. Let's figure out this mask."

There was a light tap on the door. Everyone froze. Gaia's gaze flew to Pearl, whose rigid expression told Gaia it was not Mace outside. Silently, Pearl pointed Gaia toward the stairs, and Gaia flew up them as noiselessly as she could, stopping near the top where she could crouch to peer back down. Her heart thudded in her chest as Pearl turned out the light, and then Gaia heard the big door open.

"Please," came a whisper. "Let me in."

Gaia clenched her hand on the banister.

"We're closed," Pearl said sternly. "Come back in the morning."

"Wait!" the voice came again, more clearly. "Derek Vlatir sent me."

Gaia's heart leaped in recognition and then fear. Leon! Why had he come? She couldn't see anything down below except a faint beam of moonlight falling on the floor. Pearl opened the door to let him in. The moonbeam widened, then vanished as Pearl clicked the lock closed.

"Oliver. A candle," Pearl said.

There was a scratching noise and a match flared. Leon stood just inside the door, his back to the wall.

Pearl had a knife pointed at his heart.

"You'd best explain yourself, son," Pearl said.

Oliver lit a candle and placed it on a brick that protruded from the oven. He held a cleaver in his other hand. In the faint light, Gaia could see Leon's face and disheveled clothes. His jacket and hat were gone. From her angle, she couldn't see his eyes under his messy bangs, but wariness was visible in his motionless form and the tight line of his unshaven jaw.

"What do you want with us?" Pearl said quietly.

"Mace Jackson knows my father."

Pearl was standing very straight. "We do not have the honor of being acquainted with the Protectorat," she said.

Leon kept his hands against the wall behind him. "My real father is Derek Vlatir. He sent me to you."

Pearl slowly withdrew the knife. Gaia, gripping the banister, came down a step and saw Leon's face open with surprise when he glanced up. She almost believed he was happy to see her, and then his expression dimmed.

"You're here," he said quietly.

Pearl glanced sharply at Gaia. Gaia came down the rest of the stairs and went to stand beside Yvonne, who slid her arms around her waist. Confused emotions kept Gaia silent, but her breath came quickly, and she peered intently at his lean, disheveled appearance. The single candle flame cast a weak light over his skin and the black of his shirt while he held himself motionless.

Leon turned back to Pearl. "Derek Vlatir was questioned tonight because the Protectorat believed I would go to him for help. He was right, and the guards nearly caught me. But Derek sent me back through the wall, and now—" He stopped. He shot another look to Gaia. "He thought Mace would help me."

Gaia thought rapidly. If what he was saying was true, then in the last four days, Leon had unraveled the rest of the code, gone all the way outside the Enclave, found his birth father, and then returned.

"Why didn't you return to the Bastion?" Gaia asked.

"I can't."

"Why didn't you leave for the wasteland?" she asked.

"I couldn't," he said, his voice low. "I didn't know where you were."

A strange, slow flip moved in her gut. She swallowed hard. She didn't know what to say.

Pearl put her knife up on the rack and pulled the little hanging measuring spoon to turn on the light again.

"Clearly, you two know each other," she said. "Put back your cleaver, Oliver."

"But he's the Protectorat's son," Oliver said. "We're harboring a fugitive. He could get us all killed."

"You heard the boy. He's not exactly waving the Enclave banner tonight, is he?"

Oliver put away his cleaver, and Yvonne slipped away from Gaia, stepping toward the table.

"Are you a fugitive, too?" Yvonne asked.

Leon shifted his gaze to the girl, and his voice softened. "Apparently."

The girl nodded, and Gaia breathed more easily. Pearl moved to the oven and opened the door to stir up the coals. She moved the pot of soup that had cooled on the hearth back into the embers.

"Have a seat," Pearl said. "Let's hear what news you have."

Leon hesitated, as if waiting for a cue from Gaia, and with a nod she beckoned him forward. He accepted a chair and brought it up to the table. Gaia uneasily took a place opposite him. In the brighter light, she could see his black shirt was of a rougher quality, like ones men wore outside the wall. Though he smiled slightly at Yvonne when she drew up a stool near him, Gaia could see the edginess in him.

"I know where your mother is," he said. "She's alive and in fair health."

"In the southeast tower," Gaia said.

He tapped a slow finger on the table. "How did you find out?"

"Mace told me."

He nodded, his gaze sliding toward the oven. "I also found out where your father's buried," he said.

237

Gaia waited, tense, and Pearl came to put a hand on her shoulder.

"He's in the potter's field, outside the wall," Leon said. "Where they bury paupers."

Gaia closed her eyes as sorrow, for a long moment, silenced everything inside her. It hurt to think of her father, and there was something terribly final about knowing where his body reposed. It should have been some small comfort to know he was outside the wall, but she only felt the hard stone of her grief melting inside her, which was even worse.

"There now," Pearl said. "He's at peace, honey. You just remember that."

Gaia opened her eyes and turned to Leon. "Why did they arrest my parents in the first place?"

Leon rolled his black sleeves to the elbows before resting his forearms along the wooden tabletop, and still he didn't speak.

"Did my parents actually do something wrong?" Gaia asked.

"I don't think so. No."

"Then why—"

"They kept a record. That was why they were arrested."

"But keeping records isn't illegal," Gaia said. "How did the Enclave even know about it?"

"We heard a rumor that one or more of the midwives were keeping records, and then, when we questioned your parents, they were obviously hiding something. Once your parents re-fused to cooperate with us, they technically became traitors."

She realized that he was evading her gaze, and that he had been since he'd come in. Something had happened to him in the last four days. A quickness was missing from him. She felt a barrier between them, too, one that caused a quiet coolness to settle within her.

She dropped her voice. "What's really going on with my mother's code?"

"I'm trying to figure out how to explain," he said. "It's intricate."

Oliver leaned back into one of the darker corners, idle and watchful, while Pearl brought Leon a bowl of soup.

"Thank you, Masister," Leon said.

"You might as well eat something while you answer Gaia's questions," Pearl said. "Just start from the beginning, and we'll try to keep up."

Gaia could feel him gazing past her shoulder, sorting through memories or information that was invisible to her, and then he lifted the spoon from his bowl of soup. Little Yvonne held up a finger. "Don't drip," she said.

"Imagine," he said to Yvonne, "that your mother gave you twenty-three spoons for your birthday." He slid the spoon between his lips.

Yvonne's eyes lit up. "That's a crazy gift."

He set the spoon back on the rim of his bowl. Gaia pulled her sweater more securely around her and leaned back, watching him answer the girl.

"Yes," he said to Yvonne, his voice warming. "But they were very interesting spoons, all made out of chrome, and each one was a little different from the others so you could tell them apart. And then, to your surprise, you opened your father's birthday gift, and it was twenty-three more chrome spoons. When you looked at them closely, you could match up your father's spoons with your mother's spoons into pairs."

Yvonne scrambled off her stool and came back with a couple of spoons. "Like this," she said, setting them on the table under the light.

Leon nodded. "Yes. But remember, there are forty-six all together, half from each parent."

"Chromosomes," Oliver said, coming reluctantly forward from his corner. "We learned about this in school. The chrome

239

spoons are chromosomes, and we have them in every cell of our bodies."

"Go on," Pearl said.

Leon held his soupspoon up toward the light so that its edges gleamed. "Each spoon has dents all along its length, so many you can hardly see them all, each right against the next, some longer and some small. The dents are genes. How a dent on one spoon interacts with its matching dent on its matching spoon determines what traits you have, like brown eyes, or connected earlobes."

"Or blood that clots properly," Pearl said softly.

Gaia looked over to see her watching Leon closely.

"Yes," he said.

Gaia expected Pearl to mention Lila, but she said no more. Yvonne fidgeted restlessly beside her, and Gaia patted her knee reassuringly.

"Are we getting to my parents?" Gaia asked.

"I said it was complicated," he said.

Her pulse jumped at the slight edge in his tone. That was more like Leon.

"We'll get there, Gaia," Yvonne said. "What's DNA? That's what I want to know."

"It's the chrome of the spoon," Leon said, running his finger-tip along the whole length of the spoon. "It's what makes up every dent, the basic material of every gene, from one end to the other. I'm not saying everything about you is determined by your genes, but they matter a lot."

That fit with what she knew, Gaia realized, with her eyes fixed on his spoon. She had never quite understood what DNA was, but with the chrome in all the variety of those spoons and dents, she could easily see that each person's DNA was unique.

"Okay, go on," Yvonne said.

240

Leon frowned briefly. "There's another part of the story. They've found an Enclave boy, a toddler named Nolan. He has the genes that say he should have hemophilia, but he doesn't have it. His blood is fine."

Pearl gasped. "How can that be? Did they cure him?"

"No," Leon said. "His parents brought him to Mabrother Iris's lab when his older brother's hemophilia became apparent. His was mild, but they worried Nolan's would be bad. Instead, the lab determined that Nolan was born with some beneficial suppressor gene that's counteracting the hemophilia." He paused. "It's like there's a dent on some other spoon, far from the hemophilia dent, that cancels out the hemophilia."

Gaia frowned. "Is that possible?"

"Yes. And that's why Mabrother Iris is so excited." His voice darkened. "Nolan's mother is from the outside. And she has a freckle tattoo on her ankle."

Gaia exhaled an enormous breath and leaned back in her chair. "Oh, no," she whispered. Focus on the freckle tattoos would bring more attention to Western Sector Three, which could only make things worse for people there.

"I still don't understand," Yvonne said. "Why does that matter?"

Leon brushed back the hair over his ear, and turned toward the girl. "There are really three steps for what happens next. First, the Enclave has to identify more kids like Nolan who don't have hemophilia even though their genes say they should. Second, they want to identify the suppressor gene," he said. "They can find it one of two ways: breed Nolan with other kids like him, or track back through their family trees to narrow in on the gene by a process of elimination. Of those two options, the second one is far more humane and faster, too. Once they identify the suppressor gene, they're ready for the third step: they can test everyone to see who has the suppressor gene, and

241

those people can be selected to marry hemophilia carriers to eliminate hemophilia in their children."

Gaia watched him stir his spoon once through his soup, as if he were losing his appetite.

"My head's spinning," Pearl confessed. "What does this really mean for us? For all of our friends inside the wall right now?"

Leon set the bowl aside. "They're taking the freckle-tattooed girls and boys to test them to see if they're like Nolan, carrying the suppressor gene. It won't be very invasive. They'll just take some blood and a swab sample from inside their cheeks. When they identify a few more people like Nolan, then they'll locate their parents."

"From outside the wall?" Pearl asked.

"Yes. From outside the wall. And they'll work back from those parents to study the family trees."

"But the freckles aren't a guarantee of anything," Gaia objected. "There's no connection between the tattoos and the genes."

"I know," Leon said. "And Mabrother Iris and the Protectorat know that. But the people with freckle tattoos are the only ones we can work with, the only ones with known birth parents."

"Because of my mother's code," Gaia said.

He nodded. "It was the key," Leon said. "They were watching us through a camera. I should have known. Bartlett should have told me. They've deciphered it all by now."

"They were using you, too?" she said.

He nodded once. "When they saw me go into your room, all on my own, they couldn't believe their luck."

"Did Sergeant Bartlett set you up?"

"I don't know for sure. It wouldn't be like him. Not on purpose. He just knew I was interested in you."

Her heart gave another little kick. *What*, she wondered, *did Leon say to Sgt. Bartlett about me?*

"What will they do once they identify the suppressor gene and find the people who carry it?" Gaia asked.

Leon templed his fingers together, and they cast a sharp shadow on the tabletop. "They're thinking long term. Once they can identify the suppressor gene, they'll test all the babies outside the wall and take the ones who have it. They're patient," he said.

The dawning horror made Gaia momentarily speechless. "All of them?"

"They'll be the most desired, most precious advanced children ever," he said flatly. "The mothers of those children will be encouraged to have as many babies as possible, all for advancing. And when those babies grow up, they'll have their pick of the elite families to marry into."

Pearl cleared Leon's soup bowl away. "It all sounds awfully far-fetched," she said.

"Accept it. It's fact," Leon said.

Gaia leaned forward and gripped her hands together upon the table. "What happened to you, after you left me?" she asked.

A muscle clenched in his jaw. "I went to my fa—to the Protectorat and Mabrother Iris. Mabrother Iris congratulated me on my progress with you and explained the promise of the suppressor gene." His voice dropped to a low, mocking frequency. "He told me who my parents are. Always a reward with Mabrother Iris. And then he wanted to know if I could find the baby you saved, the one from the executed couple."

"You're kidding," Gaia said.

Leon passed a hand before his eyes, and when he lowered it, he still wasn't looking at her directly. "That baby could be another one like Nolan. They want you back, Gaia. They want to hold you up as a hero for saving him."

243

"No," Pearl muttered.

Gaia's breath caught.

Leon shook his head. "I told them the baby was dead," Leon said.

Pearl was leaning against the sink. "Is it?" she asked.

Leon turned to her and spoke quietly. "I don't really know. There's no trail in the black market for babies, unless Masister Khol keeps some record. And she'd be a fool to do so." He shifted back toward Gaia's direction. "That's why you have to leave. You're not safe anywhere here, not in the Enclave, not in Wharfton. If they find you, they'll use you. You won't have any choice."

Gaia sat in silence among the others, her mind reeling with the new information. The Enclave wanted to use her for political purposes. That was worse than them wanting her dead, but she was even more concerned for what would happen to the families in Western Sector Three. They stood to lose even more babies.

"They must be stopped," she said.

"How?" Oliver asked.

"I don't know. But there has to be a way."

Leon shook his head. "You can't do it, Gaia. They're too powerful. And they'll persuade people this is for the best. They always do." He closed his eyes briefly and rubbed his forehead, as if he were deeply weary. "And maybe it is for the best, in the long run."

"You can't believe that," she said.

His voice dropped low. "I don't know what I believe. I don't trust them, but I can, actually, see how finding the suppressor gene could help."

"You're saying reproductive slavery would be all right?" she demanded. "You're saying taking more babies from their mothers would be fine?"

He finally, reluctantly, lifted his gaze to meet Gaia's. If she had ever thought there was something dead inside Leon, it was nothing compared to the bleak, unfeeling emptiness she saw in his eyes now.

"What *happened* to you?" Gaia said.

His gaze dropped and his hands went still on the table.

Pearl put a hand on her shoulder. "Be easy, Gaia," she said. "It's a lot to take in. I have to tell you, if I heard there was some little boy growing up outside the wall right now who could marry Yvonne some day and they could have healthy children, it would open doors, not shut them. A lot of us trust the Enclave to do the right thing in the long run. They always have."

"If that's true, why are you helping me right now?" Gaia demanded. "Don't you realize you have to take a side?"

Pearl folded her strong arms across her chest in a way that implied she could not be budged. "I have to live here," Pearl said quietly. "My life is here. It's not perfect, but it's the best we have. I'm helping you because my heart tells me it's the right thing to do and because I can. That's enough for me."

Gaia struggled with her confusion and forced herself to think ahead. "We still have to get my mother out," she said. "That's our first priority. Agreed?"

A sigh of relief went through Yvonne and Oliver, and Pearl hitched up another stool with a shuffling noise. "Here," she said, producing a roll of wide paper.

"What's this?" Leon asked.

"A map," Oliver said. "We were looking at it earlier."

For the first time, the old Leon seemed to stir. "What's your plan, precisely?" he asked, pivoting the map to face him.

Gaia tilted her face to try to see it at his angle. The parchment was tattered at the edges, and some of the lines were smudged and reworked from repeated updates, but it was a complete map of the Enclave and Wharfton, with streets and sectors carefully marked. Gaia found it odd to see her world set out in two dimensions, without the elevation that was so much a part of rising from the unlake to the gate, or entering the Enclave and climbing gradually toward the Bastion. Still, it gave a clear perspective on how near and far things were. She traced her finger gently over the little line of Sally Row, where her home stood in Western Sector Three. Her father, she knew, would have loved this map.

"Mace has gone to ask Masister Khol to take me up to my mom," Gaia said. "I'm going to be disguised as one of the boys, carrying a bag for her. We'll take a cutting tool in case there's a lock or chains we need to deal with, and then we'll throw a rope out the window for me and my mother to climb down."

Leon looked skeptical.

"What?" Gaia demanded, crossing her arms over her chest. "Do you have a better idea?"

He cleared his throat, and to Gaia's annoyance, he couldn't quite hide a smile. "The part with Masister Khol isn't half bad," he said. "But you'll never get down a rope. Not unless you have some mountain-climbing experience I don't know about."

Oliver laughed. Gaia sat stiffly on her chair, and Pearl nudged her elbow. "We did have our doubts about them climbing down the rope," Pearl admitted.

Leon held out an upturned hand as if to say, *see?*

"You're not the only one with strong arms," Gaia said.

"I'm sure yours are quite burly," Leon said. "But how are your mom's?"

Gaia tugged the map back in her direction. "Are you going to help or not? The Bastion and the prison are here, and the southeast tower here." She pointed. "After we get my mother, we can exit either through the main south gate if there's some distraction, or here, where there's a concealed passage by the garbage pit." She looked up to see that Leon had come around to her side of the table and was looking at it over Yvonne's head.

"Why not the north gate?" he asked.

"We have friends in Wharfton. I thought they could help us hide and get supplies before we go farther on. How did you get inside the wall from Derek's?" Gaia asked.

Leon lightly touched the line of the wall in another place. "Here, by the solar grid plant," he said. He hesitated, and then pointed to first a street and then a honey farm on the map. "There's also a tunnel here, and here, that leads into the wine cellar of the Bastion, here." He pointed again.

Gaia shook her head. "That's too far from the tower to help us." She studied the map and the ominous way the roads all ended at the interior edge of the wall. "Mace offered to smuggle me out in a bicycle cart when the boys go out for wood."

Leon slowly shook his head. "We can't smuggle out all three of us. It will have to be this passage, here." He pointed to the spot by the solar grid plant, on the southeastern edge of the Enclave.

All three? she thought. Was Leon planning on going outside the wall with them? "I suppose," she agreed.

"Then what will you do?" he asked. "Have you thought about surviving in the wasteland at all?"

She traced her finger north to where the map ended. "The Dead Forest is north of here. That's where we're going. To the community there."

Leon leaned back slightly. Yvonne hitched her stool nearer and leaned far over the map, inspecting it. Oliver and Pearl exchanged a glance.

Finally Leon spoke. "There's nothing north of here but wasteland, Gaia," he said quietly. "The Dead Forest is a myth."

247

Gaia glanced at Pearl and the others, waiting for them to contradict him, but they remained silent.

"I thought so, too, once," she said. "But it's real." In the face of their doubt, she tried to remember how she knew it was real. "Outside the wall we know this," she said. "People go there."

"Because they die," Oliver said.

"No," she said. "I have this friend, Old Meg, who said she was going there." She stopped, looking at Leon and remembering how he had asked her about Old Meg the night she left Wharfton.

"And does anyone ever come back from the Dead Forest?" Leon asked pointedly.

She knew what the truth was, even if she had no proof. "No," she said.

Chapter 21
Happiness

LITTLE YVONNE LEANED closer to Gaia and put her slim arm around her shoulders. "I believe in the Dead Forest," she said sweetly.

Pearl let out a low laugh. "Come on, pumpkin. You're nearly asleep on your stool. I think we should all try to get some rest, frankly. Yvonne and Oliver, go on to bed now."

Yvonne complained briefly, but Pearl was firm, and soon the brother and sister said their good-nights and left. Gaia didn't see how she could sleep with her plans still so inchoate, and she drew the map nearer again. When Pearl braced a hand on the doorway and turned once more toward the kitchen, Gaia glanced up. Leon was on his feet, looking respectfully in Pearl's direction.

"We don't have another bed," Pearl said. "But you could sleep on the floor in Oliver's room. I'll have him leave you a blanket. I'm sorry. It's the best I can do."

"Don't worry about me, please," Leon said.

It occurred to Gaia that Leon had risen deliberately, according to Pearl the deference a gentleman routinely showed a lady. Now Pearl straightened and cast a last look in Gaia's direction.

249

"Get some sleep, Gaia," she said. "Tomorrow's going to be a long day."

"I will."

"Do you mind turning the light out? You can open the door of the oven for some light. Just bank the coals and close the door before you go to bed. I expect Mace back in another hour or so, but keep the door locked."

"Of course," Gaia said.

In another moment, there came the quiet, hollow sound of a door being closed down the hall, and Gaia knew she and Leon were alone. He flicked off the overhead light, and she waited for him to open the door of the oven before she blew out the last candle. The warm, golden light from the oven spilled out onto the floor and brought little reflections to light on the rims of pans and cooking utensils hanging on the walls. She became aware of dough rising on a rack of trays behind her, as if it were gently alive with its yeasty scent.

He sat slowly again, and pressed his face into his hands so that his dark hair spiked through his fingers. She loosened her grip on her sweater and fingered one of the little buttons of her dress. He'd hardly looked at her the entire time they'd been talking with Pearl's family, and she wondered if that would change now that they were alone.

After a moment, he slouched sideways, leaning his stubbly cheek in one palm, his gaze toward the map. He ran a finger along the lines of Sally Row like she had earlier. "Were you happy growing up outside the wall?" he asked.

The question was so unexpected she found herself letting down her guard a bit. "Why do you ask?"

"I can't help wondering if I would have been better off out there, growing up in Derek's family."

She smiled. "That's ridiculous. You've had every advantage."

250

"Have I?"

"How can you even ask that? You've had decent food from the minute you were advanced. And warm clothes and an education. Not to mention rich, powerful parents. I saw your glamorous life on the Tvaltar whenever there was a *Protectorat Family Special*, so don't tell me your life wasn't perfect."

She reached out to trace a black burn mark on the tabletop. Her eyes were slowly adjusting to the near-darkness, and as long as she avoided looking directly into the oven, her eyes stayed perceptive. She could see him well enough to realize he was back to avoiding her gaze.

"So what was it like for you, growing up?" he asked. "Really."

"Really," she echoed slowly, trying to figure out how to sum up an entire childhood. "It was pretty good when I was really little. We were poor, like everyone, but I didn't know that. Our house was at—well, you know it's at the far edge of Western Sector Three, and I liked it there, with all that room to explore and grow." She nodded toward that part of the map. "My parents worked during the day and kept me near them, but in the evening I could always get one of them to go exploring with me. I loved that, especially going down into the unlake."

"And did you have friends?"

"I had two friends. Well, one really. Emily lived across the street from me. We liked to play dress-up with my dad's scraps of fabric."

"And are you still close?" he asked.

She glanced over at him, puzzled. "Why do you want to know all of this?"

His voice was quiet in the silent room. "I'm just trying to picture your life. I'm trying to figure out how you're so different from anyone else I've ever met."

251

This surprised her. "I am?"

He shifted in his chair so that his profile was aimed toward the oven, and one of his boots extended toward the hearth. The door was propped open, and the red coals inside still pulsed with heat. The collar of his black shirt fell open slightly and slid away from the nape of his neck.

"What changed as you got older?" he asked.

Gaia tried to think what to tell him, and at the same time, she felt an odd urge to resist him, like he was pulling at something fragile inside her. She stepped over to the sink and turned on the tap for a cup of water. "Do you want some water?" she asked.

"Please."

She poured another for herself and brought them over. "Do you have any idea how amazing it is to me that I can get water out of faucet in this kitchen?"

He raised the cup to his lips, but held it there without drinking. "Explain."

She pulled up her chair again and swallowed a sip. "To get water outside the wall, I used to take my yoke pole and two huge bottles to the spigot in the wall for our sector. Usually old Perry, the waterman, was there with his big buckets and funnels, and he'd help me load up. I'd give him some basil or eggs in return. But if he wasn't there, I'd have to sit at the spigot waiting slowly to fill each bottle. The spigots are really slow, you know. Sometimes there was a line. It could take ten minutes or more to fill my own bottles, and then I'd carry them back with my yoke."

"I thought water was delivered to your family. That was one of your payments for your mom being a midwife."

She laughed. "How much water do you think a family goes through? That payment never lasted out the week, and when my father was dying fabric, we needed bottles and bottles of water."

252

She leaned her elbows on the table and took another sip from her cup.

"So you hauled water," he said. "What else?"

She shrugged. "I helped my mom with her herb garden and took care of the chickens. I'd run errands for my dad. I don't know. Cleaned. Hung laundry. Helped cook. All the kids I knew were always working."

"But were you happy?" he asked.

She didn't know how to answer him. Would he want to know that she'd had nightmares for months after one of the neighborhood boys died from a fever? Or that kids teased Gaia endlessly about her face? Those walks with the loads of water were the worst, when she couldn't run, couldn't use her hands to defend herself, and any pig of a boy who wanted to throw something at her could. She'd been starved for ideas and information, never able to sate her curiosity. There had been the slow, burning grudge against injustice, too, as she'd grown to realize people on the other side of the wall weren't struggling like they were in Wharfton.

Then again, she'd loved her parents deeply and joyfully.

Gaia set aside her cup, grateful when he didn't press for an answer. Good or bad, happy or not, that life was over for her now. She couldn't exactly go back and resume her duties as midwife of Western Sector Three.

Her hair was loose, her bangs falling irritatingly into her eyes. She reached up to plait some of the ends into a little braid, adding in just enough so that she could make some of the hair stay behind her right ear, at least until it all slipped free again. "I'm sure you were happier inside the wall than you would have been outside," she said. "You know, you could probably still work things out with your family. You haven't done anything too unforgivable, have you?"

"I needed to think and find my real father, so I left. Does

that sound unforgivable? They sent soldiers to track me down."
He shifted again to lean an arm on the table and drum his
fingers once on its surface. "We should work out our plans for
tomorrow."

She nodded. "I'll go up with Masister Khol to get my
mother and try to come right back down the stairs with her.
Then we'll bring her back here and at night we'll figure out
how to get outside the wall."

"If you need to, you can go into the Bastion. There are interior doors to the tower." He pointed to indicate the direction
on the map.

"That's good to know."

"If you don't come back out, I'll go in to find you. If you
run out of options, try to work your way upward, toward the
roof. They won't expect that. And I'll start looking for you
from the top down."

It was there, unspoken between them. Why would he help
her now when he hadn't helped her before? Sgt. Bartlett had
found a way to help her out of the Bastion. Why couldn't Leon
have done the same thing?

"I'm still taking the rope," she said.

"Go ahead. Just don't get your neck broken. I don't suppose
you'd let me go in for you instead."

She shook her head. She wouldn't trust him to do it right.

"That's what I thought," he said. "Even if you do think I
have strong arms."

Startled, she glanced up to find him watching her. "I didn't
exactly say that as a compliment."

"No?"

A bit of ember shifted in the oven, making a brief flare of
light, but otherwise the room was still. She didn't know what
to make of him, or how to feel, but it was far more confusing

when he was inspecting her with a curious, receptive expression.

"Are you teasing me?" she asked.

He started slowly to smile. "Should I?"

She was momentarily speechless. Then she frowned. "What do you know about Sergeant Bartlett?" she asked.

"Besides that he helped you out? That messed up everything, you know."

"That depends on your perspective," she said.

"Are you friends with him?"

"Sort of," she said. "What's he like?"

Leon stood and took a knickknack off the mantel: a tiny eggbeater that looked more like a toy than a tool. He spun the little wheel. "Jack's like a lot of guys. Works hard. Not a bad shot. I guess he likes to sing. Why?"

Gaia wished she'd had a chance to know him.

Leon gave the wheel such a spin that one of the beaters broke off. He swore and reached for the little piece. "Forget it, Gaia. He's not your type."

"And how would you know what my type is?" she asked.

"It just isn't Jack."

"Why, because he's nice to me?"

He shoved the little pieces of the broken eggbeater at her. "Can you fix this?" he asked.

"He's my brother, all right? Jack Bartlett is my brother, Odin Stone."

Leon sat again, his expression puzzled. "Jack is? But he doesn't look anything like you."

"Thank you. Brilliant observation. Very useful."

"All right. No need to get touchy."

"Jack Bartlett got me out of the Bastion. Jack Bartlett didn't leave me there with no way to get out and no explanation."

She reached for the little pieces and began to arrange them in a row on the table. Leon lifted his empty cup and turned it in his hands, and as the silence stretched out, she knew she had to know, even if she revealed how vulnerable she was.

"Why did you leave me?" she asked in a tight voice.

She watched him slowly turn the cup once more and loop his thumb in the handle. When he looked at her this time, his eyes were alive with regret. "I'm sorry," he said softly. "It was a mistake."

"But why did you do it?"

His fingers stilled. "I thought I could negotiate for you and your mother. When I saw the girls in the courtyard, I realized Mabrother Iris must already be acting on your information somehow, and I thought he would be grateful. I thought I could persuade my father and Mabrother Iris to let you go."

"But they wouldn't?"

He shook his head. "They refused. They wanted me to persuade you to return to them, like I said before, as their newest hero."

"And you said no."

His eyes flicked away. "Gaia," he began. "It was utterly hopeless. I felt like I'd betrayed you completely, like they completely manipulated me. And then they started explaining about the suppressor gene and how much your mother's records mean to them." He glanced back, his lips parted. His cheeks had taken on color with the warmth of the oven, and his blue eyes were dark and alive. "My father's an incredibly persuasive man. I'd forgotten."

"And that's when he convinced you their plan is okay?" She could feel her anger percolating up again.

"I don't know," he said. "I don't know what I think. If your father told you something he was completely convinced of, wouldn't you listen to him?"

"My father's dead."

She shoved her chair back with a jerk. She was trying to understand Leon, but it was hard. It all seemed to come back to his relationship with his father. Much as he tried to deny it, the Protectorat really was his father. He was the one who had raised him, and he was the one who still had strings in him, even though they'd been estranged for years. That much was clear to her. It seemed terribly unfair to her that he still had his father, even as difficult as that relationship was, when her own father was lost to her.

"I'd like to hear about your family now," she said. That would only be fair.

"It's a boring story."

"Just any old thing," she said. "I told you about my childhood."

"All right," he said slowly. "Maybe you'd like to know a secret about the *Protectorat Family Specials*."

She guessed from his tone that they weren't all they'd seemed to be. She could still picture the sunny scenes of the family in the Bastion gardens, the boys with their impeccably white shorts and clean knees, the twin sisters in matching yellow dresses. A particular apple-picking scene came to mind. It had been her favorite, with the kids swinging from the low-hanging, apple-laden branches.

"We practiced them for weeks," he said. "There was not one unstaged, genuine moment in any single one."

"You're kidding."

"Believe me. We kids hated doing them, and finally, when Rafael was around seven, he flatly refused to do any more. It was the only time I was grateful he could throw a fit."

"What about your sisters? Did you play with them when you were a kid? Hide-and-seek in the Bastion?"

"Hide-and-seek," he said slowly, and she could hear the

257

weight of complex emotions behind the simple words. She would have liked to see his eyes, but he turned toward the oven again.

"We did play hide-and-seek. And chess. And all sorts of games. They liked it when I lost." He touched the door of the oven with his boot. "It's Fiona and Evelyn's birthday tomorrow," he said.

Gaia was surprised. "You mean, today?"

"Yes. I guess today. This is the first year they've celebrated since Fiona died," he went on. "Evelyn's turning fourteen. The family's invited half of the wealthiest families to the Bastion for a party. There's supposed to be fireworks at the end."

"Are you supposed to go, too?" she asked.

He shrugged and gave half a laugh. "Evelyn invited me, but I was told quite clearly not to come."

She waited, hoping he would continue. "Tell me," she said softly. "I want to know more. What were you like when you were little?"

He smiled slightly. "I was the most uncoordinated kid imaginable. When I started playing soccer, I would fall every time I kicked the ball. I mean, actually fall down. But I stuck with it. Then it took me forever to learn how to read. I couldn't keep the letters straight. They thought I was stupid. Even Rafael learned to read before I did."

"I didn't know that."

Leon shrugged. "They didn't put that in the specials. I made up for it later, though, once I finally got the hang of it. I loved school."

She envied him that. One by one, she clicked together the pieces of the little toy eggbeater. "How much younger than you is Rafael?"

"Genevieve had Rafael when I was four, and the twins showed up the year after that." The golden light from the oven reflected along his nose and jaw. His gaze was pensive. "Gene-vieve is really the only mother I've ever known, and she was very kind to me when I was little. I'll give her that. But my father absolutely doted on his new family, and I was, well—" He paused. "It was natural, I suppose, for the rest of them to be close."

It was curious to see Leon become more serious as he talked about his family. Gaia tried to remember the boy version of Leon in the Tvaltar specials, the dark-haired, older one, usually positioned in the back. She'd always been captivated by the little sisters with their bright curls and laughing faces, so it had been natural to overlook him. It wasn't hard to believe that Leon had been subtly excluded from his own family.

"So, Fiona?" she asked. "Do you miss her?"

Leon shook his head briefly. "I don't talk about her."

She remembered what the women of Q cell had said, and wondered if she could get to the truth behind the rumors. "And your aunt?" she asked.

He turned, his expression puzzled. "Aunt Maura? What about her?"

She swallowed thickly and wished she could take it back.

"What have you heard about my aunt?" he asked, his voice colder.

"Nothing."

"No. You've heard some rumor, haven't you? What have you heard?"

She looked miserably down at her hands and gave the toy a little spin. It worked perfectly. She could feel the heat rising in her cheeks.

He let out a sharp laugh. "I should have known," he said. "I'm telling you about my family, things I've never told anybody, and you just want to know if the rumors of incest are true."

"I didn't say that."

"They're not. Okay? I haven't slept with anyone, related to me or not. I don't much care if you believe me, but there it is."

She wanted to sink down into a pool of black slime and evaporate. "I'm sorry."

Leon stood, took the miniature eggbeater to return it to the mantel, and moved to the sink. She heard him quietly cleaning out his cup, and the faint squeak of the faucet. Something about his controlled, quiet movements made her feel even worse. When he held out a hand for her own cup, she passed it to him wordlessly. He washed it, too, and turned it upside down on the rack.

"You don't have to help me tomorrow," Gaia said.

He turned, folded his arms, and leaned back against the counter. "You know what? You're pretty good at pushing people away from you. Did you know that? Maybe that's why you had only one friend growing up."

She shook her head. "That's mean."

He ran his hand back through his hair, gripping it above his forehead. He looked tired, and exasperated, and hurt. Gaia had no idea what to say or how to take them back to the comfortable feeling they'd had before. She only knew she didn't want him mad at her. And that made her feel weak and vulnerable, which she didn't like at all.

She stood and backed toward the stairs that led to the room she shared with Yvonne. "It's late," she said lamely.

"Fine. Go to bed, then."

"Are you going to sleep in Oliver's room?"

"No."

She glanced back at the table, chairs, and stools, and the totally utilitarian space of the kitchen, knowing there would be nowhere comfortable here for him to sleep. She was about to protest when she heard a soft click from the hallway and then quick footsteps. Pearl entered the kitchen doorway.

260

"Is Mace here?" she asked in a worried voice. "I thought I heard him coming."

"No," Gaia said. But a moment later, a noise came at the door, a low, distinct pattern of knocking.

"Close the oven," Pearl whispered.

As soon as Leon did and the room was dark, Pearl unlocked and opened the door to the outside. Mace Jackson slipped inside, followed closely by a woman in a long white cloak. A fresh swirl of cool air spiraled through the kitchen as the door closed again, and then the dim room was very still. The fiery flickers around the edge of the oven door were the only light.

"Pearl?" Mace asked in the darkness.

"At last," she said.

When Gaia struck a match to light the little candle on the brick of the oven, Mace and Pearl were in each other's arms. With Pearl's broad shoulders and Mace's powerful bulk, they were like two bears embracing. Gaia had to smile.

"Who's this?" Mace asked, his voice deep and low, his black eyes directed over Pearl's shoulder toward Leon.

"He's a friend of Gaia's," Pearl said quickly.

"He's Leon Quarry," Mace said severely, releasing Pearl. "Do you have any idea what would happen to us if they found him here?"

Gaia stepped slightly in front of Leon. "It's not like that," she said. "I'm sorry, Mace. I never meant to—"

"Derek Vlatir sent me," Leon interrupted. "He's my father. He told me to come to you."

Mace peered at Leon closely, and then he picked up a knife. "I don't care what Derek said."

"Mace," Pearl said firmly, with a warning hand on his arm.

"Please," Gaia said. "He's with us now. With me. We just want to rescue my mother, and then we'll leave."

Mace's eyes flashed to Gaia, and he looked pained. "Not

261

him, Gaia. He's worse than scum." His voice dropped in warning. "You don't know what he's like."

"Yes, I do," she said. "And I'm telling you to trust me."

She turned to Leon beside her and saw his eyes were tight with restrained anger. He said nothing to defend himself. Mace made a disgusted noise and jabbed the knife back in its block. Then the woman in white who had remained by the door moved forward into the candlelight. Gaia recognized Masister Khol. Her lips were turned down with disdain.

"Who would have guessed? Both of you here," Masister Khol said, looking first at Gaia and then Leon. "The whole city's looking for you."

Leon's voice was carefully neutral. "Have you come to help us or threaten us?"

Masister Khol stiffened into a more imposing figure. "I didn't know you were involved with the girl," she said to Leon.

"Wait. Please," Gaia said, stepping forward again. "We just need your help to get me to my mother. That's all. If you'll just do that much, we'll be grateful."

"It's never just that much," Masister Khol said. "I passed you a note once from your mother, but did it end there?"

Gaia didn't know what to say. She turned to Pearl, and Pearl moved beside Masister Khol, speaking too softly for Gaia to understand her.

Gaia glanced at Leon, but his face was impassive. Mace tugged on the overhead light. Crowding past Leon and ignoring everything else, Mace washed his hands. Then he pulled a wide, flat board from a shelf, set it on the table and dusted it with flour from a sack on the counter.

Gaia stood helplessly, watching Pearl and Masister Khol, until finally they turned.

Masister Khol spoke to Mace as if he were the only person in the room. "Sometime this morning, I'll be crossing the

Square of the Bastion with a heavy basket. If I see a boy there to carry it for me, I'll take him with me into the southeast tower. Nothing more. He can stay for five minutes. I have important work to do for the Enclave and no time for this nonsense. I refuse to be implicated if a crime is committed."

Mace bowed his head briefly. Gaia had a million questions, but Mace gave her a hard look, and she remained silent.

"Thank you, Joyce," Pearl said. "I appreciate it. I really do."

Masister Khol turned to the door. With one hand on the latch, she paused and turned her face toward Pearl. "If I could lessen your real loss, Pearl," she said, "you know that I would. I wish you wouldn't deceive yourself that a stunt like this makes any difference." A moment later, she was gone.

Pearl dashed the back of her hand across her eyes and clapped her hands together once. "You heard Joyce," Pearl said. She reached for her apron. "We've got no time at all. She'll take you up, Gaia, but the rest is up to you. She'll have to be able to say she was tricked just like anyone else. Let's get Oliver and Yvonne."

Everyone jumped to action, moving as swiftly and quietly as possible. Oliver was sent to find some of Jet's apprentice clothes for Gaia, and some of his own for Leon. Yvonne was braiding lengths of laundry line into a sturdy rope. Mace worked the dough before him with silent, unhurried movements, and when the next trays of risen dough were in the oven, he started to load the cart to take to the market. Pearl wrapped a long swatch of brown cotton cloth around Gaia's torso, bulking up her waist and shoulders with padding. When Gaia slipped on the apprentice's blue shirt and pants, followed by a white bak-er's apron and a brown coat, Yvonne turned from her web of laundry line and giggled at her.

"You look like Jet on a bad day," Yvonne said. "Even the hair."

"Thanks," Gaia said.

She took a couple of strides in the pants, getting used to the feel of them. Women in Wharfton wore pants occasionally, if their work called for it or the winter turned cold, but it wasn't common. Gaia hadn't worn leggings since she was a girl.

"You have to walk with your legs apart, like this," Yvonne said. She demonstrated, giggling.

Pearl had whipped together a quick, thin batter, and it hit the flat skillet with a hissing noise as she poured a super-thin crepe.

"Hat," Pearl said curtly, and Yvonne sprinted upstairs, returning shortly with a boy's deep-brimmed brown hat.

Gaia twitched in her clothes, trying to get comfortable, and she watched Pearl lay two thin crepes to cool on a flat, clean towel. They were circular and light, with a flexibility and texture that were surprisingly like skin.

"They're too pale for her," Leon said, pausing as he passed through the kitchen with an armload of baguettes.

"What do you know? Get out of my way," Pearl said. "Go shave, why don't you?"

Leon shot Gaia a quick look, almost a smile, and then he and Oliver and Mace were busy with preparing the cart. They kept opening and closing the front door of the shop as they normally did when loading up on market day, and the cool air brought goose bumps to Gaia's arms and neck.

"Sit," Pearl said, pointing Gaia toward a stool directly in the light. She touched Gaia's chin, and Gaia obediently tipped her face upward, closing her eyes. She felt cool dabs of a pasty substance being applied to the scarred skin of her left cheek, and she was amazed by the firm tenderness of Pearl's touch. Next she felt a cool, damp, suffocating fabric cover her entire face, and she had to fight back an instinctive fear. An instant later, the right side was lifted away, and Gaia realized Pearl had laid one of the crepes on her face and bisected it down her nose. With her eyelids still closed, Gaia was intensely aware of Pearl working closely over her face. She could feel the woman's breath against her neck, and sometimes her ear, and she could hear a faint clicking noise Pearl made in the back of her throat as she concentrated.

Next there was a brush of powder that Gaia felt distinctly on her right cheek and forehead, but as only the faintest pressure on her left side. Pearl made a dissatisfied sound, and Gaia heard her turning back to her flour and spices. A moment later, Gaia felt more brushing, and Pearl blew sharply on her face so that Gaia winced.

"It's awful," Yvonne said, and Gaia's eyes shot open in alarm.

Yvonne was grinning at her, and Pearl, inches away, was frowning as she touched the masklike new skin on Gaia's left check.

"Well, it's obviously a speed job," Pearl said. "But it will do, if you keep a hat on and they don't look too closely." She sat back on the opposite stool, and Gaia cautiously sat upright. She kept expecting the crepe to fall off her skin, it was so lightly applied. Yvonne passed her a mirror, and with bright eyes, she watched Gaia over the rim of the glass.

Gaia looked at a young boy in the mirror, a tanned, round-faced boy with long lashes, pale lips, and a broad forehead. There was an awkwardness to his nose, as if he'd had it broken once, and there were faint shadows under his eyes, as if he hadn't been sleeping well. As she peered more closely, Gaia saw the seam edge of the crepe where it started on her chin, ran around the left perimeter of her lips, up her nose, under her left eye, and all across the top of her eyebrows to her right temple. Her own brown eyes peered out from between black lashes. She reached up gingerly, but Pearl stopped her hand.

"It's fragile," she said. "Don't touch it. And don't try to smile or it will buckle around your mouth."

"It's amazing," Gaia said, and saw in the mirror that her left cheek looked odd when she spoke. She would have to avoid talking, too, as much as she could.

"Well," Pearl said with a modest cough. "I think making you a little darker was a good idea. Here. Put some on your hands, too. And settle your hat on. Yvonne, is that rope ready?"

Pearl made Gaia take her coat off again, and stuffed the rope and an extra cloak of Pearl's for Gaia's mother into the back of Gaia's shirt. When Gaia's brown coat was on again, she looked even more like a round young boy who had just started his growth spurt. Pearl shook her head. "Your hands are all wrong," she said. "Too slender."

Just then Mace yelled from the doorway to the shop. "Pearl!" he called. "We're going to set up at the market. Where's my apprentice?"

Gaia's heart froze with fear for one instant, and then Pearl gave her fingers a quick, hard squeeze. She drew her to the front doorway.

"We'll be waiting for you here," Pearl whispered. Yvonne came forward for a hug, but Pearl held her back. "No, don't mess her," Pearl said in warning. "Take these," she said to Gaia. She thrust three little white cubes into Gaia's palm.

"Sugar?" Gaia asked, puzzled, stepping out and holding them toward the moonlight on her open palm. They were smaller and denser than sugar cubes, and Gaia looked back at Pearl curiously.

"They're not sugar. They're for sleep and pain. They work fast and they're powerful, so be careful."

Gaia slid them into the right pocket of her trousers, her mind racing to anticipate how they might be useful. "What are they? Are they for the prisoner in the tower? For Masister Khol?"

"Yes," she said. "Or for you, if— Well, you can use your judgment."

Yvonne's young face was a pale blue in the shadowed doorway. "They're all we have left over from Lila," she explained.

"Oh," Gaia said softly. She searched Pearl's face, unsure if she should take them.

"Go," Pearl urged her. "We don't need them." The older woman squinted toward where Mace and Leon, now dressed in Oliver's clothes, were waiting with a cart in the narrow lane. Oliver was out of sight.

Gaia spared one last glance for Pearl and Yvonne, who gave a little wave and a big smile, and then she hurried after the cart like a late, contrite apprentice.

Chapter 22

The Women of the Southeast Tower

T HE MONUMENT LOOMED over the Square of the Bastion, a heavy, black presence against the predawn violet of the sky. Gaia's ears were full of the rattle of the cart as its broad wheels traversed the damp cobblestones, and beside her Leon's breath came in a steady rhythm as he and Mace pulled the cart toward the southeast tower. That was their goal: to be the cart nearest the tower when Masister Khol chanced by and needed a boy, any convenient, trustworthy boy, to carry her load up the tower steps. Gaia palmed the crown of her hat to push it down more steadily on her head, glancing forward under the brim. In her pocket, her fingertips curled around the small cubes of white powder Pearl had given her.

In a corner of the square, two guards stood by the great wooden door to the southeast tower of the Bastion. Gaia tried not to look at them. On the opposite side of the square was the familiar arch to the prison, and she avoided looking at that, too, hoping she'd never enter there again.

There were a few other carts already in the square, and more were arriving for market day: a vegetable vendor, a poultry farmer with eggs and clucking chickens for sale, the clock-maker who occasionally brought his wares outside to Wharfton and now set up a small stand beside the base of the monument. Later the colors and smells would be vibrant, but now, in the gray light, even the copper bottoms of the pots were the soft, indistinct color of ash. Gaia kept her head down and helped Mace.

"When do you think Masister Khol will come?" she asked.

"I don't know. But we're in a good place for when she does. Remember, bring your mother back down to us quietly," Mace said, reviewing the plan they'd finally agreed upon. "If you can walk out naturally, she can sit here in Pearl's cloak, under the sun shade, as if she were one of us. Then we'll leave all together in an unhurried way."

"What if the guards notice?" Gaia whispered. "Which way do we run?"

"That way," Mace said, nodding over his shoulder. "Through the market, and cut over to the arcade and through the candle shop. They have a back door. Is your mother a fast runner?"

Gaia remembered her mother's gentle, steady manner and her graceful, unhurried movements in her brown skirts and dresses. She was a thickset woman nearing forty, strong and fit, or at least, she had been before her arrest. "If she has to be. For a short distance," Gaia said tensely.

Mace smiled, passing her a pair of loaves to arrange. "Then let's hope the guards notice nothing unusual. Remember, there are other doors into the tower from inside the Bastion, which people use regularly, coming and going, so having an extra woman come out should be okay. Be ready."

The square gradually filled with more vendors. The sun topped the buildings to the east, and as the morning hours progressed, it slowly shrank the line of shadow until the entire square was in the full sunlight of noon and the scorching July heat. Mace had her help set up two awnings, one for customers in front of the cart and one for them behind. Cicadas started up their slow, whining song of heat. Several times people came out of the door at the base of the tower, passing the guards, but no one went in.

Gaia was afraid every moment that someone would come along and notice her or Leon, but they stayed at the back of the stand and Mace handled the steady stream of slow-moving, heat-soaked customers. Gaia grew almost sick with the alternating anticipation and disappointment every time she saw someone who looked like Masister Khol.

"She wasn't lying, was she?" Gaia asked Leon. "It must be noon now, and she did say she'd come this morning, didn't she?"

He had shaved, and his blue shirt made his eyes seem lighter than she was used to, even in the shade of Oliver's borrowed hat. "She's a busy person, but she'll come. She has her own twisted kind of honor."

Mace wiped sweat from his forehead. "I'm almost out of bread anyway. If she doesn't come soon, we'll have to go back. This is already longer than I usually stay."

Finally, across the square, Masister Khol's white figure was visible, walking awkwardly as she carried a round, lidded basket. Gaia was so relieved she could have run to her with tears of gratitude. Masister Khol stopped a few feet from the door of the southeast tower, and set the basket down. With one hand poised at her back, she frowned toward the square. Gaia felt an itch in the back of neck, waiting by Mace's cart. The guards straightened to imposing posture.

"I'm here to check on the prisoner in the tower," Masister Khol said.

One of the guards stepped forward. "What do you have there in the basket?"

Masister shoved it forward a pace. "A gun and a few knives," she said sarcastically.

The guard laughed, and lifted the lid. "Sunflower seeds and potatoes? What kind of diet is that?"

"It's not a whole diet," Masister Khol said disdainfully. "It's a supplement. She needs more vitamin B6."

He shook his head. "It's always something. When's the baby due?"

"Not for another month," Masister Khol said. "Listen. Do you want to carry this up for me?"

He shook his head, and so did the other guard. "Orders," the first one said apologetically.

Masister Khol put a hand on her hip and turned in irritation toward the square. Gaia had been listening avidly to the exchange, and now she nearly jumped out of her shoes when Masister Khol addressed her.

"You, there!" Masister Khol said.

Gaia looked up, and then, trying to look natural, she glanced at Mace. Around them, the normal hubbub of the market continued.

"Yes, you, boy," Masister said. "Come here and carry this basket for me."

Gaia set down a loaf of bread. Her fingertips tingled with nervousness.

"Leave your apron and hurry along," Mace said to her. "Don't make Masister wait for you."

Gaia untied her baker's apron, threw it to Leon, and made her strides longer as she went to pick up the basket. She had to lean her body away to balance the weight.

The guards laughed.

"That will put a bit of meat on you, boy," the guard said. "Along you go, then," he said, opening the door for Masister Khol. The guard bopped Gaia's hat brim down lower on her forehead as she went past, and laughed again. Gaia had a moment of terror, feeling the mask on her forehead press oddly, but then she tried to react as a boy might. She jerked the hat back up, and shot the guard an annoyed look.

"That's the way," the guard said, his voice teasing but not unfriendly.

Her disguise had worked. Secretly delighted, Gaia hurried after Masister Khol, hauling up the basket. The steps spiraled upward in a clockwise fashion, with walls of stone on each side and with oblong windows in the outer wall every dozen steps. She passed several landings with closed doors, as well. The basket grew heavier with each step, but Gaia hitched it up her arm and kept going until her heart was pounding. Her breath came in gasps. The thought that every step was bringing her closer to her mother drove her upward, even as her leg muscles burned. She kept her eyes on the back of Masister's white skirt and the heels of her scuffing, black-soled shoes as she ascended the steps right in front of her. Just when Gaia thought she could go no farther, they reached a triangular landing and Masister Khol stopped.

Masister Khol paused to catch her breath, saying nothing, and a moment later she slid aside a little panel on the door and spoke through the opening.

"It's Masister Khol," she said. "We're coming in."

Gaia watched her pull one heavy iron bolt to the left, and the door swung outward.

They were in the tower at last. Gaia's heart lifted with anticipation. *My mother! Which one is my mother?* She glanced first at a woman who sat in a rocking chair. Persephone Frank, with her distinctive moon-shaped face and brown hair, lowered her knitting and looked up casually at Gaia. Gaia was shocked to find her there. Weeks ago, Leon had told her that Sephie was free and back home, practicing medicine. Yet here she was.

Either Leon had lied, or Sephie had chosen to serve the Enclave as a watchdog. Sephie drew her splayed fingers along her yarn to loosen it and resumed knitting.

Gaia's gaze flew to a second woman, who was lying on the farthest cot with a thin blanket covering her. The unfamiliar woman was sitting up slowly, one hand in a magazine, and her long brown hair slipped over her shoulder in a messy braid. She was a rotund young woman with heavy-lidded eyes, and not what Gaia expected in a political prisoner.

"Who is it?" the woman murmured.

"It's Masister Khol, you slugabed," Sephie said. "See if you can't make yourself presentable."

When the third woman, on the nearest cot, did not bother to roll over to see who had come in, Gaia's heart ticked faster with fear. Gaia set down her basket and stood by the door, afraid to do or say the wrong thing. With a quick glance upward, she located the tiny white box that matched the one she'd had in her Bastion room earlier, and she knew it was the surveillance camera. It was more than probable that Mabrother Iris or one of his assistants was watching the room closely. She inwardly groaned.

"Come now, Bonnie," Masister Khol said, and her voice cajoling, almost tender. "See the sunflower seeds I found for you. When's the last time you ate a sunflower seed?"

The form on the bed did not move. "I'm not hungry."

Gaia's heart leaped at the familiar voice, and it was all she could do not to rush over to her mother.

Then, as Masister Khol urged the prisoner gently to sit up, Gaia saw something she could not believe: under her blue dress, her mother's belly was swollen with the round, expansive bulge of pregnancy. Gaia inhaled sharply. It could not be. Or could it? The truth hammered home: her mother was not the attending midwife here. Her mother was the political prisoner. Impossible as it seemed, Gaia's mother must have been nearly five months pregnant when Gaia last saw her outside the wall, without Gaia knowing. A tiny, left-out voice at the back of her mind wondered why her mother hadn't told her, and then empathy rose in Gaia to wipe out everything else. She took an involuntary step toward her before she could stop herself.

Gaia's mother lifted tired, apathetic eyes in Gaia's direction, and Gaia was shocked by the other changes in her. Her once vibrant, sunny mother looked exhausted and totally disheartened. Her arms, formerly strong and agile, were thin and bony. Her cheeks and lips were the same colorless hue, and deep rings underscored her lackluster eyes. Her long braid was gone, and instead her limp hair grew in straggly clumps to her neck. It seemed all the life had been drained out of her body and concentrated into her belly to keep her child surviving, leaving only a shell of the mother behind.

"Who is this?" Gaia's mother asked in a dead voice.

"A boy from the market," Masister Khol said.

Gaia's mother looked vacantly away, and Gaia ached for her.

"Come along now," Masister Khol said. "We need a urine sample."

"We don't need anything." Gaia's mother turned to lie down again.

"No," Masister Khol said, quickly catching her. Sephie rose to help Masister Khol, and between the two of them, they brought Gaia's mother tottering to her feet. Sephie guided her feet into two brown slippers.

"It will just take a minute," Sephie said in a low voice. "Really now, Bonnie. You must. For the baby."

Bonnie's lips came tightly together, and she allowed Sephie to lead her into a little side room while Masister Khol hovered behind.

The awful truth hit Gaia again: her mother was pregnant.

And terribly weak. How on earth was Gaia going to help her escape?

"All set, Bonnie?" Masister Khol asked.

Gaia tried to think why Masister Khol hadn't mentioned that her mother was pregnant, and then she realized Masister Khol would have assumed Gaia already knew.

"Let's give her a little privacy," Sephie answered. She closed the door as she came out, then resumed her seat in the rocker by the fireplace and took up her knitting. Her needles made a pleasant clicking in the little space, and as Gaia looked around the room for other ideas, she realized what an unusual cell it was. The room was almost comfortable. The curved walls were made of dark stone, but a small fire for cooking glowed at the back of the fireplace, and a soft, rose-patterned carpet covered the floor. White curtains hung in three windows, framing the bright afternoon sky, and a cupboard held cooking gear and a few books. Above, from the apex of the conical, wooden rafters, a ceiling fan hung down and turned quietly, curving patiently into the air to stir it upward.

Sephie reached for a kettle that hung near the fire. "Care for a cup of tea before you go, Joyce?" she asked.

Masister Khol was rummaging through the basket Gaia had carried, and now she triumphantly lifted a little black tin and shook it. "I had a feeling you'd ask," she said. "It's a nice blend with a hint of vanilla in it."

The other woman smiled and pushed her hair back. "You're a miracle."

While Sephie slid off the lid of the teapot and took the tin from Masister Khol to shake some tea inside, Masister Khol turned to the third woman.

"How have you been, Julia?" Masister Khol asked.

"I've had better jobs. This is a bore, mostly," Julia said. She was rebraiding her hair with deft fingers. "I thought she was supposed to be a danger to herself and everyone around her."

Sephie's eyebrows lifted once in what Gaia guessed was dismissive contempt for Julia. Sephie was laying out three cups and saucers before the fire when she looked again at Gaia, and her gaze narrowed suddenly.

"You, there," Sephie said.

Gaia's heart stopped. "Yes, Masister?" She kept her voice low.

Sephie frowned at her and Gaia waited anxiously. She steeled herself to keep her gaze steady on the older doctor, and when Sephie silently angled her face to her left, Gaia resisted the urge to mirror her motion.

Sephie's eyebrows lifted, she winced briefly, and then she made a clicking noise in the back of her throat. "I had a helpful assistant once," she said lightly. Then her voice changed. "Make yourself useful, boy," Sephie said as she poured. "Pass these around. And then you should go."

Gaia's heart slammed on again in double time. Sephie must recognize her, but she wasn't initiating any alarm. Why not? Gaia suddenly remembered what Cotty had once said about Sephie: she did whatever was easiest. But what would be easiest for Sephie now, to raise the alarm against Gaia, or to wait and see what evolved? Gaia didn't know. She fingered the small white cubes in her pocket, wondering how quickly they would dissolve in hot water and, more importantly, how quickly they would work.

"You heard her," Masister said sharply. "Don't stand there like an idiot. Are you deaf?"

"He probably wants some sunflower seeds," Julia said, giggling. "I know I do."

The bathroom door started to open. "Wait, Bonnie," Sephie said, rising from beside the fire. "Let me help you."

When Sephie reentered the bathroom, Gaia knew she

couldn't delay. Stepping near the fire, she picked up the first cup and surreptitiously dropped a white cube of powder inside. She handed this to Julia, and then repeated the maneuver for Masister Khol. As her mother reappeared, supported by Sephie, Gaia turned her back to the camera and dropped the third cube into the last cup of tea.

Gaia's mother looked more exhausted than ever, and she sat on the edge of the nearest bed, her hands gripping the edge of the mattress as if to keep her balance. Gaia came forward hesitantly, holding Sephie's teacup. When her mother reached for it, Gaia froze, withholding the cup until her mother looked up, questioning.

"No, Bonnie," Sephie said, taking the cup from Gaia's tight, trembling fingers. "The last thing you need right now is a diuretic."

Gaia almost laughed with relief.

Her mother was watching Gaia in a puzzled manner. "Do I know you?" she asked her daughter.

Gaia clicked her jaw shut, shaking her head.

Sephie laughed. "You think you know every child in the Enclave just because you saw a few of them for an hour when they were born," she said. Then she turned to Gaia. "You've had your visit with our pregnant celebrity. Now, I told you to go."

Gaia understood: Sephie was allowing her a harmless glimpse of her mother, and nothing more. Gaia looked in alarm at Masister Khol, but she was calmly sipping her tea as if she had no interest in Gaia whatsoever. Despair shot through her, and she looked desperately at her mother. Her mother's head was hanging wearily.

Gaia's mind raced. "If she can't have tea, should I get her some water, then?" Gaia asked, keeping her voice low.

Sephie looked up, her eyes narrowing cautiously. Then, as if making a decision, she nodded. "Here's gallantry," she said, and pointed to a cup on the shelf. "Fetch her some."

While Gaia took the cup into the bathroom to get water from the tap, she tried to think how else to delay her departure. The women were talking of news outside the tower. Julia's voice was light, with occasional laughter, and Masister Khol's tones were lower and steadier. Water rushed into the little metal cup. If she could find a way to get her mother out while the women continued acting normally, she might buy time before anyone behind the security camera realized anything was wrong.

"Pass me that blanket, will you, Joyce?" Sephie said to Masister Khol. "She's tired again. I think what she really needs is more iron, by the way. Not to mention a little sunshine. Bed rest doesn't mean she has to lie indoors every second."

"Do you want to tell the Protectorat or shall I?" Masister Khol asked.

Gaia came through the bathroom doorway with the cup of water.

"If he came up here, I'd tell him myself," Sephie said. "Since he doesn't, it'll have to be you." She dropped the blanket around Bonnie's shoulders, and with a pale hand, Bonnie drew it closer across her chest.

"I'm a little sleepy myself," Julia said, with a yawn and a stretch. "What I wouldn't give to walk around the market for a bit."

"Why don't you take another snooze?" Masister Khol said dryly.

Julia appeared to miss the sarcasm. "No, no," Julia said, laying her head on her white pillow. "I want to help Sephie." She tucked her feet up onto the bed and her face went slack with sleep.

"Well, of all the lazy nerve," said Masister Khol. A moment

later, her head tilted back to rest against the back of her chair. Gaia watched in grim astonishment as her eyes began to close. Her teacup tipped, spilling liquid into her lap, but Masister Khol was so deeply asleep she didn't notice.

"You viper," Sephie said softly to Gaia. "I kept up your cover. I let you have your little visit."

Gaia watched Sephie stumble toward her rocking chair and grip the armrest as she sat heavily. She lifted her heavy-lidded eyes to Gaia.

"Take her, then," Sephie said. "At least they can't blame me."

She was asleep.

Chapter 23

Maya

"**W**HAT'S HAPPENING?" Gaia's mother asked, a new alertness in her eyes.

Her hands flying, Gaia bunched the extra blanket and a pillow into a heap on the bed and threw another blanket over them to fake a sleeping form.

"Quickly, mother," Gaia said, gripping her arm firmly and guiding her upward. "We have no time at all."

"Gaia?" her mother asked, her voice lifting in wonder.

"Please," Gaia whispered urgently, wrapping an arm around her waist and practically carrying her toward the door. "We have to get out. Now. Before they see."

"Oh, Gaia!" her mother said breathlessly. "I can't believe it's you!"

Gaia wrenched open the handle, pulled her mother out to the landing, and shut the door. The maneuver from bed to landing had taken no more than six seconds, and if anyone in surveillance had happened to look away during that instant, they might not see that anything was wrong with the people in the tower cell—not until they looked closely at the women and saw they weren't talking, but sleeping.

"Oh, Mom," she said, hugging her as hard as she dared. She inhaled the scent of exhaustion and desolation that lingered on her mother's skin, while her mother's bony, swollen body shivered under the thin fabric of her blue dress.

"I can't believe it's you," her mother said again. Her narrow arms pressed around her daughter, trembling. Then she peered into her face, gazing in wonder. She touched Gaia's cheek. "What happened to your face?"

"Be careful. It's a mask. Quickly, we have to leave." She drew her mother's body alongside her own and held her firmly around the waist as they started down the steps.

"I'm so weak," her mother whispered. "I'm sorry."

"It's okay," Gaia said, her mind racing. She couldn't take her mother out the door she'd come in with Masister Khol because the guards would immediately be suspicious. But she had to get to Leon or Mace Jackson somehow. Her mother stumbled, and when Gaia caught her, she groaned.

"Are you all right?" Gaia asked.

"I've had some spotting," her mother said. "I've been on bed rest. This is the most exercise I've had in I don't know how long."

"How did this happen?" Gaia asked, helping her down another step.

Her mother gave a faint laugh. "In the usual way. A lifetime ago."

"But, I mean, it's Dad's, right?" Gaia asked. She had to ask. "Why didn't you tell me you were pregnant?"

As they approached an oblong window, her mother gripped the sill and the sunlight dropped on her pale hand, giving it a translucent blue color as she braced herself against the darker stone. Gaia couldn't believe how small and fragile her mother looked.

"I'd had so many miscarriages," her mother said, her voice

thin. "I didn't hardly dare to hope myself. But we were about to tell you. Your father was so excited. It feels like a lifetime ago now. And then, when we were arrested, the baby saved my life. Your father—"

A clattering noise rose from below. Gaia clutched protectively at her mother and could feel her trembling. Her mother's arm was slung around Gaia's neck, and she silently pressed her face against Gaia's right cheek.

A peal of laughter echoed up the tower staircase. "I can't believe you!" came a merry, girlish voice. "What kind of a present is that?"

There was the sound of a scuffle, and then a man's quiet laughter, and then a sharp, jingling noise.

"I mean it!" the young woman said again playfully.

There was an indecipherable grumble, and then a low voice: "You'll be the death of me, Rita. I swear."

"Shhh!" Rita said. And then, "Okay. Now."

There was a shuffling sound of footsteps, and then a thud of a door closing, and then silence. Gaia was certain she'd recognized the voice of the pretty girl Rita who had tried to warn her not to get involved with the executed couple. Her mother bent over suddenly and gasped.

"Oh, no," she groaned.

"What is it?" Gaia whispered.

Her mother turned beseeching eyes on her. "Leave me, Gaia. Leave me here. Hurry down and you can escape." She slid her pale, blue-veined hand under the curve of her belly.

"No," Gaia protested, resisting panic. Her mother couldn't be going into premature labor, not here, not now. She held her mother more closely than ever. "I'm not leaving you. We'll find a way."

Her mother came down a few more steps with her, then a half dozen more, and then Gaia felt her sag. Sweat broke out on

Gaia's forehead under the mask, loosening it. *What am I going to do?* she wondered desperately. Her mother slowly sat on one of the steps, lowering her head into her hands and holding very still, as if concentrating in pain.

Gaia couldn't just deliver her mother's baby there on the steps. It could take hours, and soldiers would be coming as soon as one of the women in the tower above recovered enough to raise an alarm.

"Should I take you back up to Sephie?" Gaia asked. "Mom?"

Her mother shook her head. It was hardly a definitive answer, and Gaia was torn, trying to think what would be best for her mother.

"Are you sure?"

"I'm not going back," her mother said.

Below, Gaia could see the door that Rita and her boyfriend must have come through. It could only lead into the Bastion, to one of the upper floors, she guessed, since it was the first door they'd come to. It would lead them farther from freedom, but Gaia didn't see any other choice.

She hurried down the steps to touch the latch, and it lifted easily. She peeked out the door and saw it led to a hallway much like the kind she'd traversed on her way to the yellow room. The peaceful yellow walls and runner carpet looked deceptively welcoming.

"Come with me, Mom," Gaia whispered, beckoning.

"Where are we going?"

"We have to find a place to hide you," Gaia said, hoping she sounded more confident than she felt. "Are you okay?"

She nodded. "For now." She held one hand to her stomach, and Gaia reached for the other.

Gaia checked down the hallway once more and looked along the ceiling for camera lenses, seeing none. She had no idea how to find her way out, but she knew generally where the courtyard

283

and the school she'd escaped through before must be, and she headed in that direction, north through the building. Her mother couldn't go far. When she came to a corner, she looked again for camera lenses and saw none. Either Mabrother Iris didn't see a need for surveillance in the secure, upper hallways of the Bastion, or the Bastion's inhabitants insisted on their right to privacy.

They passed several doors, hearing nothing behind them, and then the hallway opened onto a long, covered balcony.

"Let me rest," her mother said, leaning over.

Gaia could see a courtyard three stories below. At Gaia's level, arched openings and pillars led all around the upper perimeter of the courtyard in one continuous balcony. Voices carried upward, and Gaia ducked down behind the balustrade, bringing her mother with her so they would be out of sight.

"Where are we?" Bonnie asked.

"Near the school," Gaia said. "If we can cross around to the opposite side of the balcony, we'll be above the school, and there might be another way down."

A whistle blasted and loud voices came from below.

"Attention! We have an escaping prisoner. Let no one in or out of the Bastion. All guards to your stations! Immediately!" The whistle blew again.

Gaia heard a flurry of footsteps along the hallway behind them, and when she turned, she found Rita and a young man skidding to a stop before them. Her red, sleeveless dress was askew, and the buttons of his brown shirt were half undone.

"Oh, no," Gaia whispered, sheltering her mother behind her where they crouched.

Rita's honey-colored hair was tumbled around her face, her expression grim. The young man hurriedly stepped forward, shielding Rita behind him.

"It's them!" the man cried.

Beside Gaia, her mother moaned quietly again, and Gaia lifted pleading eyes to Rita. The man leaned toward the balcony, clearly intending to yell an alarm, but Rita clutched his arm.

"Not a word, Sid," she said in a sharp low voice. "If you call down, they'll find you and me together. Is that what you want?"

Sid backed away from the balcony, his expression openly confused and angry. "But, Rita—!" he began.

"Be quiet," she snapped. Rita came forward and crouched beside Gaia. Gaia felt her frowning, penetrating gaze. "It's you," Rita said in a flat tone. "Why am I not surprised? Are you insane?" She scowled at Gaia's mother, and then back at Gaia. "What are you doing with her?"

"She's my mother," Gaia said.

Rita's almond eyes widened in shock, and then she glanced quickly at her boyfriend. "Give me a hand," she said. "Quickly."

Sid hesitated another moment with his powerful arms crossed, and then he angrily moved behind Gaia's mother. "You're going to get us both killed," he whispered to Rita.

Rita was leaning over. "No, *you* are, moron," Rita said to Sid. "Hey. She's in bad shape, isn't she?"

Gaia guided her mother up with Sid's help, and then pulled her mother's arm around her neck and braced her against her hip.

"Come on," Rita said.

But Gaia's mother let out another moan and her knees buckled. Sid swore and scooped her up into his arms.

"Where to, genius?" he demanded.

Rita turned back the way they'd come and hurried them along a narrow hallway, then up another staircase. They were going farther from the only way Gaia knew out of the Bastion. Yet she had no other choice than to trust Rita, and a few moments

285

later, Rita pushed open the door of a small room. Gaia, and Sid with his burden, followed her closely inside.

As Gaia shut the door, Sid knelt on the floor and gently laid Gaia's mother on the wood where she sagged, her face contorted in pain. Gaia was dimly aware that they'd entered a long, narrow room with shelves along the walls. She crouched beside her mother, taking her hands. "It's okay, Mom," Gaia said.

She glanced up at Rita, who was passing her a pile of white towels and sheets. "Here," Rita said. "We have to go. I'm sorry, but this is the best I can do. I have to get Sid out of here somehow. Sid," she said to him. "We're going past the library, to the school. You're going to be okay."

They heard more shouting noises and loud footsteps passing in the hall. Gaia saw Sid's face go chalky with fear, and she was certain hers was the same. Rita had her hand on the doorknob, waiting. As she tucked a strand of her blond hair behind her ear, Rita looked utterly unflappable.

"If you make it until dark," Rita said, frowning, "I might be able to come back. But don't count on it."

"Thank you," Gaia said. It was still hard to breathe normally. "You saved our lives." She slid several towels under her mother's head for a pillow and glanced up again at Rita.

"I heard what you did for that convict's baby," Rita said. "That was the bravest thing."

"What?" Sid said, obviously confused.

But as Gaia understood, she was filled with gratitude. "I just had to," she said.

Rita gave a determined nod, and her eyes flashed once more in Bonnie's direction. "Take care of her."

"What baby?" Sid insisted. "How do you know this guy?"

Gaia realized he had not yet recognized who she was.

Rita took Sid's arm. "Are you ready, my sweet troglodyte?"

"You're the one slowing us down," Sid said.

Gaia watched them hesitate one more instant by the door, and then Rita opened it and they were gone.

As Gaia focused again on her mother, she saw that her eyes were closed. Her face was relaxed in the relief and exhaustion that came between contractions. It was frightening how quickly her contractions had started up, and how intense they were. Gaia knew, since her mother had had three children, that this fourth child could arrive more quickly and with less pain than the earlier ones, but she was also alarmed. She had no assis-tance and no tools to use during the delivery.

"It's okay, Mom," Gaia said softly, when her mother moaned again.

"Heaven help us," her mother said. "What have we come to?"

Gaia glanced more carefully around the room to see what there might be to use, and mentally thanked Rita again for her quick thinking. They were in a kind of laundry room or giant linen closet, with rows of shelves where towels, sheets, and blankets were neatly folded. At the end of the room, two large, white cloth bins stood on rollers, and from the way their sides bulged, Gaia guessed they were full of dirty linens. At the end of the narrow room, a tall, thin window let in enough sunlight for Gaia to see easily. A look at the door showed her there was no bolt. Anyone could come in at any minute to discover them.

Gaia took a quick look at her mother's closed eyes and hurried to the end of the room, near the window. She rolled aside the two bins and quickly layered blankets and sheets into a pad against the wall. Here, with the bins arranged to block the view, they would be shielded from a cursory glance into the room.

"Mom," Gaia said, and her mother opened her eyes. "Can you move with me, down there?" She pointed.

Her mother nodded and held up a hand. Gaia gripped tightly, and helped her mother to a hunched, standing position. Carefully, moving slowly, they passed the shelves, and her mother sank onto the makeshift mattress. Gaia bunched fresh towels under her head, and collected the others from where they'd first come in. With the bins arranged at Gaia's back and the window above her mother, Gaia had the sense of being in a sort of laundry nest. She pulled off her jacket so the extra cloak and the rope fell out of her shirt. When she tossed off her hat, she felt a piece of the mask along her forehead break free with the brim.

"There you are," her mother said gently with a crooked smile.

"I'm sorry, Mom," Gaia said. Her throat tightened. "I didn't know you were pregnant when I came for you. You would have been safer if I'd left you with Sephie. Should I go back for her?" She remembered Sephie was drugged into sleep. "Or find another doctor?"

Her mother shook her head and touched a finger to Gaia's cheek. "I want to be with you," she said. "Couldn't be in better hands."

Gaia let out a choked laugh. "How early are you?"

"I'm around thirty-five weeks. It'll be a small one. But it's strong." Her mother caught her breath, and Gaia put her hands on the bulge under her mother's dress, feeling the contraction tighten her belly. When it eased, Gaia gently lifted her mother's gown out of the way. Blood was seeping out of her mother, oozing onto the white towels. Gaia's heart froze, and then started up again in alarm.

"Don't worry, Mom," Gaia whispered. "I'm going to see how dilated you are, okay?"

She nodded, and Gaia examined her, feeling the hard knob of the baby's head. She forced herself to smile at her mom, and wiped her hands on a clean towel. Her mother had another contraction, visibly gritting her teeth with the strain. She stopped, panting.

"I'm almost there, aren't I?"

Gaia grabbed her hand, holding hard. "Yes," she said.

Her mother's face was an awful, pale color. The contractions came steadily then, one wave after another. Gaia helped as best as she could, waiting for the first moment her mother would cry out and knowing the noise would bring the guards. With a shaking hand, her mother reached for one of the towels, and before the next contraction, she put it between her teeth. When next the pain came, she bit into the towel, and at that moment, her baby's head slipped out. Gaia quietly encouraged her, and with one more contraction, the rest of the body slid out.

Gaia's mother collapsed backward in relief, turning her colorless face toward the light of the window. Gaia was concerned by the blue, mottled color of the baby, but awed by its astonishingly small, perfect shape. She swiped a finger through its mouth and rapped it smartly on its back. Nothing. Laying it on a clean towel, she compressed its chest several times, then covered its tiny mouth and nose with her mouth and breathed lightly. The baby jerked. Gaia breathed again and gave the baby one more smack, and then it cried, a tiny, mewing, peevish cry. Relief washed through Gaia, and her mother turned her face to see.

The baby's color began to change with each more assertive cry.

"Oh, Gaia," Bonnie said, reaching. "Let me have him."

"She's a girl," Gaia said, and passed her over.

Gaia's hands were trembling. She watched the loving, tender way her mother drew the little baby close to her face, and she smiled at the abrupt silence when the baby stopped crying and instead made a soft, smacking noise with her tiny lips. This was one of the smallest babies Gaia had delivered, and like other early ones, it was also covered with a cream-colored substance. Beneath, her skin was deepening to a healthy red.

Gaia refocused her attention on her mother, and saw there was something terribly wrong with the way blood continued to pulse slowly out of her. Gaia cleaned up the afterbirth and massaged her mother's abdomen, guiding the womb to contract. She did everything she knew to make it stop, but still the blood was coming, more than it should.

"Mom," she said. "You're still bleeding. What am I supposed to do?"

"Do you have any shepherd's purse?"

Gaia shook her head. "I don't have anything here. Nothing at all."

Her mother winced, and seemed to be holding her breath. She licked her lips and turned her gaze to Gaia, who couldn't bear it when her mother tried to smile.

"Come on, Mom. What else can I do?"

"It's all right, Gaia," her mother said.

But it wasn't all right. Gaia could see that. She massaged her mother's abdomen again, harder, and watched her mother's face crumple in pain. Gaia's guilt was an exquisite, piercing blade as she realized this was all her fault; if she hadn't tried to rescue her mother, if she'd left her in the tower, her mother would most likely be safely resting right now instead of hemorrhaging her lifeblood into the white towels.

"Let me go get you some help," Gaia said.

"No. Don't leave me."

"But this is all my fault. At least in the tower you were safe."

"You couldn't be more wrong. Now take care of this baby."

Gaia wiped back a tear with her knuckles and ripped off a narrow band of linen to tie off the baby's umbilical cord.

Her hands were shaking, clumsy, but her mother only smiled at her.

"Sorry, Mom."

"You're doing a fine job," her mother murmured. "Pack a fresh towel against me, there, and let me rest."

Gaia rolled a clean, soft towel between her mother's legs and tried to make her comfortable. She had practically forgotten where they were, or that anyone was looking for them, until she heard a sharp clatter and a noise in the hallway.

This is it, she thought. And she was glad. Someone would help them now. Someone would save her mother. She leaned her face down beside her mother's, shielding her weary body with her arm, and curving her hand over her mother's where she held the newborn. In this position, she heard the door open and knew someone was looking into the room. Inches away, her mother's eyes flashed to meet hers and held, keeping her silent.

There was a disgruntled noise. "Man," somebody said. "They better catch up on this laundry."

"Is it empty?" came another voice.

The first voice was receding. "It stinks. Close the door."

As the door clicked closed, Gaia blinked at her mother, amazed.

"Idiots," her mother murmured, smiling.

"Let me get them," Gaia said softly, pressing her mother's hand. "They can bring a doctor."

"No, Gaia. I don't want anybody else."

Gaia wrapped her fingers in the sleeve of her mother's robe. "Please, Mom," she whispered.

Her mother exhaled heavily and closed her eyes, still smiling. "I want you to name her Maya."

Gaia bit back a sob and tipped her forehead against her mother's shoulder. "That's a pretty name," she said, trying to sound calm. "Why Maya?"

"It means *dream*. She's my dream, all the things I never thought I'd see."

"Oh, Mom," Gaia said, her heart breaking with grief.

"Besides," her mother said with a little laugh. "It rhymes with Gaia. Your dad would like that."

Gaia felt her mom's fingers gently patting her hair, soothing. "Come, Gaia. You've got to be strong."

Gaia sniffed and straightened up. Her mother's complexion had become impossibly wan, but her eyes were as vibrant as ever, even luminous in the diffused afternoon light of the little space. Gaia folded the towel more securely around little Maya's sleeping form. The skin of her mother's arm was strangely clammy and cool.

"Take care of her for me," her mother said. "Don't let anything hurt her."

Alarm shot along Gaia's nerves. "What do you mean?"

Her mother lifted a hand, and Gaia felt her cool fingertips against the skin of her left cheek. Somewhere during the birth, the rest of Gaia's mask had fallen away, and now her scar felt newly sensitive.

"I'm sorry about your face," her mother said.

Gaia felt a lump form in her throat and couldn't speak, but she closed her lips and shook her head, looking away.

"No," her mother said. "Look at me, Gaia. We thought it would save you. We never guessed how much you would suffer, in so many different ways. It was selfish, I know, but your father and I, after losing Arthur and Odin, we wanted so badly to keep you. The closer we came to the day we might lose you, the more we just couldn't take the chance, and it was the only way. Will you ever forgive us?"

Gaia swallowed thickly while loss and anguish warred in her heart.

"You hurt me on purpose?" she asked.

"Oh, darling. I'm so sorry. So very sorry."

Gaia struggled to grasp, in a moment, all that might have been different if she'd never been scarred, if she'd had a chance to be advanced, if she'd grown up without her parents. And it was inconceivable to imagine life without her parents' daily love.

"It's okay. You did the right thing. Just what I would have wanted," she said. "Don't leave me, Mom."

Her mother's face contorted in a moment of pain, and then her features eased again. She looked almost peaceful. "I want to be with your father," she said softly. "And now you've come to take care of Maya. Keep her safe for me. Promise."

"Mom, please," Gaia pleaded. "You can't. Wait, I found Odin here in the Bastion. He's tall and blond and a soldier. Sergeant Bartlett. Did you ever see him? I discovered who he was just a few days ago, and he got away. He left the Enclave, and he hasn't been seen again. We need you. All of us do."

But her mother patted her hand. "Are you sure?"

"He has Dad's twitchy fingers. He likes to sing."

Her mother let out a faint laugh. "If only I could have seen him. That's all I wanted, to just see him once and know he was all right. They kept promising, if I behaved, I could see my boys, but they never let me." She stopped to blink sleepily. "So many mistakes we made."

Gaia dropped her head down upon her mother's chest, hugging her frail body tightly. "No, Mom. Please."

She could feel her mother's gentle hand on her hair, patting smoothly. "Such a good girl," her mother murmured. "So beautiful."

Gaia let out a sob, squeezing her eyes shut. This could not be happening. Her mother's chest went very still, and Gaia lifted her eyes to gaze at her ashen, quiet face. A pulse throbbed in her neck, and she took a last, deep breath. Gaia watched her, waiting, hoping for another breath that never came. She glanced down at her mother's legs, and then quickly away. Blood had saturated the towel and the skirt of her dress. Gaia searched her mother's face again, willing her to breathe, but her gaze was fixed on the window above, unseeing, and when the baby wiggled a tiny hand against her mother's cheek, she could no longer respond. The pale skin of her neck was even, pulseless.

"No," Gaia whispered, closing her eyes again. "What was I supposed to do?" she said, her voice ragged with pain. There must have been some way to save her mother, something different she might have done. "I need you, Mom," she croaked, smoothing her face and hair. "Please." Her fingers trembled, and her heart overflowed with grief. She leaned back against the wall and hugged her arms around herself, while her mother's still body slowly began to give up its warmth.

Chapter 24
A Perfectly Circular Pool

MORE THAN ANYTHING ELSE, Gaia longed to sink her head down beside her mother's and simply stay there, giving up the fight. But when her bleary gaze fell upon her infant sister, she knew the darkness would have to wait. She couldn't bear to look at her mother's face, or the tender, worn skin of her knuckles. She could not stay there, beside her mother's body, for long. The guards might come back, or even the people who regularly took care of the laundry might come to deal with the bins of dirty sheets and towels. Most pressing of all, the baby would soon need sustenance, or she, too, would die.

Gaia shifted carefully away from her mother, and leaned over to gently lift the baby from her mother's lifeless arms.

"Hey, little sister," she whispered. Her mother had asked Gaia to take care of her, and she would. No matter what it took.

Maya was tiny in her hands, a wobbly parcel with solid weight but no coordination. Gaia wiped her as clean as she could and wrapped her securely in a clean white towel. She rested her on a pile of sheets, and then she looked down at her blood-stained trousers and jacket. No one would take her for a baker's apprentice in these anymore, but she had Pearl's cloak. She dropped the jacket in a laundry bin, followed by the last bits of mask from her face and the rope she'd never found a use for. She kept on the blue shirt, rolling up the cuffs to hide other smears of blood.

Quickly, she rolled up the legs of her trousers to the knees, and then she took one of the clean sheets and folded it in half. Ripping part of the seam for a tie, she wrapped the fabric around her waist to fashion a skirt and tied it tightly. It looked awful, but she could do nothing more, and at least it gave her the semblance of a skirt beneath Pearl's deep blue cloak. She picked up her sister and cradled her close.

Stepping to the window, she peered past the ghostly silhouette of her reflection to try to get her bearings. Clouds had moved in to obscure the afternoon sun. She gazed down at the solar panels on the roofs, seeing from their south-facing angles that she must be on the west side of the Bastion, far from the southeast tower and the school. She had no clear idea how to get out, or what to do once she did, but with a sort of numb urgency, she knew she had to try.

Gaia was keenly aware of her mother's body lying in a heap in the corner of the linen room, unnaturally still. When she was ready with the baby in her arms, she looked for a last time at her mother, and then bent down to cover her face with a clean towel. She couldn't say good-bye; the words lodged in her throat, but she knew this was the last time she'd ever be with her mother, and for a moment she slouched against the wall, overcome with grief. An invisible weight pressed in upon her from all sides, and she closed her eyes, unsuccessfully, against the tears.

I'll try to be brave. She hugged her sister close and took in a deep, shuddering breath.

Then she turned away and pushed past the laundry bins to

the door. She blinked hard, trying to concentrate and listen for noise outside the door. When she heard none, she pulled it open an inch, looking down the hallway. *How can I do this?* she wondered hopelessly. *You must,* came her own reply. She tiptoed stealthily to the end of the hall, fearing any second that another group of guards would come around the corner. And then she realized she was making a mistake: cowering was the last thing she should do if she hoped to escape detection. She must act like Masister Khol who strode with firm, unapologetic authority.

Drawing a deep breath, Gaia twitched the hood of her cloak forward and started down the hall at a steady clip. At the next staircase, she headed down, and when she'd passed several landings she arrived suddenly at a bright, sunny solarium with a high, arching, glass ceiling. It took her only an instant to recognize the French doors and realize that on the other side of them lay the foyer of the Bastion, where the grand double-staircase descended toward the main doors.

White, wooden arches framed the solarium, while the lush foliage of ferns and the gurgle of running water created an oasis of peace and rich beauty. The loveliness, contrasted with the horror of losing her mother, was almost more than she could bear. Gaia paused in an open archway, breathing in the fragrant, humid air and marveling sorrowfully that such a place could exist. Green leaves of every shape, colorful corollas, and tempting fruits spread in a vast array around her. *Is this,* she wondered, *what the earth once was like?* She was drawn irresistibly forward toward the sound of water and found, in the center of the solarium, a perfectly circular pool. Its serene surface reflected the undersides of the bordering ferns and a touch of sky. She'd never seen water used simply for beauty before, and it stirred a mix of resentment and awe inside her. She fingered a pale yellow bloom, dazzled by its fragile petals, and her

297

gaze lifted to where a palm tree soared against the arching, glass-paned ceiling. The water and energy needed to maintain this space defied her imagination.

A bird chirped, and then voices approached from her left. Gaia backtracked quickly. She skirted to the right down the nearest hallway and walked directly into the entrance foyer of the Bastion.

The familiar white and black tiles expanded before her feet like a minefield, where any single step could result in her detection. She teetered in one last, indecisive moment of fear, and then she decided to walk directly across it, in the direction of the school. She hadn't taken four steps before she heard voices coming down the stairs, and she glanced up to her left to see the family of the Protectorat descending, all dressed in impeccable white: the blond, teenage girl Gaia had seen once before, the older brother, Genevieve trailing a light finger on the banister, and beside her, the Protectorat himself. Gaia was halfway across the white tiles, aiming for an open doorway on the other side of the foyer, hoping desperately that no one would recognize her, when the front door on her right was thrown open and two guards rushed in with a loud shout. They threw a man to the floor before them so that he landed roughly on his knees and one shoulder. Gaia gasped, pressing back tightly to a pillar.

The girl on the stairs shrieked in alarm, and the Protectorat hurried down ahead of his family.

"What do you think you're doing?" the Protectorat roared.

"Mabrother," the guard said firmly, in a loud voice. "We found this man trying to break into the Bastion." He jerked off the man's black hat.

Gaia's gaze shot to the figure on the floor, the young man in rough blue clothing who even now was straightening upward, his hair a shock of dark brown and his blue eyes blazing.

Despite having his hands tied behind his back, Leon Grey regained his balance and pushed himself up to his feet.

Genevieve gasped and Gaia instinctively took a step forward. Leon's eyes flashed in Gaia's direction, taking in her clothes and the baby, and then with grim fury he faced his father.

"Gaia," Leon said. "I'd like you to meet my mother, Genevieve Quarry. This is my sister, Evelyn, and my brother, Rafael." His voice ground to an ironic undertone. "The Protectorat you already know."

He didn't call him his father. The Protectorat was a tall, distinguished man whose even features were accented by a black mustache. His salt-and-pepper hair was closely trimmed, and his white, tailored suit delineated a strong physique. Gaia had seen his image at the Tvaltar, projected on a screen twenty times larger than life, but he was far more commanding in person. Cool, calculating power emanated from him, as if he could charge the air particles around him even when he stood motionless. Every instinct in Gaia told her to shrink away, to run and hide, but she took one step forward and forced herself to stand straight.

"How do you do?" Her voice came out as little more than a whisper.

The man ignored her.

"Leon," Genevieve said, coming down the last few steps. Her voice was low with bewildered compassion. "What's happened to you?"

"Hello, Mother," Leon said evenly. His gaze never left the Protectorat.

"Stay back from him, Genevieve," the Protectorat said.

She paused beside the newel post, and her daughter joined her. To Gaia's left, the doorkeeper silently appeared with Mabrother Iris, closing the door behind him.

"Take the infant to the Nursery, Winston," the Protectorat said quietly. "Then take the other two downstairs and shoot them."

Leon's face drained of color, and Gaia hurried across the tiles to stand beside him.

"No, Miles. You can't," Genevieve said quickly, grabbing the Protectorat's arm.

Winston was coming closer, and Gaia pressed nearer to Leon, guarding the baby in her arms.

"She's right, father," Rafael said. "He's the one person you can't eliminate. It would be political suicide."

Gaia glared at Leon's brother. It was no surprise that he bore no physical similarity to Leon. His even features and carefully combed, light brown hair were familiar to her from the Tvaltar specials, but there was something in his intense expression that drew her attention. Perhaps it was in his bearing, or his innate sense of entitlement, but in some elusive way, the younger brother resembled Leon.

"I appreciate your concern, both of you," the Protectorat said dryly. "But I'll take my chances."

"Miles, think," Genevieve urged him. "He's more important than ever right now—your own advanced son from outside the wall. He even has the freckles. He's the future. And Gaia Stone is practically a hero. Look at her!"

"Dad, please! You can't kill them!" Evelyn said.

The Protectorat's mouth closed in a grim line, and his flat eyes yielded nothing. Winston was hovering just behind Gaia, and when he put a hand on her arm, she jerked forward.

"You're despicable," Gaia said to the Protectorat, a catch in her voice. "A man who would kill his own son. How can you call yourself the Protectorat?"

The Protectorat barely looked at Gaia before turning to his wife. "He's not mine. He's never been mine. I tried to reason with him four days ago, and what did he do? He ran. He's a catastrophe waiting to happen," he said. "Not to mention that he's acquired a mouthy, low-born slattern from outside the wall."

Leon angled toward Genevieve and spoke softly. "How can you bear to stay with him, Mother?" he asked.

With two steps forward, the Protectorat backhanded his fist against Leon's jaw. Leon's face whipped to the side and he stumbled back.

"You'll be silent," the Protectorat said.

Gaia saw Genevieve's complexion whiten, and Leon's sister gasped, covering her mouth. A trickle of blood came from the corner of his lip, but Leon was straightening again with slow deliberation.

"Enough of this nonsense. Who is the baby?" the Protectorat demanded.

Mabrother Iris stepped forward and nervously adjusted his glasses.

"It's Bonnie Stone's child," Mabrother Iris said. "I was just coming to tell you we've located the body of the prisoner in the third-floor laundry room. The infant, as you know, has as good a chance as any from Western Sector Three to have the suppressor gene. Just as the girl here does." Mabrother Iris turned to Gaia. "Is it a boy or a girl?"

"It's mine, you bastard," Gaia said. "You're not taking it."

The Protectorat turned again to Winston. "The girl was raised outside. You can see what she's like. Dispose of her already."

"But, Father. Think of the gene pool," said Rafael, coming to stand near his father. "You have to think of her genes."

To Gaia's alarm, the Protectorat suddenly grabbed her chin, jerking her so that she stumbled forward, her face clearly exposed for inspection.

301

"Would you have this?" the Protectorat hissed at his son.

Rafael's gaze narrowed in a slow inspection while she stared defiantly back. Rafael's gaze faltered, shot briefly toward Leon, and then down. His answer was obvious: no.

And in spite of everything, in the face of all the other more important dangers that threatened her, it still stung that someone, some boy, found her ugly. Gaia burned with sudden hate for all of them.

The Protectorat saw. He smiled slightly.

"I thought not," said the Protectorat, releasing her with a flick. He turned back toward his family. "I can't thrust her on any family I know, no matter what her genes are. She's a freak, not a hero. I'd rather make a hero out of Myrna Silk."

Leon had been standing tensely throughout this exchange. "I'd take Gaia," Leon said, his low voice resonating in the space.

Gaia caught her breath and turned to find him watching her with his steady, intrepid gaze. She realized he had hardly spoken a word in the Protectorat's presence, as if Leon despised him and distrusted him so completely that he wouldn't give his adoptive father the satisfaction of seeing Leon try to defend himself. But Leon was defending Gaia.

Leon's father laughed derisively. "Perfect," he said.

"He's right, Miles. Can't you see?" Genevieve said. "Think how it would appear if we took them in. He'd be reclaimed, totally submissive, and she'd be the hope of the Enclave. They might even have a child, one of the children you need, all under our guidance, and we, we'd be the heroes."

The Protectorat's face hardened. "You forget what he did," he said bitterly.

There was a silence during which the baby made a small, sucking noise in Gaia's arms and wiggled briefly. She instinctively drew her closer, shushing her.

"I haven't forgotten," Genevieve said quietly.

Gaia's gaze flew from one tense face to another. Genevieve's hands clenched to her chest, and a bit apart from her, Evelyn seemed lost inside herself. Rafael, also standing aloof, had his hands buried in his pockets. The Protectorat was a stone. Finally she turned to see Leon's jaw rigid, his vivid eyes bright with defiance. For a fleeting moment, Gaia felt the presence of the missing sister, an absence as palpable as if a live twin had just descended the staircase beside Evelyn, only to vanish.

A touch of color rode high along Leon's cheekbones. "For the last time," he said softly. "I never touched her."

The Protectorat spoke distinctly and slowly. "You're a pervert and a liar. As far as I'm concerned, you might as well be a murderer." He abruptly turned away. "Do it quietly, Winston," he said. "Now."

Gaia felt Winston and the guards closing in on them, and Evelyn gave a shriek of protest. But Genevieve and Rafael had run out of objections, and Gaia realized with a shock that Leon stood frozen, doing nothing to resist, as if something his father had said proved he deserved to be killed. What was this insidious power his father had over him?

"No!" Gaia said.

On impulse, she pulled Leon's arm in the one unexpected direction, bolting forward toward the stairs. The Protectorat grabbed for them, but Genevieve lost her balance and pitched forward into his arms. Gaia shoved hard into Rafael, and when he gripped her arm, she jerked down and free. Then she and Leon ran up the great, curving staircase, gaining crucial seconds on the guards who wove through the family to follow.

Gaia sprinted up the stairs two at a time. Near the top of the staircase, Leon overtook her. His hands were still tied behind him, but he led rapidly to the right.

"Quickly!" he shouted to Gaia, and she flew after him,

around another corner and bouncing off the wall of the hall-way with one hand for leverage. He slid to a stop before a small, half-size door. "Open it!" he commanded, and Gaia jammed her thumb into the latch and yanked. She followed him out in a blind crawl, closing the door behind her, and for an instant she feared they were trapped on a balcony. A second look showed her they were on the roof of the solarium, and a narrow iron catwalk led over the arch of the glass panes.

Leon stepped out ahead of her. "Follow closely," he said. "Take my hand."

She reached to where his hands were bound behind him and felt the firm clasp of his fingers. If he slipped or lost his bal-ance, he would have no way to catch himself before he crashed through the glass and fell fifty feet to the floor of the solarium below.

"I've got you," she said, and hitched the baby closer in her arm.

She forced her feet forward on the narrow rails. From be-hind came the noise of guards running in the hallway. She could only hope that they overlooked the little door. She and Leon reached the apex of the roof and started down the other side. Terror urged her to go more quickly than she would have dared, and she sucked in her breath as her balance teetered. Leon jerked her back in line and then wobbled himself while she clung to him.

"Forward," he said fiercely. "Now, Gaia. Don't pull me back."

They reached the far side of the roof with its corresponding little half door just as a voice called out behind her, and then a bullet blasted into the wall beside her face, scattering a spray of burst stucco.

"Hurry!" Leon urged her as she reached for the door handle, and then he was nudging her ahead of him. Gaia pulled him through, and then they were running again down another hallway, to another staircase, one that spiraled downward into increasing darkness. Windowless walls of stone echoed the clatter of their hurrying feet. She stumbled once and gasped, slashing her hand against the wall.

"Gaia!" he called, turning back for her. "Are you all right?"

"Yes," she said, feeling the sting along her palm, and dimly perceiving a dark line of blood. She repositioned the baby in the nook of that arm, so her good hand was free. The air was cool and smelled stale, of old sawdust and onions. "Where are we?" she asked.

"It's the wine cellar," he said. "It should have lights. Ah." They'd turned the last corner, and a motion detector flicked on a light bulb, revealing a long, low-ceilinged room with masonwork arches. As she hurried behind Leon, twisting between a dozen tables and shelves loaded with old pots and potatoes and turnips, Gaia glimpsed catacomb-like cavities filled with bottles and barrels. Leon gave a savage kick to a tall, wooden worktable that had a row of drawers.

"In here," he said to Gaia, over the rattling. "See if there's a knife."

Gaia glanced back at the doorway, hearing footsteps.

"Hurry!" Leon commanded.

She ripped open drawer after drawer, scattering their contents on the floor, until Leon tapped his boot onto a sharp, serrated knife. Gaia laid the baby on the table and grasped the knife. She slipped it into the rope that bound his wrists, and with three jagged tears, she had him free.

"Yes!" Leon hissed, curling his freed wrists in front of him.

Gaia snatched up the baby just as the first guard appeared. "Stop there!" he yelled.

"Here!" Leon said, grabbing her hand and ducking into one of the niches. A gunshot exploded, and another bullet hit the wall beside her. She hit the floor. Leon was yanking barrels away from the back wall, and she had a terrifying moment of suspecting he'd led them to a dead end, but then a deeper blackness opened in the wall and cool, dank air touched her face. Leon grabbed her shoulders and pushed, and she stumbled forward into nothingness, bracing her body to protect the baby as she fell against a stone wall.

She felt Leon fall against her, and then the door slammed shut behind them and they were pitched into the black of utter darkness.

Chapter 25
The Tunnels

GAIA'S EYES WIDENED against the darkness, searching for any glimmer of light, but the black was complete. She could hear Leon shoving something by the door, and then sharp banging noises and muffled voices came from the other side.

"Help me push," Leon said.

Completely blind, she put out her hand and felt him wedging something solid and hard against the door. She put her shoulder beside his and pushed as best she could with Maya in her other arm. The door shuddered but didn't move.

"It won't hold them long," Leon said.

The baby felt even smaller in the dark, and Gaia wrapped both arms around her. "Where are we?" she asked.

"It's the tunnel from the wine cellar," he said. "Remember the map?"

She heard a scratching noise, and then brilliant light burst from the tip of a match. Leon's frowning face appeared in the glow before he lifted the wick of a candle. A violent, battering noise came from the door, and Gaia jumped. She saw they'd wedged a bench into the woodwork of the door, but already it was buckling.

"They're following us!" Gaia said.

Leon grabbed a couple more candles from a box on a shelf, and then he was moving. He lifted the candle toward a narrow tunnel carved into the bedrock and shielded its flame with the cupped fingers of his other hand. "Hold on to me."

"Just go. I've got you."

She gripped the back of his shirt and flew after him. The one flame was enough to reveal the dark stone walls and ceiling of the tunnel, where, at intervals, wooden beams had been added to support the walls and ceiling. She once dared to look behind, where their forms cast a huge, frightening shadow back into the blackness. Once the tunnel forked, and Leon took the right tunnel. Then it forked again, and he went left.

There was a crashing, splintering noise behind them, and loud voices.

"Hold tight! Hurry!" Leon said, speeding faster so that the flame flickered wildly.

With each turn, the voices of the men fell farther behind.

"Quietly!" Leon said, slowing his pace hardly at all.

Gaia stumbled forward, gripping even more tightly on his blue shirt for balance.

He stopped. "All right?"

"Yes," she said, regaining her balance.

He started on again. As the distance between them and the guards increased, their voices diminished and then vanished entirely. Gaia could hear only her own labored breathing and her footsteps chasing Leon's over the uneven ground. In places, the tunnel had caved in, and they had to scramble over and around dusty rubble and stone. Maya gave a little whimper in her arms, and she saw Leon look back over his shoulder to her.

"All right?" he asked again.

"Are we lost yet?" she asked.

He let out a laugh. "Fiona and Evelyn and I used to play down

308

here," he said. His voice had an eerie, muffled quality against the close walls. "Remember how you asked about hide-and-seek? Here. Take my arm now beside me. It's a little wider here."

"It's just kind of creepy," she said. A feather touch traced her face, and she looked up to see the ceiling was lined with spider webs, ashy thin in the darkness. She looked back the way they had come. "I don't hear anybody," she said.

Leon nodded and lifted the candle in the still air. "They'll come," he said. "They'll just be slower because they'll have to figure out which way we turned at each fork." He started forward again, shielding his flame. "Hold tight."

"Where are we going?"

"There's a place ahead where we can decide. If it's not caved in," he said.

She sped with him several more minutes in silence until they came to a widening of the tunnel, an area where the path diverged again. When Leon finally stopped, she released her grip on his arm and peered around her. Several wooden wine crates were arranged in a rough square, enclosing a little area beside the nearest wall. At her feet, an old gray cushion had been used for a mouse's nest, laced with black feces and seed husks. Leon was lighting a couple of fresh candles from the stub of the old one and he passed the first to her.

"Here," he said.

She lifted her candle to cast light into the crates. Shreds of chewed paper lined the boxes, the remains of comic books and magazines, and mixed in with these she saw the distinctive shapes of a yo-yo and a handful of scattered jacks. One shelf higher up contained piles of papers. A map of the Enclave and Wharfton, coded with colored marks and stained with damp, was fixed to the wall. The cool, earth-scented air was chilly to her, uninviting, and it was hard for her to imagine children playing here. Normal children, at least.

"What is this place?"

"Command central. Our fort. Fiona and Evelyn and I used to hole up here, long ago." With the toe of his boot, he pushed at a tin container and marbles rolled inside. "Fiona was obsessed with figuring out who my true parents were and where they must live. Especially when I turned thirteen. That's when I had to decide whether to live outside the wall or not, but of course, no one ever does. It was a game with endless possibilities and no solution." His gaze shifted from her face to the map on the wall. "How ironic to be here now, when I finally know the answer. We only have a few minutes, but from here we have a choice which way to go. You okay?" he asked.

She nodded. "Good enough, considering."

"I take it you found your mother," he said.

Gaia tried to form the words to say she'd died giving birth, but they wouldn't come. Instead, she glanced down at the baby and saw her murky blue eyes were focused on the candle in a vacant, dreamy way.

"It was bad, wasn't it?" he said. With his sleeve, he wiped at the corner of his mouth, erasing the trace of blood from the Protectorat's blow.

"I couldn't save her," Gaia said, and then stopped before her loss could overwhelm her.

"I'm sorry, Gaia. I wish I could have done something."

He had tried, she realized. He'd been caught trying to get to her. Later, maybe, she could let herself think of her mother, but now she had to save her sister. "Maya will need food soon," she said. "Where do these tunnels go?

He lifted his candle to the left. "This way goes northeast toward where the wall meets a cliff. It ends in the cellar of a bar. If we could make it out of the bar, we'd be close to the wall, and we could run for it." He nodded toward the right.

"This way cuts a bit south and east, to the cemetery near Ernie's café where I saw you that day."

"Near the garden with the boulders?" she asked, stepping close to the old map on the wall. "The café's here on this little square?"

He nodded. "Yes. The tunnel collapsed in places, but we might be able to get through. When I was last down here, it was passable, but that was a few years ago."

"Who else knows where the tunnels lead out?"

"Half a dozen people, probably. My sister Evelyn, for sure. The Protectorat must know of the bar exit. This was an iron mine long before the Enclave was built here, but most of the tunnels have fallen in, and they're not safe."

Gaia had learned that the founders of the Enclave had drilled deep, deep below a defunct iron mine to reach a source for geothermic energy and steam, but she rarely thought about it. She tried to look down the tunnels for a clue as to which way to go. It sounded to her like they were trapped.

"Is there anywhere else?" she asked, examining the map.

"Only one other tunnel branches off this one," he said, "but it leads away from the wall, back toward the Bastion, to near the Nursery and the honey farm."

"The Nursery?" she said.

"Fiona found the way. She liked to go see the babies." He tapped a place on the map that was just north of the Bastion.

Gaia's gaze skimmed across the old colored markings on the map, mainly little X's scattered around Wharfton, and then she went still inside while her mind swirled. A terrifying, brilliant idea occurred to her. There was a faint, distant noise from behind, and she started in alarm.

"Leon," she said. "You wanted to find your birth parents when you were a kid, but what information did you have?"

"None really, besides my birthday. Fiona was trying to find families outside the wall who had siblings a year or two on either side of my birthday, but no kids my age. It was like trying to find where there were *not* pieces in a jigsaw puzzle, with none of them put together."

Gaia nodded. "That was because you didn't know the information about birth parents from outside the wall. You didn't have my mother's code."

"I know," he said. "Nobody had your mother's code. We searched through our family records, but there was no information about my birth parents. Sometimes I thought I could remember something from when I was an infant, but it made no sense."

"But there was information about who adopted you," she said.

The candlelight pooled around them, shifting across his features as he watched her curiously. "Of course. What are you getting at?"

She seized his arm. "All my mother wanted, all she really wanted, was to know my brothers were all right, but she couldn't find out who they were inside the wall. Oh, Leon." A thrill shot through her. "We have to get to the Nursery. I have to try to get the records of who adopted the advanced babies once they came inside the Enclave."

"Who they became inside?" he asked, with a flicker of puzzled concentration.

There was another noise behind them, closer this time.

"It's the reverse of my mother's code," she said urgently. "It's the information we need for the people outside the wall, people like my mom. And there will be formula for Maya there. We have to *go*!"

Leon took her arm and sped down the narrowest tunnel.

She gasped as hot wax spilled across her fingers and her candle went out.

"Sorry," he said.

"It's fine. Go ahead. I'll hold on again. Hurry."

She gripped his shirt again while he led the way with his candle. He veered left at another turn, and then, gradually, she had a sense that they were ascending. They passed the dried-out bones of a small animal, and then, just where the tunnel grew wider again, its condition became worse. Huge boulders tumbled in places where the ceiling had collapsed, leaving only narrow, jagged passages. Once Leon scrambled through first, leaving her in near darkness, and she passed the baby through a hole and climbed through after. Twice they stopped to listen for noises behind them, and all Gaia could hear was her rapid breath in the straining silence.

"What if they cut us off at the opening?" she asked.

"I don't know," Leon said.

In the dark, time lost meaning, and it seemed to her that she'd been scrambling forever over and around the twisted, ancient tunnels of the mine. Maya made tiny, plaintive noises, but rarely moved, and with only rare glimpses, Gaia had to trust that she was okay. Eventually, she thought she perceived a gray glow in front of her, and then they took another turn and she could see, far ahead and slightly higher, a reflection of gray light on the rock.

Leon blew out his candle, and they scrambled forward and upward. The tunnel narrowed again, turning, and the gray reflection expanded and grew brighter. The floor of the tunnel slanted upward as one great, uneven slab, with water trickling in its crevices. She had to crouch, bracing her free hand against the gritty stone wall, and Leon crawled ahead of her. They were in a natural cave, and when she turned around, she could see no evidence of the tunnel hidden behind. As they approached the light, the sound of water grew louder, into an echoing rush. The opening to the outside was hardly large enough to crawl through, and a tangle of roots and vines further concealed the opening. Through the roots, she saw a curtain of steady rain that poured loudly onto the hard ground, and beyond, barely discernable, the hunched, boxy outlines of hives.

"It's raining," she said in wonder.

It had been months since there had been any rain. Months! Rainwater transformed life outside the wall, like pure wealth falling from the sky. And the smell of it! She could taste the sweet moisture, as if the wet earth itself had become a spice.

"Leon, look," she said.

"I know," he whispered, his voice near her ear barely audible over the drone of the rain. He braced a hand on her shoulder in the tight space, and leaned toward the opening. "Let me check if anyone's out there. Wait a minute. I'll be right back," he said.

Before she could object, he was gone. A flash of lightning was followed closely by a sharp clap of thunder, and she jumped in her skin. The baby let out a tiny squawk of discontent. Gaia cradled her against her neck, wrapping the edge of her cloak around her as she supported the little warm head. A minute passed, and Gaia listened intently for the sound of a shot. Leon suddenly reappeared outside the opening.

"Don't do that again!" she yelled.

"Gaia! Quickly!" he said. "There's nobody's here. Come with me!"

She blinked as she crawled out into the dense rain, and by the time she scrambled to her feet she was deluged with water. She pulled at her cloak to cover the baby. Leon took her hand again, and they ran through the honey farm, passing between the hives and under the drenched trees. Lightning blazed the sky around them, and thunder crashed, stopping her pulse in her chest. She shrieked and let go of Leon to hold the baby more securely.

"Where do we go?" she asked, as they reached the edge of the farm.

"It's just ahead, a few meters," Leon said, yelling over the sound of the rain.

They ran down an alley and around a corner. Rain sloshed and poured around them, inundating Gaia's shoes. She could barely see the pavement in front of her, and the rushing tumult filled her ears.

Then Leon pulled her against him and pressed her hard against a wall. An overhang of low roof provided a few scant millimeters of shelter and she licked her lips, tasting rain. She glanced down at the baby in her arms and saw her sister's mouth pushed into a tiny pout.

"We're here," he said. "This is the Nursery."

She gazed along the length of the wall and upward to where the rain slanted against the upper windows. The Nursery was a small, white, two-story house, with dark green shutters and four window boxes of geraniums that had streams of rain pouring from the corners down into the street. Gaia was surprised. For some reason, she'd expected something larger, more institutional, but this looked almost friendly. The area where they stood contained several tall bins, and the distinct odor of bleach and soiled diapers mixed with the scent of rain.

"How did you and Fiona get in to see the babies?" She asked.

Leon pointed to a balcony that jutted beneath an upstairs window. "They're up there."

A flimsy trellis lined the wall, and Gaia gulped as she

imagined climbing up there with Maya in one arm. "You climbed? Were you insane?"

"Fiona did," Leon said. He tugged her wet sleeve. "Come on. There's a back door."

She peered to the right as another curtain of rain washed down the street toward them, pummeling the wall and the ground and rattling on the overhang above them. He pulled her around the wall, pushing through a wooden gate to a narrow backyard. A couple of chickens let up a squawking noise from a coop along the back wall. Faintly, above the noise of the rain and the chickens, she heard a baby's cry. Leon led her around another corner to where a couple of steps led to a back door.

"I'll go in," he said. "I know where the office is. I'll see what I can find."

"We're staying together," she said. When he turned to face her, clearly ready to argue, she wiped the rain out of her eyes. "That's not negotiable," she added.

"You can't, Gaia," he said. "It's suicide. If anyone recognizes you, they'll call the guard."

"What about you? Aren't you wanted, too?" she demanded.

"I can talk my way out of things."

His arrogant certainty almost made her laugh.

"Really. This I'd like to see," she said.

"Masister Khol might be in there."

"I left her drugged in the tower."

"But that was hours ago," he argued.

Gaia had no idea how much time had gone by, but she knew she couldn't stand there in the rain with her baby sister a moment longer. She gripped the metal knob of the door and turned it, surprised when the door was unlocked. Waiting for no further invitation, she stepped inside and found herself in a dim, neat kitchen.

Leon came in behind her and closed the door, shutting out

316

the deafening rush of the rain. In the vacancy of sound, a drip from the faucet was surprisingly audible. The counters and table were clear, except for a colander of beans that stood beside the sink. A braid of garlic hung from a hook by the window. The far wall was made of stone, with an inlaid oven and fireplace, and a wide, stone hearth. The room was pleasantly warm, and Gaia saw a small fire had been lit in the grate. A row of shallow boxes had been built in along one counter, and little blankets rested, some rumpled, inside them. Gaia's gaze focused in on a dozen glass baby bottles that stood drying upside down on a rack of spokes.

"Hello?" came a woman's voice. The sound was weary, but unalarmed, and her voice carried with a high, flutelike quality. "Franny, is that you?"

Leon moved toward the sound and at that moment, a young woman in a red dress came through the door, holding a baby against her shoulder and patting its back with firm, steady fingers. She stopped, obviously surprised.

"Can I help you?" the woman asked Leon. She has hardly more than a girl, only a few years older than Gaia, with full, rosy cheeks and plump hands. Her gaze scanned quickly from Leon to Gaia, and her expression softened when her eyes fell on the baby. "My name's Rosa," she said. "Have we met?"

"Is Masister Khol in?" Gaia asked.

Rosa inspected her wet garb curiously. "No. What happened to you? And what are you doing letting a baby get all wet?" She set the child in her arms in one of the crib boxes on the counter and curled a loose lock of her black hair back neatly behind her ear. Then she reached for Maya. "Come here, sweetheart," she crooned.

When Gaia instinctively backed away, Rosa looked up in confusion. She turned for a moment to Leon, and then her expression sobered. "You're Leon Quarry. Or Grey. Right?"

Leon said nothing. Rosa's gaze flicked again back and forth between him and Gaia, and then she looked down at Maya. Gaia was about to speak, but Leon shook his head in warning.

The young woman cleared her throat and looked again at Leon. "Well," she said, and her voice was slightly lower, with a hint of knowing. "There's a first for everything."

Before Gaia realized what he was doing, he reached for a clay pitcher on the counter and lifted it in a quick, heavy arc to land against Rosa's skull. The impact caused an uncompromising thud, and he caught her as she began to fall. Rosa didn't let out the least bit of noise, not even a grunt of pain.

Gaia's eyes rounded with shock. "Is that what you call talking your way out of things?"

He shuffled Rosa's limp form to the ground and grabbed an apron from the back of a chair. Astonished, Gaia watched as he rapidly bound Rosa's wrists behind her back.

"Stay here," he said, picking up the pitcher again.

"But what are you doing?"

Already he was crossing through the door Rosa had entered, and a moment later, she heard his quick footsteps mounting the stairs. There was a brief cry, and then another sound of a body being dragged. Gaia was staring at the captive on the floor, trying to see if she were still breathing. Rosa's eyes were closed and her face was pallid in the firelight, but her lips were open and her chest moved.

Leon came down the stairs again and pivoted into the kitchen. "That's all of them," he said. "We only have a few minutes until one of them comes around. You get supplies for your sister upstairs, and I'll go through the office. I have an idea. Gaia?"

She dragged her eyes away from Rosa and hugged her sister tighter.

"Did you have to do that?" she whispered.

318

He tilted his face, regarding her intently and without apology. She realized it shouldn't have surprised her how swiftly he'd acted. He was in the guard, trained. He'd always been capable of decisive violence.

"I'm sorry," she said.

He looked over his shoulder, listening, and then he took a step toward her and spoke more gently. "Do you want to take care of your sister or not?"

His reminder reawakened her sense of urgency. She dropped Pearl's soaked cloak on the back of a chair. She looked briefly at the baby in the crib on the counter to see it wasn't fussing, and then, side-stepping Rosa, she slipped out of the room and hurried up the stairs. Leon headed for the office.

Little natural light reached the narrow, steep stairs. At the top, two doors stood open on either side. The room on her left was darker, with a row of cribs. She turned toward some faint, indefinable sound in the right-hand room and stepped into a small, clean, low-ceilinged nursery. A faint, fragrant scent of lavender soap and cotton laced the air. Rows of small cribs lined the walls, side by side, more than a dozen, but Gaia saw that only a handful were occupied by babies, all sleeping. *What are the chances of that*, she thought. Did they know how to keep infants on a schedule here? Rain streamed down two large, multipaned windows that let in the cool gray light. A flash of lightning flickered outside, followed shortly by a muffled boom of thunder, but the weather only emphasized how safe and warm it felt inside.

Then Gaia turned to the last corner of the room. An elderly woman clad in white lay slumped over in a rocking chair, her chin on her chest, her wrists tied to one armrest. In fascinated fear at what Leon had done, Gaia watched the woman closely to she see her chest rise and fall. Beside her stood a table that was piled with diapers and blankets and a basket half full of little clothes. One of the babies made a soft, sucking noise, and Gaia instinctively patted Maya. Any moment now, one of the babies would wake up, and the cries could wake the others, and then who would take care of them? Gaia didn't dare take the time to undress and clean Maya, but she wrapped two fresh blankets around her securely, then quickly snatched some diapers and blankets. She tossed them into the basket of clothes, and grabbing the handles, she hurried out of the room again as quietly as she could.

She tiptoed rapidly down the stairs.

"Leon?" she whispered.

She peered around another doorway. A cluttered desk stood in the middle of the front office surrounded by cabinets and shelves. A couple of empty cribs stood against the wall as if even here someone might need to set down a baby safely. The rain was a muffled drone, and a small, green-shaded lamp on the desk pushed back the afternoon grayness. Leon was seated at the desk, his fingers clicking over a keyboard, while the glow of the computer screen cast a pale blue light onto his cheeks and the backs of his hands.

"Have you found anything?" she asked.

"Not yet."

Gaia knew she should get formula, but Maya had drifted to sleep again and she couldn't help taking a quick scan around the room. There were notices posted on a corkboard over a cupboard, and in the right corner, a familiar booklet of paper that looked like an invitation, only thicker. She peered closer.

Summer Solstice 2409
Extant Members of
The Advanced Cohort of 2396
Are Hereby Invited to Request
Unadvancement

320

Gaia flipped back the first page and saw columns of names. *I've seen one of these before*, she thought, trying to remember when. The print was small, and there were several pages. She calculated quickly and realized there were more than a hundred names.

"Leon," she said, plucking it from the board. "What is this?"

He typed a few more keystrokes and then stopped, his fingers poised above the keys. He glanced up and squinted at her, then at the paper in her hand.

"It's an unadvancement notice," he said. "The Enclave puts one out every summer for the thirteen-year-olds. It's a formality. For appearances."

"But isn't it a list? Of all the babies from a certain year?" A light dawned. "Didn't you find one of these in my father's sewing kit? Back when you first arrested my parents?"

He reached out a hand and she gave it to him. "We did," he said, considering. "It is a list. But it doesn't have any birth dates."

"What year was it from, the one my father had?"

"It was a notice from one of your brother's years. The younger brother, as I recall."

"So it wasn't just a paper for pins," she said. "My father had a list with my brother's name on it?"

"That's right. Maybe he hoped he could eventually figure out which name was the right one," Leon said, and then he turned his face, alert. Gaia held still, too, listening. A sleepy but distinct baby's cry came from upstairs, just once, and then fell silent. Leon's gaze riveted on Gaia.

"Oh, no," Gaia breathed. It would be only a matter of seconds before the baby let out a louder, more peremptory call, and then the other babies would start waking. "I have to find formula," she said.

"I'll be right there."

Gaia was already running toward the kitchen as another, louder wail came from up above. As soon as Gaia stepped back into the kitchen, she saw that Rosa had moved closer to the gray stone fireplace. She had her legs curled for leverage and was trying to roll over so that she'd be able to rise. The red material of her dress was bunched awkwardly around her knees.

"Don't move," Gaia said.

Rosa turned her face in Gaia's direction. Her black hair fell half across her face, and a strand of it stuck in the corner of her mouth. "You have to let me go," she said, her voice still a clear soprano. "I have to take care of the babies."

The infant in the crib on the counter was waving one hand and making a gurgling, playful noise. Another cry came from above and was joined by a second baby voice.

"Where's the formula?" Gaia demanded, scanning the kitchen for likely containers. One wall was lined with cupboards and closets. She set the basket and Maya on the center table and began opening doors as fast as she could. The first cupboard held adult food, the second dishes, and the third was stacked with lidded clay canisters. Gaia pulled one out and lifted the lid with a sucking sound: cream-colored powder.

"Don't take that," Rosa said. "We need it."

Gaia dipped her pinky finger into the powder and tasted it, then grabbed one of the canisters and put it in the basket. Taking three of the bottles from by the sink, she filled them with water and twisted on the nipple tops as more cries came from upstairs.

"Leon!" she yelled, tucking the bottles into the basket with the baby blankets. She picked up her sister again and gripped the handles of the bulging basket. "Is there a list of the babies' birth dates?" she asked. "A record anywhere?"

Rosa let out a laugh. "You think I'd give it to you? You know they're going to catch you," she said, shifting again, inching her body toward the fireplace. "And they'll hang you right in the Bastion Square while I watch."

"Leon!" Gaia called again. She couldn't tell what distressed her more, the increasingly urgent wails of the babies upstairs or the sinister predictions in this girl's clear, high-pitched voice.

He appeared in the doorway. "I can't find anything," he said. "It must all be restricted." He reached into one of the closets and pulled out a couple of red cloaks. "Take this."

"She knows where there's a list," Gaia said. "She won't tell me."

For a moment Leon looked into Gaia's eyes, as if weighing something important. *Do it,* Gaia thought. *Do whatever you need to.*

"You'll never get outside the wall," Rosa piped from the floor. "They'll have people watching out every window and guards everywhere."

Leon slipped a cloak around Gaia's shoulders, and she hunched into the warm, soft material. Then he dropped the other cloak on the table and reached for the handle of a knife that protruded from a block of wood. Its sharp, short, serrated blade gleamed blue in the light from the rainy window. As the cries from upstairs grew desperate, he took a step nearer to Rosa, still bound on the floor. He aimed the knife in Rosa's direction.

"You wouldn't," she said. Her eyes rounded with fear.

Leon flipped the knife once in his hand catching it deftly. "Where's the list?" he said.

Gaia sucked in her breath, biting her lip. Rosa was pushing back from him as much as she possibly could. Her voice lifted even higher in alarm.

"I don't know!" she said. "I really don't!"

The baby on the counter began to cry, adding a grating, discordant counterpoint to Rosa's pleading.

Leon took another step toward her and stooped to touch the point of the blade to the middle of her throat.

Gaia clutched her sister, terrified of how far Leon might go.

"Tell me," he said, his voice low and unflinching. "And I don't mean in the computer. A written record. I know Masister Khol would have a backup."

The blade stroked downward along the skin.

Rosa let out a gasp of fear. "Don't hurt me! Check the bottom drawer of the big cabinet. By the far wall," Rosa said. "I swear there are some ledgers. The bottom right drawer. Go look! Please!"

Leon glanced up at Gaia and nodded.

Gaia set her sister and the basket back on the table again and flew into the office. She wrenched open the lowest drawer of the biggest cabinet and there was a pile of thin ledgers. She flipped rapidly through the covers, seeing each book spanned five years, and a quick glance showed her there were names and birth dates inside in precise, small script. She swept the entire pile into her arms.

By the time she returned to the kitchen, Rosa had tears in her eyes. Leon hadn't moved a millimeter.

"They're here," Gaia said. "Leon. I've got them. Let her go."

Chapter 26

White Boots

H IS COLD, steely eyes yielded nothing, but he turned the cusp of the blade away from Rosa's throat. She burst out a sob as Leon straightened to his full height. From the crib on the counter, the baby's cries subsided into a hiccupping, lonely noise, while the other babies upstairs continued to cry.

"You're a monster," Rosa said, half choking on her words. "A freak. Just like they've always said."

He tossed the knife on the floor. It landed just behind Rosa's tied wrists, where she would be able to reach it and work herself free.

"Come on," he said to Gaia, grabbing the handles of the basket and tossing the other red cape over his shoulders. He opened the back door, and she teetered with him for a moment on the doorsill, facing the cold rain. She shivered once, hard, all through her body and gazed up at Leon's unrecognizable face. How completely he'd changed, how ruthless he'd become during those moments he'd held Rosa at knife point. How much of that had been genuinely him, and how much of that had been him acting as Gaia's tool? She had to accept that some of the responsibility was hers, and she didn't like it.

"You ready?" he asked, and she was relieved to hear his voice had lost its merciless edge.

She nodded. He took the ledgers from her and pushed them into the basket. With a twitch, he settled the hood of his cloak around his face, and the contrasting red made his cheeks seem even paler.

"You'll never look like a girl," she said.

He gave the faintest hint of a smile. "This way," he said, and led her around the building.

The rain was lessening, and with the dry red cloak around her, she no longer felt every raindrop pounding along her head and shoulders. She tucked Maya under the fabric, and hugged her close to her side.

"Where are we heading?" she said.

"To Mace Jackson's. Do you have a better idea?"

She didn't. But when they reached the turn for the street with the bakery, a group of soldiers stood at the corner, and Gaia stopped in alarm.

"Hey!" a soldier called.

"Quick! This way," Leon said, pulling her back with him. They ran down an alley, and then he pushed her through a narrow door into a garden. She flew past the sodden vegetables and into another little yard and out another gate. A staircase curved up the side of a building, and Leon took her hand to lead her up. At the top, a flat roof was covered with laundry lines, all bare now, and they ran to the other side. A cistern was full and overflowing with rainwater, and behind it a plank utility bridge accompanied a water main that crossed to another roof.

"Can you make this?" he asked.

Compared to the run over the top of the solarium, this was nothing, and Gaia held out her hand. They were across to the next roof in a flash.

Gaia caught a glimpse of the obelisk and the Bastion towers, but then she and Leon turned down another staircase, and Gaia was back at street level, in another alley. They paused, looking for soldiers, and then they dashed across the road and up a lane. Leon stopped against a familiar metalwork gate.

He thrust his arm inside, and at that moment, Gaia recognized the walled garden where she and Leon had stopped once before.

"We can't," she said. "It's a dead end. A death trap."

"We have no other choice. We have to hide somewhere while we come up with a plan."

He shoved the gate opened, and she flew in behind him. The wet gate closed with a click, and she looked fearfully toward the house. Gray, blank windows merged with the rain-soaked stucco, and she looked to Leon, surprised. "They're gone?"

"They must be at my sister's birthday party," he said. He started toward the terrace, but Gaia shrank back.

"No, Leon. We can't go in there."

"We need shelter, Gaia. We have to figure something out."

She backed away, shaking her head. "Let's hide out here, in the garden, just until we can figure out a way to get out of the wall." She sniffed as a big drop of rain fell against her lashes, and then she wiped it away.

"If you insist," he said. "At least it should be drier under the tree. Come on."

She barely recognized the garden as he led her toward the back, toward the big pine tree. Light from a streetlamp flooded over the wall in one place, illuminating the wild cascades of rain, and the pummeling effect of the rain on the bushes and flowers, but otherwise the garden was a maze of drenched shadows. A gust of wind blasted into her face, stealing her breath, and she leaned into it.

"Here!" he said, and she squinted into the gloom. They had

reached the giant pine and the deep, dry shadow beneath. She had to hunch to move beneath the lowest, sloping branches.

Maya let out a cry, and with her open mouth, the infant rubbed her cheek against her towel, rooting instinctively for food. Gaia wiped her finger on the wet fabric of her cloak and put her littlest finger upsidedown in the baby's mouth. It was a trick she'd learned from her mother, but it was still startling how hard the baby could suck.

"She needs a bottle," Gaia said.

"We don't have time."

"I can't exactly take a crying baby down the street."

He frowned toward little Maya and the finger Gaia had in her mouth. "What do I do?"

Gaia told him to dig out one of the bottles of water and explained about adding the powdered formula and shaking the bottle to mix it.

To her left, a sheet of gray rain marked the edge of the cliff, and she could just make out the blurred buildings below. With Maya in her arms, she huddled to the ground. A few streams of rainwater ran through the dead, fragrant pine needles. When Leon handed her the bottle, she nudged it into Maya's lips, and the baby latched on vigorously.

"Hungry little monster," Gaia said softly. She licked the rainwater from her lips.

He was sitting on his haunches beside her. "Did you notice the guards didn't take any shots at us back there?" he asked. "We were in range. I wonder if they have orders to capture us, not kill us. The Protectorat was willing to have us executed when he could do it quietly, but he might not want us gunned down in public."

She glanced up from the baby to find Leon's face near enough for her to see the individual drops along his cheekbones. "That's good then, isn't it?"

He squinted at her, nodding. "Yes. But they'll have guards combing every corner of the Enclave and all around the wall, too."

She thought this over and shivered.

He moved nearer and put an arm around her shoulders. "Cold?"

"Not so bad."

He gave her shoulder a squeeze and then pulled her a bit nearer so that she could feel the warmth of his torso along her arm through the wet cloak.

"I think we might have a better chance if we split up," he said.

"What?"

"They're looking for the two of us together. If you just go yourself, right up to the south gate, like you have business outside the wall, you might be able to get close enough and then run."

She blinked over at him. "You've lost your mind."

"What do you think we should do, then?"

Gaia didn't know. She wished there was a crowd. If they could get lost in a crowd, they might stand a chance. Maya was almost done with her bottle, and her eyes were closed as if she would slip right into sleep. "I don't know," Gaia said. "Isn't there any other way out of the wall?" She remembered the way she'd come in originally, and the guard tower just above it. That would be no good. "Didn't you say you got in by the solar grid plant?"

"That's clear on the other side of the Enclave. We'd never get that far."

"So there's no way out."

"Aside from blasting open our own hole, no."

"How about where the wall meets the cliff? Could we go down the cliff?"

"Not unless you have a— I don't believe this. Where's your rope?"

She let out a laugh. "I left it in the Bastion. With my mother."

"It wouldn't work anyway," he said. "There are guard towers along the cliff, too."

Gaia lifted her face as the rain lightened even further, and gazed out toward the cliff, to where she would see the unlake if the rain and the darkness didn't obscure it. Night was falling, and the gleams of streetlamps shone below. "So, we're stuck," she said. "Do you still have the ledgers?"

"They're right here," he said.

She gazed at the hastily assembled basket of supplies, realizing she might never have the chance to use them all, few as they were. It was almost funny, in a way, to feel so safe for an instant while guards must be closing in on them from every direction. Something slowed down inside her and grew peaceful, as if she'd accepted a great boulder.

"I would have liked to get the list outside," she said. "To the people in Wharfton. They have a right to know what happened to their babies."

"Gaia. You sound like you're giving up."

It didn't feel like that to her. It felt like she was facing her future realistically. She just hoped they could be killed quickly and not have to go through a scene in the Square of the Bastion with a formal execution. She wouldn't like that. "It's just reality, Leon. There's no way out. The only one who could get us outside the wall tonight would be the Protectorat himself, or maybe Genevieve. And I don't think they'd want to leave Evelyn's birthday to offer us an escort," she added wryly.

Leon loosened his arm from around her and stood. "Incredible," he muttered.

"What?"

"We've been thinking like fugitives. We need to think like royalty."

"I beg your pardon?"

"Stay here," he said.

"You're not leaving me!" she said.

He crouched beside her again and gripped her shoulders. "Listen," he said. "It's the night of my sister's party, right? The wealthiest people from the Enclave are out tonight, heading toward the Bastion. The guards are looking for us in red, desperate and soaked. All we need to do is dress in white, Gaia. We just have to act like we're part of the guest list. Guards would never stop a couple in white."

The peaceful boulder began to break up around her heart, letting hope in again, and with it fear.

"But what about the baby? What about my face?"

Leon stood and helped her to her feet. "It will all work out," he said. "Come on."

She gathered her sleeping sister more closely in her arms as he lifted the basket of supplies, and then they were hurrying through the garden toward the house. The rain had lessened to a drizzle, and a roll of thunder was more distant. Even though she knew that the house was lightless and empty, it still frightened her to creep up onto the terrace. With a stone, Leon made a sharp tap against one of the windows of a French door to break the glass. A moment later, he had the door open and they were inside. It was hard to see more than the forms of furniture and the openings of doorways, but Leon seemed to know his way, and she followed him up the stairs to a bedroom.

"How do you know this place?" she asked.

"One of my friends from school lives here. Tim Quirk. His family is friends with my family. I've been here a hundred times, though not lately." He was closing the curtains, blocking out the last bit of light, and a moment later she heard a click as he pulled a light switch in the closet. Gaia was afraid to touch anything, especially once she saw that everything in the closet was white with only the slightest other pastel shades for accents. There were special shelves for hats, and a dozen compartments just for shoes.

"Here," Leon said. "Pick something out. I'll get something from Tim's room."

"I don't have the least idea what to wear," Gaia said.

He turned to her, frowning, and she could just imagine the picture she made, dripping wet, in the red cape and with a baby rolled in blankets in her arms. Her hair was wet and probably messed, and under a layer of mud, she still wore Jet's bloodstained trousers and her improvised sheet-skirt.

"I wish we had time for showers," he muttered.

She laughed. "Well, we don't. Let's not think that much like royalty."

Leon turned again to the closet and whipped out a long, slender, creamy sweater with soft, narrow sleeves. Next he pulled out a white dress that would sweep below her knees. "The style's probably not right for a young girl like you, but it's all we have. Here's a cape. I don't think it's waterproof, but the rain's stopping, I think, and it has a good hood. Can you pick out some shoes?"

"How about the boots?" she asked, pointing down at the row of boots, some tall, some ankle-high, all in spotless white.

"Let's hope they fit," he said, and pulled out a pair of the low ones. They reminded Gaia of cowboy boots from the Tvaltar, but shorter, dainty.

"Okay," she whispered, and let her red cape fall to the floor. She couldn't wait to get out of her snug, water-soaked clothes. She set the sleeping baby on top of the bundle. As she reached for the dress, she looked over her shoulder to see if

Leon had left yet. He stood by the doorway, his eyes scanning her body with unguarded interest, and she wondered for a moment if he were judging whether the clothes would fit.

"What?" she said.

His gaze flew to hers, and then he turned sharply away.

"I'll be right back," he said.

That was . . . odd, she thought. *To say the least.* Gaia stripped off her wet clothes and pulled on the dress. There were buttons along the back, and her cold fingers trembled as she snagged her hands behind her to reach them. In the dark, with only the light from the closet to guide her, she worked quickly, and then tiptoed in the little boots over to a full-length mirror that gleamed beside the bed. She looked over her shoulder to make sure she'd gotten all the buttons, and was surprised by the graceful way the white material clung to her form. She looked like someone else. Someone privileged. Especially with only the right side of her face to the mirror.

"You're perfect," Leon said.

She turned to see him in the doorway and smiled. Aside from his black boots, he was dressed in impeccable white, with a tailored jacket and trousers. He had hitched his blazer open to rest a fist on his hip, and she saw a short dagger that hung in a sheath from his belt: a fitting military accent. He gave his sleeve a twitch. "The coat's a little short," he said.

She laughed. "You look incredible. Certainly good enough to fool any guards. Now what about the baby?"

He produced a gilded bag made of paper. "I found this," he said. "She might fit inside for a present."

Gaia was doubtful.

"See if you can do something with your hair," he said. "Like put it up or something? I don't know. I'll see what I can do with Maya."

"Here. Let me do this much." Maya's blankets had come

333

loose, and Gaia refolded them securely around her sister so that, from a compact little cocoon, only the baby's face showed.

"Thanks," Leon said.

Gaia stepped over to a dresser where she found a brush and a couple of clips. Hastily, she brushed the worst knots from her wet hair and swept the short strands up in back, securing them on top of her head as best she could. It felt strange to leave her face so exposed, but when she pulled on the sweater and then the white cape, she saw it looked passable. Her scar would only be noticeable to someone who looked directly into her hood, to her face.

"We're good," Leon said.

He was standing with a gift bag casually tucked in one arm.

"Can she breathe in there?" Gaia asked.

He tilted the bag to show her the baby's sleeping face was upward, and the ledgers were tucked in with her, too. She looked cozy, warm, and content. Gaia couldn't believe how tiny she was.

"It's a little bulky, and there's no room for formula," he admitted. "But if she stays asleep and doesn't move, we'll be okay."

We just have to make it outside the wall, she thought. Nothing else mattered.

When he turned out the closet light, she naturally reached for his hand in the darkness. Together they crept back down the staircase and rounded the corner to the front door. Leon unlocked the door, and when he opened it part way, they looked out at a drizzle. A sconce light mounted on one of the entryway pillars lighted the path toward the road.

"It's almost stopped," she said.

"We should wait another minute," he said.

She nodded, postponing the next plunge into risk by standing in the temporary shelter of the quiet, dark home. He released her fingers to reach for a white hat on a peg behind the door, but then he took her hand again and brought her close to his right side, tucking her fingers into his elbow. The baby parcel looked secure in his other arm.

"This is how we'll walk," he said.

"So you actually have a plan?"

She glanced up to meet his eyes under the white brim. He was regarding her with his usual concentration, but his mouth curved in the slightest smile.

"I have to say, I'm tempted to take you back to the Bastion and walk right into my sister's party. You belong there."

She let out a laugh. "Now I know you've lost your mind."

He tilted his face slightly. "I should have met you long ago."

"Outside the wall?"

"There shouldn't even be a wall in the first place," he said.

"But there is," she said, looking back out to the drizzle in the lamplight.

"Listen," he said. "If something goes wrong, if we get separated, I want you to go ahead with your plan to go into the wasteland. Head north."

"We're not splitting up."

"I know, but if we do—"

"Leon," she said, gripping his arm. "It's not happening. We're staying together."

She expected him to nod, but instead his gaze was directed again toward the open door. She wondered if it really made any difference whether they waited a few more minutes or not. They were almost certain to get caught once they reached the wall, if not before. Still, she'd rather be caught this way than bedraggled and desperate.

"You should know something about me," he said quietly.

She gazed up at him, waiting.

"I'm not sure if I'm doing the right thing for you," he added.

335

She touched back a strand of her dark hair, uncertain how to reply. "What do you mean?"

"I just want to be sure you're making your own choices. I'm not the best judge of what's right for someone else."

She loosened her grip on his arm. "What are you saying?" she asked.

Just beyond the pillars the rain was falling softly on the sidewalk and grass, washing everything with a gray, sodden hue. Leon seemed to be looking through the dimness to another time, and though in one way she felt like he was leaving her, she also felt she was on the brink of being closer to him than she ever had. He turned slowly to the narrow table that stood in the hallway, gently set down the gift bag with Maya inside, and crossed his arms.

"Two years ago," he said, "when my sister Fiona was only twelve, she and I were playing chess one night in the solarium. There was an enormous storm, like this one."

A cool mist came through the open doorway, but she felt an even deeper coolness within her as she sensed he was confiding something he'd never told anyone else. She tried to imagine what it had been like under that glass ceiling with all the rain pounding down. "Why didn't you play somewhere else?"

"She liked the storm," he said. "It felt like electricity charged the air, and she liked that. But then the power went out. There was nothing but black, as dark as the tunnel without a candle. Then these wild, random, crashing flares of lightning shot through the room. It felt like the glass of the ceiling was crashing down on top of us."

"It must have been terrifying."

He nodded. "Fiona completely freaked out. She was terrified, way beyond anything I'd ever seen. She couldn't even breathe. She climbed onto my lap and begged me to hold her. She was almost hysterical, and I was—well, I was kind of laughing at her. I wasn't very nice at all, but I didn't know what to do with her. She'd become this crazy cat of a kid. And then she gripped me in a kind of panic, and then—" He stopped.

Gaia bit her lips inward, waiting. His posture had grown stiff, and his face was aimed toward the rain again so that she couldn't read his eyes.

"She was my sister," he said, his voice low. "She kissed me. Not the way a kid does."

Gaia watched the strange, cold detachment that settled in his features, like a death mask. She could see he'd replayed this memory a million times. "What did you do?" she asked.

"I was in shock. I didn't want to hurt her feelings. I couldn't just push her away. She had me by the collar and I—I was trying to back away when Rafael found us."

"Oh, no," Gaia said. Her instinct told her to reach out to him, but he stood aloof.

"It gets worse," he said, his voice leaden. "She had a diary. She'd kept a list of every nice thing I'd ever done for her, no matter how small. She had developed a whole logic about how we weren't biologically related, so the laws against siblings marrying didn't apply to us. She'd imagined an entire life for the two of us, in a cottage, outside the wall." His eyes closed. "When Fiona saw what trouble I was in, she tried to deny it, but it was too late."

Outside the door, a gust of wind brought a shower of bigger drops from the nearby trees, spattering them into the puddles on the sidewalk.

"I think they would have believed us, eventually," he said. "But Fiona died."

Gaia shivered, drawing her cloak more securely around herself. He finally turned to her, his eyes dark and troubled, his voice a low murmur.

337

"Gaia," he said. "When my little sister came to me to apologize, when she wanted to try to make it right with me, I was furious with her. I told her she was sick. A sick little girl. And that's when she did it." His voice dropped to an agonized hush. "My sister killed herself because of me."

Gaia shook her head, disbelieving. It was too terrible to imagine. Fiona had been only twelve years old! And how could Leon blame himself for her death? Such a tragedy couldn't be blamed on one cruel comment.

"But it was an accident," she said.

"No," he said. "Evelyn saw it. She couldn't stop her. It wasn't an accident."

"I am so, so sorry," Gaia whispered. She could understand now how wild rumors had spread. Leon's family, shattered by the suicide of one twin, must have been completely devastated. In that tangle of disbelief and confusion, how easy it would have been to focus their rage and pain on Leon, to blame him. He'd absorbed it all in, every bit of it. How many people knew the real truth?

"The worst thing of all is, I think she really was sick," Leon said. "I've thought about it, and I think she needed help. I think she was terrified, and not just the night of the storm. Her moods were swinging crazier all the time. Some days she couldn't even get out of bed, and other days she had all this wild energy and she didn't know why. She was trying to ask me to help her, but I couldn't see. I just made it worse." He turned his face away again, peering toward a distance that Gaia couldn't see.

"What happened wasn't your fault," she said. "I don't know what was wrong with Fiona, but she should have been getting help from someone far more knowledgeable than you were. Did Genevieve know what was going on? Did the Protectorat?"

"You're missing the point," he said. "My sister is dead. If I

338

hadn't mistreated her when she needed me most, she would be alive today." Leon's voice was low, with a hollowness that came from deep within him. "You once wondered why I became a member of the guard. Honestly? There was no point doing anything else. There was no point doing anything, period. I took a job. I didn't question any rules or orders. I didn't care."

She twisted her hands together, and looked up at him, unflinching. "That was your only mistake," she said. "Giving up yourself like that. You shouldn't have done that."

He let out a brief, bitter laugh and stepped away from her. "You're judging me?"

Gaia didn't know what to tell him, but she knew in her heart that his sister's suicide was deep enough of a loss, without adding his own guilt to drive it even deeper. Then again, she felt uncertain. How could she ever truly know what he'd felt? His whole family had been ripped apart by losing Fiona, and he'd been disowned when he must have needed them most. He'd had to grieve alone. She didn't know how she would ever handle such loneliness, such sadness. "I'm sorry," she said slowly. "You've lost so much, Leon. Not just Fiona." She thought sadly of her own parents and how she'd never see them again. Not even once, for a moment. It was more than she could bear. "I'm sorry," she whispered again. It was that simple.

From the present on the table beside her came a hiccup. Gaia glanced inside at the little infant, and then heard it again. Gingerly, Gaia extracted the baby from the gift bag and lifted her to her shoulder to burp her. The little, endearing hiccups vibrated through her hands, and she had to laugh, even though she felt broken inside. She glanced up to find Leon watching her, his gaze a mix of puzzled tenderness.

"You're good with her," he said.

Her lips curved. "She's my sister," she explained.

He shook his head, as if she'd said something remarkable.

"See that? You know," he said. "I was fine, really. I was doing just fine until one night, when I was sent outside the wall to interrogate a difficult young midwife."

She caught her breath as a thudding started in her chest. "I wasn't so bad."

He laughed. "You were utterly fearless. And impossible. Look at all you've done," he said. "You got into the Bastion tower to save your mother. Who else could ever do that? I couldn't. Face it, Gaia. When you decide something's right, there's nothing that can stop you from doing it."

"I killed my mother in the process," she said, her voice low. "Don't forget that."

"*That* I don't believe. And I doubt you really believe it, either. Would your mother blame you for anything that happened?"

She looked down at her hand, turning it slowly, as if it should have bloodstains on it still, but it was clean. "No," she said softly.

"See?" he said. "That's how we're different. You have nothing to blame yourself for. You never will."

She shook her head. "Don't turn me into some paragon, Leon. That's not who I am."

"No. You're more real than that." He lifted a hand against his forehead, tipping the hat back. Then he readjusted it again slowly and frowned. "I hated knowing you didn't respect me. Even when I could save your life, back when you were first arrested, it didn't matter to you."

She searched his face and the strange, uncertain loneliness behind his eyes.

"That's not why I respect you now," she said.

"Is that all you do? Respect me?"

In the dim light, his cheeks had turned a chalky, blue hue, but there was nothing cold about his expression. A fine tension

340

emanated from him, like a soundless buzz, and he took a step nearer again. She was holding her baby sister awkwardly before her, strangely nervous, like she might drop her.

"Leon," she said. "I don't know what you want from me."

In answer, he took one more step, until the rim of his hat came just above her forehead. She knew that if she looked up, his eyes would be near.

"Who said I want something?" he asked, and took off his hat.

She could feel heat rising in her cheeks, and still she kept her gaze down. He closed the distance between them and slid his arms around her and the baby. When his warm lips touched the sensitive skin of the scar on her temple, she felt something give away inside her. She angled her face, bringing her mouth nearer to his, and then his lips touched hers in the lightest, most tender kiss. She inhaled a quick breath, and he kissed her again. An ache rose in her throat, and she lifted her chin, meeting his lips more directly. Outside, another loud spattering of huge drops fell on the bushes and sidewalk. Once she had wondered if anyone would ever kiss her, and if she would know what to do. Now she could hardly think at all. She felt Leon's hand shift to the back of her hair, and then his kiss deepened. She felt the world tip, and then her sister gave another hiccup.

Gaia pulled back. Leon was watching her under heavy eyelids. "You are so, so sweet," he said tenderly.

"You're not supposed to kiss me," she said. She was surprised at how low her voice had become.

"I beg to disagree." His lips touched hers again.

She struggled to focus. "We have to get out of the Enclave."

His eyebrows lifted. "Right now?"

She pulled back more decisively, and he loosened his arms to let her go. "It's stopped raining," she said. "This is our chance."

341

He glanced regretfully out the door. "You don't like me after all."

"Leon!" She socked him in the arm.

He smiled crookedly. "Okay. Just checking." Then he reached to help her settle baby Maya back in the gift bag. The paper was a thick, durable type, but it was definitely getting crinkled from handling. Gaia watched carefully as he repositioned the bag in his left arm. She wished it would look right for her to carry it herself, but it was logical for a gentleman to offer to carry it for her.

She fetched his hat from where it had dropped to the floor. "Here," she said. "There's a basic problem with our plan, you know. When we head toward the gate, we'll be going the wrong way, away from the party."

"You're getting picky." He put on his hat.

Gaia slid her fingers into his right elbow and before she knew it, he dipped near for another soft kiss on her cheek. "I wish we had more time, Gaia," he said.

She nodded, and passed with him through the doorway.

Chapter 27
Trust

WITH HER HAND IN HIS ELBOW, Gaia and Leon walked down the wet streets, winding their way ever closer to the wall. When they came upon a group of soldiers, Gaia instinctively hesitated, but Leon drew her smoothly along, barely looking at them, and though she kept expecting every instant to be stopped, the guards gave them only a cursory glance.

Gaia exhaled in relief when they turned the next corner.

"See?" Leon said.

The sky had grown dark with nightfall, but an eerie luminosity glowed ahead of them as if a surfeit of white light was bouncing up to reflect off the low-hung clouds.

"They must have the wall lit up," Leon said. "So the surveillance cameras won't miss anything."

"Are there cameras tracking us here?"

"There are cameras trained at most streetlamps," he said. "We've probably been picked up a half a dozen times already."

"So are we tricking them?" she asked.

"I don't know. They might just be waiting to pick us up by the wall."

They walked down another wet street and crossed to a

343

narrow lane where the shop awnings reached out over the sidewalks. Drips fell from the awnings, and Gaia ducked her head each time they passed beneath one.

"How's the gift?" she asked.

"Good."

They passed a second group of soldiers that appeared as unconcerned as the first, and Gaia began to feel some hope. But as they rounded another corner, she heard the sound of footsteps behind them.

"Are they following us?"

"Don't look back," Leon said.

Gaia kept walking, turning with Leon onto a wider street that descended in a wide, gentle arc toward the south gate. White storefronts, streaked gray by the rain, lined the street, and streetlamps cast paths of reflections in the wet cobblestones. From some apartment above, the spicy scent of curried stew mixed with the smell of rain, and tauntingly reminded her that the rest of the world was going on with routine dinner preparations while she might well be walking her last steps. Gaia stretched her stride to avoid a puddle. There were guards on the parapet of the wall and in front of the gates, but the doors of the gate were wide open. Gaia even had a glimpse of Wharfton through the open archway, a row of drab, gray houses, wet and hunched against the night. There was motion out there, people passing by.

"It's a trap," Gaia whispered. "They're waiting for us."

"Keep steady," Leon said.

At that moment, a couple of men in white came out of a doorway on the left. They glanced curiously in Leon and Gaia's direction, and then one of the men stopped. He lifted his hand in a brief wave.

"Hey! Grey!" he called. "I didn't realize you were going to the party. You've been far too reclusive lately."

"We have to go!" Gaia whispered.

But Leon released her and held out a hand to shake with the two men. "How've you been? We thought we'd get a look at the fireworks from the wall," he said.

"Are they still having the fireworks with the rain?"

"That's the plan." Leon said.

The men were looking curiously at Gaia. She kept her face turned toward Leon so they wouldn't see the scarred side of her face.

"You remember my friend Lucy Blair," Leon lied smoothly. "From archery class. This is Mort Phillips and Zack Bittman."

The men looked surprised, but they offered their hands to shake. "Of course!" the first one said.

"Nice to see you," Gaia said shyly.

"Are they really going to let you up on the wall?" Mort asked. "Looks like they're busy with something. Have you heard anything about fugitives?"

"Nothing lately," Leon said casually. "Good to see you. Let's catch up at the party."

"Sounds good," Mort said. He pointed a finger at Leon. "I still have that book you loaned me."

"Forget about it. I knew you'd never give it back," Leon said, his voice droll.

The men laughed and started up the road. Leon offered his elbow again, and Gaia slid her fingers into the corner of his arm.

"Do you know everybody?" she whispered.

He gave her a smile but his eyes were watchful. "Yes."

He's a far better actor than I could ever be, she thought. The guards behind them had stopped during Leon's conversation with his friends, and they had their heads together now. The guards down below had turned uncertainly toward their leader, a tall, white-haired man with a distinctive Adam's apple.

"Even Lanchester?" Gaia asked.

"What?"

"I know the head guard, Sergeant Lanchester," she said.

They were almost upon the gate now, almost near enough to run through. Gaia thought her heart was going to beat out of her chest. The guards, more decisive now, were lifting their rifles. The ones on the top of the wall already had theirs cocked and pointed at Gaia and Leon.

"Do you trust me?" Leon asked.

"Yes."

She did. Implicitly. She met his intense, searching gaze with absolute certainty.

"Then take this," he said, and passed her the gilded gift bag with her sister inside. In the next instant, he grabbed her left arm and jerked it up behind her, twisting her hard up against him, and with the other hand, he bared a knife before her chin. She let out a shriek and instinctively struggled, desperately clutching her sister.

"Let me through or I'll kill her," Leon called.

"Let her go," Sgt. Lanchester called.

The men were moving into the archway to block the exit, their guns aimed at Leon and Gaia. They closed one of the massive doors.

"Clear out of the way!" Leon said. He wrenched her arm upward painfully and she let out another scream.

"Stop!" she said. "Oh, please! Stop!" And then she was silent because the knife was biting into her throat.

"Move!" Leon said again, edging closer to the archway.

"Step back!" Sgt. Lanchester said to his men. "Don't fire! Don't risk killing the girl! Gaia, is that really you?"

She was too afraid to speak. Leon was half carrying, half jerking her toward the great open gateway, and she was terrified that she would drop her sister. Already she was certain

346

the bag was ripping. Leon jerked her arm again, and she gasped out as pain shot up her left shoulder. Sgt. Lanchester was shifting closer, his gun aimed at Leon's head. Leon held Gaia as a shield before him, and still edged toward the gate.

"Just let her go," Sgt. Lanchester said, his voice deliberately calm. "She never did anything to you. Just let her go, and we'll talk about this."

"Don't get any closer," Leon said. "Put up your gun."

But Sgt. Lanchester came even closer, and his pistol was leveled at them. Gaia could see down the black of the barrel.

"Don't shoot!" she begged. She felt tears brimming her eyes. She didn't think she could bear the pain in her shoulder any longer. She could feel her grip on her sister loosening, and still Leon was jerking her toward the archway.

"Please, Leon," she whispered. "You're hurting—" she gasped again as another twist of agony ripped through her, and then she closed her eyes as her head began to spin with pain.

"Let her go!" Lanchester said again.

As she felt a minute yielding in Leon's grip, she opened her eyes and was stunned and to see they'd reached the archway. They were practically through the door. Practically free! He still held her pinned against him, his cheek alongside her ear, his knife at her throat. For an impossibly long moment, her hope was as intense as her raw pain.

"Run," Leon said softly.

She didn't understand.

He released her completely, pushing her stumbling out of the Enclave. She took half a dozen running steps before she realized he wasn't with her. She turned around and saw him swinging the door closed. With himself still inside.

"No!" Gaia said. "Leon!"

She stumbled back toward the door, but through the narrowing gap she saw a rifle butt crack hard into the back of

Leon's head, and he was falling. For one, unblinking instant, Gaia couldn't think at all, and then she turned away from the lights and the wall. She gripped the ripping bag with her baby sister to her chest and ran blindly.

Chapter 28
Returned Property

AS ANGRY VOICES from the top of the wall followed after her, Gaia ran tripping into a crowd of people. They called
after her, too, reaching out for her, but she pulled away and ran.
There were groups of people everywhere in the streets, sitting in
lines along the curbs and on stools they'd brought outside. She
nearly fell over a group of children, and their parents shouted at
her as well. It was bizarre, surreal, and she couldn't pause to try
to make sense of it. All she could do was keep to the darkness,
avoiding any lights that might expose her to the surveillance
system, and run as fast as possible. Her left arm was still limp
with pain and almost useless. A shrill, interior screaming de-
railed any normal thought in her mind and kept her fixated on
the last glimpse she'd had of Leon falling, unconscious or dead.

"He can't be dead," she whispered.

She stopped to catch her breath and braced herself against a
building. A light exploded in the sky and then a loud pop came
from behind her. The crowd around her broke into a satisfied
"Ooh!" She turned in amazement to look back in the direction
of the Enclave, and saw a firework disintegrating in the foggy
sky above the tower. As a second firework exploded, she real-

ized finally what was happening: the celebration of Evelyn's birthday had gone on, uninterrupted, even as she and Leon had been scrambling to save their lives.

She peered around to get her bearings and realized her feet had brought her to Eastern Sector Two, near her old friend Emily's home. The moist air tasted of wood smoke. While more fireworks boomed into the sky behind her, she swerved left and ran down two more streets to a small house at the end of a row. She rapped on Emily and Kyle's door, gasping for breath.

When the door opened, she practically fell inward, and strong hands grasped her.

"Gaia Stone!" Kyle said in astonishment. "Emily! Come quickly."

She felt a strangled desire to scream again, and a new ripple of pain shot through her left shoulder joint. Kyle guided her to a chair by the fire. Emily was coming from the back room, wide-eyed. As he closed the door, the booming noises were muffled.

"Gaia!" she exclaimed. "What happened to you?"

Gaia turned back the bag in her arms, scrambling to get a clear look at her sister. The baby's eyes were open but otherwise she was still. Gaia let the ripped bag and the ledgers fall to the floor as she lifted the baby before her, holding her head gently in her palm. "You okay, Maya?" she asked.

The infant's eyes blinked, and she made a little pursing face with her lips. Gaia sighed with relief, and snuggled her sister closer into her arms again.

Emily and Kyle exchanged a glance, and Emily slid next to Gaia, wrapping an arm around her shoulder. Gaia winced in pain.

"Kyle," Emily said. "Go see if anyone's following her."

Kyle grabbed a coat from a hook. "I'll tell the others and get your father. Don't worry, Gaia. We'll watch for them. If the guards are coming, we'll get you out of here."

Gaia looked at Emily clearly for the first time and saw her

face was fuller, her auburn hair longer than when she'd last seen her. Her eyes were the same rich blue and as full of concern as ever.

"Are you okay?" Emily asked. "What's happened to you?" She plucked gently at the fine white fabric of Gaia's cloak.

"I need to change," she said, slowly. She needed to think ahead. Leon wasn't with her. He wasn't coming. He couldn't. It was still only barely believable to her. "I need to leave as soon as possible. Do you have any formula? Any supplies I can take into the Dead Forest?"

Emily looked amazed. "Of course," she said. "But are you sure you want to go?"

Gaia hardly knew where to start, and when she tried to sum up everything that had happened to her since she'd gone inside the wall, she couldn't do it. There was too much: her father, her mother, Leon. "I can't explain it all," she said. "But I do know I have to go."

"We knew they were looking for you," Emily said. "They've been posting your picture on the Tvaltar, but they didn't explain why. What trouble are you in?"

"It's not safe for me here," Gaia said. "It's also dangerous for anyone who helps me. I just realized—they know you're my friend. I'm sorry, Emily. I shouldn't have come here." She turned toward the door and started to rise.

Emily hushed her and pulled her down again. "Don't say that. You can't leave like this. We're glad to help, and I'm sure Kyle's got someone watching for us."

Gaia rubbed her left shoulder, trying to squeeze out some of the pain.

"You're hurt, aren't you?" Emily said. "Here. Let me help you into some other clothes. Does your baby need a bottle?"

Gaia's heart was still racing, but she was able to breathe more regularly now. "Not yet. She's my sister. Maya."

"Your sister? Where's your mother?"

Gaia gazed down at her sister's little face, infinitely sad. "She's dead."

"Oh, Gaia."

Gaia searched out her sister's little hand and lifted the fingers into the firelight. More muffled booms came from the Enclave. If she started thinking about her mother, the tears would start coming and she didn't know if they'd ever stop.

"I'm so sorry," Emily said softly. "She was a wonderful woman."

Gaia closed her eyes hard, feeling the tears start to brim despite her determination to keep them back. "Please," she said. "I can't think about her. I can't."

"Of course not," Emily said kindly. "Just wait right here. I'm going to put Maya in something clean and dry, and I'll grab some things for you. You want me to take her?"

Gaia nodded mutely. Carefully, she passed over the infant, and her hands felt emptier than they ever had. Emily passed quietly out of the room. Gaia slumped down onto the bench near the fire and let her face drop forward into her fingers. Every bone, every muscle in her body was weary from pain and exertion, but it was deep in her heart that she was most worn with misery.

There was a sharp burst of staccato explosions outside, and a glimmer of light outside the window signaled the finale. Soon the streets would be a madhouse as people headed for their homes. She reached slowly for the pile of ledgers that had fallen to the ground at her feet and settled them in a pile on her lap. They didn't seem like much of a prize when she'd lost so much. She opened the top ledger and scanned the first page. It was the list of adopted babies, a simple line for each:

Jan 4, 2385	Healthy boy.	Lauren and Tom McManus.	"Tom, Jr."
Jan 16, 2385	Healthy boy.	Zoe and Nabu Nissau.	"Labib"
Jan 17, 2385	Healthy girl.	Lucy-Alice Mairson and Stephen Pignato.	"Joy"

And on and on, year after year they went. This was what she had to leave behind of her mother and father's legacy: a guide, or a way to open the wounds of loss for every parent outside the wall who had ever wondered what had happened to an advanced child. Now, if they chose to, they could know who had adopted their children and, if they investigated further, if they were willing to risk pursuing information within the Enclave, they could discover if their children had thrived or died. How many parents, she wondered, would really want to know? Her Mom, of course, would have died for these records. In essence, she did.

Gaia flipped the pages and slowly ran her finger down the column of dates until she came to the one entry that still mattered most:

Feb 12, 2389 Healthy boy. Jodi and Sol Chiaro. "Martin"

That was her brother Arthur. He had become Martin Chiaro. Little good it did her to know; he was as lost to her as ever.

Gaia closed the cover, and as she did, she noticed something shiny on the floor, mixed in with the gilded paper and a blanket that Leon had tucked into the gift bag. She reached down and pulled at a bit of chain, lifting it into the glow of the firelight. At the bottom of the loop a familiar disk of metal rose and pivoted slowly in the golden light: her locket watch.

353

"Oh, Leon," she murmured.

She could practically hear his voice insisting that it belonged to her, especially now that she was free. She flipped open the tiny catch to see the words engraved within the cover: *Life First.* She wrapped the chain slowly around her fingers and gripped the cool watch, pressing her fist against her forehead. It was ticking. She would not cry. She would not.

"You okay?" Emily asked, coming in again with Maya and an armful of clothes.

Gaia shook her head. She was not okay. She didn't know if she'd ever be okay again. She wiped her wrist against her eye.

When she glanced up at Emily again, she noted the sway of Emily's back as she held the baby, and the subtle curve of her belly. Gaia frowned. "Are you expecting again?"

Emily laughed. "How like you to notice."

Gaia glanced around the room more carefully, seeing the simple furniture and a high chair in one corner. The sound of people laughing passed in the row outside. "Where's your baby?"

"Paul? He's down for the night." She smiled again. "Or so I hope. Here. Why don't you change? I mean, you look like a princess, but that's not very practical out here."

Gaia slipped off her white clothes and dressed slowly in a brown dress and a blue, white-flecked sweater. She had to be careful with her left arm, but it didn't feel like anything was broken.

"Here, you take her," Emily said, passing Maya back to Gaia. "I'll get you some stew."

"I'm not hungry. I don't have time. Honestly."

"You'll eat anyway."

Emily bustled around, taking away Gaia's white discards and bringing her a steaming bowl with a spoon. As her fingers closed on the spoon, Gaia founds she was shaky with shock and exhaustion.

"What are those?" Emily asked, gesturing to the ledgers.

"I want you to take care of them," Gaia said. "They're the records of the advanced babies and who adopted them inside the Enclave."

Emily's forehead creased in disbelief. "Are you serious?"

Gaia lifted a spoonful of soup before her lips and blew gently on it. It did smell good, salty and rich with potatoes and meat. "Yes," she said. "Can you make copies somehow? Do you have people you can trust? Your parents?"

Emily sat beside Gaia and turned a few of the pages. "This is incredible," she said, nodding. "There are a few of us, not too many, but a few of us that have started meeting up." Her expression grew more somber. "A few weeks ago, something frightened me badly."

"When the raven was shot? On the shore?"

Emily turned to her slowly, her amazement obviously. "How do you know about that?"

"They were showing me," Gaia said. "They wanted to make a point."

Emily's voice dropped. "They made their point. They've gone too far, Gaia. Taking your parents, and then raising the quota to five. A baker was roughed up in Eastern Sector One the other day by a couple of guards. People are starting to talk. Fireworks are not going to be enough to keep everyone happy."

"You think there might be a revolt or something?" Gaia said, swallowing her stew.

"It's too soon to say. But this," Emily tapped the ledgers. "This could change things. What if people could actually take back their children?"

"And the baby quotas?" Gaia asked. "What about them?"

Emily settled her hand over her stomach. "I couldn't do it," Emily said. "I couldn't give up my baby. And I know two other mothers who feel the same way. I don't know what we're going to do if—" She lowered her gaze. "I mean, I know it's your job," she continued.

Gaia set aside her stew. "No. Never again."

Emily looked surprised.

"It's out of the question," Gaia said.

Gaia gazed down at her sister, who had fallen asleep again peacefully. Her nose was still flattened, and she had only the faintest indications of eyebrows. A fierce, possessive power rose in Gaia as she cradled her sister in her arms. "I have Maya to look out for."

Emily drew her fingers into a fist on top of the ledgers. "This is an awful idea," she said. "But do you really want to take her into the wasteland? I could keep her for you. She'd be safe here."

She didn't have to spell it out for Gaia to understand: Emily believed they were going to die. Gaia couldn't think that way, and she couldn't leave her sister behind. She'd had enough of separating families.

"Thank you, but we're staying together," she said.

There was a quick knock at the door, and Emily rose to let in her husband. Behind him came Theo Rupp.

"Gaia!" Theo said. "Amy and I have been that sick with worry! Are you all right? Where are your parents?"

Gaia stood and felt his big arms encircle her and the baby in a great hug.

"Is anybody coming?" Emily asked Kyle.

"The guards are searching for you house by house," Kyle said to Gaia. "They lost you in all the crowds, but now they're coming. I've got Rufus watching outside."

"Then there's no time to lose," Gaia said, turning to Emily. "Help me get ready."

"I don't understand," Theo said. "What's happened?"

Emily set a hand on Gaia's arm. "Gaia's leaving, Dad. Jasper and Bonnie are dead. She wants to go to the Dead Forest with her sister."

The others exchanged looks, and then Theo took off his hat. He circled it in his big hands. "I'll go with you," he said.

Gaia shook her head. "You can't, Theo. You have your family here."

"But, darlin', do you even know the way?"

"Do you?" Gaia asked.

Theo's helpless expression was echoed in the faces around him. "That's what I thought," Gaia said.

Emily's family began gathering things to put in a pack. Emily brought a sling of gray cloth that she had used with her son, showing Gaia how to arrange it over her unharmed right shoulder and down to her left hip so that she could carry the baby snugly in a pouch of fabric across her chest. Kyle packed a box of matches and a knife, a small pan and a sack of corn meal, a slab of mycoprotein, and a bag of pecans into the backpack. Then he filled a couple of water bottles and added those. Theo rolled a tarp and a couple of blankets into a tight bundle and attached it with straps to the outside. Emily added diapers, three canisters of baby formula, and two baby bottles, until the pack was stuffed full.

"Take this in case it rains again or gets cold," Emily said, handing over a clean gray cloak that swept to her knees. The fabric had been worked with beeswax to make it water-proof.

"You're better off traveling light and trying to make some distance," Theo said. "If you can get yourself far enough north, the wasteland changes into forest. There's water there. That's what you'll be needing most."

"The Dead Forest," Gaia said.

"Yes," he said. "That's what we've heard."

Gaia looked around at the cozy home and the strong, loving

family, and she felt a pang that was half loss, half envy. She was leaving this place forever, and everything here that might have been.

"Thanks," Gaia said. "All of you. More than I can say."

"We'll take you as far as the edge of Wharfton," Kyle said, shouldering her pack.

She looked up at him, seeing his determination, and couldn't refuse. "Look after those ledgers," Gaia said to Emily.

"I will. I promise. And you look after yourself, will you?" Emily gave her a tight, fierce hug. "I'll miss you."

Gaia wordlessly hugged her back, and then she, Kyle, and Theo slipped out the door.

The rain had stopped completely, and the streets of Wharfton were quiet. Only a few groups of people still lingered after the fireworks. Mist clung in the air, and there was a tang of acrid smoke from the explosives. Once Gaia heard loud voices and knocking, but as they hurried farther from the wall and closer to the unlake, the sounds diminished. She and the men walked quickly, avoiding the few lights that might make them visible to a camera lens. Gaia had no doubt that Mabrother Iris was at his screen desk, watching for any flicker, ready to command his soldiers to converge upon them.

When they reached the unlake, they turned west. The expanse of the unlake was a heavy void of darkness on her left that sucked down the streams and trickles of water crossing beneath her feet. Soon they passed Sally Row and Gaia's old neighborhood. For a moment, she remembered her old home, the shady back porch, the smell of fabric drying in the sun, the tinkle of the wind chime. She could hear her father working the treadle. She could see her mother rinsing out her blue teapot. She tried to picture what life would have been like if the guards had never arrested her mother, if she'd been able to stay home, pregnant and healthy, enjoying this late little baby girl with her husband. Then she looked in the direction of the potter's field, invisible in the night, and wondered if they would bury her mother there, too, beside her father.

Gaia peered into the darkness, keeping her gaze forward, until they reached the last row, the last house, the last yard.

"This is good," she said.

Kyle transferred the pack to Gaia's back. She hitched it forward, settling the weight to minimize discomfort to her sore left shoulder, and checked that the sling with her sister in it was still balanced along her chest. She hitched her skirt up a bit, and laughed as she realized she was still wearing the white boots. At least they were comfortable.

"Good luck, Gaia," Kyle said softly. He gave her a quick hug and passed her along to Theo for another.

"You have everything?" Theo asked.

She felt for the locket around her neck, tucked inside her dress. "Yes," she said. "Give my love to Amy."

"And you know your stars?" Theo asked.

She looked up at the cloud-filled, dark sky. An area of pale glowing showed the moon was behind the clouds, and that they were moving fast. "I will," she said. "When they show up."

Theo gave her one last hug. "You're a brave girl," he said.

She didn't think so. She was just doing what she had to do. With a last wave, she headed out alone into the night, finding her eyes had adjusted and there was just barely enough light for her to avoid tripping over the stones and grasses. The road became rougher and narrower, then finally vanished altogether. Crickets sounded in the damp night. When she'd gone on for some distance, she turned back to see if the others were still watching her, but she couldn't make out anything but the lights of the Enclave, spreading up the hillside toward the Bastion.

She wiped a strand of hair out of her eyes, and her fingertips grazed the familiar scarred skin of her left cheek. She adjusted the baby's warm weight in the sling, and then turned away again, lifting her boots carefully for each step as the ground began to rise.

Rain run-off trickled between the stones, and a fragrant, stone-scented mist was rising from the ground. She could sense the open expanse in the night ahead of her: not a tree, dead or otherwise, this side of the horizon.

At the top of the first rise, she paused one last time to look behind her. The white, curving line of the wall was clearly visible under the distant floodlights, dividing the hulking hillside into two sections. Below, there was a faint scattering of reflections and rare, isolated lights. Above the wall, pinpoints of light dotted the Enclave all the way up to where the towers of the Bastion reached toward the dark sky. From this distance, the lights looked cheery, welcoming, as harmless as fireflies, but Gaia felt a residual shiver of fear ripple through her.

Where is Leon now, she wondered. Had they put him in the tower where her mother had so recently been captive? Had they killed him?

He'd saved her. She did know that much. He'd given the guards a new target just long enough for her to get away. She couldn't help wondering how long he'd planned it, or if he'd known when he kissed her that he would be sending her ahead without him. She hoped, if he *was* still living, that he believed his sacrifice was worth it, and even more, she hoped she'd be worthy of it.

Leon had told her to head north, to the Dead Forest, to a place he didn't even believe existed. Maybe he'd decided he did believe. If ever he could find her and join her again, that would have to be where.

Gaia peered south, toward the unlake, and heard a bird chirp somewhere to her left. She pivoted right, and sensed the vast, open space of the wasteland stretching before her under

360

the opaque sky, a darkness as thin and final as the velvet lining of a shroud. A touch of wind lifted against her cheeks and ruffled her skirt. The little bundle of her sister was solid and warm against her chest. "Let's start north, Maya," she said.

As she walked through the dark, stepping softly through the wet stones, she looked ahead to where the first cautious star managed to blink through the clouds.

Acknowledgments

I wish to thank my students at Tolland High School, who make me want to write. I'm grateful to Kirby Kim, my agent, and to Nancy Mercado, my editor, who brought me deep into Gaia's story. Special thanks to Amy Sundberg O'Brien, Nancy O'Brien Wagner, and my mother, Alvina O'Brien, for input on the earliest draft. Thanks to Kate Saumweber for her midwifery insights. I thank my son William for his boundless encouragement, my son Michael for his wisdom regarding irony and the map, and my daughter Emily for insisting I not kill off babies.

Finally and always, I thank my husband, Joseph LoTurco, for everything.

Caragh M. O'Brien
March, 2010

Pondering Questions *from author*
Caragh M. O'Brien

*Warning! These are total spoiler questions
for after reading the story. —Caragh*

1. Considering what you know about poverty, wealth, technology, the likelihood of being infertile or having a child taken from you, hemophilia, education, surveillance, and everything else in the world of *Birthmarked*, on which side of the wall would you rather live?

2. Which side of the wall do you live on now?

3. Why do you suppose Leon likes Gaia?

4. One of my favorite moments in the novel occurs when Gaia is in the Square of the Bastion, just after the hanging, when Gaia has to choose between going to her mother and trying to save the criminal's baby. Her choice changes the entire course of the story and defines who she is. What's your favorite moment in the novel?

5. Hemophilia and infertility are real health issues in human populations that have inbreeding, and they certainly exist for people now. The founders of the Enclave made a ruthless decision to have no hospitals at all. How far should our medical system go to save people's lives or help them have babies?

6. What object in the novel would you like to have for your own?

7. Considering that Gaia takes a baby away from her mother in the opening chapter, she risks being an unsympathetic character, yet many readers tell me they like Gaia. When and why did you start liking Gaia?

8. When I originally wrote the story, I had Leon leave for the wasteland with Gaia and the baby (and I figured privately that all of them were goners). However, when I was offered the chance to write a trilogy with a bigger story arc, I changed the ending. Now, even if *Birthmarked* weren't part of a trilogy, I would keep this ending. What would have been lost by having Leon go into the wasteland with Gaia and the baby?

9. *Birthmarked* was deliberately left with a few loose ends, such as Gaia's grandmother, the Dead Forest, and, of course, Leon, who was last seen getting bonked over the head. Poor guy. If you were going to write the second book, what people and problems would you carry over, and what would you add to make it new?

10. What are the walls that now limit what you can do and who you can be?

Feel free to visit the author's blog for updates on her writing and occasional stories about characters from the world of *Birthmarked*.

www.caraghobrien.com

∗ ∗ ∗

GOFISH

Caragh M. O'Brien

What do you do on a rainy day?

I write and bake chocolate-chip cookies, and then I eat chocolate-chip cookies while I'm writing. Like everybody else, I prefer the raw batter. It's so sweet and chunky.

Rainy Day

Are you rich?

More than one teenager has asked me this, so I guess people are curious. The answer is: Yes. I have a sweet family, a home in a quiet neighborhood with decent schools, enough food, health insurance, a few friends, my civil rights, and work I love. I could not be richer, and I'm thankful every day for my good fortune.

Do you know all the words in *Birthmarked*?

I do. I tried to write the best book I could, which included using the right words.

Why did you write this book?

For fun

For whom did you write it?

I wrote it for myself and my kids, and I was thinking about my ninth-grade English students, too. I'm an impatient reader, so I was aiming for a fast read with a good story. Gaia interested me right from the first chapter, and then I threw in a bunch of my favorite things, like a code, a disguise, a sicko with weird eyes, towers, cloaks, candlelight, executions, babies, and fresh bread.

Did you always like to write?

I suppose so. In seventh grade, I started a journal as an assignment, and I kept up with it until writing and thinking became the same thing. I feel like the words on the computer screen are my mind working there. Writing fiction is, for me, the coolest way to experiment with the truth. And revising. I adore revising. I've revised this paragraph about eight times.

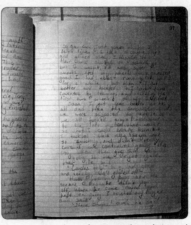

I saved my seventh grade journal and still keep one.

What was your favorite thing about school?

The library. I used to go there to nap on the floor between the fiction shelves. It had a blue carpet back then. Sort of smelled like rubber and dust.

What makes you laugh out loud?

Just about anything. Unfortunately. Especially when I'm not supposed to. Like when we're singing at a gerbil funeral.

Who's Hair, our extant gerbil

Which of your characters is most like you?

Okay. This question's more serious. My characters aren't like me, really, but I wish I were more like Gaia. She's made me braver. I took a risk and resigned from teaching because of her. I spoke my mind recently in a sensitive conversation when it used to be I would remain silent to avoid conflict. I thought that was the polite thing to do, but I can be polite and still have a voice, in person and in my writing. To be more precise, I'm actually still afraid, but now I speak up more than I once did, despite my fear.

I work on a couch.

What would readers be surprised to know about you?

I'm just like anyone else who has reached these words on this page, right here, right now. We all have the capacity to laugh and create and make the world around us more just. Life is just starting, for all of us.

Everything Gaia believes in is at stake when the people
of Sylum capture her. If she wants to see her sister again,
Gaia must accept the moral codes of a matriarchal culture
where a kiss is a crime and curiosity is punished.
How will she survive in this dystopian society?

Turn the page to read an excerpt from *prized*

CHAPTER I

the wasteland

SHE GRABBED THE HILT of her knife and scrambled backward into the darkness, holding the baby close in her other arm. Beyond the fire, the wasteland was still, as if the wind and even the stones had frozen in the night to listen, and then she heard it again, a faint chink, like a footfall in pebbles. Someone or something was out there, watching her.

Gaia turned the knife in her palm, resetting her grip, and peered toward where the far edge of the firelight touched the boulders and the gnarled, wind-stunted trees of the gulch. Without dropping her gaze, she felt by hand that the baby was secure in the sling across her chest, her warm, light weight hardly more than a loaf of bread. She'd left the baby bottle on a ledge of rock, out by the fire, and she hoped whoever was watching her wouldn't take that bottle, whatever else they might do.

The chinking noise came again, drawing her gaze to the far side of the fire. Then a head, an enormous, animal head, big as a cow's but long of face, appeared at the edge of the firelight, looking directly at her. *A horse?* she thought, astounded to see an animal she'd believed was extinct. She checked its back for a rider, but there was none.

Inadvertently, she lowered her knife. In that instant, a powerful hand closed around her wrist and another touched around her throat.

"Drop it."

The voice came softly from behind her right ear. Sweat broke out along her arms and neck, but still she clasped the knife. His grip did not move, did not lessen or increase at all, conveying his confidence that he simply had to wait until she obeyed. So completely, so imperceptibly had he crept up around her that she stood no chance of fighting back. Below her jaw, she could feel her own pulse beating against the firm, pernicious pressure of his thumb.

"Don't hurt me," she said, but even as she spoke, she realized he could have killed her already if that had been his intention. Rapidly, she imagined trying to twist free of him with a kick, but the baby might get hurt. She couldn't risk it.

"Just drop it," came the voice again. "We'll talk."

With a sense of despair, she dropped her knife.

"Do you have any other weapons on you?"

She shook her head.

"No sudden moves," he said, and his hands released her.

She sagged slightly, feeling the adrenaline still coursing through her. He picked up her knife and took a step toward the glow of the fire. A broad-shouldered, bearded man, he wore clothes and a hat of the same worn, dusty color as the wasteland.

"Step forward where I can see you properly," he said, and held out a hand to invite her forward. "Where's the rest of your group?"

"We're it," she said.

Gaia stepped into the firelight, and now that the burst of fear that had given her strength was receding, she doubted she could stand for long. The campsite, she knew, must reveal how she'd been reduced to the last, pathetic shreds of survival. He picked up the baby bottle. She watched his gaze settle on the sling that crossed her chest and the protective hand she kept there. He jogged up the brim of his hat with his thumb in obvious surprise.

"You have a baby?"

Gaia braced a hand against the tree trunk. "You don't have any baby formula with you, do you?"

"I don't usually carry that. What's in this?" He gave the bottle a little shake, and the translucent liquid caught the golden firelight.

"Rabbit broth. She won't take it anymore. She's too weak."

"A girl, even. Let me see her."

She curved back the edge of the sling for him to see, and as she had done a thousand times since she'd left the Enclave, she checked her sleeping sister to see if she was still breathing. Firelight flickered over the little, pinched face, bathing it in brief color before sending it back to black and white. A delicate vein arched along Maya's right temple, and a breath lifted her little chest.

The man touched a finger to the baby's eyelid, lifted it a moment, then let it go.

He gave a sharp whistle, and the horse came nearer. "Here we go, then, Mlady," he said. Decisively, the outrider lifted Gaia from the ground and up to the saddle. She grabbed the pommel to balance herself and Maya, and swung a leg over. He passed her the bottle and her cloak, then collected her meager things into her pack and slung it over his own shoulder.

"Where are we going?" Gaia asked.

"To Sylum as directly as we can. I hope it's not too late."

Shifting, she tried to arrange some of the fabric of her dress between herself and the saddle. She could feel the dark, cool air touching her legs above the tops of her boots. When the outrider swung up behind her on the horse, she instinctively leaned forward, trying not to crowd against him. His arms encircled her as he reached for the reins, and then he kicked the horse into motion.

"Hey, Spider."

The horse's movements seemed jerky to Gaia at first, but when her hips relaxed into the horse's stride, the ride became smoother. Behind them, the gibbous moon was low on the western horizon, casting a light strong enough to create shadows in their path, and Gaia peered to her right, toward the south, to where the Enclave and all she'd left behind had long ago dropped beneath the dark horizon.

For the first time in days, Gaia realized she might live, and hope was almost painful as it reawakened inside her. Inexplicably, she thought of Leon, and a lightless, lonely feeling surrounded her, as real as the outrider's unfamiliar, protective arms. She'd lost him. Whether he lived or died she would never know, and in a way, the uncertainty rivaled the unhappiness of knowing definitively that her parents were dead.

Her sister could well be next. Gaia reached her hand into the sling, easing her fingers between layers of fabric so that she could feel the baby's warm head in the palm of her hand. She made sure the cloak couldn't smother the little face, and then she let her eyes close. She nodded gently with the rhythm of the horse.

"Maya is dying," she said, finally admitting it to herself.

The man didn't reply at first, and she thought he must not care. But then there was a careful shifting behind her.

"She may die," he confirmed quietly. "Is she suffering now?"

Not anymore, she thought. Maya's crying, before, had been hard to bear. This was a much quieter, more final form of heartbreak. "No," Gaia said.

She slumped forward, dimly aware that he was helping, with singular tenderness, to support her and the baby both. Why a stranger's kindness should amplify her sadness she didn't know, but it did. Her legs were chilled, but the rest of her was fast becoming warmer. Lulled by despair and the soporific, distance-eating gait, she gave in to whatever relief oblivion could bring, and slept.

It seemed like years passed before Gaia became dimly aware of a change around them. She ached everywhere, and she was still riding, but she was leaning back against the man whose arms were supporting her and the baby securely. The baby's body was warm. Gaia took a deep breath and opened her eyes to search Maya's face. The baby's skin was translucent, almost blue in its pallor, but she still breathed. When sunlight flickered over the little face, Gaia looked up in wonder to see that they were in a forest.

Tiny dust motes floated in shafts of sunlight that dropped through the canopy of leaves and pine needles, and the air had a lush, humid luminosity that changed breathing fundamentally, filling her lungs with something warm and rich each time she inhaled.

"What is it, in the air?" she asked.

"It's just the forest," he said. "You might be smelling the marsh. We don't have much farther to go."

Even when it had rained in Wharfton, the air itself had remained sere between each raindrop, aching to suck away any moisture, but here, when she lifted her hand, she could feel a trace of new elasticity between her fingers.

"You talk in your sleep," the outrider said. "Is Leon your husband?"

The thought of Leon as her husband was too ludicrous and sad to bear, no matter what she might say in her dreams. "No," she said. "I'm not married."

She glanced down, checking to see if the necklace Leon had returned to her was still around her neck. She tugged the chain so her locket watch rested on top of the neckline of her dress and loosened her cloak. As she straightened, the man let her go, using only his right hand to hold the reins. His fingers, she saw, were clean, with stubby fingernails.

"Where are you from?" he asked.

"South of here. From Wharfton, on the other side of the wasteland."

"So that still exists?" he asked. "How long have you been traveling?"

She thought back over a daze of time in the wasteland. "The formula for Maya lasted ten days. I lost track after that. I found an oasis and caught a rabbit. That was, I'm not sure, maybe two days ago." There'd been a corpse at the oasis, a body with no visible wounds, like a harbinger of her own pending starvation. Yet she'd made it this far.

"You're safe now," he said. "Or almost."

The path rose one last time, turned, and the earth dropped away on their right. Stretching far toward the eastern horizon was a great, blue-green flatness that reflected bits of sky between hillocks of green.

She had to squint to see it clearly, and even then she could hardly believe what she was seeing. "Is it a lake?"

"It's the marsh. Marsh Nipigon."

"I've never seen anything so beautiful," she said.

Lifting a hand to shade her eyes, she stared, marveling. Gaia had spent much of her childhood trying to imagine Unlake Superior full of water, but she'd never guessed it would be like having a second, broken sky down below the horizon. The marsh expanded across much of the visible world: part serpentine paths of water, part patches of green, with three islands receding into the distance. Even from this height, she could breathe in the cool freshness of it, laced with the loamy tang of mud.

"How can there be so much water?" she asked. "Why hasn't it all evaporated?"

"Most of the water *is* gone. This is all that's left of an old lake from the cool age, and the water gets lower every year."

She pointed to a swatch of dark green that rippled in a slow-motion wave as the wind moved across it. "What's that area there?"

"There? That's the black rice slue," he said.

The path took a long, left-handed turn along the bluff, and as they rode, Gaia could see where the landscape dipped down to form a sprawling V-shaped valley. At the wide end, the forest descended to meet the marsh. A patchwork of woods, farmland, and backyard gardens seemed to be stitched together by dirt roads and pinned in place by three water towers. Where the path curved down to meet the sandy beach, a dozen groups of men were working around canoes and skiffs.

"Havandish!" the outrider called. "Hurry ahead and tell the Matrarc I've brought in a girl with a starving baby. She needs a wet nurse."

"We'll meet you at the lodge," a man answered, swinging onto another horse and bolting ahead. People turned to stare.

"Who's the Matrarc?" Gaia asked.

"Mlady Olivia. She runs Sylum for us," he said.

He steered his horse rapidly up the shore and through the village, and for the first time, the horse stumbled. Gaia clutched at the pommel, but the horse regained its footing.

"Almost there, Spider," the outrider said. "Good boy."

Caked with sweat, double-burdened, the horse flicked back an ear and pushed onward. The road turned to abut a level, open oval of lawn, edged with oaks and ringed farther out by sturdy log cabins. Simply dressed people paused in their work to follow their progress.

Ahead, a sun-scorched strip of dirt separated the commons from a big lodge of hewn, dovetailed logs, and in this area stood a row of four wooden frames, like disconnected parts of a fence. Puzzled by the jumbled sight, Gaia stared at a hunched form in the last frame until understanding came to her: they were stocks, and the dark form was a slumped prisoner, passed out or dead under the noonday sun.

"Why is that man in the stocks?" she asked.

"Attempted rape."

"Is the girl okay?" Gaia asked. *What sort of place have I come to?*

"Yes," he said, and dismounted from behind her. Rugged and lean, bearded and strong, the outrider ran a hand down his horse's neck and turned to look up at Gaia. *He isn't old*, she thought, surprised by her first clear look at him. She'd seen the outrider only by the light of the fire, and she was curious now to see how this man, to whom she owed her life, matched his voice and clean hands.

He tilted his face slightly, regarding her closely, and she waited for a question about the scar that disfigured the left side of her face. It never came. Instead, he took off his hat to rake a hand through hair that was dark with sweat. Decisive, perceptive eyes dominated his even features with inviting candor. Beneath his beard, the corners of his mouth turned down briefly with a trace of regret.

He donned his hat again. "I hope your baby makes it, Mlass," he said. "For your own sake."